Looking *for* Lough Ine

Kieran McCarthy

Acknowledgements

I extend my deepest thanks to all those whose support I have accumulated over the nine years of work on this project, first and foremost to my friends and family, for their continued interest, encouragement and patience. For more recent involvement, I want to thank Ms. Tessa Gibson, for taking the time to review my work and suggest some valuable changes. To journalist and fellow writer, Conor Power, and his family, I thank you for your advice and direction, and for inviting me into your home that day, even after it took me hours to find it.

And to my elusive but good friends, David, Sacha, Patsy and Daisy Puttnam for their words of wisdom, inspiration and motivation, and for introducing me to the concept of 'audiobooks', 'public readings' and other ideas which will no doubt prove very useful in the near future.

I am indebted to Mr. Micheál Hurley, Celine O'Donovan and Kevin O'Hanlon, for seeing me through the difficult times, helping not only the story, but the storyteller. I take this opportunity to promote their fantastic service, *Employability* for those who need help realizing their potential.

Also, to a woman I've never met, but whose provocative book, *Be Your Own Life Coach*, empowered me to make this dream a reality. Thank you, too, Fiona Harrold, wherever you are. And of course, to the people at Choice Publishing, for doing what I consider a top-notch job.

It has been an adventure, made all the more exciting by the people with whom I shared it.

Contents

Prologue

One night was all it took for the course of the world to change forever. One night... one little trigger. And once it happened, it was not to be undone. No one saw, no one heard, no one could have envisaged, for on that night, the change began happening in a place Man no longer cared to value - the wild.

A bitter wind swept across the ocean, towards the land, lifting up waves and dashing them relentlessly against the rocky coast. The mighty waves rose and fell, spraying and hissing over the sharp rocks, a white foam bubbling up around each one, as the ocean heaved and tossed in a furious rage. Onwards, the wind gusted, gathering strength and fury.

On the tip of the southern Irish countryside, rich white snow whirled down from the pitch black sky, landing in heavy piles all over the land. The ground was as hard as iron, and gleaming brightly under sheets of snow and ice. Every pond and puddle was frozen solid. Pine trees creaked and swayed, trying to withstand the cruel blizzard. The tall, deciduous trees, such as the ash and the hawthorn, stood bare and bent, glowing in their new white overcoats. The air was sharp and thin; unbearably cold.

It was the last breath of winter, and no living creature dared to stir - save for one.

Scarlet, the vixen, stood on top of a high hill, gazing down at the farm. With the wind billowing past her face, it was safe to assume no one could see her. Not that anyone else would be out on a night like this.

She panted. It had been a long trek through the frozen fields and hedgerows. Still, she gazed down at the farm; all surrounded by wire mesh fencing; at the corrugated iron roofs of the barn and the milking parlour, where outside, a big red tractor was parked. And of course, the chicken coop.

Scarlet's eyes narrowed. The chicken coop sat near the farmhouse. Smoke rose from the chimney of the small, stone faced cottage; thick grey puffs mingling with the white haze of the blizzard. Someone was home. Scarlet would have to make this quick.

She took a deep breath. The frantic pounding of her heart was the only thing keeping her someway warm. She set off down the hill.

The sub zero temperatures had been debilitating enough, but the food shortages! It seemed every tasty little creature had been driven underground, or even abroad. The hedgehogs and field-mice were off hibernating, while the rabbits and rats were lying low until the storm passed. Birds, such as the swallow and the swift, had long flown south for refuge. Insects had retreated further into the bowels of the earth, out of reach. Crops had spoiled; berries, nuts, all rotted. And with the ponds and lakes frozen over, fishing was impossible.

Scarlet wouldn't have cared otherwise. Ever since her mate, Laoch, had fallen to a speeding car, she wouldn't have thought much of starving.

But Scarlet wasn't doing this for herself…

Under the mesh fence, the beautiful, brazen, young vixen crept, and into the forbidden zone. She scanned the area with her hazel eyes; thoughts of danger stiffening her fur more so than the cold. She sniffed along the ground and sure enough, came across the frosted droppings of cows, bulls, cats and - *dogs!*

Over to the door of the chicken coop, she scurried, and then –

FLASH!

Spotted already?

The whole barnyard became flooded by a luminous yellow light. Scarlet fell with her back pressed to the door, eyes squinting. And then, relief. It was a simple porch- light, automatic, fixed above the door of the farmhouse. No one had seen her. Yet.

Scarlet felt an empty space behind her, and turned to see a chunk of wood missing from the bottom corner of the door. She considered. She stooped and tested it with her head. It needed widening. Especially for the job she was about to do. As quietly and as delicately as she could, Scarlet began chewing around the edges of the hole, spitting out sawdust and splinters, until she had formed her entrance.

With all the stealth she could deploy, the vixen slid under the doorway…

It was surprisingly warm inside. Stacks of bales and hay gave the place a comfortable atmosphere. Empty swallows' nests clung to the rafters above near the ceiling where busy spiders had weaved curtain after curtain of cobwebs. But Scarlet couldn't afford to let her guard down. Silent as a spectre, she glided along the straw covered floor, watching all the sleeping hens and roosters as they lay snuggled in their little nesting compartments, oblivious to her presence. Had they been awake, they still would not have seen her as she crept through the darkness. She scanned the loft with her eyes, targeting a fine, plump, brown feathered hen.

Enough for five!

Step by step, the vixen edged her way up to the unsuspecting hen, with bated breath, poised for the big kill. Her shadow loomed over her to-be victim. Then-

POUNCE! Before the hen could open an eye, Scarlet was down upon it, throttling it, jaws clamped tightly around the bird's neck. The hen was shaken, ravaged, sending a cloud of feathers into the air like a burst pillow!

By now, every hen and rooster in the coop was wide awake, flapping, flitting, shrieking and shrilling, in a panic and utter confusion. They clumsily ran in circles, crashing into and clambering over one another, tumbling out of their nesting boxes, in a mad tangle of wings, claws, beaks, feathers and tails. Wasting no time, Scarlet squeezed out through the gap in the door, with the dead hen dangling from the side of her mouth, bouncing up and down as she made a break for the fence.

The entire farm was now in turmoil. The air was filled with mooing, hissing, whinnying, barking, squealing, honking. Hooves and paws battered the ground, tails swished with excitement. The farm bustled with frenzied animals.

A light went on in the house. The Farmer came to the door, holding a ready-loaded shotgun. He had heard all the racket outside and knew instinctively – it was a *wild* animal causing the commotion.

The Farmer's name was O' Connor: a short, thin, bald headed man in his late forties. He was also a wicked, cruel man. He hated wild animals and everything about them. Oh, they were just useless pests, out to make farm life more difficult for him. Often, he laid down poison in his fields, or set traps in the hope of depleting their numbers. But nothing tickled his blackheart's desire more than *hunting* them.

People of the local village often said of O' Connor: 'That man hates animals so much it's surprising he hasn't shot his own cuckoo clock!'

For this sport, he used his three vicious hounds.

In only his pyjamas and slippers, The Farmer dashed out into the snowstorm, calling their names: Ripper, Gnasher and Thrasher.

They needed no bidding. The dogs had already sprung from their kennels, their bloodlust long roused by the noise of the farmyard, and the smell of fox! Each hound was starved and hardened. They lived only for chase, and the thrill of the kill. They all looked more or less the same; crossbred beyond identification; brown silky coats, dark, amber eyes; ears tattered, fur patchy. Around their necks, they wore red collars of pyramid spikes.

They stood now on their hind legs, scrabbling and gnawing at the mesh fence, barking and slobbering.

O' Connor lifted the iron lock and swung the mesh door open, stepping back with caution as though he had released three hungry lions. The hounds sped away into the night, sniffing around and baying their malice.

Meanwhile, Scarlet was having trouble making her getaway. The hen she carried was much too large to fit under the fence she had used upon her entry. It ended up stuck in the relatively narrow gap. The vixen's first instinct was to dive out through the fence, herself first, and drag the hen behind her. But no time. So she opted to charge through the gap, hen and all, bird in front. But this proved disastrous. Not only did this lessen the chance of a good dinner, it also sealed Scarlet's exit! She struggled for a while, pushing, shoving, maneuvering, until she heard the terrifying sounds of barking and howling approaching from nearby. The vixen aborted her plan and fled.

Ripper, Gnasher and Thrasher leapt from the snowy haze, spotted Scarlet immediately, and the chase was on.

Scarlet desperately tore off around the farmyard, fast and light, only skidding when she turned corners. The hounds were heavier and clumsier, but nevertheless, just as fast. They nipped at the vixen's heels, snarling and yapping furiously.

Scarlet knew she couldn't outrun them for long, as she led the stampede. There was only one thing for it: stall them.

One more lap of the farmyard, and Scarlet shot straight into the barn, which was packed tight with cattle! The hounds grinded to a halt, sniffing and slavering, before they too, charged into the barn.

Scarlet zoomed through a long aisle of iron bars, clinking against each other, upsetting every cow in her wake. The great beasts mooed and screamed, casting their heads about. Scarlet stopped to catch her breath, only to look back and see the three hideous, manic faces hurtling towards her. Off she went again, with an aching chest. Running up against a dead end of blank brick wall, Scarlet spied a stack of boxes and buckets.

On came the hounds.

Without a thought, Scarlet threw herself at the stack, sending an avalanche of boxes and buckets tumbling along the floor. The hounds faltered, dodging aside or jumping over the barrage, and setting off again.

One hound, however – Thrasher- ran with his head wedged inside an iron bucket!

Scarlet hopped onto the long concrete bank of the feeding trench, and negotiated her way between the cows, dodging the massive heads that swung for her.

Ripper and Gnasher pursued at either side, worrying the cattle into breaking their chains and pulling down the iron braces that held them. Two cows now ran amok through the barn.

Thrasher, who was still running with a bucket on his head, received such a headbutt, he was sent into the wall. The bucket rang like a bell, as he slumped silently to the ground.

Reaching the end of the trench, Scarlet spotted an open window across from her. An impossible jump… unless.

Ripper and Gnasher galloped to either side of her, barking like demons. Scarlet took a breath and leapt onto the great flat back of a cow!

The animal shuddered.

From there, Scarlet launched herself neatly through the window! There was no time to enjoy the brief feeling of weightlessness, as she soared from the warm barn back into the freezing cold. No sooner had she landed, than Ripper and Gnasher came gallumphing around the corner, tongues lolling from their mouths.

Scarlet picked herself up and made a bee-line for the milking parlour.

The room was tiny. Barely big enough for the bulky, shiny machine it housed. Scarlet executed a three-point jump – from the ground to the wall to the top of the machine. She shrieked, as Ripper arrived in time to tear a clump of fur from her tail.

The vixen found herself cornered, looking down at the two enraged hounds from the top of the machine. They jumped up and down, swiping with their claws, yapping furiously; salivating at the thought of a kill. Scarlet's eyes darted restlessly around the little room. Nothing. There was nothing. She was trapped.

Hold on!

A plank of wood rested against the wall, at a promising angle, not far below. Scarlet did some mental calculations. Again, no time. She dived down onto the end of the plank, all four paws balancing on a strip of wood no more than two inches thick! Using her rump, she forced the plank into falling. Ripper and Gnasher stood back but continued to bark, as the plank whooshed down, vixen and all. It smashed the pressure valve of the milking machine.

Before they knew it, the hounds were being plastered to the wall by a gushing torrent of MILK! The snow white, ice cold liquid spewed with powerful velocity, from a deceivingly small hole, as the vixen slipped outside unnoticed.

Scarlet had reached the wire mesh fence and begun digging, by the time Ripper emerged alone from the parlour.

Presumably, Gnasher was lying on his back somewhere, bloated from an overdose of calcium. So now, the single hound, dripping with both milk and hatred, set off after the vixen.

She abandoned the hole she was digging and resumed the chase, now feeling fatigue set in. Feelings of despair and hopelessness also slowed her down. The mesh fence – it was too high and too strong. There was no time to dig under it. How was she to escape?

Ripper's crazed barking behind, snapped the vixen to her senses. As she approached the barn again, she noticed the door of the tractor was open. And that's when a plan, fully formed, fully fledged, came to her.

She veered off the path and bounded towards the tractor. Ripper followed like a heat-seeking missile.

Scarlet reached the step of the tractor and flung herself inside- the door still wide. She watched the hound advance. She held her ground. Ripper clambered up the steel step, his hefty form filling up the tiny space under the cab all by itself. Scarlet ducked as his great snapping jaws hit the window. She darted under the hound's legs and slid out of the tractor again.

And – all in the fraction of a heartbeat – all in the half blink of an eye –

Scarlet spun around, stood on her hind legs and pushed the tractor door shut with her front paws, trapping the berserk hound inside.

She stood back and watched him, scrabbling and scraping at the window, barking his throat out, the glass dripping with drool.

Scarlet's legs trembled as she watched. Her heart hammered in her chest. Her stomach, twisted. She felt as though she would never catch her breath. There was only one thing left to do.

Wait.

Ripper shifted back and forth inside the tractor, hopping from seat to dashboard, from seat to dashboard. Then, his leg slipped, and he came down heavily on the brake. Very soon, the tractor itself began to roll forward. Down the gentle slope it rolled; the immense metal beast with its giant, grooved hind tyres, vertical exhaust pipe and heavy carrier box.

Scarlet stepped aside and watched the tractor pick up speed, Ripper inside, panicking.

Yes. Come on.

The tractor, as she'd hoped, made its way gradually towards the wire mesh fence, and crashed headlong into it.

All around the northern side of the farm, the wire fence came down; pulled from its iron poles; nails shooting out here and there, until it lay flat in the snow.

Freedom called, but Scarlet had unfinished business to attend to. Searching along the ground, she located her hen, and was away.

It was then, and only then, she allowed for celebration, laughing inwardly.

Hmm. That went well.

Sadly, it was not to be…

O'Connor stepped from the light of his porch. His long, inky shadow stretched off up the hill where Scarlet had run, covering her.

Sensing his presence, she ran faster.

The Farmer marched to the fallen fence, now dressed in a coat and wellingtons, and aimed his shotgun precisely. The air was severed by a loud, echoing bang, as smoke belched from the barrel of his gun.

The pellets streaked past Scarlet's ear, narrowly missing. While bells rang in her head, the vixen tore off up through the white capped hill, stumbling and sliding with the hen in her mouth.

No. No you don't.

O'Connor took a step forward and fired again. The red-hot pellets thudded into the ground just behind Scarlet, sending up a fountain of snow. The vixen was almost out of sight and range.

O'Connor cracked open his shotgun and frantically reloaded, shoving in two fresh cartages. Then steadying himself and lining up his target, he pulled the trigger…

Scarlet shrieked with sudden, incredible pain, and tumbled to the ground. She dropped the hen, leaving it to slide back down the hill, followed by a trail of blood.

…that's not the hen's blood.

A mist of silence descended on the hill. Nothing much could be heard now. The wind seemed soft and light. Trees continued to sway in the breeze, crouching over, as if in grief.

One by one, the vixen found her senses disappearing. Touch. The pain was gone. Smell, taste, gone. Sight – there was only white, a bright, all-consuming white. Conscience remained. She worried, she worried about those she was leaving behind. And she felt anger.

Thwarted by Man again.

Hearing. She could hear the sounds of paws and boots jogging up the hill towards her. But by the time they reached her, Scarlet could hear no more.

O'Connor nudged the carcass with the tip of his gun. The three hounds sniffed at it excitedly, tails wagging. Snow drifted down, flecking the red fur with white. Despite the onslaught of snow, the tracks were visible; the tracks it had left on its way in; distinctive pawprints with four claw marks.

'Filthy creature.'

The pawprints led from the farmyard all the way up through the white wilderness… O'Connor rested his gun under his armpit and clapped his hands. The hounds were off.

'Did you hear that?'

'Hear what?'

'Something's digging.'

In the middle of a cluster of hawthorn trees, tucked down at the bottom of a little hillock, four young fox cubs had been sleeping soundly in their den.

'Go back to sleep, it's nothing.'

'But there's definitely something up there.'

'It's probably Mother with some food. Pretend to be asleep or she'll be angry.'

The cubs had been born in early summer but had never strayed far from the den. Scarlet had ever been extremely protective of them, not wishing to let them go the way of their father. By autumn, she was almost ready to let them go; to pursue separate, independent lives. But with whisperings of the most dreadful winter of all time looming, she could not bear to turn them out. In a most unusual decision, Scarlet held onto her cubs, continuing to nurture and pamper them.

Only recently had they been weaned. Tonight would have been their first big meal.

'That's not Mother.'

'How do you know?'

'Mother doesn't have that many legs.'

All four cubs were small and plump, roughly the size of a fully grown cat. They each had fluffy coats of brown-red fur, four short legs and short dumpy snouts. Their faces were round and chubby.

'Uh –oh.'

'What now?'

'I think the ceiling's falling.'

This den was not a new den, though Laoch had discovered and refurbished it. It had sheltered generations of foxes, badgers, rabbits and stoats.

Until tonight.

Flllllllllllllump!

Soil, rocks and pebbles sprinkled down as the ceiling bulged. Roots popped out and hung loosely, others snapping.

Now frightened, the four little cubs, two males, two vixens, sprang from the warm dry grass of their sleeping chamber and made their first unguided dash up along the shaft to the exit. They hurried out into the bitter cold, only to discover to their sheer horror, that the same fate awaited them outside as inside.

Three monstrous hounds towered over them, eyes glowering menacingly, teeth flashing.

The cubs huddled and froze. The hounds barked and set upon them, all the time watched by a tall figure in the shadows, smoking a cigarette.

The cubs broke up and fled in all different directions: one running in mad circles, trying to shake off her pursuer, one dashing around the hawthorn trees, another diving foolishly back into the den, and the last one galloping up the side of the hill, towards the safety of the outside world. Only a loud BANG pursued him.

But the hounds had little difficulty during their second chase of the night. The four young foxes were small and slow, and had been taken by surprise. Their short legs could take them neither fast nor far, and their small sizes offered no chance of fighting back. The hounds were on them instantly.

Ripper chased one, Gnasher chased another, and Thrasher went for another.

In the end, only one young fox escaped with his life.

And with his life, that young fox was to become- the bringer of change.

BOOK ONE
- PART ONE -

Looking for Lough Ine

First Steps

He opened his eyes and saw nothing but bright white. He drew in a deep cold breath. He shivered and tried to move, but his bones were frozen stiff. The surviving young fox cub had spent the entire miserable night sheltering under the giant root of an old ash tree. When he awoke the following morning, from a fitful, jittery sleep, he knew nothing of the world around him. Everything was amazing. Everything was new. This was the beginning of his life.

Slowly and cautiously, the cub crept from beneath the tree root and stretched his aching body. He arched his back and flexed his little claws. Then after shaking his head, he looked around.

It had stopped snowing. All of the surrounding fields, hedgerows and bushes were pure white, sparkling like diamonds. The clouds in the sky were slowly clearing away, and the sun was at last coming out. All seemed still and peaceful.

The cub was quite transfixed for a while. He pricked up his ears, which were still quite large in proportion to the rest of his baby features. He had been the slowest to mature in the family. He then sniffed the air. The scent of the hounds appeared to be gone. He had been pining for his family throughout night and hoped they were okay. He decided to chance going back to the den.

By following his own paw prints, the cub found his search much easier. He padded through the snow for a while, in an awkward toddler's gait, pausing every now and then to peer around for danger. Onwards he moved, across the white fields until he reached a tangle of bushes; hawthorn, holly and ivy; their leaves were powdered with snow. Through them, and down a small slope, the cub went, and there he found what was left of his home. But instead of the gracious reunion he was expecting, the cub was met with crushing disappointment.

The place was empty. And quiet. The den was destroyed A gaping hole had been tunneled through the top of it. The chambers and passages were flooded with earth and melted snow. It had become muddy and slushy. The entrance had been buried after the cave in.

All around the place, paw prints, big and small, trailed along the ground and circled the trees, indicating there was a terrible chase. The ground was ripped up and flattened in places, littered with leaves and twigs - the telltale signs of a struggle. Not a strand of hair was left of the young fox's family. They were gone, all gone.

The little survivor moped around the area, inspecting the ground and the ruins. He sniffed at the paw prints and the tree bark, before slumping down by the entrance of the den and weeping for his family. Grief and confusion clawed at his heart for the first time. How he missed them, even after only one night. He would never again be able to play with them, or snuggle up with them at night in the warm bedding. He would never again wait with his siblings in the den for Mother to arrive home with a live mouse to play with. Those simple, carefree days were over, torn away, just like that. And where would he go now? What would he do? Who will feed him? Who will play with him and protect him? These were questions the little fox couldn't bear to ponder. Turning away, he left his ravaged home and walked on through the bushes and into the field, not knowing where he was going. All he knew was that he had nothing left to leave behind…

First Steps

Be strong, my little darling
There'll be time enough for tears
So step outside your shelter
And rise above your fears

Standing on the threshold
Of two lives you've come to know
The pain of hanging on
Is worse than letting go

Innocence is fleeting
Now it's time to say goodbye
*Your name has made the list_*
And the world is in your eyes

So off you go, my darling
To light the day for weak and small
When you find out who you are
To win, you'll lead us all!

The day brightened ever more. Sunshine escaped through the white clouds and illuminated the countryside. The winter had been long and arduous. Although in its finishing stages, it was determined to go down fighting. A series of violent snowstorms had plagued the land for days, but thankfully were now over.

For what seemed like ages, the lost cub wandered the snowy plains by himself, daunted and bewildered. Nothing made any sense. He didn't know what anything was, or where he was, or where he was going. It was all so surreal, like he'd been born all over again, to a place less cosy. The surface world seemed too big, too dangerous and full of too much mystery. He didn't even know anything about himself. All he could remember was lazing about at home, with his brother and sisters around him, suckling milk from his mother and sometimes going outside to play in the late summer grass. Everything else was a faded blur. He couldn't tell the difference between his dreams and his memories.

As he wandered aimlessly, the young fox wondered what his mother would have wanted him to do. He remembered her mentioning something called 'hunting' several times. But what did that mean? He had no idea. Without his beloved mother to guide him, the cub would never know how to live and behave like a real fox. He was on his own, free to make his own decisions and choose his own path to follow. But it took him time to realize this.

The countryside began to unfold. It appeared the little fox was not entirely alone after all. A number of birds were seen flitting around or singing. A little black headed bird perched on a gorse bush nearby, flicking its tail and uttering its *tick- tick* call. A red breasted bird landed on a bramble bush and sang for all to hear. A pair of brown, dip tailed birds bounced along the ground ahead, in a hopeless search for insects, before taking to the air again. Blue and yellow capped birds fluttered from bush to bush, nibbling on berries and preening. But the most amazing creature the cub had the fortune of seeing was a great, mottled brown, golden blotched falcon. It was spotted hovering elegantly above the hedgerows, waiting for prey to pass by below. The cub admired these odd little creatures for some time, but his wide chocolate eyes were beginning to droop over. For as he resumed his blind journey, the cold air and hunger began to take their toll. The cub wandered on for as long as he could, until he became so weary, he gave up and collapsed at the edge of the field, falling fast asleep.

Not Without Company

When he awoke again, a short time later, the cub could feel something breathing warmly on his face, and a big wet nose nudging his forehead. At first, he thought it was Mother making a miraculous return. But after coughing and opening his sticky eyes, he realized to his utter shock, it was the most unmotherly creature he had seen all day! It was big, grey and hairy with long sharp claws. It had a black face with a white stripe running from the top of its head, all the way down its chest and belly. The cub gasped and sprang to his feet, startled. But ironically, the creature too, stumbled backwards as if frightened.

'Whoa, don't hurt me,' it pleaded, backing away. 'I was only checking to see if you were still alive!'

The two animals sat nervously apart, eyes fixed on one another, both panting heavily.

The little fox looked at this creature, now more puzzled than frightened. It did not seem dangerous, but instead friendly; with its warm, welcoming eyes and voice that initially sounded quite young and innocent. What was it? And why was it pleading for its life? The cub had no intention of hurting anyone, nor did he know how.

The creature relaxed, once it found that the cub posed no threat. It climbed to its feet and brushed the snow from its thick coat.

'Sorry about that,' it said, in a calmer voice. 'But you can't blame me for being curious. After all, you *were* sleeping on my roof!'

The cub lowered his eyes to the ground and discovered he had been lying on top of a mound of earth riddled with holes.

'I could smell you from my sleeping chamber,' the creature went on. 'So I thought I'd have a peek outside and see what it was. It was a little unusual seeing a 'fox' lying unconscious on my carpet. At first I thought you'd died of hunger while looking for food.'

The cub blinked and whispered to himself;

'A fox? Is that what I am?'

The creature eased itself down into a comfortable sitting position.

'So what's a fox like you doing out here in the middle of the day? Aren't you nocturnal?'

The cub did not understand this question and stared blankly.

'You don't know eh,' the creature chuckled. 'Fair enough. Just having a look around? Well I hope you're finding it easier than me. I usually can't stand daylight. Like all us badgers, my eyesight is quite poor.'

The cub listened to this 'badger' rambling on. For a creature who looked so young, he sounded very mature. The cub did not know what to make of him.

'So I take it you're hunting, then?' he said. 'Out looking for a rare winter bite?'

Again, the cub did not know what to say, and simply nodded at the badger's casual questions.

'I see,' said the badger, who then swivelled his head to look around at the ground. 'You're probably wondering what all of these holes are for,' he said, rather off- topic. 'Well, this big one here is the entrance to my network of underground tunnels, and all of those little ones over there are my *latrines*. I use them whenever nature calls.'

After this, there was an awkward pause in the one - sided conversation.

The two young animals sat opposite one another, in silence, peering around at random trees and bushes. Then at last, the badger spoke:

'I'm sorry,' he confessed. 'I'm just a tad nervous. It's been a long time since I last spoke to a creature my age. It can get really lonely out here by yourself. Sometimes I just chat with any living things I can find - beetles, worms, snails - and then I eat them! It's not the best way of making friends, but it keeps me alive.'

The cub gave a broad smile. He was quickly adjusting to this newcomer. But the badger soon began to sound uneasy again.

'So,' he said nervously. 'Where's your family?'

'Ummm,' choked the cub timidly, searching for a response. 'Gone.'

'Gone?' gasped the badger, scratching his head. 'That's sad, how are they gone? No wait, let me guess, it was The Farmer, right? The Farmer took your family, or his dogs?'

The cub nodded: Yeah.'

'It's awful isn't it,' said the badger, with a touch of genuine sympathy in his voice. 'I know how you feel. My family are gone too, you know. I remember when The Farmer and his dogs raided my sett. I think he was angry coz he thought we were spreading disease among his cattle. I was the only one to survive, out of three brothers. The dogs killed them both, and later The Farmer, along with others, tied my mother to a wooden post and watched her do battle with the dogs. Of course, my mother didn't stand a chance.'

'But why?' asked the cub, in his tiny voice.

'Pardon?' said the badger.

'Why does The Farmer not like us?'

The badger sighed; 'I really don't know. I suppose we just get in his way. Humans are a mystery to me.'

The cub muttered another new word to himself;

'Humans'

'So how exactly did you lose your family?' the badger asked.

The cub was now glad he could share his plight with another animal.

'Mother never came home,' he groaned. 'Then the dogs came and gobbled everyone up, 'cept me.'

The badger gave a knowing nod.

'Well,' he said. 'At least *you* made it.'

There was silence for a moment, as the two young animals ran out of thing to say. Then again, the badger spoke:

'I take it you have no friends?' he enquired.

'No,' said the cub. Then, 'What's a friend?'

The badger shook his head and turned away momentarily, as if embarrassed,

'It doesn't really matter,' he mumbled. 'I don't have any either. I've been wandering this land for as long as I can remember and I've never come across another of my kind. I've always been alone. But, you get used to it.'

More silence followed, as often happens when two individuals meet for the first time. And again, the badger spoke:

'Anyway,' he said conclusively. 'I'm awake, alert and rather hungry now. Wouldn't mind looking for a daytime snack before The Farmer lets his cattle into this field... want to join me?'

'Okay,' said the cub as he followed the badger out through a gap in the ditch, into a different field. Here, the layer of snow on the ground appeared to be thinning. Many blades of bright green grass could be seen piercing through, towards the light, soon giving way to whole healthy bunches of grass, as the fox and the badger padded further along together.

It wasn't long before the badger turned back to the cub.

"Out of curiosity,' he said. 'What's your name?'

The cub stopped and pondered for a while, now more tongue-tied than ever. What *is* my name? he asked himself. Do I even have one? His mind raced in a panic, searching frantically for what should have been an obvious answer.

'Well?' said the badger, patiently.

'Am,' said the cub at last. 'It's, err... *Fox?*'

'Fox?' gasped the badger. 'That's it?'

'Err, yeah,' smiled the cub, awkwardly. He felt truly foolish:

'Well what a coincidence!' the badger laughed. 'I don't have a name either! Call me *Badger;* that's what I am, that's who I am!'

The cub sighed with relief.

So for the time being, the two animals went by those simple names, Fox and Badger.

But how were they to know, that the path on which they walked would lead them to even more nameless faces; faces that would come to shape everything in their lives.

The two youngsters strolled through the hedgerows together, seeing that winter had already slackened its grip in some places. Treetops and bushes burst through the snow and ice, refusing to be hidden. As they went, they watched flocks of the usual birds fluttering and dancing amid the brambles. The place no longer seemed dull or lonely. Underneath its bushes and rocks, the countryside teemed with life.

'I just had a thought,' said Badger, as he walked with Fox up a tall, heather covered hill. 'Since we seem to have a few things in common; both survivors, both nameless, both without families... maybe if we stuck together, we could find a new home, you know, somewhere far away from humans.'

'Yeah,' said Fox, nodding. The thought of a new home made no difference to him. Anywhere was better than the den.

'I just reckon it's a good idea,' said Badger. 'I'd like to find a place where I know I'm out of harm's way.'

Fox agreed of course.

As they both neared the hilltop, Badger asked Fox;

'One thing, have you ever seen what the world looks like during spring?"

'What's spring?' Fox asked.

Badger grinned while still trundling through the bushes.

'Only every animal's favorite time of year. Follow me, this'll all be new to ya."

When Fox gazed out over the edge of the hill, he was stunned. Lying there before him, and stretching across as far as the eye could see, was a vast and rugged landscape. Green fields flourished and hedgerows grew sprightly. Everywhere, long, lush grass blew in the wind. The place was a blend of green, white and purple, for dots of resilient wildflowers still huddled together, their splendid colours more than compensating for the large patches of snow that were still to be seen. Nature thrived. Fox was overwhelmed.

'You see,' laughed Badger. 'There wasn't enough snow in the sky to cover everything! That means winter is coming to an end. Hello - spring!'

Fox continued to stare in awe at the wonder and majesty of this place.

'I know it *looks* nice,' said Badger, breaking the cub's trance.' But unfortunately, we can't stay here."

Fox withdrew his eyes and looked at Badger in disbelief. 'Why not?' he enquired.

'Because it's too dangerous,' Badger explained. 'This land belongs to The Farmer. He has the place riddled with traps and electric fences. And if he ever catches us here, he'll set his dogs on us, or shoot us with his 'gun'.

Fox felt somewhat disappointed. He did not see the dangers that this place was hiding. He saw only its peace and elegance. He would have loved to spend his days here. But Badger, despite his young age, seemed to be an animal of natural wisdom, and Fox believed his views were correct.

'Sorry if I got your hopes up,' said Badger. 'But this place isn't as nice as it looks. Where there're humans, there's danger. It's that simple. I've been finding it hard to survive here by myself; I do what 1 need to do; only coming out at night to feed on a few measly insects and tree roots before going back underground - but always with a sense of fear, like fear is watching me. I really don't think it should be that way! I dream of a place where I can stay out all night doing whatever I want without worrying about stepping in an iron jaw, or eating a toxic berry; a place where I can dig out a brand new sett and find a nice female to be my mate.'

'What's a female?' asked Fox.

Badger sighed politely, growing tired of Fox's infernal questions, still glad however, that he had finally found someone he could share his knowledge with.

'You have so much to learn," he said.

Badger led Fox down the other side of the hill, and together, they explored the land.

The lack of snow in the area conjured up some of Fox's earliest memories: The place was a mad tangle of shrubs, plants and bushes, all growing and dancing, free of their winter shackles.

While trekking through it all, Badger taught Fox everything he knew about life in the wild, as quickly and as concisely as he could. He showed him many different types of trees, plants, flowers and insects, and told him what they were called.

But there was only so much Fox could take in before he became delirious from starvation. It had been days since his last square meal. His stomach no longer rumbled, as if it had given up hope of ever seeing food again.

Once he mentioned it, Badger dropped everything and the hunting lesson began. 'I can't teach you how to live like a fox,' said Badger. 'But I'll show you how *I* live.'

That day, Fox learned how to dig for worms, by seeking out the moistest areas with the darkest soil. He learned how to roll away rocks and find insects, how to find the end of a tree root by following it from the base, and how to pick berries off the end of a bramble bush without getting hurt - the trick is, try not to worry, because you're going to get hurt anyway.

By the time dusk had settled on the land; when the air grew chilly and moist and when the sky became covered in a dark shade of red, the two young animals were beyond tired. It had had been the busiest day of Fox's short life. He and Badger decided to take a break and rest in a pocket of unsnowed grass for a while.

Fox lay on his back across from Badger, his chest heaving from eating so many beetles, worms and berries. But he felt good. His belly no longer ached from hunger. His strength was returning. It would not be long before he could run again. (And he'd need to.)

Not much was said between the two animals as they lay half asleep, Fox deep in the grass, Badger lying under a nearby hawthorn tree.

'I'm bushed,' he chuckled, resting on his back with his paws folded over his chest.

The evening was blissfully quiet. Not much could be heard, save for a few blackbirds twittering in the bushes and treetops. The sky was aglow with the setting sun, saying goodnight to the fading scenery.

'Looks like I won't have to go hunting tonight,' Badger yawned. 'I have it all done now. And maybe tomorrow night, after a good rest, we'll start looking for that new home.'

'Yeah,' Fox mumbled, struggling to stay awake. He was very satisfied with his day. The cub felt enraptured having met Badger. Before him, the last animals he'd seen were the hounds, and now a friendly face was most welcome, especially one this friendly. He felt safe and secure with him, and felt he was learning. But right now, he needed a break from the rambling.

The stillness of the evening lingered peacefully on for some time, but was snatched away when the two animals suddenly felt a slight tremor in the ground. Shaking off their exhaustion, they both sprang to their feet, fully alerted.

'What was that?' Fox gasped, standing firm and peering around with his ears and tail erect.

Badger didn't respond, but with a serious look on his face, cocked an ear up, listening carefully.

The trembling in the ground was becoming more intense. It appeared to be coming from the distant road; a small, narrow dirt track behind a row of blackthorns. There they could hear a clattering, sort of 'marching' sound, which at first, seemed far and low, but grew louder and louder.

'What is that?' cried Fox. 'What's happening?'

Badger turned to Fox, looking extremely anxious.

'We have to get out of here,' he said. 'Be quiet, lie low and make no sudden movements!'

'WHY?' cried Fox in a panic. 'What's happening?'

'The Farmer is letting his cattle into this field,' Badger whispered. 'If we're lucky, it's only cows, but if there's a bull, we have to be extra careful. I've seen this bull before and he's a real mad one. And by mad, I actually mean he's not right in the head! He chases and tramples anything he sees moving!'

The two animals dropped to the ground and began creeping through the long grass. The exit fence seemed so painfully far away...

Not far behind them, they could hear an iron gate creaking open and O' Connor's harsh voice yelling as dozens of cows milled into the field.

'Hoah, hoah, hoah, move along, come on now, move along, you too

Mister, move along, get going, all o' ya."

The ground rumbled under the many moving hooves as the cattle barged through the gate and onto the wide open plain. The air was filled with mooing and puffing.

Not daring to look back, Fox and Badger continued to sneak towards the faraway fence, as stealthily as they could, knowing that they were being surrounded by a big herd of cattle.

While crawling along on his belly, Fox suddenly gasped with fright, after catching sight of a pair of cows behind him, having never seen any before.

They were massive, white creatures with splashes of black and full, heavy udders dangling between their legs. They stood like tall pillars, grazing lazily.

'They're gia-normous!' the cub squeaked.

'Don't be afraid,' said Badger, reassuringly. 'The cows are quite harmless.

I'd be more worried about the bu - oh no, there he is!

Fox turned to his left and peered over the tall grass, in the direction Badger was looking. In his head, he shrieked.

Not far from where the two youngsters hid, a giant, muscular built brown bull stood, barrel-chested with shoulders like boulders. As was typical, he had a steel ring in his nose and two nasty horns on his head. He snorted and stomped his heavy hooves on the ground, stating his place as dominant male (which the cows found annoying, because he was the only male).

In a panic, Fox shot to his feet and tried to make a break for it, but Badger quickly caught him by the scruff of the neck and dragged him back down.

'Don't let him see you!' he hissed, his brown eyes flaring. 'Just stay down and keep quiet. We'll slip past him by going slow. And I reckon we should stop all this movement before-'

Badger was cut off by the unmistakable sound of heavy hooves thumping the ground, drawing closer at an alarming speed.

The two animals daringly poked their heads above the grass and saw to their horror that the great bull was already making a drive for them! Head down, horns pointing out like a pair of spears, he advanced.

'That didn't take long,' said Badger, in disbelief.

'What now?' asked Fox, trembling.

'We run!' cried Badger.

Both youngsters broke cover and took off across the field, as fast as each of their four legs could carry them, with the battle hardened bull catching up rapidly. He snorted, puffed and roared while in pursuit of his quarry.

He had been waiting a long time for a bit of excitement and two, tiny defenseless cubs seemed an ideal source. His aim was to catch them, toss them in the air with his horns and then run them over after they'd landed.

That would surely be amusing. Onwards he galloped.

The two little animals sprinted across the field, with the smaller Fox in the lead. He dived under the barbed wire fence, followed shortly by Badger.

Thinking they were safe, they scrambled on through the second field. But Badger's analysis of the bull proved correct. He was indeed, a nutcase.

When most other bulls would give up here, this particular bull wasn't willing to let these wild intruders escape. Hyper, nothing else would satisfy him until his targets were destroyed. He frantically paced the length of the fence, searching for a way around the barbed wire, but ended up smashing through a wooden pallet! Bits and pieces of timber showered down all around the beast, as his hard head rammed through. The chase was far from over.

Fox and Badger looked back and saw him approaching, looking more full of rage than before. He caught sight of the two animals and thundered on, picking up even more speed as he chased them down a slope. His terrible hooves punched deep holes in the ground.

Fox and Badger, still tired from their busy day, struggled to keep moving. Only fear drove them. Their joints ached and their hearts raced. It even hurt to breathe. As they ran, they could feel the ground shuddering beneath them. A massive shadow loomed over the two helpless creatures as the bull finally caught up! He lowered his monstrous head and prepared to scoop them up in his dreadful horns. Fox and Badger both let out a petrified howl, believing it was all over.

But without a second's warning, a small, furry figure flew from nowhere and darted across the bull's path, distracting him from the job at hand. The bull grinded to a halt and stood up on his hindquarters, roaring, before setting himself back down again to see where the furry figure had gone.

It blazed across the field at an incredible speed, in a flash of brown and white. A long line of dust trailed behind it. It was a truly awesome sight.

Feeling challenged, the bull reared up and bounded after it, this time, not standing a chance of catching up.

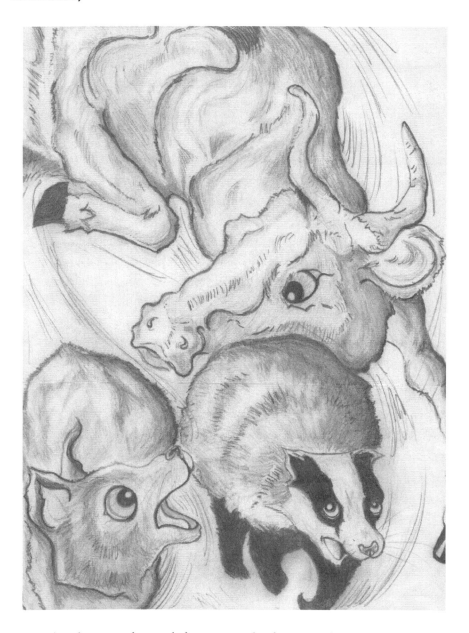

Fox and Badger wearily crawled into a patch of gorse and watched the chase from their safe distance.

The bull was led around and around the field by this newcomer. He galloped in mad circles around every mound and bush in the field, with the little brown thunderbolt zipping and zooming far ahead, acting, for all the world, like a red rag! This crazy chase pattern was repeated over and over again, until the bull was both exhausted and dizzy.

Then, the furry figure turned and veered uphill, past a large, convenient boulder. It lay the biggest, among a heap of man- dumped stones, hidden by last year's ivy. The still determined bull gave chase, but being in such a muddled state, ended up careering headfirst into this boulder! Fragments shot out here and there and those watching couldn't tell if they were bits of rock, or bits of horn! The bull now stood, dazed, wobbling in circular motion. He groaned with pain, took one step, and slumped to the ground, unconscious.

Fox and Badger kept themselves hidden for a while longer. They could not believe what they had just seen. What a spectacular show!

When all seemed peaceful again, Badger carefully emerged from the gorse patch. Fox stood up to follow but Badger insisted he stay put.

'Wait here,' he hushed. 'I'll be back soon.'

Badger made his way up the slope, through all of the hoof holes and skid marks. He then edged his way up to the mysterious furry creature, who by now had emerged from behind the boulder and was crouched over the silent bull.

The creature, although very young, was quite tall and handsome. It had enormous, strong hind legs, two, long, spoon shaped ears, a white fluffy tail and was coated from ear to paw in reddish brown fur. Its build was slim and lanky.

It turned around and spotted Badger, then chuckled in a high, comical voice.

'Is this what the world is coming to?' it joked. 'You can't even go for a nice evening jog without being hassled by bullies!'

Badger smiled. He could immediately tell this creature was friendly. And from its eyes, he could tell it was almost as daft as the bull.

'You're awful brave,' Badger remarked.

'I know,' said the creature proudly, checking its nails.

'Well,' said Badger. 'Thanks very much for saving our tails."

'Ah it was nothing,' the creature gloated, standing up on its hunkers with its eyes lightly closed. 'I could've done that with four paws tied behind my back!'

15

Wait, what do mean by *our* tails? I spotted only one of you earlier.'

Badger turned around and shouted down to the bushes; 'It's okay, you can come out now!'

Fox timidly poked his orange head out of the gorse, much to the surprise of the long eared creature.

'Aaaaaahh!' he shrieked, jumping backwards and losing all of the bravery he had previously shown. 'A fox, run!'

Badger stood in the creature's way, preventing him from fleeing. 'Calm down,' he hushed. 'He's with me.'

'What?' gasped the creature. 'You're hanging around with a fox?"

'It's okay,' said Badger reassuringly. 'He won't harm you.'

The long eared creature was not convinced.

'I'm getting out of here,' he shouted. 'There's a fox coming over here, and I'm not in the mood for being eaten today. Good luck!'

But Badger continued to bar the creature's way.

'Listen to me,' he explained, sounding more assertive. 'This fox is harmless. I only met him this morning but he's really friendly. Let him come over.'

The long eared creature turned and watched Fox approaching from the bottom of the slope, looking slightly self conscious.

'This is mad,' he continued, turning back to Badger. 'Why are you letting this fox follow you around? It's- it's dangerous and stupid. Are you trying to impress a female? If you are, I don't think she's worth it!'

'Stay,' Badger insisted. 'And give him a chance.'

The long eared creature shuddered with nerves as Fox sat down in front of him.

The cub blinked a few times, eyeing the two animals in front of him, feeling unsure. No one moved or spoke for a moment. Then:

'See,' said Badger. 'I told you he was harmless. You have no reason to be afraid.'

'Still,' said the creature, his eyes locked on Fox, his voice quivering. 'A friendly fox - not something you come across every day. I've had nothing but bad experiences with this lot; being chased and scared out of my fur.'

Fox stood in between the two animals, glancing from side to side as each one spoke. He felt awkward, being the subject of their conversation. He wished they would speak *to* him, and not *about* him.

'Please,' said Badger gently. 'You have to understand. He hasn't had it easy. He lost his whole family to The Farmer, just like I did. So I've been teaching him how to survive.'

After hearing this, the creature seemed to relent.

'Really?' he gasped, looking at Fox but still talking to Badger. 'You both lost your families?'

The two animals nodded.

'Oh,' he said. 'I suppose I can relate.'

'You've been upset by The Farmer too?' said Badger.

'Have I?' exclaimed the creature. 'When I was just a newborn leveret, my dear mother was shot dead out in the open field.'

'Where were you?' asked Badger.

'At home in my nest, with my brothers and sisters,' replied the creature.

'We heard the shot. It was only a matter of time before the hounds found us. And they did. We were huddled together, small, naked, some of us still blind...'

'What happened next?' asked Badger, engrossed, and of course devastated.

'I'm not too sure myself,' said the creature. 'I was too busy crawling through a patch of grass by myself, looking for somewhere safe to hide. By the time I found a rock to shelter under, the hounds were already finished with my family. Since then, I've been alone, wandering, no real home, taking care of myself.'

Badger became grave.

'I'm very sorry,' he said.

The creature forced a smile.

'Don't pester me with your sympathy! I'm not that alone. I reckon the spirit of my mother is still here, guiding my steps.'

Fox and Badger were both deeply moved by this newcomer's story of loss and survival.

'Yep,' he concluded. 'Those humans are a strange bunch. I don't know what The Farmer didn't like about my family. Maybe he thought we were rabbits, and wanted to protect his vegetables. Who knows.'

The three youngsters sighed, nodded and looked at the ground.

'Well, stranger," said Badger. 'This was sure a funny way of meeting for the first time. Do you mind if I ask your name?'

'Name?' grunted the creature. 'Huh, why would I need a name? I don't know anybody, and nobody knows me. I have no one to address me.'

'Not with that attitude,' Badger mumbled. 'Well in that case, can we just call you *Hare?* I mean, you are a hare, right?"

'Of course I'm a hare!' snapped the creature. 'What do I look like to you, an oversized mouse with a really bad ear infection?'

Badger sniggered, and then introduced himself.

'I'm Badger,' he said.

'Oh really?' exclaimed Hare, raising his eyebrows. 'You don't have a proper name either?"

'Neither of us do,' said Badger. 'And even if I did have one, I've long since forgotten it.'

'Sad," said Hare. 'Very sad. That lousy human really messed us all up. I'd love to see him being chased by his own bull. I wouldn't help him. In fact, I'd be riding the bull!'

Badger sniggered again.

Hare then turned to Fox.

'You're Fox I presume?' he said.

The cub nodded, happy now at being acknowledged.

'Well Fox,' said Hare, in a sorry (but playful) tone. 'I apologize for getting the wrong impression of you. It's just that any other fox would want me to spend the night in his belly. But you seem alright.'

The cub smiled, not quite grasping Hare's rapid speech.

'Good to see that you're not afraid anymore,' said Badger.

'Hah,' Hare shrugged. 'I never was afraid. See, I just took down a giant bull. Why would I be scared of this little fella?'

Badger chuckled;

'He's still bigger than you!"

'Quiet,' Hare hushed, in joking tones.

The two youngsters laughed, Fox giggling to fit in.

'So,' Hare went on. 'Do you two outlaws have any plans together?'

'Yes I think we do,' Badger beamed. 'Fox and I were planning on leaving this place tomorrow in search of a new home. It's kind of a long shot, but I figured we might as well. This place isn't exactly paradise anymore.'

'Hmmm,' Hare muttered, swivelling his shiny, marble eyes around. 'That's odd. I was planning on doing the very same thing.'

'You were?' said Badger anxiously. 'Do you know of any places we can go?"

Hare paused for a brief moment, and then a smile of childish excitement broke across his whiskery face.

'Well there is *one* place...' he muttered.

'Where's that?' asked Badger, with deepening suspense.

'Apparently,' Hare began, sitting down and looking up at the two eager faces staring back down at him. 'A few miles north east of here, there's a little nature sanctuary. I've never seen it of course, but I often hear birds talking about it. Supposed to be very beautiful- fine forests, green hills, a lake. They call this place *Lough Ine.*'

'Lough Ine?' gasped Badger.

'That's what it's called, apparently,' said Hare, rising to his big feet. 'And if we want to get there, we should leave now instead of tomorrow.'

'Now?' Badger groaned. 'But Fox and I are exhausted. We've had a long day of exploring and hunting and being chased. Why now?'

'Because it's safer if we go now,' Hare explained. 'While there're no humans or machinery around. Plus night is always the best time for us animals anyway; foodwise and what not.'

Badger grunted, 'That's true. And I do love the darkness. Daylight can really give me a headache.'

'So it's settled then,' Hare concluded. 'We leave right away.'

'What?' asked Fox, having not spoken for a while. 'We're all going? Now? Together?'

'Sure,' said Hare, already turning to leave. 'Isn't that what friends do?'

'Wait,' Badger moaned. 'Can we please wait a while? My paws are seriously sore.'

Hare sighed and sat back down, his excitement temporarily quenched.

'Fine, we'll rest for a bit first.'

A loud snorting sound startled everyone. All eyes turned to see that the bull had finally come to. He opened his eyes and shook his mighty head. Hare grinned; 'Or not!'

The three young animals turned and sped off into the wilderness.

On the Trail

After meeting Hare, things started happening fast!

Through the thick, marshy, sticky tangle of the mysterious countryside, the three companions, Fox, Badger and Hare travelled together far and wide, all in search of the same place: the promised land of Lough Ine. Had anyone out walking spotted them, it certainly would have been an odd sight; a small group of natural enemies wandering along together, as if content in each other's company.

But because each of the three animals was so different, it made the journey a great deal more difficult. Badger was a creature of the night, who preferred to come out only after sundown to feed, and of course, dispose of what he had already fed on. Hare was a creature of the day, who was happier roaming the hills in broad daylight, nibbling grass and chasing the wind. And Fox - he wasn't too sure. However, these contrasting hunting and sleeping patterns also made the journey more interesting. At the outset, the animals decided to alternate. One day, they would travel through the night, the next, the morning, and so on. During the time they were not on the move, they would sleep. And while travelling, they would also seek food. But committing to this timetable was easier said than done. For none of the friends knew how long their journey was going to be - nor how dangerous.

On that first night, as he struggled to keep up with his two new companions, Fox's head buzzed with a thousand thoughts and questions; he wondered if he was doing the right thing by following these two creatures whom he had just met, to a place he wasn't sure was real or not. Furthermore, he wondered if his mother would have approved of him socializing with animals that were not of his own kind…

During what seemed like many long hours of cold air and bright silver moonlight, the animals picked their way through many a field. The grass was long and dew drenched. They crossed a number of cold, trickling streams, sometimes stopping to have a drink, before proceeding.

Onwards they went, through wild and bushy hedgerows, barely pausing. The brambles, ferns, heather and gorse were annoyingly clingy, despite being withered and in some places snow-caked, so the animals had to wrestle and tear through them. More fields followed. The friends hobbled across each one, stumbling and faltering. The hoof prints in the ground, left over from a herd of cattle formed deep holes, which the companions could barely see in the dark, and kept stepping in.

Later, they passed under a row of maple trees, which were framed against the glowing moon. They pressed on, frequently running, and then slowing again. Hare often took breaks to be alone.

Fox and Badger would watch as he fought invisible enemies; punching air, and roundhouse kicking in the darkness. It appeared a hard-bitten life of solitary wandering had made him wary; wary of a world where friend was tragically outnumbered by foe.

So the friends went on, resting, moving, resting, moving. At one point, they took a break to feed. Badger sharpened his claws on one of the maple trunks, and then using them, tore off strips of bark, revealing an assortment of delicious creepy crawlies; woodlice, slugs, larvae and beetles. He and Fox polished them off, while Hare helped himself to a patch of clover and sedge. After a final drink in one of the nearby streams, the journey continued.

So came the morning of the second day. From behind the distant, ice capped mountains, the sun slowly rose high into the sky, thawing out what was left of the cold winter snow. The countryside brightened under its faint heat.

As always, birds flew busily over a patchwork of fields, meadows, hedgerows and bog land. Cows grazed lazily on the plains, without a care in the world. In one of the emptier fields, two brown horses galloped side by side; a mare and her foal. They neighed and snorted happily, while now cantering along together, with their long manes fluttering in the wind.

But the three young animals that had been out the previous day were nowhere to be seen. The dull day drifted on without them.

Then came the evening. The sun still shone, but was hidden behind a white veil of clouds. It was not as bright as it had been earlier. The air was damp and chilly.

From underneath a blanket of shrubbery. Fox, Badger and Hare poked their sleepy heads out. The morning and afternoon they had spent resting. Now they were ready.

For all of the other creatures around; the birds and the farm animals, the day was nothing special or interesting. It was just another peaceful day in the open country. But for the three travelling youngsters, the *day* had plans for *them!*

'Cracked as da Crows!'

'Come on fellas,' shouted Hare as he sped up the hill. 'You're lagging behind. You'd be faster hitching a lift with a snail! Get a move on!'

Panting and gasping, Fox and Badger followed their quick - legged companion up and over the grassy plain, on a cold but bright day. All around, the grass was undulating in the breezes, and the distant hedge borders nodded their heads, as if urging them on.

Hare whizzed along excitedly, through the short, trampled grass and halted at the edge of the precipice.

'Let's see,' he muttered, gazing out over the seemingly endless landscape. 'Looks like we'll have to tackle a few more fields, and, oh goodie, we get to cross a river!'

Badger hobbled up beside him, struggling for breath.

'What do you see?' he groaned. 'All this daylight is blinding me.'

Hare laughed; 'Keep your fur on, ya big whinge-pot, as soon as we make it over that river we'll stop for a rest in the shade.'

Fox plodded awkwardly across the lumpy field with his two friends. Every moment now was a challenge and a thrill. Already, he'd had to teach himself things he never knew before- such as how to swim. The journey had broadened his awareness greatly, so much so, that he now rarely asked what many would consider 'stupid' questions. Still, the journey was young, and so was he, and he still had so very much to learn.

When the trio reached the river, they stopped, wondering how to get across. The distance to the other side was an impossible jump. It looked as though the ground had divided during an earthquake, both banks being so spaced apart.

When the friends peered down over the side of the first riverbank they gasped and took a step back. It was a frightful drop. Sharp rocks seemed to grow out of the gushing, foamy water far below. Occasional leaves and driftwood rode the current, disappearing downstream at high speed. In some places, the river plunged into deep pools, creating creamy mounds of suds.

'Well this is certainly a kick in the bucktooth,' said Hare, in a strangely calm tone.

'We'll never make it,' Badger groaned.

'Hah, maybe *you* won't,' Hare smirked. 'But watch me!'

Hare backed up with his tail in the air and prepared to vault over the chasm, but Badger stood in his way.

'Don't risk it,' he protested. 'You'll fall and splat yourself off those big rocks down there.'

'So what will we do?' asked Hare, miffed.

'Search for a way around, I suppose,' Badger suggested.

Badger and Hare had been sharing the role of 'leader.' They frequently took turns trying out different ideas and suggesting different routes to take. So it only seemed fair that Badger got to make the decision.

'Fine,' grunted Hare reluctantly. 'We'll search for a way around. But if I had jumped I would have made it. Probably.'

The trio walked slowly along the riverbank, which seemed to wind on forever. It was lined with clumps of new hogweed, hemlock, reeds, sedge and cat's tail. The opposite bank was just as lush, and it stood there as if teasing them.

'I don't think there is a way around,' said Hare.

'Don't worry,' said Badger. 'We'll find one.'

Just then, Fox, who was trailing a short distance behind his friends, spied an old, lice infested log to his left. It stretched from one side of the river to the other, and was obscured under an over - hanging blackthorn tree.

'Hey,' squeaked Fox as he hurried over to it, wagging his tail. 'What's this?'

'Well done, Fox,' Hare joked, now spotting it himself. 'Maybe we can use that log as a raft and sail to Lough Ine!'

Badger ignored Hare's joke and shuffled up beside Fox and stooped to inspect the log. It may have been an old sycamore tree, now dead and rotting from the inside out. Its grooves were wide, and covered in layers of soft, green moss and crab - eye lichen. There were also clusters of fungus' growing on the ancient, hollow trunk; knobbly black balls called 'King Alfred's Cakes' and 'birch polypore.' The log was sagging in the middle, barely taking the weight of all the green stuff.

'Hmmm,' Badger muttered. 'Looks like this log's seen too many seasons. It mightn't be strong enough to hold all of us at once. We'll have to cross over one by one.'

Hare sighed, combing back his ears;

'This is so predictable. Two of us'll make it, and whoever's last, will fall like a pig trying to fly.'

Badger turned to Hare with a look of surprise;

'What makes you think that?'

Hare shrugged;

'I dunno. I can just imagine it happening, that's all.'

Badger laughed. 'Well thanks for your great words of encouragement. Come on, we'll give it our best.'

Hare went first. Swift as a breeze and without any trouble, he was on the other side.

'Hah,' he laughed triumphantly, jumping up and down. 'At least I won't be the one who goes tailly uppy!'

Badger turned to Fox. 'Do you want to give it a shot?'

Fox nodded nervously and stepped onto the old, wobbly log. It sort of rolled from side to side as he tried to steady himself. He then found his balance and stood still for a brief moment. Then Badger called him back.

'Oh, and Fox,' he asked politely. 'When you get to the other side, could you do one thing for me?'

'What's that?' asked the cub.

Badger grinned;

'Slap Hare.'

Fox smiled and proceeded to edge his way across the river. The sound of the roaring water below was terrifying but he dared not look down. Breathing lightly and carefully placing one paw in front of the other, the cub made steady progress. His tense, thumping heart did not distract him. Forward he moved. Soon, his ordeal was over and he was on the other side with Hare who was dancing a jig and singing;

We made it, we made it
With no stopping or stalling.
We made it, we made it
To see Badger falling

From the other side, Badger shouted:

'Hare, when I get over there I'll catch you by the ears and dangle you over the edge!'

Hare sniggered defensively.

'Oh really? Let's see you make it over here first!'

Badger, who was the heaviest of the three, stepped onto the log bridge and began waddling along slowly, trying hard to stay balanced. The log sounded like it was in pain; bending, creaking and splintering under his great weight, but so far, it remained in one piece.

'Any second now,' Hare joked. 'That log is coming down! Timberrrrrrrrr!'

'Oh you're dead,' Badger muttered.

'I hope you're a good swimmer,' Hare quipped, continuing to heckle his friend.

Badger halted in the middle of the log and cackled; 'I'm half way there, Hare, and it hasn't broken yet. You'd better start running!'

And sure enough, to put him right, a large split appeared across the bottom centre of the log. Badger could feel himself descending. Soft orange chunks poured from each side of the log as it gave way and snapped completely in half!

Badger frantically scrambled onto one half of it and leapt onto the ledge of the riverbank, barely hanging on with his claws, while both halves of the log dropped down and smashed off the rocks below. Hundreds of woodlice and earwigs swam for their lives.

'Little help!' cried Badger, as he slid hopelessly down the bank. His plump body dangled over the edge, while his claws desperately ploughed through the earth.

Fox and Hare gasped and dropped to their knees and peered down over the edge at Badger, who was suspended over the treacherous water and rocks.

'Grab my ears!' cried Hare as he bent over and hung his head upside down, just about close enough for Badger to reach. Badger desperately reached out with one paw and took hold of one of Hare's long ears, but being so heavy, ended up dragging him down over the edge too! Hare shrieked as he tumbled down over the bare, earthy riverbank and caught onto Badger's short, stumpy tail for safety. Badger flinched with pain and dug his claw deeper into the bank. His arm seemed to stretch. Now both friends were in distress.

'Badger,' Hare begged. 'Please don't let go. If you do, *I'll die!*'

Badger growled,

'You're lucky I didn't drink much today.'

Knowing he was their only hope, Fox recklessly dived down onto the ledge, slipping and sliding. Soil and pebbles skittered down the embankment, to be swallowed up by the current. The thought of danger did not cross his mind. It was simply courage over instinct. He turned and beckoned Badger to grab his tail. Badger did so, and almost pulled the cub down on top of himself. Digging his tiny claws into the earth, Fox struggled furiously to climb the steep bank, with the weight of *two* animals on his back. His tail was on the verge of ripping. Squinting and hissing with agony, the cub pressed onwards, inch by painful inch. His limbs quivered under the pressure. Badger held on tightly, eyes hardened with fear and uncertainty. Would Fox manage this daring task, being so small and puny?

Hare still gripped Badger's tail; eyes squeezed shut, while muttering in prayer;

'Okay, I can tolerate falling, or drowning, or landing on a sharp rock, but please, please don't let Badger land on me!'

With an almighty final surge of energy, Fox hoisted himself, Badger and Hare up over the edge and back onto flat land. Fox wailed and collapsed. The muscles in his stomach, legs and tail were red- raw. And so the three lay in the bed of rushes, panting and wheezing. From that moment, they knew things weren't going to be plain sailing. They took time to catch their breath and calm their nerves.

After a short while, Hare sat up and burst out laughing; Hahahahahaha, 1 was right! Hahahahahaha, the log did break! Hahahahahaha, Badger did fall, didn't I say he would! Hahahahahaha -ouch, what was that for?'

The day wore on.

As the three youngsters went, the land began to rise. It wasn't long before they found themselves standing on a high windy hill, which was overgrown with rich blankets of thorny heather and tall, spiky bushes of gorse. Getting through it, they found, was an unpleasant task.

'Ow, my paws,' Hare groaned. The sharp thorns of every bush dug into him as he and his companions struggled to pass through. 'Ow, my ears. Ow, my whiskers!'

'Quit whining,' Badger snapped, looking back. 'Your whiskers can't feel pain!'

Thorn bushes are said to be a haven for wild animals. They provide homes, safe passage, shelter (from weather, or when chased) and are ideal for resting under. But animals only use them out of instinct. They would much prefer to be out in the open.,

As soon as the messy wave of bushes became unbearable, the friends halted. Gorse towered above and around them, while heather lay thick beneath them, growing up as far as their waists. Their fur was riddled with tiny spines.

'How do hedgehogs put up with this on a daily basis?' Hare grumbled.

'We all feel the same way,' Badger growled, while ploughing through the branches with his big body. Fox and Hare followed in the path he was creating. They plodded along over the trampled heather and broken twigs, until they came to the edge of the hill.

They then took time to recover from that short trial. Fox sat combing the thorns out of his ears with his paws. But instead; this caused his paws to become lodged with thorns. Then using his mouth to remove the thorns from his paws, the cub soon found his *tongue* riddled with thorns!

While Fox and Hare proceeded to groom themselves, Badger snooped around the ground, searching for an easier route to take. The steep hill offered a splendid view of the landscape, but Badger's eyes were unable to see that far. He was now constantly dazzled. Even when he turned his head away, orbs of colour still floated before his eyes, like he was looking through stained glass. Only the nearest fields were within his scope. Peering around, he announced to his friends:

'Well we don't have many choices. We could go through that marsh over there, but we might sink in all that mud. Or we could go through that hedgerow, but it's awful close to a human's house. Or, we could go through that field, but there's a herd in it.'

Hare stopped grooming for a moment and looked up.

'Heard of what?' he enquired.

'Herd of cattle,' said Badger.

Hare chuckled; 'Of course I've heard of cattle.'

'No,' said Badger, sternly. 'I mean a 'cow' herd.'

'A cow heard what?' asked Hare.

Badger rolled his eyes, as if trying to seek help from above.

After shaking the last of the thorns from their coats, the animals chose the nearby trampled field as their next path. The cattle were huddled at the other side, too lazy and too comfortable to care about three small vagabonds passing through.

They made their way down the slope and across the plain, trying to follow the trail of shade.

Again, Badger led the way, trying to adjust the setting of his eyes. A breath of cool wind drifted through the short grass. Leaves whirled around in the breeze. The land was beginning to level; becoming smoother and flatter. Up ahead, the aqua blue mountains were constantly in sight, drawing closer with every step the friends took.

But suddenly, there was a faint rumble. The friends stopped in their tracks and froze.

'Another bull?' gasped Fox.

'No, not a bull,' said Badger, in a bashful tone. 'That was my belly. It seems like the more I eat, the hungrier I get. This journey is taking a lot out of me.'

Fox nodded, and then he and Badger noticed that Hare was staring at something in the distance.

'Look,' he gasped, with a strand of drool hanging from his mouth. 'An apple tree!

All three heads were now fixed upon a distant shrub, with the distinctive flat- topped shape and gnarled, rickety features of a crab apple tree. Only it happened to be growing inside a picket fence, on the lawn of someone's property. A tall, white, two storey house blotted out the sunlight.

'Tempting,' said Badger. 'Very tempting.'

'Come on,' Hare pleaded. 'I'm tired of eating only grass. I've never tried fruit'

'Hmmm,' Badger mumbled, stroking his chin, wondering if and how he and his company could undergo this daring feat.

Fox peered around.

'But there're cows over there,' he said. 'All around the fence.'

'I'm not worried about them, said Badger. 'There's no bull. I'm more worried about whatever humans might be living in that house. And another thing, can any of us climb trees?'

'We'll figure that out when we get over there,' said Hare. 'And besides, there might be some apples on the ground'

Badger pondered for a time more and then gave up.

'Fair enough,' he sighed. 'Let's go for it. We can regret it later.'

The three youngsters set off towards the apple tree. But their first task was to get through the cattle, which were gathered outside the picket fence, grazing on the extra long grass.

'Easy does it,' Badger whispered. 'Just take it slow, and keep away from their rear ends!'

Hare sniggered to himself:

'Pat on the head.'

Carefully did Fox, Badger and Hare move through the forest of long legs and swishing tails. The cows rose up around them like black and white giants. Yet they seemed quite docile. They simply stood there, chewing the cud, most of them unaware of the three small animals creeping around their hooves. Suddenly, one cow lifted its tail and emptied its bowels all over the grass.

'Yuck,' Hare cringed. 'You disgusting-'

'Keep going, keep going,' Badger hushed 'And ignore the smell.'

As soon as the fence was reached, the friends slipped in through a gap between the wooden planks. Badger was the last in of course. He had to squeeze his big, hefty form through with some difficulty.

Behind the fence, they found themselves in a little garden. The house was surrounded in tall Lawson cypress trees, and below lay a rich and colorful flower bed, with all sorts of weird and exotic winter flowers; yellow clocks of winter jasmine, healthy bunches of darley dale heath, bright red tangles of firethorn. Even some odd looking 'garden gnomes' stood on guard among the colourful display. A mixed herbal smell hung in the air, which certainly made a change to the not- so- pleasant smell of the cattle outside.

The three companions were enchanted. They peered around at their new and unusual environment, feeling slightly insecure.

'Why are we doing this?' gasped Badger. 'This is crazy. Humans live here.'

'This isn't the best time to start having second thoughts,' said Hare, nervously. 'We're here now, and we're not leaving empty pawed.'

The three animals craned their necks to look up at the apple tree. It didn't look too promising. There were very few leaves, and those that were there were brown and crispy. The outer branches displayed no apples, and it was impossible to tell with the inner branches, for there were too many twigs in the way.

Badger tutted.

'I have a bad feeling about this,' he sighed.

'Search the ground,' Hare suggested.

The trio crouched down and began combing through the dark, damp grass with their snouts. All they could find were five apples; five soft, spongy, rotten apples.

The friends then rose to their feet and looked at each other.

'I wouldn't feed these apples to a bluebottle,' said Badger. 'Looks like one of us will have to climb the tree. It's our only hope.'

'But who?' asked Hare. 'I can't'

'Neither can I,' said Badger. 'I can hardly run.'

Badger and Hare then turned and rested their eyes on Fox, who then quivered.

'What?' he asked, a little taken aback.

'It looks like you're the only one who stands a chance,' said Badger.

'Why me?' asked Fox. 'Why can't you climb?'

'You think we don't want to!' cried Hare. 'I tell you, if we hares could climb trees, we'd frickin' well live in them!'

'But I can't climb either,' Fox protested.

'How do you know that?' enquired Hare. 'You've never tried'

Fox shook his head.

'Ah ah,' he said dismissively. 'Too dangerous.'

'We'll catch you if you fall,' said Badger reassuringly. 'All we want you to do is climb the tree, find a few apples and toss them down.'

'But what about me?' asked the cub.

'Don't worry,' said Hare. 'We'll save an apple for you.'

Again, the cub shook his head and took a step back.

'Come on,' pleaded Badger. 'You're light and you have good claws. I'm too heavy.'

'And my claws are too short,' added Hare.

Fox paused, and then replied sternly; 'No.'

'I know you can do it,' said Badger. 'And I'll tell you why. I was out grubbing for worms one evening and I came to a copse of trees. I stopped at one of the trees to sharpen my claws, but when I looked up the first thing I saw was a fox; fast asleep on the base of the branches, with his tail hanging down. You see! He was able to climb a tree. And he was so confident he managed to have a nap up there!'

Fox gulped. He hesitated no more and gave in, just to please his friends and test his own abilities.

Positioning himself at the base of the tree trunk, the cub took a deep breath and looked up.

The tree trunk itself was quite short. The only parts of the tree that were long were the two main branches that stretched off in opposite directions, forming a perfect 'Y' shaped structure. The entire tree was hard and knobbly, covered in lumps and knots. This provided good grip. Fox looked back at Badger and Hare who were standing side by side, giving him encouraging smiles and nods. The cub smiled back, having found just a morsel of courage, and then bounded straight onto the tree. Instantly, his claws sprang out; a natural reaction. They gripped the trunk firmly, supporting the cub's weight.

He quickly took control and pulled himself upwards, scrabbling with his hind legs and clinging on tightly with his front. After reaching the safety of the top of the trunk, Fox looked down at his friends.

'Good stuff,' cried Badger, craning his neck upwards.

Fox grinned gleefully, and then shuddered. His friends seemed a fair distance below now. He decided to not look down anymore. Onwards he progressed, onto one of the long sturdy branches, standing upright, digging his claws in deep and maintaining his balance. He then stopped and scanned the treetop for any sign of apples. All he could see was an endless tide of twigs and lichen. There were no apples to be found whatsoever.

'There's nothing,' he cried. 'Are you sure this is an apple tree?'

Below, Hare took his eyes off Fox and glared at Badger, who had a paw clapped over his face.

'Of course,' he gasped 'This is the wrong season! Apples only grow in summer! We've just barely finished with winter!'

Hare grunted with annoyance. 'Now he tells us!'

'This was mainly your idea!' Badger remarked.

'Never mind that,' Hare sighed. 'Let's just leave this place.'

Meanwhile, up on the tree, Fox was wondering how to come back down. He nervously edged his way backwards and then stopped to turn around. But on doing so, despite his efforts to be careful, he lost his footing and dropped off the side of the branch! With lightning reflexes, he grasped back on with his claws and dangled above in the air.

Badger and Hare froze in horror.

'Fox!' they cried as one, not knowing what to do.

Fox's claws scraped against the side of the branch as he slid further and further down. He kicked his hind legs and waved his tail in a panicked frenzy. Then, knowing it was hopeless; he released his grip and plummeted into the soft flower bed below.

Badger and Hare rushed to inspect the sunken patch of pink and red flowers, where a cloud of petals sprinkled down from above. Before they could get close, a perfectly unharmed Fox popped his head out of the flower bed, and shrieked with surprise when he came face to face with a crude looking gnome!

'Don't worry,' Badger panted as he reached his friend and plonked himself down beside him, 'It's not a real human. And even if it were, you could take him!'

Fox forced a nervous laugh, whilst still trying to catch his breath.

'Good show,' said Hare warmly.

'Yeah,' added Badger.' That was real bravery.'

Fox nodded, and allowed his companions to help him up. The gnome seemed smaller now that Fox was standing. He imagined it winking at him, from under its red cap and white beard.

The three animals then crept through the garden, in search of an exit, keeping as low and as quiet as they could. The frightful thought of humans and dogs still hung over them.

Badger halted promptly. His powerful nose detected something.

'You smell something?' asked Hare.

Badger sniffed deeply and looked around 'Yes,' he replied. 'I smell something alright.'

'Oh no,' Hare sighed 'If it's a dog, we're done for. I don't see any openings!'

'Not a dog,' said Badger, moving forward in the direction of the scent. The friends were led around the corner of the house, to the back garden. There, they stopped up overjoyed at the sight that met their eyes. There in front of them, lay a small, ripe, vegetable patch. It lay like a soft green mattress, filled with numerous broad leaves and stalks, indicating a treasury of food below the rich soil.

Badger turned and faced his comrades.

'Okay, okay,' he said excitedly. 'Let's make this quick. Grab what you can and leg it!'

The three friends seized their opportunity and plundered through the vegetable patch; they uprooted carrots, turnips, parsnips, and beetroot, leeks, onions, celery. Lovely, moist earth dripped from each vegetable as it left the ground for the first time.

'Oh wow,' Hare trembled. 'I think I'm gonna die with excitement.'

'Ssshh,' Badger hushed. 'Let's hurry this up. Come on!'

The animals pulled as many vegetables out of the ground as they could and did not dare to linger. They hastily finished their raid and galloped to the front of the house as fast as the weight of the stolen food in their mouth would allow. After finding the gap in the fence from which they had entered, the three daring youngsters dived out through and back into the wilderness. Badger had to toss his prize over the fence and follow it through the gap.

Out in the middle of the field, in the shade of an old well, a feast took place.

The three companions sat in a circle and happily tore into their stolen goods.

Fox had managed to swipe four onions, which he soon found tasted revolting. They stung his eyes and made his mouth water furiously. But Hare, who had greedily nicked three carrots, was happy to share one with the hungry cub. And as for Badger, he managed to take only one turnip. But being so large, it proved a meal in itself.

And so, the friends sat nibbling and munching. Fox and Hare finished their carrots, while Badger struggled with the second half of his turnip.

'I can't... manage any more,' he panted, lying on his side, bloated. 'I'll have the rest later.'

After a quarter of an hour, the animals shakily climbed to their feet and the journey continued.

The field was the biggest they had yet come across. It stretched ahead, beyond their line of vision, forming a straight horizon. As they walked, the ground became harder and the grass shorter.

The lack of trees in the area left the animals fully exposed to the cool sunlight. Badger, who was still carrying the leftovers of his turnip, trailed behind his friends, using their bodies as shade. Hare led the way. The trio soon came to a long line of tractor tracks. They lay pressed into the ground, full of mud puddles from which the animals stopped to drink. Forward they moved, following the track which seemed to lead on without a break or turn. The friends found this part of their journey both tiring and tedious. But they were blissfully unaware of the sinister eyes that watched them from a distance.

High up in the air and lined all along a telephone wire, a murder of hooded crows were perched. The filthy, black and grey feathered birds sat cawing and chattering amongst themselves. Although most hooded crows were native to the countryside, these particular crows had come from the local town in search of better food. All they were used to was rubbish and road kill.

Their story was a sad one, but nothing worthy of pity. It was simply in their genes to be outcasts, having no friends other than their own kith and kin. Perhaps it was their egotistical nature and violent outlook that set them apart from other creatures. If it wasn't a crow, it was hated.

Their leader, 'Corvus', was a sly and dangerous individual. He had a fiery temper and a lust for stealing, mobbing, fighting and even killing. He was feared and reverred by all of the smaller birds in the area, whom he often bullied and robbed from. Even his own followers dared not defy his orders, for they were terrified he might peck them bald (this was a punishment Corvus often carried out on fellow crows whenever they made mistakes or disobeyed him).

Today, the gang leader was perched on top of the pole, as he would on a tall building or warehouse, ruffling his ash grey feathers and preening. Beneath his feet lay the messy remains of a baby sparrow that he had snatched from its mother's nest. But it simply wasn't enough to keep out the hunger.

So Corvus and his gang waited above on the wire, surveying the land.

Suddenly, three peculiar looking figures roaming the distant plain caught the attention of the gang leader himself; a shaggy, grey, hairball, a floppy eared, fluffy tailed rodent and a ginger colored puppy of some kind. They all appeared very young and lost. It took Corvus a moment to put labels on them. And then he noticed one of them was clutching the remains of a perfectly good turnip...

'Jaypers, would ya lookit dat,' he said discreetly to the crow beside him. 'A fox, a badger an' a rabbit all walkin' t'gether. Pretty quare in't it?'

The other crow, who was called Razor, leaned forward and lowered his eyes down on the three passer byes. He snorted:

'Huh. What a dose.'

Corvus wiped the sparrow blood from his long bill and gave a devious grin.

'Look, look,' he went on, in his usual raspy voice. 'One of 'em's got a shnack. Hope he wouldn't mind us scabbing our share.'

'But boss,' the other crow protested. 'What about da fox?'

Corvus glared at his companion.

'What about de fox, exactly,' he said, unperturbed. 'Lookit de size of him! I'd say his mammy just let him out! Shir, we can flake 'em no bodder!'

'I dunnah, boss,' sighed Razor, unsure.

'Ah, come on, willa,' Corvus laughed. 'It'll be a ball! They're just babbies! And I don't see any ould ones.'

Razor still sounded reluctant.

'Boss, I'm all fer fighting, like, but j'know, foxes and badgers are a bit much in fairness-'

Razor stopped when he saw the insane expression on his leader's face. Corvus hissed threateningly:

'If ya want t'keep your head feathers, y'll do what I say! Roight!'

Razor nodded fearfully. 'Whatever ya say, boss.'

Corvus cackled.

'Right lads!' he announced to all the other crows. 'Y'see them young scuts down dere? Dem ones crossing de field? Fancy an ould barmey with em?'

The crows of course, devoid of free will, who had forfeit their sorry lives to please a most unworthy leader, had no choice but to consent. They all erupted into cheering, cawing and cackling, bumping their chests together and head-locking, after which Corvus announced his wicked plan.

'Alright bies,' he bellowed. 'This is de scoop- we catch 'em by surprise, rough 'em up, and we take de tornup! And if any o' dem die, we eat *dem* too!'

More fiendish laughter burst from the gang of crows, which was soon followed by Corvus's orders:

'Reaper, Diver, Glugger, Dumpster, Scabbers- you follow Razor! The rest o' ya, come with me! This oughta' be class!'

Meanwhile, Fox, Badger and Hare were nearing the edge of the field. A dense area of shrubbery came into view up ahead. Brown, withered ferns lay in untidy heaps all over the hedgerow, with long, sharp brambles sprouting out through them like a miniature jungle canopy.

'Finally,' sighed Badger with relief. 'Shelter.'

The three friends stumbled onwards, in the direction of the hedgerow, when all of a sudden a large shadow was cast over them. Looking up, they saw a flock of sinister looking birds pass overhead. Their silhouettes resembled little lumps of coal being spat from the sun.

'What kind of birds are they?' asked Fox.

'Hooded crows,' Hare replied. 'The gangsters of the countryside.'

'Are they friendly?' asked Fox.

'Hmph,' said Badger, dropping his turnip. 'In all my time wandering this place, I've never come across a friendly hooded crow. Nothing but a thieving, grasping, greedy bunch of thugs and murderers; the whole miserable lot of them.'

Fox gulped fearfully;

'And, err, why are they coming this way?'

The three companions watched in mounting suspense as the wave of crows turned and swooped down towards them, before breaking up and forming a giant ring, which then dropped from the air and alighted on the ground. Fox, Badger and Hare - were surrounded.

They stood together in a tight little circle, glancing around at all of the cawing, snapping birds, with their black feathers and grey jackets, sharp, curved beaks and pointy talons.

Corvus stepped forward from the great rally, with a devilish grin on his ugly face. His eyes could not be seen. They looked more like empty sockets.

'Story bies,' he jeered. 'Howz da craic?'

The three companions were now consumed by a mixture of fear, confusion and even a sense of rage. Badger stood over Fox, protecting him from the monstrous, noisy rabble of newcomers. Both friends were stiff with nerves, but Hare, on the other hand, struck up a boxing pose.

Corvus turned back to his followers.

'Whatcha reckon, lads?' he grinned. 'Easy meat or what?'

The crows all cackled raucously,

'It's okay Fox,' whispered Badger, into the ear of the petrified cub. 'We're bigger and stronger than them. We'll get through this.'

'Sorry what was dat?' hissed Corvus, hopping over to Badger.' Y'think ya know a way outta this hames, is it? Go on, so, I'd like t'see ya try!'

Badger glared coldly at the gang leader, who then focused his attention on Hare.

'And is this yer fluffy bunny friend?' he mocked, sticking his beak close to Hare's nose, in an intimidating manner.

Hare smirked arrogantly and squared up to him.

'Who're you calling a bunny, you ignorant, dung faced, thrash eating feather bag!'

Corvus laughed with spite.

'Oh, we got ourselves a chancer here, bies. Still, nothing we can't sort out!'

Turning around again, Corvus ordered; 'Take de tornip!'

Two crows hopped forward and landed on the leftover turnip. They looked at Badger and cawed nastily in his face before rolling the turnip into the crowd.

'Less fer ye ta carry,' laughed Corvus, looking at the three trembling animals. He then fixed his hateful gaze on Fox, who was cowering in Badger's shadow.

'Ah, isn't this de cutest thing ye've ever saw?' he mocked. 'A fox following a badger an' a rabbit around like they're his buddies!'

More loud, irritating laughter boomed from the gang of crows, egging their leader on. Corvus looked Fox in the eye. Fox shivered and stared at him, utterly terrified.

'What's wrong witcha?' the gang leader jeered. 'Why aren't ya chasing that rabbit an' eating him? Shir he's not yore friend. He's yore food!'

Suddenly, Badger's paw shot up and gripped Corvus tightly around the neck and pulled him towards his face. Corvus gasped for breath.

'Now listen to me you scum!' Badger seethed, frothing at the mouth. 'We've just wasted a lot of time being hassled by you and your empty headed goons, while listening to you talk rubbish! I think you're familiar with the word *rubbish* right? It's where you came from! Now let me put you right; for starters, he over there is no rabbit. He's a hare; the land's fastest runner. And this fox, believe it or not, is one of us. He's not going to kill us; he's not going to eat us. Now you and your low life 'buddies' better back off and fly away while you still have your wings!'

With that, Badger released Corvus and pushed him back into the stunned crowd. It took the gang leader a second to regain his composure.

'Big mistake, badger boi,' he said in a venomous voice. 'Right lads, millie up!'

The crows, with no minds of their own, practically had to be told how to feel, so seeing that their leader was ready to fight, they switched from fear back to aggression. They cawed and screeched furiously, beating their wings and scraping the ground with their talons. Slowly, they closed in on their prey.

Fox, Badger and Hare grouped together in a defensive circle, watching the crows advance. This was it. The flashpoint

'Nice speech, Badger,' said Hare, with his guard up. 'But I don't think it did a whole lot of good for us.'

Badger stood with his back arched, and each of his hairs standing on end, making him appear twice his size. He snarled ferociously, bearing his teeth and claws. His eyes were glazed over with red fury. All of the natural fighting spirit that made him an animal showed. Fox stared open mouthed at him for a while, spellbound by the display of bravery his friend had just shown. Inspired, he insisted on copying him.

'Right, here's the plan,' Hare announced, as the crows continued to psyche themselves up. 'Fox, you take the seven on the left, and Badger, you take the seven on the right. And that gabby little crow in the middle, the one who called me a bunny- he's mine!'

'Any better ideas?' Badger growled.

'Fair enough,' Hare sighed, 'Fox, instead, you take the one on the far left, and Badger, the one on the far right. I'll deal with the last thirteen!'

Badger sighed:

'This isn't working. Let's just have some fun, shall we?'

The three friends recklessly charged at the marauding gang of crows and crashed headlong into them, lashing out with everything they had; clawing, biting, tearing, snapping, kicking.

A cloud of black and grey feathers exploded into the air as the hooded crows were stormed. They flapped, fell and scrambled to their feet, some running in panicked circles, others fluttering about idly, most making an

attempt to fight back against the three raging young animals.

The air was filled with loud hissing, spitting, squawking, snarling and barking, as a furious clash ensued. The three friends were trapped in a deadly jumble, being shoved against each other as the crows hemmed them in. No matter how many horrible beaked faces they knocked aside, several more popped up immediately, before they could think. Everything moved so fast, the world spinning as their heads were jolted about. The crows pranced around, pecking, poking and jabbing with their bills, aiming for the eyes, but were no match for their larger, stronger foes.

By throwing his weight, and swinging his heavy fists, Badger laid the crows out flat, one after the other. Mobs of them clambered up his big hairy back, raking him with their sharp beaks, but all Badger had to do was roll over once and flatten them.

Hare was in his element. Summoning all of his natural skill, he stood firm and levelled every crow that came upon him, with lightning punches and head butts, parrying their blows and using his powerful legs to drop- kick them from one end of the scrum to the other. It was a fit of blink- and -you'll- miss-it fury. More crows queued up for the same punishment.

Five surrounded Fox. But after watching Badger's brave performance only moments ago, he too had little difficulty in meeting his hectors. Allowing anger and bloodlust to take hold, he growled in his little voice and threw himself at the crows, tackling two to the ground at once. Out the corner of his eye, he spotted the rest, and cracked one across the face with his paw, sending it into a spinning descent. He then landed his full weight down on top of the remaining two. They let out strangled squawks as his paws pinned them down. Fox grinned through his panting. What a rush!! He allowed the crows to fly away, shedding feathers in their wake. No one had any regard for life or pain now. It was a free- for- all brawl.

Fox, Badger and Hare were scratched, bloodied and bruised all over. Every crow was mortally wounded. Three lay dead. The crowd had broken and dispersed.

Corvus rushed around, yelling orders; 'C'mon lads, they're only kids, like, make an effort - ouch!'

Hare sneaked up behind the gang leader and cuffed him hard on the side of his head, using the flat of his paw. Corvus toppled over and buried his beak in the turf.

'Come on,' Hare growled, hopping from side to side. 'Fight me, you son of a turkey!'

Corvus rose and went for Hare with his dagger like bill, but Hare swiftly jumped aside, allowing the gang leader to blindly pass him by. Hare then seized his chance and pounced on him from behind, tackling him to the ground, where they grappled for some time.

Fox and Badger stood side by side in the clearing, and watched all of the weary crows hobble towards them, unwilling to surrender. The two friends looked at each other and nodded, before hurling themselves back into the heat of the fray. They delivered lethal bites and blows, thrashing and mauling, shattering wings and breaking beaks. The surviving crows knew it was hopeless and retreated. Broken and battered, they struggled to fly. Badger released Razor and Dumpster from a firm double- headlock, and watched them limp along into the distance, fleeing from the animals they had underestimated

Corvus broke free of Hare's grip and gave him a deep gash on the eyebrow with his beak, before flapping his wings and taking off.

'Come back here you little dip stick!' Hare shouted.

43

Corvus laughed to himself while soaring along, pursued by a vengeful Hare. But the gang leader was far too injured to fly very high, and ended up gliding close to the ground, where Fox and Badger had joined the chase. The three sore, exhausted animals struggled to catch up to their fleeing opponent, who was still rankling them.

'What's wrong witcha, like? Ah?' he cackled, looking back. 'Were we too much fer ya? Hehehehe.'

Soon, once the animals were out of sight, Corvus set himself down and began running through the short grass by himself, still looking back and laughing.

'Hehehehehe —oomph!'

In the midst of his excitement, the gang leader did not look where he was going, and foolishly ran directly into a low hanging electric fence, shocking himself. His black and grey body clung to the wire as currents of energy surged through him. By the time Fox, Badger and Hare reached him, Corvus was already dead.

Badger crouched down to examine the carcass, which was still sparking and smoking.

'What a shame,' he panted. 'All that chasing for nothing. Anyway, is everyone okay?'

'No not really,' Hare groaned, rubbing his forehead.

Badger assessed the gash closely.

'Looks like that's going to be a permanent scar,' he said, gravely. 'But don't worry, once your fur grows over it, no one will notice.'

Hare sighed: 'That lousy crow. He's just lucky the fence got him before I did.'

Fox sat licking a wound on one of his front paws.

His head was still reeling from the excitement of the battle. He trembled, his heart still pumping, as if it was not yet over. He could hardly believe what he had done; what he was capable of. Through it all, he had felt as though he was standing beside himself, watching someone else, being everything he wasn't. What a thrill, what an absolute pleasure it was to know he had strength within him, resistance.

Though his body leaked with wounds and throbbed with bruises, he felt no pain just yet. They were medals. He hoped this numbness would never wear off. He wished his heart would never slow down.

'You're an animal,' Badger laughed, as he sat down beside the cub. 'Seriously, you did great today,' and looking him in the eye, he added, 'Your mother would have been proud.'

Fox smiled happily.

Walking in the Ruins

Evening time rolled in quickly. The air turned a biting cold as droplets of dew sprinkled down all over the land, moistening every inch of greenery. The red sky became cluttered with thick, navy clouds. The last light of the sun still burned intensely through the settling darkness. The black hills were now hunched against the sky, gradually fading from view.

Ever since being delayed, the little company of animals had been covering much ground. Every paw ached, every stomach rumbled. They hobbled together up a wide grassy slope, through dim thickets of reed and rush. Mounds of shrubbery cast shadows across their path as they moved slowly upwards.

A family of starlings warbled in a nearby alder tree. A magpie rattled out its harsh call somewhere below the line of hills. A woodcock launched itself from the shrubs, rising upwards in twisting flight, before levelling itself and soaring off on steadier wings, while whistling its distinct tune.

When the three friends reached the top of the slope, they took time to gather their bearings.

The sight of the vast green downs below them was although very beautiful, incredibly demoralizing. The friends simply felt too overcome with exhaustion to go any further. They decided on stopping for the night. But where to rest was the question. They turned and backtracked down the slope and searched for a place.

Their search led them underneath a rusty iron gate and across a large puddle of mud. It squelched between their toes as they waded across to the other side, where a low stone wall stood in front of them. Each stone was marble white and perfectly smooth and round, worn down from old age. Badger crouched beneath it and allowed Fox and Hare to stand on his back, one at a time. They leaped onto the wall and then, bending their backs, helped Badger up too. The trio then climbed down the other side and proceeded to venturing through some dense moor grass. Weary and footsore, they made it through to the other end, only to come across something they could never have expected: the ruins of an old village. There it stood, only a few meters from where the friends gazed; no more than eight tiny cottages with no roofs, no windows and no doors. They were built of the same stone as the old wall the friends had just climbed over, only weathered and moss covered. Weeds and brambles grew up around and out through the seemingly ancient stonework, sprouting through window sills and coiling around arches. Piles of debris lay scattered around the area. And, in some parts of the walls, they noticed shiny black balls embedded in the stone…

The village itself stood on the edge of a cliff, facing the sea.

'It doesn't look like anyone's home,' said Hare, breaking the deathly silence. 'What do you reckon? Want to spend the night here?'

Badger shuddered at the thought of doing so.

'I don't know,' he said. 'It looks fairly well haunted if you ask me.'

'Haunted?' Hare scoffed. 'By what - the ghosts of dead humans! I tell ya, it's the living humans we have to watch out for.'

'I know that,' said Badger stiffly. 'But still, we don't know what could be living in there.'

'Nothing is living in there,' Hare snapped. 'Why would anything want to live in a place so old and shabby; no shelter, no trees, no food? And as for ghosts -I don't see any! I think you're being a little paranoid.'

'I'm being cautious,' Badger protested.

Hare sighed.

'Okay you win. It's been a long day. Let's just leave this place and spend the rest of the evening wandering around getting wetter and dirtier and hungrier so we can find a little hole to snuggle up in together and - '

'Alright,' Badger barked. "We'll go inside, if it'll keep you from whining!'

'Thank you,' said Hare with a spiteful tone. 'And don't worry. I promise I won't let any ghosts harm you.'

As usual, Fox had no voice in the matter. He just sat waiting for Badger and Hare to stop bickering.

Into the gloomy old village he followed them, unaware that Badger was right. Usually the village *was* empty. But not today…

In only a short space of time, the three companions settled comfortably on the outskirts of the ruins. Hare squatted down in the corner of one of the overgrown cottages, munching contentedly on clumps of long wet grass and clover. The walls were weeded over with maidenhair spleenwort, navelwort and dusty ivy veins. And outside, grass grew long and in thick clumps, providing the animals with cover from the breezes that bombed in from the sea. Fox and Badger lay outside near the edge of the cliffs among patches of tussock sedge and water dock.

The homebound seagulls had already flown, leaving a wondrous view. The ocean was enchanting. It lay below and across from them, vast beyond measure, like a vision of pure clarity. So calm, so soothing, occasionally swirling in the breezes. The friends felt like they were on the edge of the Earth. The sight was enormous yet empty.

Not as much as a rock or a vessel tainted its perfection.

Red was its colour, reflecting the darkening sky. The setting sun dipped towards the west horizon, creating bright, silver wavelets that drifted out into eternity. It was an evening of peace and solitude. Even Hare couldn't help stopping by to admire it for a moment.

'Look at that,' Badger mused, marvelling at the endless stretch of water. 'I wonder what it would be like to live in there.'

'Cold, probably,' said Hare. 'And wet. I'd say we're better off up here.'

'With that. Hare returned to dining in the cottage.

Fox stared blankly out at the slow, tranquil waves, his eyes wide open, his whiskers twitching every now and then. His mind was elsewhere. It was the first time he was able to relax and think.

'I wonder where they are now,' he said to himself out loud, unaware that Badger had heard him.

'You wonder where 'who' are?' he enquired, looking over from the pile of rubble where he was sitting.

'My family,' said Fox, his voice faltering.

'Oh your family,' said Badger smiling as he made his way over to the cub and sat beside him. 'You shouldn't worry about them. They're happy where they are now.'

'Where's that?' asked Fox.

'The place above the clouds,' Badger replied, lying back and gazing skyward.

Fox was puzzled.

'The what above the what?' he asked.

'Spring Valley,' said Badger cryptically.

'What's Spring Valley?' asked Fox.

Badger paused for a bit to gather the correct words.

'Apparently', he went on. "It's a place where our lost loved ones can go and find peace.'

The look in Fox's eyes said: 'Do go on'.

'Well I don't really know much about it myself,' Badger retorted. 'I've never been there. But from what I can remember my mother telling me, Spring Valley is supposed to be so wonderful not even imagination can grasp it; so huge, and green, and fresh. It's a place where all those who died are born again, and are free to run wild!'

Fox narrowed one eye, but kept listening.

'When we arrive at Spring Valley,' Badger went on, 'and we will, we're greeted by all the good creatures we ever knew, only they'll be young again, and healthy and happy all the time.

There's nothing to be afraid of there; no guns, no traps, maybe even no humans. Trees can never fall, rivers never dry, and it's never winter so the flowers are always in bloom. Animals that used to hunt each other become friends, and they share the grass. Berries and mushrooms grow to be the size of pumpkins, and sometimes, when it rains, it rains warm milk! Because our mothers won't be able to give us any! They'll be cubs just like us! Don't you see? In Spring Valley, we can be young forever!'

Fox sat wide eyed for a moment. 'Are my family really there?' he asked.

'I'm sure they are,' said Badger. 'They're probably watching over you right now, from one of those purply clouds up there.'

Fox, although happy with this idea of paradise, was reluctant to believe it. Even at such a young age, he could not allow himself to be fooled by amazing stories.

'How can we be sure Spring Valley is a real place?' he asked.

'We're never sure,' said Badger. 'But it's a nice thought isn't it? If we choose to believe in it, we feel safer. The idea of a place like that being out there, waiting for us, kind of gives us hope, you know? Something to look forward to.'

Fox pondered, wrinkling his eyebrows with frustration. He then shook his head.

'I still don't know,' he muttered.

"Well think about it,' Badger continued, 'Is this really all we have? One life? One life full of danger and difficulty; that we can lose in the blink of an eye? I think not. I reckon we deserve some kind of reward, don't you? If Spring Valley isn't real, then what is this life leading to?'

Fox paused again. An afterworld certainly was a lovely thing to believe in. A strange sense of warmth and security began to well up inside him. Fox had to shuffle his body a little to calm it.

'I know Spring Valley is a difficult thing to believe in,' Badger concluded. 'But it's better to *think* there is one, than to *know* there isn't.'

Fox looked up at the bright crimson sky, now surrounded in the massing clouds of nightfall. The sky gave an unusual feeling of comfort. A streak of blinding yellow light pierced through the dark clouds, as if opening up to a different world. Beams of light shone down in straight lines, like a giant golden staircase. This pleasant sight helped the young cub make up his mind.

'Maybe there is a Spring Valley,' he said finally. 'In fact, I know there is now!'

Badger smiled; 'You see! I bet you feel better already.'

'So I'll see my family again?' Fox asked cheerfully.

'I'm sure you will,' Badger replied. 'And hopefully, I'll see mine.'

'I can't wait,' squeaked Fox excitedly.

'Be patient,' Badger hushed. 'You're not dead yet!'

Suddenly, a familiar brash voice interrupted them from behind;

'What are you two fat hens clucking about over there?'

Hare came bouncing out of the ruins, with his mouth full of grass and flowers. Daisy and buttercup petals clung to his face and whiskers.

'If I didn't know better,' he joked. 'I'd say you two were plotting something against me. Well be warned- I have eyes on the sides of my head!'

Badger rolled his eyes and laughed.

'Not at all, Hare,' he joked back. 'Just sleep with one of those eyes open tonight!'

Fox giggled and followed Badger into the ruins, leaving Hare behind to feel paranoid.

'What did you mean by that?' he cried. "Come back here!'

When nightfall had well and truly settled on the land, Fox, Badger and Hare nestled safely inside the remains of one of the old farm cottages. They each rested in separate corners of the little room. Badger dug himself halfway into the ground and snuggled deeply into the softened earth. His thick coat provided good enough insulation from the cold. Hare scratched out a small but fairly comfortable nest in the opposite corner. He carpeted the hard stone floor in leaves, grass and moss, before lying down on it for the night. Fox chose a clump of sedge growing in the third corner. He wrapped himself up in the long grass like a make-shift blanket. And so the three weary travellers rested there for a time, nursing their wounds and aching joints, and cleaning their muddy paws. And then, they put their heads down for sleep.

The night was dim and moonless. Above in the ink black sky, the stars were veiled. Outside the relative safety of the cottage, the wind was howling madly. An unmerciful gale gusted in from the sea, roaring across the land. No rain or snow followed, but its strength was enough to flatten the grass and rattle the very structures of every cottage in the lonely, secluded village.

Fox was the last to fall asleep. He found himself staring absent mindedly up at the wall, where one of those shiny black balls was wedged. It was then, he wondered for the first time,

'What happened here?'

As exhaustion began to enfold him in its drowsy embrace, Fox could have sworn he saw images in the hard black vault above him; glowing green blotches, taking the form of strange, bow shaped vessels. Faint sounds accompanied these images as Fox drifted further out of consciousness; sounds of peril; screaming, shouting. Jets of smoke boomed from the vessels, and Fox's vision swivelled to show him- a little stone village, being levelled to the ground. The cub eased his eyes shut, and was off to sleep.

But his heart suddenly lurched, when he heard a terrified voice up close. It was Hare.

'Badger,' he cried, paws cupped over his mouth. 'Look behind you, a ghost!'

Frightened, Badger sprang up and turned around, only to come face to face with a blank stone wall. But no ghost?

He turned back to Hare, who then burst into a fit of laughter. He clutched his belly and rolled around the floor.

'I was only pulling your tail!'

Fox and Badger were both gulping for breath.

'Not... funny... Hare,' Badger panted. 'I do believe in ghosts, you know.'

'I'm sorry, Badger,' sighed Hare with a hangdog look. 'If I had known you scare so easily I never would have- oh my, Badger, behind you, a real ghost! He's making faces!'

Again Badger spun around, startled, falling for the same trick,

'Hah, hah, hah, you're too easy,' Hare cackled, now sitting on the floor and holding his feet. 'I could keep this up all night. In fact, why shouldn't I?'

Badger clutched his racing heart and trembled.

'You're evil Hare,' he yelled.

But even Fox couldn't help giggling this time.

Once he caught his breath, Badger looked up and, quite unexpectedly, staggered backwards with a look of dismay on his face.

'Hare, behind you!' he shouted.

Hare didn't move. He simply sniggered, folding his arms smugly.

'If you think I'm going to fall for the same trick I played on you just now, then you truly are hopeless.'

Badger's eyes were transfixed with fear.

'No, I'm serious, look behind you!'

'Honestly, Badger,' Hare sighed. 'I expected better from you. You're smart; there were lots of other pranks you could have played on me; you could have tied my ears together in a knot while I slept, or buried me under a pile of earth. But this- this is just sad.'

Fox was frozen with fear. This was no joke.

Up high on the window sill, a pair of glaring white eyes loomed over Hare in the darkness.

Badger now screamed urgently:

'Hare, please trust me, I'm not kidding, look behind you!'

Hare grunted, reluctantly turning around and then started as a big brown *rat* emerged from the shadow, hissing and spitting. Its body was hunched and silky and its eyes were cold and crafty. It had grown fat on farm produce, and possibly seabird carcass. It had sharp, dirty claws, a long, worm like tail and two jagged, yellow fangs.

The three companions stood like statues, wondering what to do. The rat was clear in their night vision, crouching over them, looking intimidated with all the eyes staring back up at it.

Without warning, it squeaked and dived down on top of Hare, gripping him by the back of his neck! Hare shrieked and shook his head as the rat's fangs dug into him.

'Get him off me, get him off me!'

Fox and Badger leapt into action. They galloped around Hare, jumping up and down, trying to swipe the big rat off with their paws, but Hare was in too much of a frenzy to stand still. He danced around, kicking his legs like a horse gone mad, and waving his arms as if on fire, swinging the heavy rat back and forth. But the stubborn little beast  refused to let go. Hare dropped to the ground and began rolling along, as Fox and Badger tried in vain to stamp on the rat with their paws, but they missed with every attempt. Hare's panicked screams mingled with the screeching wind outside. Furious, he scrambled to his feet and took off, running at top speed around the room. He scampered up and down the walls, sending old stones rolling onto the floor. He dashed in and out of the fireplace, scattering ancient ashes. Fox and Badger stood back to back in the middle of the room, feeling dizzy as Hare's fleeting image zoomed around them in circles. The rat was dragged along, collecting bits of slate and clay in its fur, still hissing through a mouthful of fur. Savagely, it sunk its teeth deeper into Hare's flesh and held him tighter as he ran. It would not let go.

Fox shook the dizziness from his head and steadied his body. Getting into pouncing position, he waited until Hare slowed down. Once Hare grinded to a halt and began screaming again, Fox bravely seized his opportunity. He lunged at the rat and tore it away from Hare's neck, and wrestled it to the floor until it could fight no longer. But before Fox could stop himself, he began *eating* the creature. He did not know what possessed him to; he simply did it without thinking. Fox was famished and did not stop gorging himself until the tasty rat was gone.

Hare roused himself from the floor, rubbing his throbbing neck. It felt such a relief to be liberated from that little tyrant.

'I have to admit, well done,' he said, looking at Badger. 'That was a really, really clever trick. How did you do it?'

Badger did not reply. He just stared. Hare followed his gaze and saw Fox crouching over the skeletal remains of the brown rat.

'What did I just do?' he gasped, his snout covered in blood.

'Oh no,' muttered Hare to himself. 'This can't be good.'

That night, while Fox lay in his grass bedding, tossing and turning in an uneasy sleep, Badger and Hare remained wide awake, watching and talking about him from underneath the window sill where they were sitting.

A draught of cold air crept in above their heads as the violent wind continued its rampage outside.

'Look at him,' whispered Hare. 'He looks so peaceful and harmless. Hard to believe he can turn on us at any time.'

Badger gasped;

'No, he won't turn on us. We're all he has. Surely he knows that.'

'You saw what he did to that rat,' Hare pointed out. 'It's only a matter of time before he discovers what real foxes are - hunters - and when that day comes, he'll kill us.'

'No he won't,' Badger hushed. 'Fox only killed that rat because it was attacking you. That's proof he cares about you. I'm sure he would've done the same for me. I just can't see him turning.'

'Hmph, easy for you to say,' Hare complained. 'Foxes don't even eat badgers, do they?'

'No,' Badger replied, sounding unsure. 'I don't think so. I hope not. Oh, I really hope not!'

'Hah,' said Hare grinning. 'I knew you were scared.'

'Yeah,' said Badger shamefully. 'But I don't want to be. Fox is my first and best friend. No offence.'

'None taken,' Hare smiled. 'But seriously, don't be surprised if Fox turns. By right, all three of us should be enemies. Of course it's nice that we're not, but Fox over there has the heart of a hunter, and when that heart starts beating, we're done for.'

'Maybe Fox is different,' Badger snapped. 'Maybe we all are. Look at us; we all survived The Farmer's hounds, we all met on the same day and we're all on the same journey to the same place. I have hope that Fox will always be our friend, after everything we've been through so far.'

'That's what worries me,' said Hare. 'If we make it to Lough Ine, Fox might meet another of his kind. He'll learn what it's like to be a normal fox and he'll become one. He'll find out that hares and badgers and all other animals are his natural enemies and he'll soon come looking for us. That's when the trouble starts.'

'I'm trying not to think like that,' said Badger. 'I knew Fox was different from the morning I met him. There was no aggression, no treachery about him. I saw a peace lover, like me. I reckon he's capable of being something more than a regular fox. And he's no fool either. He knows his friends. Look how much he's helped us already- he rescued us from falling in a river, he tried getting us apples, and of course he sorted out that rat. Would a traitor do that? No. No way.'

Badger paused to conclude. 'No matter how strong he grows, no matter how wise he becomes, I doubt Fox will ever betray us.'

Hare looked over at the sleeping cub, still kicking and grunting in his sleep.

'I hope you're right, Badger,' he muttered.

Home

'*Keeeeaaark! Keeeeeeeaaark!*'

Light bore through the darkness at dawn, mopping up the shadows that lay in and around the village. Cool sunlight shone from behind the white haze above. The stormy winds had at last abated. Below the line of cliffs, the ocean stirred gently; waves pouring around the rocks, in hissing foam, dragging in blankets of seaweed and rubbish. Herring gulls screeched and squawked on a distant island.

When morning was well underway, the three travellers took the next steps of their journey. Down the grassy little mound they went, yawning and flicking their ears. They took one last look back at the ruins, glad to have left the dreadful place.

'Any sleep last night?' asked Badger as he caught up with his companions. 'Um, a little bit,' said Fox. 'The wind kept waking me up though.'

'Hmph, well I didn't get a wink,' Badger grumbled. 'I'll never get used to sleeping at night when I should be out hunting and doing my business. And a lot of that wind you heard was just Hare snoring.'

'Well excuse me!' snapped Hare. 'But running around with a rat on your back after a long day's hike can tire you out!'

'Sorry, sorry,' Badger hushed. 'I'm just not a morning animal. Anyway, what route do you think we should take today?'

'Beats me,' Hare shrugged. 'All these paths look the same. We'll just have to keep moving forward, by going through obstacles instead of around them.'

'Makes sense, I guess,' muttered Badger as he, Fox and Hare reached the bottom of the mound.

And so, a long hard day of travelling unfolded.

North east, they headed, guided only by instinct. None of the three travellers knew where exactly Lough Ine was or what it looked like, so their only option was to continue moving forward until they came upon a site that resembled the place that Hare had spoken of earlier. The path of their journey now lay through a vast area of steep, rocky hills. Here, the wind was sharp and thin, and the grass constantly short and dry. Very little shelter was found as the hills were barren and exposed to the elements. The three friends spent much of the day lumbering over every wind battered hill face, climbing and stumbling awkwardly. Each step in this new terrain was as strenuous as four steps in their previous terrain. The altitude and the strong wind set them back repeatedly.

There were no places for them to rest; no bushes, no trees, no holes. And stopping to rest on the hills was simply too uncomfortable and unpleasant, the ground being so hard and thorny and the wind so cold, biting at their faces. It was one long, unforgiving hike.

As the morning faded into afternoon, the three youngsters felt themselves heading downwards. The long stretch of hills was at an end. Ahead, lay a wide open area of swampy, boggy land. Fox, Badger and Hare slid down the side of the last hill, through bristling stalks of heather and gorse, and into the bog. Their environment had changed in an instant. The ground was now soggy and murky. Beneath the yellow green grass, mud squelched and gurgled. The friends waded on through, the mud deepening with every step. They tripped and faltered, making slow but sure progress, as the thick gunk climbed up their legs and threatened to suck them under. The paw prints they left behind were deep black holes, gradually filling with water as the ground closed in.

Purple moor grass and branched bur reed grew in bunched patches scattered throughout the bog. The friends decided to use these as 'stepping stones,' even though they were clearly not stones. The clumps of grass were the only parts of the ground that were solid, and so, pulling themselves from the clingy muck, the three companions began hopping from clump to clump across the smelly mire.

Fox and Hare zipped and bounced along quite fast, finding it much easier than Badger, who was the slowest and clumsiest of the three. He kept tripping and splashing back into the festering ooze whenever he tried to catch up with them. Nevertheless, all three made it safely out of the bog. After quickening their pace and keeping their balance, they reached a dense mass of blackthorn trees. Here, they took time to rest and clean themselves up.

Warm afternoon sunshine slowly spread out across the landscape like a giant yellow blanket, stippling the grasslands with patches of light and shade.

The only movement around was the swaying of the long grass in the breeze, and a curious kestrel perching herself on a nearby hawthorn bush, dipping her fan like tail up and down. Somewhere, on a far off road, a car could be heard purring along further into the distance.

When it was thought they had rested enough, Fox, Badger and Hare achily pulled themselves from the shade of the thorn bushes and carried on the remainder of their journey.

Across hundreds of acres of green pasture land they steadily made their way, now finding their journey rather repetitive. It seemed no matter how far they ventured, they were met with the same terrain and the same challenges: bumpy, grassy and occasionally bushy land. In spite of this, they continued to push on through; tearing through shrubs, crawling under barbed wire, crossing shallow brooks, climbing over rock mounds, eventually putting some two miles behind them.

It was only when they had emerged from a certain field that they came upon an entirely new enigma: a long, flat, straight and narrow section of ground, stretching off in both directions. Close to nothing in the form of vegetation grew on its hard grey surface. A gentle wind brushed over this strange thing with a sprinkle of dust.

The three wanderers stood cautiously at its edge, finding this place eerie and discomforting.

'It's so... barren,' Badger commented.

'And empty,' Hare added.

'Same thing,' Badger retorted.

For a short while, the friends sniffed at the strange thing and peered around, not wishing to make a quick and false move. Sure enough, on the other side lay more fields and bush land, things they were used to. But this - what was it?

'It seems safe enough,' said Hare. 'It's hardly going to open its jaws and swallow us. Let's just cross over already.'

Badger remained the more vigilant one.

'I wouldn't be so careless, Hare,' he pointed out. 'It's obvious that humans built this. This could be one of their tracks.'

'So?' Hare quipped. 'I don't see any humans.'

'Not now you don't,' Badger warned. 'But this is their run. If we use it, we could be spotted.'

'Hardly,' Hare protested.

'Well alright,' said Badger, giving in. 'But let me go first, just to test it out.'

The hard concrete layer was so different to the soft clay ground that Badger was used to. His paws ached more than ever. He trundled across to the other side as fast as he could, and right away, he heard a rumble.

'Oh no,' he breathed, popping his head up and stiffing his ears. The ominous sound of an engine roaring was growing in volume. The ground was beginning to vibrate.

'Metal monster!' Badger screamed urgently. 'Get across now!'

Fox dashed over the narrow concrete strip as if being chased, and scurried to where Badger stood beckoning him.

Hare followed immediately but couldn't help freezing once he was out in the middle of the concrete strip. All sounds, all surroundings suddenly became very distant. He stood on two legs, sniffing, peering around. It was fascinating, like everything he ever knew had vanished. So he dawdled there, enjoying the sensation of rock beneath his feet, and ignoring Badger's frantic shouting.

But, the metal monster never came. It had obviously taken a different turn. Hare eased out of his trance- like state and joined his friends at the roadside. Badger was livid.

'What were you playing at!' he scolded.

'I don't know,' said Hare dreamily.

Badger didn't pursue the issue. This was no place to argue. They needed shelter. Fast.

After they'd recovered from that nerve-racking false alarm, they made their way up the road, making sure to keep to the side, hidden from view behind the long grass and overhanging fuchsia.

They searched all along the roadside verges for a way back into the commonlands. The road was lined with high, weed covered stone walls and row upon row of tall thorn bushes, making the fields behind inaccessible. They tried climbing several times, but kept sliding back down or falling. It seemed they were locked out of the wilderness; the world split in half, until they came upon something that gave them all an idea.

Lying at the end of some person's driveway was a set of cattle grates.' A deep square pit was dug into the ground, right at the entrance to the drive, with eleven iron bars lying across it. There was a space of roughly three inches between each one. Its purpose was to prevent passing cattle from wandering into the owner's garden.

On the other side, the usual fields and hedgerows were clear in view. This looked like the only way to reach them.

'Come on,' said Hare, cheerily. 'We've done stupider things.'

Backing up and steadying himself, Hare cleared the cattle grates in one leap.

'Easy,' he announced, looking back at his friends. 'A grasshopper could do it. Who's next?'

Badger grunted, reluctant.

'We probably should have planned this first,' he said, questionably.

Hare laughed wryly.

'What's to plan? It's a hole. Jump over it!'

Badger hesitated, but Fox, feeling a little cocky, decided to give it a go.

He stood back and hurdled most of the bars, but unfortunately, did not have the size or the stamina to finish the jump, and fell short, smack- bang into the edge of the pit. He scrabbled and panicked, but instead of going forward, he began retreating back to the first side.

Badger and Hare could only watch, with paws on heads.

On his way, Fox put a paw between two bars and went down fast, walloping his jaw off the wrought iron.

By the time he was back on the ground, he was a quaking mess. He lay curled up, quivering and whimpering at Badger's feet. His jaw smarted.

Badger nuzzled him all over, looked at the grates, and then at Hare, who looked very apprehensive.

Badger shook his head.

'Hare, you'll have to come back here. It won't work if you can make it and the rest of us can't.'

Hare relaxed and sighed. 'Aw, I knew you'd say that.'

The trio were back on the road, at the end of the driveway. Clueless, as to how to continue their journey, they stayed by the roadside, sniffing around, checking the walls up and down.

Badger frequently asked Fox how he was, and Fox nodded; afraid his jaw might fall off if he opened it.

'Maybe we'll spot something from the other side,' said Hare as he hopped across the road - just as a familiar rumbling sound could be heard. The car came barrelling down the road at the speed of chain lightning! It practically lifted off the ground, seemingly indifferent to what got in its way.

Fox and Badger dashed behind a clump of grass, and from the other side, Hare ran to join them.

Badger roared:

'HARE, STAY WHERE YOU ARE!'

But the iron giant thundered recklessly past, drowning out his voice. Fox and Badger were already lying behind the grass, hugging with eyes shut, and did not see what happened. They shakily poked their heads up, hearts racing.

A cloud of dust trailed along the road, taking a moment to fully settle. The sound of the engine was now fading from ear. Silence descended again. The two survivors scanned the area. Empty.

For a while, Fox and Badger were rooted to the spot.

'Hare?' shouted Badger. No reply.

Fox's throat closed with worry.

'HARE!' Badger tried again.

More silence... and then a cough.

'I'm over here!'

Fox and Badger hurried across the road and found their companion lying in a stream, waist deep in leaf mulch. The place was sheltered under branches of buckthorn and fuchsia. The two friends peered in and heaved a huge sigh of relief.

'We thought we'd lost you,' said Badger.

Hare smiled and stood up, his bottom half muddied brown, even his fluffy tail.

'Hmph, you should have both jumped in front of that thing and saved me!' he joked.

Fox and Badger both smiled at their bedraggled companion, who seemed unhurt.

'Oh yeah,' he added. 'You, err, might want to come look at this.'

Curious, Fox and Badger slid down into the stream and found what Hare was looking at. Or into.

It had many names - a drain, a pipe, a culvert. But to the three companions, it was a deep, dark and mysterious tunnel. It opened out wide, as if drawing them in, with promises of leading them somewhere nice, but more likely to lead them down into the throes of darkness and entomb them forever. The stream flowed in, carrying leaves, petals and twigs off into the unknown.

'What do you make of that?' said Hare.

Badger was in two minds, but it was clear Hare had already made up his. 'I'd take my chances in there, rather than up on that death- trap we just came from!'

'Okay,' murmured Badger. 'How bad can it be? It reminds me of my old tunnels. Minus the water, and the width.'

'As long as my whiskers don't touch the sides, it's fine by me,' said Hare. 'Then so be it,' said Badger.

Off they went, into the underground pipe of mystery. Animals rarely suffer from claustrophobia, but Fox, for some reason, felt ill-at- ease. He walked nose to tail with Badger and Hare. Now this, he thought, is the place for rats.

It wasn't as dark as they thought it would be. The clay walls were slime-slicked and up in the drier parts, cobweb covered, the ceiling *drip, drip, dripping*. The friends were up to their ankles in black running water and each step they took caused mud clouds. But nothing, nothing was more offensive than its smell.

Think of a basket of rotten eggs, sitting in a barn full of flatulent pigs, wallowing in pools of month- old milk, on a hot day. And you're not even close!

'This place looks like the inside of a horse's nose,' Hare griped.

Badger muttered. 'Yeah, and smells like the back of a horse's - Fox, where are you, oh, there you are, good.'

On they walked, the water deepening, the stench worsening, cloying their nostrils.

Fox now kept turning back sharply.

'What is it?' Badger finally asked.

'I-I hear footsteps,' said the cub.

'What, impossible!' said Badger. 'No human could fit down here.'

'But there are definitely footsteps,' the cub insisted, in a tremulous voice.

The three companions stopped to listen.

'I hear nothing,' said Hare impatiently.' Now can we please get going, this smell is making my fur fall out!'

'Alright,' said Badger, as he and Fox slowly moved off. And sure enough, there it was again, the *clip clop* of footfall. Fox halted.

'Surely you heard that!' he cried.

'Wait,' said Hare. 'Let me try something.'

While Fox and Badger stood and watched, Hare took two paces forward and instantly, they all heard another *clip clop*.

'Ah, you see!' he announced, crouched by the wall. 'There's a reason we only hear it while we're walking!'

Fox and Badger noticed it now - the water lapping against the sides of the pipe made a sound akin to boots against a hard surface. Fox sighed with relief.

Badger laughed.

'Well, it doesn't hurt to be cautious.'

After another meter, came a sight that lifted their hopes - light. But not at the end of the tunnel - above it.

They splashed on ahead, and found themselves between two pipes. They were at the bottom of a square pit, and above their heads, eleven iron bars split up the sunlight, patterning the ground with lines of shadow.

They were, of course, now *under* the cattle grates.

'Who'd have thunk it,' said Badger. 'If we were a bit smaller. And better climbers...'

'And completely boneless,' Hare added.

'We'd stand some chance of squeezing through,' Badger concluded. 'Well, now's no time to be daydreaming, let's keep going.'

The animals set off, into the second dark pipe, which appeared to be disconnected from the first. Their eyes had to adjust from light, to dark, to brief light, and now back to dark.

But the water appeared to be shallower: The ground was heading upwards, up a hill. However, the stench was showing no let up.

Hare was at the front, breathing rapidly through his mouth.

'Think of flowers, think of flowers, think of flowers!' he mumbled.

It was a long way to the top of the hill, but the companions never made it that far. And it was probably just as well they didn't, for if they did, they'd have been poking their heads up someone's toilet!

The animals were experiencing a day of bad timing.

For at that moment, a fly was pulled up. A handle was pulled down. And the toilet flushed.

The three animals were still plodding miserably up the shaft. They smelt it before they heard it.

From around a corner up ahead, a wave came crashing! Brown, chunky water, with whorls of psychedelic green slime, gushed down the tunnelway! Fox, Badger and Hare were seized by indecision, watching it power towards them like a wall of death. They bumped into each other and fussed about, before turning on their heels and legging it! Back down the shaft they ran, Badger shouting 'huphuphuphup!'

The wave swept and plunged right behind them, at nearly twice their speed, splish, splash, sploshing off the narrow walls, gathering mud and rainwater to fuel its attack.

The three friends ran until they came underneath the cattle grates again. Without a thought to share, they leapt up and grabbed hold of the iron bars, in any way they could.

The awful *poo- nami* washed right under them, tickling their tails, until it passed by down the shaft, thinning out into fetid puddles of who- knows-what.

The three runaways still dangled from the ceiling, unwilling to come down. Badger had hooked his arm around a bar, and hung like a monkey, as Hare did. Fox was found clinging to the corner of the pit, his claws set in the ground outside the grates. His hind legs scrabbled to stay up. They all panted, and closed their eyes in silent thanks.

'Well,' said Hare. 'That idea worked better in my head.'

'What now?' squeaked Fox, losing his grip.

'I don't know,' said Badger. 'But I'm not going down there again.'

Seconds later, it was becoming agony holding on. They didn't want to wade through all that sludge, but they didn't want to be suspended above it all day either.

'My arms are on fire,' Hare whined. 'And so are my nostrils. This really stinks!'

'Think, think, think,' muttered Badger, cudgelling his brain for a solution. '...Wait.'

Badger noticed the bar he was hanging from was loose. It sort of rolled from side to side in its place.

'These bars,' he cried. 'They're detachable!'

'Meaning?' Hare demanded, his arm slipping another inch.

'Meaning they slot in from the top,' said Badger. 'Too heavy to lift out from there. But down here, we can push them out!'

'I'll do whatever it takes,' whimpered Hare with desperation.

Badger used both his paws now, to monkey - bar his way over to Fox, whose claws were now furrowing the earth as he slid.

'I'm gonna fall!' he cried.

'Hang on,' said Badger, as he hugged the bar with his forelegs and used his hind footpaw to push out the bar next to him- the bar nearest the edge. Hare sidled up beside him, looking like he was using Badger's bar for chin- ups, and used both his great feet to push out the last bar. Fox threw his weight forward, and reset his grip in the ground. Now he was able to use his head for pushing.

'All together now,' Badger ordered, as the three of them gave all their might to roll the iron bar out of its slot and onto the driveway.

Fox was the first to clamber out. He caught Hare in his teeth, right before he fell, and dragged him up. The cub winced, remembering how much his jaw hurt. Badger squeezed his stripy head up towards the light, and pulled his great podgy body out of the hole with his front paws. So they all sprawled out on the gravel together, filthy, smelly, panting, trembling, and no longer caring if they were being watched.

The last light of the day was beginning to die as twilight shades fell. Dull blue clouds closed in around the sky and even a thin mist began to settle. A light rain drizzled down, making the very air damp and thick. It wasn't until the companions made their way into a new field and up a steep slope that they realized how truly exhausted they were. They had been on the go all day with only a few rest stops and little food. And now that the weather had turned against them, they felt their spirits drooping. Too tired to even hunt for a snack, the weary trio slogged their way through several more fields, light headed and paw sore. And as soon as they reached the top of the slope, their morale took another crucial blow.

Standing before them, as if to deliberately taunt them, was yet another hill. Only this one was the tallest they had yet encountered, rising majestically up into the sky, its peak shrouded in the white foamy mist. Had they been able to see the top, they would have viewed it as less of a hill, and more of a mountain.

Hare let out an anguished groan, giving in to his lassitude. 'Forget this!' he shouted. 'I'm going home!'

With that, he fell forward on his face theatrically.

Badger sighed loudly. 'Hare, you realize what you said makes absolutely no sense. Home?'

'Whatever, there's no way I'm climbing that,' he moaned.

'Okay, I hear you,' Badger sighed, emphatically.

Indeed, this hill was of monstrous height and could not be tackled now.

Turning around, the three dispirited companions limped away mournfully, searching for a place to rest and debrief.

While doing so, Badger gazed up at the dark, dismal sky, guessing where the moon would have been appearing shortly.

'Looks like I'm going to miss another night,' he muttered to himself.

The animals found shelter at the edge of a field, under an abandoned, upside down feeding trough. One by one, they squeezed under the rusty old apparatus and curled up together, struggling for warmth. In time, they settled and stopped shivering, now ready to sleep. Yet, in the moody silence that followed, each of them couldn't help feeling a strong sense of disgruntlement and hopelessness.

Time passes much slower for animals, each day feeling like a score of days, and for some animals, each year equating to seven years, so the friends had lost count of how many days they had been travelling and searching. Yet there seemed to be simply no sign of this so called 'Lough Ine' place.

Perhaps it was only a legend. Perhaps it was only an old yarn, fabricated by some creature who liked the idea of a safe haven for wildlife. So the companions had done naught but chase the wind, risking their lives for nothing; a place that existed only in folklore.

While these gloomy, defeatist feelings weighed heavy on their hearts, the friends ignored the growling of their stomachs and slumped into a deep yet dreamless sleep. They did not care for the morning to come. But they were unaware of how close they were.

Irish weather is certainly unpredictable. Fox, Badger and Hare realized this the next morning when they poked their throbbing heads out from underneath the feeding trough and opened their crusty eyes to see that the mist and rain had completely vanished, as if they had imagined it all.

It was like a day in summer. The sun poured down onto the wet fields, causing last night's rain drops to shimmer like blinding lights. The saggy grey clouds had dispersed, allowing a pure blue sky to glow down freely. Birdsong trilled softly from the surrounding hawthorns and hazels. Even in the distance, the fading arc of a rainbow was still visible, shining down on the rugged green landscape, through which the three animals had already come.

'That's nothing short of a miracle,' said Badger, shielding his face with one set of claws.

The company of animals snaked out of their feeding trough shelter and into the warm, radiant sunlight. Hunger led them across the field, to a shady elm tree. They refused to take another step without a decent top up of food.

Badger scraped the moist ground with his long claws, scooping out great chunks of earth. The damp soil gave him just what he wanted. Plugging his snout into the hole he had dug, Badger sucked up a fat juicy worm, then began digging for more. Hare chomped through patches of short grass and primrose shoots with relish. Fox joined Badger in excavating the ground, digging little holes and rolling aside rocks. Together they made short work of a number of worms, slugs, snails, woodlice and ant larvae. Hare stopped suddenly, belched, and then continued his attack on some clover leaves. All three of the animals chewed their way through some spurge and parsley roots, until the capacity of their bellies had been utterly filled. They lay together in the shade of the small elm, waiting for their strength to return, allowing the music of the song thrush to keep them entertained all the while.

And then the time came.

Climbing to their feet, as slow as the snails they had eaten, the three bloated animals made their way back across the field, towards the great hill. Despite the intensity of the sun's glare, Badger felt it was his turn to lead. He trotted ahead of his companions, under a barbed wire fence and into a bristling sea of heather, clearing a path for them to follow. The climb was painstaking and arduous, the hill being so immense and rugged.

Yet the companions felt more uplifted now that they had eaten, and since the rain had stopped. Their will to move on had been rekindled.

Even Hare was feeling his usual gabby self again, hopping just behind Badger throughout most of the climb, prattling on non stop about how amazingly brilliant hares are at everything.

'It's true, don't ignore me,' he boasted, dancing around irritatingly in Badger's shadow. 'We hares are gifted boxers! We have been known for beating the living daylights out of loads of different animals, well not loads, just each other actually - but listen, I mean it, every spring, crowds of hares get together and hold really big boxing matches! It's to impress females, you see. Ask the birds, I hear them talking about it all the time. Oh, and running, well, let me tell you, we hares can literally out run any animal, you name it; cats, dogs, bulls and I think horses, maybe, I've never tried, but we can even run fast uphill, and - ouch!'

Badger stopped suddenly, causing Hare to bump into his back. 'Ah, my nose,' he whined,' placing both paws over his face. 'I've already got a scar on my eyebrow and two fang marks on my neck. There'll be nothing left of me soon, only a fluffy tail and a bucktooth. Why did you stop?'

Badger was motionless. He stood with his nose to the wind, drawing in slow, deep breaths, frequently turning his head to sniff the air from a different direction. Fox and Hare could sense his excitement.

'Do you smell that?' he asked.

'Smell what?' asked Fox, his curiosity aflame.

Badger took another whiff.

'Trees, lots of them. Plants. And flowers, ones I've never smelt before. I-I don't think we're far!'

Fox and Hare looked at each other wide eyed, trying not to smile.

'I need someone to scout ahead,' said Badger, with a stern leader's tone. 'If I do it, it'll take all day.'

'I'll go,' squeaked Fox, piping up.

'No, me, me!' cried Hare, bouncing up and down.

Badger whispered to Fox, 'Let him have his moment.'

Fox smiled as Hare accelerated up through the gorse bushes, nearing the hilltop in only a couple of heartbeats. When the summit was reached, he grinded to a halt on top of a large flat rock face, and looked down, trying to catch his breath, only to lose it again.

Spread out in front of him, was a land he and his companions had tried so hard to picture in their minds, a land of unimaginable beauty. A little oval shaped lake lay in the middle of a vast, unspoiled, green setting, glinting like some precious jewel.

Something drifted up and clung to Hare's face. He peeled it off with his paw and looked at it - an oak leaf.

All around, from the base of the hill to nearly the peak, was another thing the three friends had never seen before - a *forest,* tall, majestic and scented with countless new plants and flowers - a new home, perhaps?

Moments later, Fox and Badger trundled up to Hare's side, instantly falling under the same spell. Hare looked at his companions.

'Welcome to Lough Ine,' he panted.

BOOK ONE
-PART TWO-

Living in Lough Ine

Settling In

Time seemed to stand still as the three companions stared helplessly at their new surroundings: the tranquil blue lake, with its several small, rocky islands, the awesome mass of the ocean beyond the green coastline, and up close, trees, taller and more numerous than they had ever dared to imagine.

Although they were aware that time could not stand still, they still wouldn't have wanted to spend it any other way.

Here on top of the enormous, densely wooded hill, the breezes were strong and icy. Each breath was like a thousand breaths at once. The three young animals were nearly bowled over. They could feel their ears and fur being stretched backwards, and their lips flapping in the driving wind. Still awe stricken, Fox, Badger and Hare made an effort to move downwards away from the peak, chancing their first steps into the mystic forest, where they immediately set about exploring...

'Wow,' was Fox's first thought. 'If Spring Valley is any better than this!'

The forest was enchanting.

Having trees over their heads gave the companions a feeling they did not have out in the fields - comfort, and safety; all the branches of the canopy mingling together like a roof, closing up the passage of the sky and wind. Above in the treetops, the breezes rustling the leaves seemed to be whispering 'You made it at last, you made it at last...' Some trees were young, others ancient. The conifers and pines had grown quite recently, but the mighty, moss covered girths of oak and chestnut had been standing proudly for hundreds of years.

Beams of bright sunlight shone down through the newly sprouted leaves, illuminating clusters of early flowers on the forest floor. Primroses, stitchwort, red campion, marsh marigold, celandine and wood anemone spiked up around the trunks and clearings. Young bracken and fern carpeted the shade and verges, unrolling from their curl- tip fronds. . A dormant bee hive hung from one of the ash branches, in an untidy tangle of twigs and sticks. A few butterflies and moths of various kinds and colours had also come out of hiding prematurely, fluttering, hovering and dancing around every plant.

As soon as he had entered the woods, Fox's nose was hit by a blast of many new and different smells. The aroma of the forest and all of its flora was over powering.

While birds chirped and twittered in the treetops overhead, Fox, Badger and Hare made their way down the steep banks of ivy and garlic until they reached a dirt track lined with brambles, and teal - green bushes of rhododendron. A little stream burbled down the slopes, falling and splashing delicately under the lime green bracken. They were nearing the bottom of the hill. The lake glinted between the larch trees. Instead of continuing on down, the friends felt they wanted to see more of the woods, and looped around, all the way back up the hill. They followed along the pathway until they came to the *other* side of the peak, the one they hadn't seen upon their arrival.

It turned out to be a festering, smelly old swamp. It lay in a grove of scots pines and sitka spruce, their blue-green needles covering the soft, bouncy ground, where mounds of moss had swollen to a great size! Several dead trees lay rotting, while at the same time giving homes to colonies of woodlice and ants. The craters left over from the fallen trees had filled with rainwater, which by now was well stagnant. Flies buzzed around the shallow, slime filled ponds.

Despite the odour in the air, the three friends took pleasure in bouncing from one mossy mound to another, laughing as they occasionally bumped into each other. The mounds were like some sort of natural cushions, and they had amazing suspension. Not even Badger's weight could deflate them. When the thrill finally died down, the trio settled into looking about the swamp.

Badger sniffed around in the rushes and spines, wondering if he'd find any early mushrooms, while Hare skirted the tree trunks, looking up at the spiky crowns. A pigeon clattered off on clumsy wings, leaving a white, ploppy present behind. The birds of Lough Ine were flitting around in a *busybusybusy* kind of way. Their nestlings were hungry, and no worm was safe!

Fox sat peering into one of the ponds. A gigantic scots pine had fallen some time ago, and now its great lateral roots opened out over the pond like a clam. The water was still, and covered in a layer of pure green slime. They say the colour green has a calming affect, and Fox felt quite at ease, just staring at it. And then, to make him sit upright, a little hole appeared on the surface. Just a little hole, bubbling. Fox watched in suspense now. A tiny, wide eyed creature poked its head up out of the water and stared Fox right in the eye.

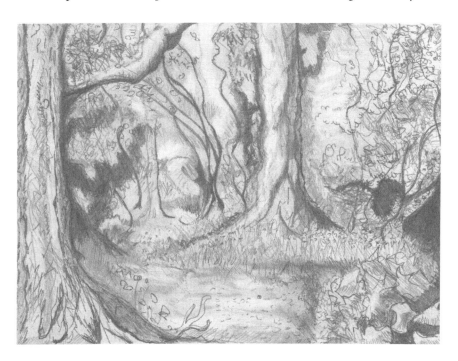

After a while:

'Hewwo,' it squeaked.

Fox fell backwards with fright, landing in a shallow mud puddle with a splash. Badger and Hare rushed to his side. 'What's wrong?' Badger asked.

Fox stood up and cautiously crouched over the pond again, and continued to examine this strange little water dweller.

It was only a baby of some sort, far too small to cause any harm. In fact, it was so miniscule, the cub had to narrow his eyes to see it. He sighed with relief, feeling foolish for having even reacted that way.

'What kind of animal is this?' he asked.

Asking Badger this question was almost cruel. His eyes had trouble enough identifying large objects, let alone ones that were extraordinarily teeny. Nonetheless, Badger was eager to find out. Leaning close and straining his eyes till they hurt, he announced:

'Oh I've seen these little fellows before. They're called 'tadpoles' Strange though, there're usually hundreds of them together. This one seems to be on its own. That's a first.'

'Oh,' said Fox, still gawking at it. 'Hello *"Tadpole."* Where's your family?' Tadpole, as he was now called, seemed quite partial to overtures. There he was, surrounded by a group of animals countless times bigger than himself- and yet he stayed put, actually enjoying their company. He shrugged, not knowing the answer to Fox's question (and probably not understanding the question!)

'Poor little critter,' Badger consoled. 'So you're all by yourself?'

'Ya - ha,' Tadpole replied, in a voice so tiny, the friends had to strain their ears, as well as their eyes, to comprehend him.

'So you have to feed yourself and everything?' Hare enquired.

The baby frog nodded, looking half proud of himself.

'What do you eat then?' asked Badger, with growing amazement.

'I wike to eat fwies and ... wikkle bugs!' Tadpole answered.

The three companions looked at each other, open mouthed. Was this tiny, seemingly defenseless infant, with underdeveloped limbs, really capable of fending for himself?

Badger gave a nervous, giddy laugh.

'I'm blown away,' he said, eyeing the young frog again. 'You do all this by yourself, hunting for food, staying alive without a giant family? I bet these 'flies' and 'little bugs' you catch are bigger than yourself!'

Tadpole giggled.

Again, the three friends looked at each other, as if appealing to each other for some kind of explanation.

'Unbelievable,' they all breathed.

When it was clear Tadpole had no more news, they decided to try having fun with him. Badger stuck his claw into the murky pond and gently began swirling the water. Tadpole found himself in the middle of a little whirlpool.

'Wahooo!' he cheered, spinning round and round, having the time of his life. When the water settled, Tadpole, for some reason, just paddled off. He disappeared behind a bed of rushes, much to the bewilderment of his audience.

'Uh, Tadpole, where did you go?' Hare called after him.

'I wanna show you stumping,' came the young frog's voice, not that anyone heard him. The three companions waited on the pond bank for a moment, until Tadpole reappeared from around the clump of rushes, pushing something in front of him. The animals watched suspiciously, waiting for Tadpole to get closer so they could make out the strange object. It was, of course, a great deal bigger than he who was pushing it. The friends noticed it was oval shaped and pure white - an, an egg?

'Can I see that?' Badger asked politely.

'Mmm hmm,' said Tadpole, as he released the egg and allowed it to float to the surface. It turned out to be much larger than the friends had thought.

They all took a startled step backwards.

'That's a bird's egg!' cried Badger. 'Where did you get it?'

'I founded it,' squeaked Tadpole. 'It was fwoating down da' stweam, so I pickeded it up and swam home wiv it. I taking good cay of it now. I waiting fo' it to hatch, so I can have a fwiend.'

'You don't have any friends?' said Fox.

Tadpole shook his head'

'Na-ah.'

'That's not a nice thing to say,' Hare remarked, in a strangely sympathetic tone. 'What are *we*, then?'

Tadpole's face was about to light up, when Badger intercepted.

'That egg won't hatch if you keep it in the cold water,' he said, matter of factly. 'Birds' eggs need to be warm and dry.'

Tadpole gaped at Badger for a while, not quite getting the hint.

'I'll show you,' said Badger. 'Could I see the egg?'

Tadpole nodded.

'Awwight.'

Badger gently scooped the egg out of the water with his fork - like paw, and placed it carefully in the dry rushes.

'There,' he said. 'At least it stands some chance now.'

All heads peered around for this 'stream' that Tadpole had mentioned. It turned out to be just a trickle, dribbling from a gentle slope into the pond.

With so much fresh mud plastering over them, nobody could see the footprints. Weeks ago, the footprints had led into the swamp, and had left again, along with a jar full of tadpoles…

There was still no telling where the egg had come from. Tadpole just stared and flicked his long transparent tail.

'Well,' said Badger to the tiny frog. 'This is looking like an interesting first day,' and he went on to say, 'Anyway, I'm Badger, this is Fox and this lop-eared nuisance is Hare.'

Hare blew on his nails and rubbed them on his chest, somehow hearing a compliment.

'We're new here,' Badger went on. 'I suppose, now that we're living here, we'll be seeing you nearly every day!'

Tadpole smiled and nodded furiously.

'Well, we'd better get going; lots more exploring to do. You just mind yourself now, and that bird's egg.'

With that, the three animals made their way out of the swamp and soon came to the edge of the wood. Outside the shade of the scots pines, lay a wide open plain, full of burrows…

Hilltop Warren

Into the wind swept meadow, the three animals happily made their way. For the first time ever, Fox led the way. He bounded excitedly ahead of his friends, through the long, curly outskirts of the plain, sending a few crane flies, dung flies and green bottles shooting from their hiding places in the grass. They took to startled flight, buzzing with annoyance. When the cub found his way out of the tall grass stalks, into a flatter area, he stopped dead in his tracks. Badger and Hare padded up behind him, about to continue the trek, when Fox turned and motioned them to lie low.

'Look over there!' he whispered, pointing his snout to the distance. The three friends could see that the yellowish slope across from them was dotted with over a dozen peculiar little creatures; some were brown, some were grey, all of them had long ears and fluffy white tails. They were huddled together around a cluster of scots pines and rowan trees, along with the usual scattering of thorn bushes.

Some were nibbling on the short grass, others were sun bathing or grooming their ears and muzzles, yet most were rollicking around and play fighting.

'Wow,' gasped Fox as he continued to watch them. 'I've never seen so many hares.'

'Hares?' gasped Hare, glaring at Fox with a look of disgust. 'I'm insulted. Those aren't hares. Those are 'rabbits'. They have smaller legs and shorter ears, not half as strong or as smart as hares! Why, we hares are tall, noble, well built, dashingly handsome, highly intelligent and of course, modest.'

'Ssshh,' said Badger, squinting his eyes at the distant rabbits. 'Keep your voice down, we don't want to startle them. If I know rabbits, they scare easily.'

Hare sniggered. 'Hmph. Typical bunnies, afraid of their own shadows. A hare wouldn't know fear if it yanked on his whiskers.'

The three friends sat for some time, observing the rabbits from their safe vantage point.

It looked as though the rabbits were running low on food. The meadow where they were frolicking seemed very battered down, the grass so short and patchy, as if it had been attacked by a swarm of locusts. Some areas had been stripped down to bare earth. Yet the rabbits were not bothered. They contentedly went about their daily routine of grazing and lazing. Some rabbits were even seen napping in the shade of the scots pines, displaying their snow white underparts. And then, some of the more plucky rabbits were seen scuttling in and out of their burrows in the hedges, or squabbling over the last leaf of clover.

The three friends were made drowsy, losing track of time as they mused over what it must be like to be a rabbit. It was a happy sight. The meadow was like a large pocket of undiscovered grass in the middle of the high - up woods. Badger was quite surprised. He had always associated rabbits with being lowland creatures. And here these ones were - half way to the clouds.

Suddenly, breaking the lull, there came an ear splitting screech from behind the row of scots pines. In a blind panic, all of the rabbits scrambled to their feet, some retreating to their burrows, others frantically running in circles and the rest crowding together in one place. Fox, Badger and Hare gasped.

One of the rabbits had been caught in a snare!

He had wandered away from his comrades, into a different field, where the grass was lusher. Only, this field did not belong to the rabbits. In fact, this field didn't even belong to animals…

The rabbit struggled and squirmed, trying to break free, but the more he pulled, the tighter the wire around his neck became. The cruel metal noose bit savagely into his flesh, denying him breath. He ran in desperate circles, pivoting around the wooden post, to which the wire was attached. But all this did was waste his energy and tire him out.

All of the worried rabbits around him were frantically wondering what to do. Some tried to dig out the wooden stake, but it was twisted far too deep into the ground. Other rabbits tried to calm their friend down, as he was now lying on the ground, kicking and gasping in a frenzy. But it was no use. The unfortunate rabbit was being strangled to death.

Meanwhile, the three companions watched on hopelessly from afar.

'We have to help them!' cried Fox as he sprang to his feet.

Before either of his friends could do or say anything to stop him, Fox took off across the field, galloping as fast as he could towards the group of distressed rabbits, while Badger desperately called after him;

'Come back, you'll scare them away!'

When the rabbits saw Fox hurtling towards them, they instantly scattered in all directions, diving into bushes, disappearing under trees, clambering and scurrying down into the safety of their burrows, all the time shrieking out warnings to those who hadn't yet spotted the danger.

The rabbits abandoned their dying comrade and vanished.

Fox halted when he reached the trapped one. He lay on the ground, still fighting for one merciful breath, whilst frothing at the mouth. His eyes were red and puffy. The metal wire embedded in his neck still held him in its tight and terrible grip.

'Go...ahead,' he managed to say, in a hoarse, bubbly voice. 'Eat me... I hope I give you... the scutters!'

With that, the entangled rabbit closed his eyes and allowed his head to thump the ground.

Fox, crouched over him, hadn't heard what the rabbit had said, and quickly searched for a way to loosen the wire. He noticed it was tied to a little wooden stake, sticking out of the ground. It was striated with teeth and claw marks from rabbits trying in vain to dig it out. But Fox would have little trouble in doing this.

Fixing his jaws firmly around the head of the stake, Fox began pulling, heaving and hauling with all his might. At first, it appeared the stake was pulling him! His hind legs skidded, churning up dirt, the wooden beast unyielding. Fox sat up, spat out splinters, and after stretching his sore neck, tried again. The rabbit was as still as stone. He did not move, he did not breathe. All hope was screaming.

Fox now twisted and manouvered, in circular motion, and slowly but surely the stake began to slide out of the ground. With a final, aggressive spurt, Fox lifted the long wooden post up out of the ground, leaving behind a deep black hole. At long last, the wire around the rabbit's neck slackened, and he was free.

It didn't look too good. The silence whispered of death. But miraculously, he opened his bloodshot eyes and took in a huge deep breath, before coughing and spluttering furiously. As he rubbed his throbbing, scarred neck, the rabbit stared at Fox, lost for both words and feelings. Instinct told the rabbit to run. But the rabbit knew full well it was Fox who had come to his rescue. 'I don't know what to say,' he rasped. 'Why would you do that for me?'

Fox sat and said nothing. He felt like he had a mouthful of nettles. Blood dribbled from his gums.

The silence that followed seemed as long as hours.

Slowly, rabbits from all around began emerging from their hiding places. It took them a while to realize that Fox meant no harm. Ears erect, noses twitching with caution, they gingerly edged their way up to him, one by one. Before long, Fox was surrounded by almost twenty brown and grey, long eared, white fluffy tailed creatures, all eying him up and down, mystified. Had this fox just saved the life of a rabbit? Such a thing was unheard of in Lough Ine, or anywhere else for that matter. This had never been seen before.

Just then, the crowd of rabbits divided in half, allowing a great big buck rabbit to come forward. He brimmed with importance. His brown coat was tinted with grey. He had a tuft of thick hair on his head, like a brown mohawk, and a great bushy mane.

Looking at a bewildered Fox, he asked in a rather deep, terse voice:

'What is your name, stranger?'

The cub shakily replied: 'Fox.'

The great rabbit grunted.

'Yes I can see you're a fox, but I asked for your *name.*'

Fox felt quite embarrassed, having to confess this in front of such an audience.

'Err, that *is* my name,' he said, timidly.

'Hmph, strange,' shrugged the rabbit. 'Well my name is 'Spruce,' Captain Spruce, leader of Lough Ine's rabbit clans. On behalf of every rabbit present, I would like to thank you for your impetuous act of kindness. You're unlike any fox we've ever seen.'

Fox smiled slightly.

Just then, Badger and Hare crept into the circle of rabbits. Startled, they all took one step back.

'And who are you?' asked Spruce.

'We're with him,' Hare panted, indicating Fox.

The Captain went silent for a moment, glancing at Fox on his left and Badger and Hare on his right.

'Have I become simple in my old age?' he gasped, placing a paw on his forehead and looking at the ground. 'First I see a fox rescue a rabbit, and then I discover his companions are a badger and a hare? What can I call you two?'

Badger and Hare introduced themselves.

'The surprises keep coming,' said Spruce, his voice reaching a new note. 'Three natural enemies travelling together as friends- none of whom have names?'

The three companions looked at each other, as if just realizing this themselves, and nodded.

'I see,' stammered the Captain, before sounding more composed. 'Nevertheless, I can't say amity between different types of animals is a bad thing. It's possibly the most superb thing I've ever seen. You're all very unusual, no doubt, but you're all very welcome here. You are 'new' aren't you?'

'Yes,' said Badger. 'We only arrived here this morning.'

'Oh?' said Spruce, scratching his chin with interest. 'From where?'

All of the rabbits leaned forward with their giant hazel eyes fully widened, awaiting an epic story.

But Badger gave only a brief account of the travels and troubles he and his companions had gone through. But this was enough to stir up a sense of awe and admiration among the crowd of rabbits. They all gasped and began chattering amongst themselves.

'That sounds like quite a tale,' said Spruce, stroking his mane with a smile. 'I'd like to hear it in full some day. Unfortunately, now is not the time. But before we retire, allow me to introduce you to your new home.'

Fox, Badger and Hare leaned in and paid attention. Captain Spruce spoke fluently of the place:

'Lough Ine consists of a number of different small regions; here, you have *Hilltop Warren,* home of the upland rabbits. To your south, and all over the hills, you have the beautiful *Knockomagh Wood.* Within the forest, you'll find *Bubble lump Swamp,* a place best avoided for those who care about personal hygiene. And finally, down below at the bottom of the hill, you'll see The Lake itself, the most cherished jewel in the land.'

Fox, Badger and Hare all gazed around at the wondrous landscape.

'Lough Ine is said to be a place of refuge for us wild animals,' said Spruce, who then looked down at the snare. 'But as you can see,' he went on, 'The humans still find ways to torment us. These cursed snares are a little too close and a little too common for comfort. Hmph. That's the last time I let one of my rabbits stray outside Lough Ine's border.

But with you three heroes living among us, I don't think we ought to worry too much anymore. You have our respect. Let it be said; if there's ever anything we rabbits can do for you in return, just give the ground a thump!'

The three companions smiled and dipped their heads with gratitude. 'Anyway,' announced Captain Spruce as he turned to leave. 'I think everybody deserves a good rest after an incident like that. Maybe later when we're finished recovering, we'll come out for a snooze in the sun.' The crowd of rabbits soon cleared away. Before long, Captain Spruce was the only rabbit left on the field. Turning back for a final word, he added: 'By the way, have you met any other any animals since you arrived?'

Hare answered this:

'We made friends with a tadpole,'

he said.

Captain Spruce chortled.

'Don't worry,' he promised. 'I'll see to it that you become acquainted with some of our other friendly residents. Until then...'

The rabbit leader disappeared under a hawthorn tree, leaving Fox, Badger and Hare alone in the middle of the meadow.

It was a while before anything was said.

'Why does that always happen?' asked Fox, feeling perplexed.

'Why does 'what' always happen?' asked Badger.

Fox sighed.

'Every time I meet new animals, they get scared of me: *you* got scared of me, *Hare* got scared of me, the *rabbits* got scared of me. They thought I was a monster.'

Badger and Hare glanced at each other with worry in their eyes, as Fox continued to sum up every suspicious hint he could remember.

'And those crows,' he went on. 'When we were attacked by those crows, I remember the big one saying that I should be 'chasing' Hare and killing him. Why did he say that? Oh, and just now, that rabbit Captain Spruce, said that I was 'unlike any fox he had ever seen.' He couldn't believe I was actually friendly. Why does everybody think I'm dangerous?'

Badger and Hare trembled. This was it, the moment they had dreaded since that night in the ruins, the moment they had wished and prayed would never come, had come! Its cold reality made their fur spike.

'Well what now?' asked Hare, looking at Badger. 'Should we tell him?' Badger gulped. 'We can't hide it forever.'

Fox gasped. 'Hide what?'

'We didn't want you to know,' Badger began. 'But you see, it's not normal for a fox to have friends.'

Fox squinted his eyes and took a step back.

'I don't understand.'

'Look,' Badger went on. 'Foxes are predators. It's in their nature to hunt and kill other animals for food. They usually live alone and hunt alone. That's why at first, we were all afraid of you. And that's why so many animals think you're strange, because you're friends with us.'

Fox was stunned.

Badger felt guilty for breaking the news.

'So now you know why we kept this a secret,' he said gravely. 'It took time for us to fully trust you.'

Still, Fox said nothing. He simply stared at the ground, numbed by this new knowledge.

'But it's okay now,' said Badger, brightening up. 'We're not afraid of you anymore. We know you'll never turn on us.'

Fox looked up from the ground. His voice carried a tinge of fear.

'But what if I do,' he said. 'What if I can't help myself one day and I end up hurting one of you.'

'That day will never come,' laughed Badger, desperately trying to lighten the matter. 'We know you too well now. You're different.'

'Well I shouldn't be!' Fox snapped. 'You said it yourself; I'm a predator, I'm not supposed to have friends!'

'You can if you want,' said Badger. "There's nothing wrong with being different if you're happy with it.'

This brought Fox no comfort.

'I remember one more thing,' he said. 'That night when Hare was attacked by a rat; I didn't mean to kill that rat. And I didn't mean to eat him either. But I did. I couldn't stop myself. If I can kill once by accident, I can kill again. I *am* dangerous; you're not safe with me!'

Fox turned and sped off into the darkness of Knockomagh Wood by himself, leaving his two friends behind, powerless to stop him.

'Fox, come back, this is silly!' Badger shouted after him, watching his friend's bushy tail disappear into the shadows of the tall scots pines.

'Fox!' Badger roared, trundling forward in a vain attempt to give chase.

'It's too late,' said Hare, restraining him. 'We've lost him. Aw, I knew this would happen.'

Old Darig

S*o* his first day in Lough Ine was an eye- opener. Under a shady alder tree in the middle of the wood, Fox sat by himself, wondering what to do. He could not go back to his friends, not after making such a show of himself.

He felt humiliated, cheated, gullible. He should have known foxes were meant to be that way. How foolish he must have looked on that journey, playing with his food. Under the tree that evening, the cub made a point to forget everything. He swore to forget his friends, and everything he'd done with them; suppress their memories, and even his feelings for them. It was time to start over, normal.

The sun was setting on the hills of Lough Ine. It retreated slowly behind the lines of trees in the distance, like an orange ball sinking in a pink pool. Knockomagh Wood was growing darker and darker as evening set in. While the air gradually cooled and while light purple clouds began to devour the sky, Fox lifted himself from the grass and made his way along the forest floor, in a state of frustration. The cub did not have the faintest idea where to go or what to do.

Tall beech trees and ash trees towered over him, their leafy crowns blocking his view of the sky. But the cub had no interest in the sky. His head was hanging down, almost between his front legs. So he wandered, gliding between the trees, forgetting he was heading upwards again, as the songbirds in the canopy finished their last tune and went home.

Coming to the grove of gnarled scots pines at Bubblelump Swamp, Fox quickly turned around and headed back down, seeing himself as a danger to the young Tadpole who lived there.

He was halfway down the hill when he found a stream, babbling along a pathway, under some mulched leaves. The cub stooped to have a drink. He gulped down its chilled, delicious water, until he could feel it sloshing around in his belly. He ended up swallowing a few beetles and millipedes with it, but that was all the better. Off he went again, until the stream led him to a clearing. It was here, he saw the cottage.

He couldn't believe it. Nothing was left of it but three low walls, and a tall yew tree sprouting up from the floor, right in its very middle. It was furred with moss, and shaded by laurel branches, and the stream just gargled by, dribbling into an almost dry, muddy riverbed.

Fox pondered over this for a while, sniffing around the inside and outside of the cottage very gingerly.

Could it be that humans once lived here in Knockomagh Wood? If so, why did they leave?

The sight and aura of the old ruin reminded Fox of the abandoned old village he had spent a night in. This cottage looked so similar, that he imagined a strong wind must have picked up one of those cottages and dropped it here in the middle of the woods.

But then, Fox's mind spun back to reality when he heard the shrubs behind him begin to rustle. Something was quartering the area, something big and heavy. Twigs and little branches snapped as the creature, whatever it was, drew closer.

Fox stood rooted to the spot, ears and tail straight with caution. He could feel his fur stiffening. The fight or flight instinct was rising. Then, out of a cluster of rhododendron bushes, it stepped - a large, magnificent fox.

His coat was thick and lustrous with fine chestnut fur. His tail was enormous and bushy, sweeping from side to side like a broom. A freshly killed rabbit hung from his mouth, as he spotted Fox in front of him, trembling.

The cub wanted to run, but curiosity got the better of him. He held his ground and stared. It was like looking at a reflection of his future self. At last, another of his kind!

The great, big dog fox allowed the rabbit to fall from his mouth, and took a step forward, with one eye narrowed.

'Who are you?' he asked in a deep bass voice, while eying the cub up and down, suspiciously.

Fox was too taken aback to answer.

'I have not seen you around here before,' said the big fox. 'Are you lost?'

Fox nodded, allowing the bigger fox to continue questioning.

'Very well,' he went on, talking slowly as if the cub had muttered something he couldn't understand. 'And were you with anyone earlier?'

Fox shook his head, now feeling he had no reason to fear violence from this creature. If it was going to attack him, surely it would have done so already.

'So you're lost and you're alone, eh,' said the big fox. 'Mind if I ask your name, little one?'

By now, Fox was too embarrassed and too nervous to answer that awful question again, and said nothing.

'So you don't have a name,' shrugged the big fox, putting his head up but keeping his eyes on the cub. 'You must be younger than you look. Come, I'll help you find your den. You don't want your mother to start fretting about you.'

The big fox was about to take his leave, when he realized the cub was standing still, looking plaintive.

'Your family don't live around here, do they?' said the big fox, knowingly.

The cub shook his head from side to side.

'I see,' murmured the big fox. 'Err, could you please show me the direction from where you came, little one?'

Timidly, Fox took a few steps forward, and pointed with his nose in the direction of the open fields and hills.

He could see the stirring feelings of awe on the older fox's face.

'From how far away did you come, exactly?'

Fox cleared his throat. 'The very edge,' he said. 'Near the sea.'

'Near the sea,' the old fox gasped. "That's where The Farmer lives. Why, your family are all dead, aren't they!'

Wondering how the big fox could possibly have known this, Fox replied in a choked voice 'Yeah.'

A reluctant smile creased the older fox's face.

'I think you and I may have a lot in common,' he said.

It wasn't long before Fox found himself walking side by side with his larger look-alike.

'Well, little one,' began the big fox. 'Since you don't have a name, allow me to tell you mine. I am Darig, or by this time, Old Darig. Being old is something you children may laugh at now, but with age comes wisdom, and I pride myself on having much.'

Fox said nothing. He just wanted to listen and learn. Now that he was in the company of another fox, he did not have to feel out of place. Darig did ask him how he had come to Lough Ine, but the cub was vague in his telling, just saying 'Yeah' to every question. Still, Darig was impressed.

'How uncanny,' he mused, as they both reached the south edge of the wood and looked out at the twilight glow.

Darig looked down at Fox.

'I know how it feels,' he said, 'to be the last one standing. You see, I wasn't born here either. I began life in a faraway town, as an urban fox. Do you know what a town is?'

Naturally, Fox was clueless.

Darig turned away.

'It is hard to describe unless you've been there yourself,' he said. 'A town is a world, alien to this one. It is where humans come from; a place tall, noisy, crowded, made of steel and concrete. So many humans, so few trees. And there I lived, in the middle of it all.'

Fox was intrigued.

'And like your family,' Darig went on. 'Mine was taken away. We'd barely survived in that place all along; hiding in boxes by day, eating rubbish by night, and in that first season alone, my brothers and sisters failed to dodge between the cars.

Very soon it was just my mother and I. She decided a town was no place for her one remaining infant, and so, we fled.

It was a bittersweet feeling; I was so used to the town. I had learned so much; I actually knew less about being a fox and more about humans and their strange ways...

We made it as far as the roundabout at the end of town, and that's where the journey ended for my mother. It was just too confusing, with all that traffic. Bless her soul; it could have been both of us...

So I made it to the countryside alone. I can't tell you everything that happened to me there, but I'll tell you this: I loved it. I could never have known such clarity.

After about two seasons, I met the vixen of my dreams. Eva was her name. Some time later, Eva and I had three wonderful cubs together; two little daughters and one hardy lump of a son. It was then I thought life couldn't get any sweeter.'

At this point in his narrative, Fox could hear Old Darig's breath becoming shallower. It sounded like he was struggling to hold in some pent- up tears. 'Until one evening,' he went on. 'I paid for a mistake that could have easily been excused. Yes, I admit it; I stole some chickens from The Farmer to feed my family! He had sprayed the crops and poisoned the rats, so I couldn't very well eat those! What are a few chickens to him, after all, he has so many!

Later that evening, The Farmer sealed up the exits of our den and dug us out from above! We'd been sleeping and took off confused. Eva was shot at point blank range, and my cubs didn't make it far either, with those hounds chasing them. Those hounds -I fought all three of them by myself, oh, how I fought! I tried leading them away from the den, into a coppice of trees, and there they cornered me.

Suddenly there was another gunshot. My son was still in the den, and the hounds ran off to investigate, leaving me alone.

They probably thought I'd die of my wounds, and maybe I should have, but no, I carried on, as far away from that place and that memory as I could until I reached here, Lough Ine.

I only wish my life here could compensate for the life I've lived,' Darig concluded. 'It is exceedingly beautiful, and peaceful, but unfortunately peace gives me time to remember. I still spring awake sometimes, after thinking I'm still in that town - all those buildings rising up around me, humans trampling on me. Survival, I suppose, comes at a price. I am sorry you lost your family, little one. But count yourself lucky. We are foxes. Only one in four of us will ever make it.'

Fox didn't know what to say. He choked on the words he failed to find.

'But the question is,' Darig brushed up. 'Why is it that some live and some die? How come we didn't join our families when they perished? Sometimes I get the feeling that I - well, *we*- were chosen to carry on, as if destined for something great'

'Like what?' asked Fox.

'Who knows,' sighed Darig, stepping out of the woods and into the open, where the sun had gone out and all was dark. He paused for a long time, deep in thought.

Fox watched him from the trees.

Darig seemed a terribly troubled figure. His tired eyes and crooked whiskers whispered of great pain and loneliness, but also of great knowledge, with whom he'd had no one to share. Fox was glad he could be that someone.

Darig was looking up at the trees, their silhouettes framed against the indigo sky.

'All we do is try to stay alive,' he muttered.

Fox wasn't sure if he was meant to hear this.

Darig kept staring through glazed eyes. 'All we do is try to stay alive,' he repeated. 'What if we tried something more...? The world is changing. Animals are changing. We now know what's happening.'

Fox tilted his head to one side, not knowing what Darig meant. But that was for another day.

The two foxes soon reached the Hilltop. The scenery below was wrapped in darkness. For many predators of the wild, nightfall meant dinnertime. Darig looked down on Fox.

'Did your mother ever teach you how to hunt, little one?'

Fox shook his head from side to side.

'You don't know how to hunt?' said Darig loudly. 'So what do you live on?'

Fox replied: 'I know how to roll away rocks and find bugs, I know how to dig for worms, I know how to pick berries and-'

'Whoa, whoa, whoa,' Darig interrupted. 'Slow down, little one. Bugs and berries aren't enough to keep you going. Why, you have the diet of a badger. What you need is fresh, raw meat.

Come, if I'm going to teach you how to be a real fox, then I might as well start now.'

So it was, the cub was swept away, away from the life he once knew, and into the bleak world of normality.

From that very evening onwards, the wise Old Darig took Fox under his wing and taught him everything he had missed out on; everything he should have been doing, as a 'real' fox.

It seemed like a long and complex training course. Fox lost track of time, as Darig allowed little time for rest or play. Every evening was spent engrossed in some new aspect of fox life. The mornings and days were to be used for sleeping, which Darig said was important for foxes as they needed to save their strength for nightfall. Fox rarely had the chance to see full daylight like he used to. During this time, the cub slept in an extra chamber in Darig's den, which was located in the thicket of the forest. It was the first time in what seemed like ages that Fox had gone underground.

And so, on the first evening of training, Old Darig decided to go easy on his new apprentice. Instead of making Fox hunt for his own meal, he kindly went to the trouble of catching him a woodcock, and then went back to the cottage ruin to retrieve the rabbit he had captured for himself earlier.

Fox thought the woodcock a guilty pleasure. Although it tasted heavenly, minus the beak and feathers, the cub had admired the bird a lot more when it was alive. Watching it shoot from the bracken, whistling and shrieking, with its stripy brown plumage and long, straight bill, was an admirable sight, only to be short lived, after Darig leapt up and snatched it out of the air, skillfully. Nevertheless, Fox felt it would be worse to let the poor bird go to waste, and in his honour, ate every last bite.

Proper training didn't begin until the following evening, when Old Darig spent much of the time showing Fox how to be sly and cunning like all of his kind. In the middle of the woods, he demonstrated how to creep silently around trees without being heard.

'The trick is,' the old fox continued. 'To try and avoid stepping on twigs or sticks, because if they snap, you'll be heard. Only tread on the soft parts of the ground, and you don't have to rush, not until necessary. Always take your time when sneaking around. It also helps to hold your breath while hiding, especially on cold days when your frozen breath can be seen. All these little techniques can save your life in the event of danger, or help you catch a snack!'

Fox practiced his sneaking moves, under Darig's watchful eye, keeping low to the ground and creeping silently along as he had been ordered to, and then dashed from tree trunk to tree trunk, trying to stay hidden.

'Don't forget,' said Old Darig, sagely. 'Strength may help you take lives, but cunning will help you keep yours.'

Being sly should come naturally to a fox, but on the journey to Lough Ine, our Fox had developed some reckless habits.

He practiced tirelessly to break them.

Over the days, Darig went about teaching the cub of the forest's flowers, plants and fungi, which ones were edible and which ones were poisonous. Although no mushrooms would grow till autumn, the cub was told that the fly agaric was deadly, and could cause him serious hallucinations, while the chanterelle was scrumptious to eat.

He also described how to recognize animal markings, such as the broken snail shells left behind after a feeding thrush, the raisin- like droppings of rabbits, and the peculiar 'owl pellets.'

After taking in this new knowledge, Fox would continue to try out his stalking and creeping moves.

When it was thought he had mastered these skills, Darig moved on to more important lessons.

'Now when it comes to fighting,' he began. 'What can I say? Only - be vicious and show no mercy! Some day, you might find yourself up against a tough stoat or even a stray dog. Yes, little one, there are creatures out there who want you dead, and remember; you want the same for them. So if you're trapped in a tricky situation with no escape, here's what you do - go for the neck!'

The two foxes spent hours out on the verge of the woods together, playfully fighting in the fading sunlight. They rolled around in the short grass, wrestling and tussling, snarling and yapping, and of course, laughing.

'Don't be afraid, little one,' laughed Darig as he stood tail- up. 'I'll go easy on you-oomph!'

Fox seemed very strong for his age. Darig wondered how he was able to tackle him to the ground so easily. It was as if the young cub had already been in a few brawls before...

Once the lesson was over, Old Darig allowed little time for rest. 'Well, little one,' he panted, examining a small scratch on his big paw. 'You certainly have no trouble defending yourself. Well done, I must admit.'

Fox smiled proudly, and then chased his tail. He was nowhere near tired just yet. But that all changed.

'Now,' Old Darig announced. 'It's time for you to dig out your own den.'

Later that evening, when the last ray of sunlight was dying down to a glow, Fox found himself underneath a large, old ash tree, down at the bottom of a deep, dark pit, which he had spent hours clearing out by himself. It was an abandoned old badger sett, cluttered with cobwebs, crusty grass, hair, droppings and the skeletons of mice and rats.

Some chambers had caved in entirely and had to be dug out all over again.

The cub was exhausted, dirty and parched, but he'd managed to snaffle up a few dozen earthworms and beetles while down there.

Darig stood at the entrance of the new den, yelling instructions down at his apprentice: 'Once you're finished digging, fill all the chambers with dry grass. It'll keep your new home nice and warm on those cold winter days.'

Fox wearily made his way up through the main tunnel, towards what was left of the evening sunshine, and emerged from the den, coughing.

Old Darig sighed, looking pitifully down at the worn out mess at his feet. 'It pains me to watch you struggle, little one,' he said in a gentle tone. 'But if I lend you a helping paw, you'll never learn to do things for yourself.' Fox was too tired to nod his head in agreement. Instead, he pulled himself from the hole and scuffed around the woods, gathering grass and bracken and whatever suitable green matter he could find. He then returned to the den and laboured on.

While doing so, Darig again sat at the entrance, giving him a lecture. 'You know, it's quite common for a fox to 'steal' the homes off other animals,' he pointed out. 'We simply find a hole in the ground, sniff it out, and if there's anything living in there, we drive it away, claiming the animal's territory as our own. Only in this case, who needs more enemies!'

Once he had finished insulating the den, Fox had no more to do.

'I'm very proud of you,' said Darig, smiling down at the cub, who was zapped of energy. 'You've come a long way since we first met. This den is a remarkable achievement for you, and always it will remind you of your progress. Have yourself a fine long rest now. You deserve it.'

Fox spent the rest of the night curled up at the bottom of his sleeping chamber, nestled deeply in his moss bedding. A gunshot would not have woken him.

The day had been long but rewarding. Fox had achieved many things; new skills, new knowledge, even a new home. He had created his very own den, a place where he could spend the rest of his life, if he so chose. But his training was not yet over and a most crucial lesson had yet to come.

To Hunt or Not to Hunt

The morning had come and gone. The wood was still and tranquil. Patches of sun and shade patterned the forest floor, where primroses had opened out fully, reaching for the light. An early chiffchaff perched on the topmost branches of a hornbeam tree, uttering its *hooeet* call. A family of chaffinches bathed and dabbled in a little puddle by the spring, squabbling and playing, undisturbed. There seemed to be no sign of any predators. The little fox that had been seen roaming the woods a lot lately was now nowhere to be seen.

All through the day, Fox remained in his underground chamber, in a deep, almost unconscious sleep. Days of learning and training had taken everything out of him. He now needed time off to rest and recharge. The day wore on without him.

By evening time however, the cub felt it was time to surface. Initially, he felt stiff and rusty all over, but he took this as a good sign of accomplishment, and after a stretch and a drink from the stream, he felt refreshed and ready to proceed. He made his way to Old Darig's den, eager to find what his next objective was.

At dusk, under a dulling, overcast sky, Fox found himself looking upon a familiar setting. He and Darig were both hiding in the bramble bushes at the edge of Hilltop Warren. It was nearly a half hour since they had begun waiting.

Outside their hiding place, the field remained empty. A gentle gust of wind crept through the short grass, ruffling the trees, chilling the air.

'Where are they?' Fox asked, peeking out through the leaves, nervously wagging his tail.

'Have patience, little one,' said Darig beside the cub. 'When the time is right, you'll know. Just remember everything I taught you.'

Fox's mind was frazzled. Since meeting Old Darig, he had had no time to think or reflect. His routine had become nothing but listen, learn, practice and sleep, then repeat it the following evening. Nothing else appeared to matter now, only learning how to become a real fox. All other thoughts had been shoved into the background.

Even during this tense stakeout, where silence was the key, Old Darig still found time to enlighten Fox with some more facts.

'We are most fortunate in having a warren right here in our back yard,' he said. 'It is a perpetual supply of food, but we must learn not to abuse it.' Fox was all ears.

'Rabbits have fed foxes since the dawn of time,' the old fox continued. 'So we must have a certain degree of respect for them, especially their great numbers. Here in this warren, I only target the old bucks, or the weaklings. It is vital that these rabbits continue to thrive, for us.'

Fox noted, but had almost lapsed into a trance while watching the deserted field.

He became alert again when he noticed a pair of long ears emerging ever so slowly from underneath the distant bushes. This was followed by two more, on either side. Very soon, all around the perimeter of the Warren, growing numbers of long ears and twitching little noses were becoming visible. The rabbits were coming out for an evening feed.

Fox watched anxiously as they casually set about nibbling on the grass and clover. The usual dozen or so rabbits were scattered throughout the field, some running from place to place, others standing still and enjoying the crisp evening air.

Darig sniffed deeply. 'Good,' he said. 'We are upwind of them. Wait till the time is right, little one.'

It wasn't long before the time was indeed, right.

'Okay,' said Darig, crouching still as stone, his eyes ever watchful. 'Here's your chance, little one. Do you see that rabbit over there? The fat brown one? He's wandering away from the rest, see him?'

'Yeah,' said Fox, keeping his eye on the lone rabbit, who was merrily hopping along and pausing every now and then to sample a dandelion. The cub now tried to suppress the strange feelings of guilt that were gurgling up inside him.

'Alright,' said Darig quickly. 'He's close, do your thing!'

Fox diligently crept from the brambles, into full view of the rabbit. But before it could run away, the cub lay down and began rolling about in the grass.

Fright became curiosity as the rabbit watched Fox playfully twist and turn on his back. It gingerly edged up to him for a closer look. Fox could see the rabbit out the corner of his eye, and contrived to bring him closer. He rolled some more, and then began chasing his tail, still pretending he hadn't noticed his spectator. The rabbit hopped closer again, wondering what on earth the cub was doing.

Then Old Darig's voice hissed from the bushes: 'Now little one, now!!'

Just like that, Fox dropped his act and straightened out, snapping his jaws! The rabbit drew back and squealed, as Fox made a drive for him. The plan flopped.

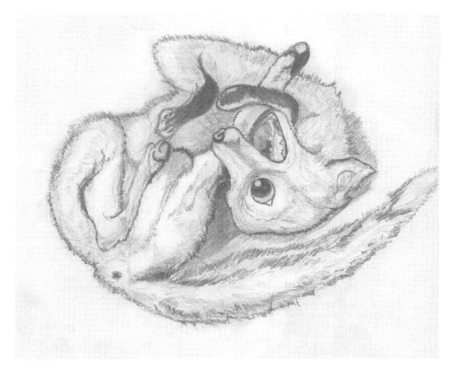

What should have been a skillful snatch, turned into a messy, chaotic chase! Although he was enormously fat, the rabbit was surprisingly quick on his feet. Fox had trouble keeping up with him, skidding on his face whenever he tried to snap him up! The rabbit scrambled around and round the meadow, sticking to the sidelines, as all of the other rabbits dashed underground, not wishing to be embroiled in the chase.

The fat rabbit could not find his burrow in such a panic, so he turned sharply and made a bee- line for the woods, with Fox hard on his heels. They ran nose to tail; the rabbit desperate to survive, and the cub eager to impress Old Darig. Both animals bounded into the dark woods, through the thick ferns, brambles and pine trees.

Fox now found it more difficult to keep up. The dangling branches and spindles repeatedly set him back, wrapping around him and getting caught in his fur. The rabbit now had the advantage and sped on ahead. Fox watched his fluffy white tail disappear into the shade of the trees. Furious at himself for not being able to stay on him, Fox tore his way through the twigs and hangers, searching frantically for his missing target. He galloped like a wild stallion, down the tree covered slope, until he spotted the rabbit just below, still running, knowing Fox was right behind. Fortunately, due to the unbelievably steep gradient of the hill, the cub was unable to slow down, and actually ran faster! His legs became blurs, as he thundered down the hill, trying not to bump into any tree trunks along the way!

As soon as the two animals reached a little clearing, Fox made his final move on the worn out, fat rabbit.

Putting all his strength into his hind legs, he lunged at his prey from behind, tackling him to the ground and rolling through the earth and leaves with him, until he had the fat rabbit firmly pinned down with his paw. Both animals panted unmercifully, exhausted from the manic chase. But Fox still had enough strength left to hold his capture still.

The rabbit, with a look of terror on his chubby face, stared up into Fox's eyes from the ground. Fox stared into his. They recognized each other.

'Why?' the rabbit choked out.

Fox's angry frown faded. His facial expression became one of bewilderment. His mind flashed back to that day when he had rescued this rabbit from the snare and befriended the entire Warren.

It was at that moment he decided he could not do it. He could not kill. He could not be a predator. He now believed he would be much happier having other animals as friends.

Lifting his paw from the rabbit's chest, he allowed him to climb shakily to his feet.

'You can go,' he sighed, still trembling. 'But don't tell anyone it was *me* who chased you. Tell them it was a different fox, and that you got away.'

Confused, the rabbit looked at Fox with his bucktooth showing.

'Just go,' said Fox, who looked equally confused.

The rabbit slowly turned and bounded back up the hill, into the trees.

Fox sat alone in the middle of the clearing for a while, trying to make sense of what had just happened.

And then, he heard a familiar voice in the distance, calling him: 'Little one, where did you go?'

In a panic, Fox frantically scanned the area with his eyes, searching for something he could use to fool Old Darig.

He struck luck when he came across a cluster of cowberries growing on a prickly bush. He immediately tore into them, chewing them up and spitting them out, licking his lips and smearing his face with red berry juice.

When Old Darig emerged from behind an alder tree, the first thing he saw was an exhausted looking cub, whose face seemed to be covered in blood.

'Oh there you are,' Darig gasped. 'Well, did you catch him?'

Still panting, Fox nodded.

'Excellent,' smiled Darig. 'And um, where is he now?'

Fox replied cheekily: 'I ate him.'

Old Darig laughed. 'You must've been hungry.'

The Legend of Arznel

A whole day had passed since the hunting lesson, as Fox and Darig walked side by side through the quiet evening wood. A startled crossbill took off at their approach, fluttering on to the nearest spruce trees, abandoning the pine cone she had spent so long trying to crack open.

The cub was just finishing a test on 'how to read the wind using one's nose'.

An unusual conversation eventually arose between the two foxes as they made their way uphill through the evergreens.

'So little one,' said Old Darig, sleepily. 'What do you think of Lough Ine so far? A nice place to live, isn't it?'

'Oh yes,' squeaked Fox, feeling suddenly gabby. 'I love it here. It's beautiful.'

Old Darig smiled down at the cub plodding along beside him. 'I know it is,' he said softly. 'But sadly, the world itself is not very beautiful. Not anymore.'

Fox's ears stood up. 'What do you mean?' he asked.

Old Darig sighed.

'I'm old, little one. I'm too old. In my time, I've seen and learned things that I wish weren't true.'

Fox tilted his head to one side, wondering what his teacher was trying to tell him.

Old Darig grunted.

'Follow me, I'll show you what I mean. It's time for your final lesson.'

The old fox led the young cub out of the pine section, up a little dirt track lined with ash trees, to the very top of the hill, which was relatively bare and exposed. Few trees grew around here, only around the crest. The Hilltop was an area of mainly heather and rocks; flat and bowl shaped. Had it been daytime, the foxes would have had a perfect view of the entire land surrounding them. But their sharp night vision served them just as well.

'Look down there, little one,' said Old Darig, with pain in his voice. 'And tell me what you see.'

Fox gazed down at the lush green landscape.

'I see trees,' he said bluntly.

'Not bad,' said Darig. 'But do keep going. What else do you see?'

Fox continued listing out everything in sight.

'Mountains,' he went on. 'And fields, oh and the Lake.'

'That's right, very good,' said Darig. 'Those are all wonderful things. If only the world could appreciate them. Now, come with me again.'

This time, Fox was led to the southern ledge of the hill, over a barren rock face, through groves of rowan trees and gorse bushes, to the very edge of the hill itself. He had not yet discovered this part of Lough Ine. It was completely new to him. He looked back at the path he and Old Darig had created in the shrubs, before the old fox beckoned him to focus. 'Now,' said Darig, seating himself behind the cub. 'Tell me what you see.'

Fox turned and gaped down over the sea of withered heather on the hillside, which led out onto a smoother area of fields. He cast his eyes from side to side for a bit, not seeing anything remotely unusual so far. Until he discovered he had been peering too low. Lifting his eyes, to look across rather than down, he immediately caught sight of something that made his heart knock against his ribs.

Lined all along the hills, standing menacingly on top of the horizon, were a number of large, square boxes. They were grey in colour and surrounded by gigantic steel spiders.

'What are they?' gasped Fox, his eyes darting back at Old Darig.

103

'Those, little one, are houses, new ones, built by humans.'

Darig turned away momentarily and hung his head.

'Perhaps I haven't told you enough about humans,' he said solemnly. 'Little one, I hate to say it, but I lived among them and learned enough to know...' Darig turned back, and his old eyes hardened.

'*They* are the reason our world is no longer beautiful!' he said bitterly. 'I have seen these concrete monstrosities before, hundreds of them, standing where fields and forests used to live! I have seen four legged knick- knacks and tall shaven poles, fashioned from the bodies of trees! I have seen rivers and lakes turned to bubbling slime and acid that would burn through the stomach of anyone desperate enough for a drink! I have seen the teeth, bones and claws of our neighbours on display for leisure, while their carcasses lie upside down on a plate, steaming! And I have seen the very sky turn purple, from the breath of so many machines – machines that steal the air we breathe and kill the trees that try to get it back!'

A bolt of anxiety shot through the pit of Fox's stomach.

'I only wish that were all,' said Darig through gritted teeth.

'What do you mean?' asked Fox, wondering how the news could possibly get any worse.

'This happens everywhere, little one,' Old Darig revealed. 'Everywhere, every day. I've seen it myself, believing I've seen the worst, but no. The birds, whom I often overhear, recount even scarier tales from around the world. It appears the world is not the vast and mysterious place we once perceived. The world is in fact, small - and getting smaller, as the humans grow!'

Fox's head was bombarded.

'But why?' he asked, breathlessly. 'Why do the humans hate us?'

'They don't hate us,' Darig explained. 'They hate each other. And they love themselves! They're so preoccupied looking after themselves or fighting petty *wars* against each other, that they are indifferent to all other life. About us, they simply do not care.'

Fox wrinkled his brow, struggling to process what he was hearing.

'It's all part of the cycle,' said Darig, sagely. 'As one race comes, another must go. I now fear our time has come. Yes, the humans are a most advanced and powerful force. I regret to say that one day, all the land, will be as noisy and crowded as that accursed town I came from.'

Fox felt nauseous. Fear and dismay seized him by the throat. Was this true?

'So here we stand,' Darig mused, overlooking the land. 'In the last of the natural havens.'

Still aghast, Fox turned to gaze across at the houses, and felt he needed a closer look. Working his body free of its numbed state, the cub made his way down through the heather, barely acknowledging the sharp thorns that were snagging him. He just moved forward, gliding like a ghost, and hobbled slowly across the field.

As he neared the building site, some time later, he realized what a deep scar the humans had left on the countryside.

To the untrained eye, it would seem that little or no damage had been done. After all, it was only a field. 'What harm if a few houses are built there?' some might say. But Fox was well aware of the amount of homes and lives that had been so carelessly destroyed.

Around the verges, hawthorn and holly trees had been brutally sawed down and sliced up. Only dry stumps and piles of sawdust remained, sitting like gravestones. Flowers and plants had been crushed under stacks of heavy concrete blocks and machine tracks. Roots and bulbs lying hidden in the comfortable ground had been churned up, snapped and mutilated. Rabbit burrows and mouse holes had been filled in and buried by avalanches of mud and concrete, birds' nests had been knocked from their places. The fresh scent of the country had been replaced by the foul stench of smoke, lime, charred timber, rusty metal and paint fumes. The view of the scenery had been blotted out by the four tall housing structures and scaffoldings. Wildfolk could no longer live here. The area was spoilt.

Fox wandered about the site, walking slowly and cautiously as if crossing a mine field, exploring its hidden treachery. The houses rose up around him like a gang of dark monsters about to close in. The cub crept around each one, sniffing pipes and cavity blocks, sticking his head into the cement mixer, leaving paw prints in the sand pile. It was the stuff of bad dreams to him.

As he looked around, tears of fear and loss filled his eyes. Such cruelty. Such a careless waste of a once peaceful part of the land. This was wrong. Surely something needed to be done.

For what seemed like an eternity, he sat in the middle of the dusty, lonely construction site, trying to adjust to his new surroundings. The sights and smells were all unfamiliar, and required time to take in. Instinct told the cub that he should turn around, and when he did, he saw Old Darig emerging from the field, making his way into the site. The old fox approached and sat himself down in front of the cub.

'I'm sorry if all of this frightened you,' he said softly. 'But you had to learn sooner than later. I just wanted you to be aware of what's happening.'

'Is there anything we can do?' asked Fox, out of pure desperation.

'Pardon?' said Darig.

'Is there anything we can do?' Fox repeated. 'To stop the humans? To save the world?'

Old Darig took a deep breath and paused.

'That's a good question, little one,' the old fox replied, gazing skyward. 'It actually reminds me of a story my mother used to tell me. A very old, very well known story; one that animals have enjoyed for untold seasons. It's about a *tiger*.'

'A...tiger?' said Fox. 'What's that?'

'A fierce and powerful animal,' said Darig. 'They live on the other side of the world. I've never seen one, of course, but according to common theory, a tiger is a magnificent creature with flame red fur and jet black stripes; not much different to a fox in its habits. It hunts, it lives alone, it's quite clever. But this particular tiger, according to the legend, was different to all other tigers. He was, as we say, unique.'

'How?' asked Fox. 'How was he different?'

'He had a gift,' Darig continued. 'A gift for long life and supreme leadership. Where he lived, all animals loved him.'

'Why did they love him?' asked Fox, becoming increasingly enthralled. 'Because he was wise,' said Darig. 'The wisest animal in the land. And the bravest. When he discovered humans were destroying the world, he refused to accept it.'

'What did he do?' Fox asked excitedly.

Old Darig grinned, savouring his next words.

'He fought back. The first animal ever to do so. When the humans invaded his home and began chopping down the cloud-forest, the great tiger went about gathering up as many strong and willing animals as he could find, to *rebel* against the humans. Many animals followed him, animals of all kinds.'

Fox was nodding his head up and down as the old fox spoke, wide eyed and waggy tailed.

'Oh, how he fought,' Darig sighed. 'One skirmish after another, outsmarting and overwhelming the loggers as he drove them further and further out of the cloud-forest. It must have been a sight to behold. Oooh, I wish I had been there!'

Old Darig then dropped his tone. 'But unfortunately, it wasn't to last. The final battle was short and simple for the humans. They had more experience and greater weapons. The *gun* had recently been invented. The great tiger suffered a crushing defeat. Most of his followers were killed and the forest, wiped out. He and the few survivors of the failed rebellion were captured by the humans and never seen again.

The humans endeavored to keep him and his triumphs a secret, but with the help of our feathered friends, his legacy lives on.'

Fox was spellbound.

'Is that the end of the story?' he gasped.

Old Darig smiled wryly.

'That's just it, little one,' he concluded. 'We don't know. Legend has it that, somewhere in the world, the great tiger is still alive, as a prisoner, waiting for some brave animal to come and rescue him, so he can be free to continue his struggle against the humans.'

Fox stammered; 'You mean...?'

'Start a war,' Darig concluded, finishing Fox's sentence. 'That's right, a huge and terrible war, and the last one ever to be fought. The tiger hopes to lead *all* animals against the humans, in one final attempt to overthrow them and restore the world to its former majesty.'

Fox went silent with amazement.

'But,' Old Darig sighed, on a more pessimistic note. 'That is, after all, only a legend. We animals may never see change. Some have their doubts that 'the great tiger' ever even existed. Still though, I suppose the story gives us hope.

Sometimes we have to make up our own endings.'

'And where did you say the tiger is now?' Fox asked. 'If he *is* real?'

'Well, like I said,' Darig replied. 'They say he is being held captive somewhere, waiting to be rescued.'

'Has anyone ever tried rescuing him?' Fox enquired.

Darig gave a short laugh; 'Oh goodness no, little one, nobody even knows where to start looking!'

Fox paused to think of another question;

'And err, what's the tiger's name?'

Again, Darig laughed; 'I thought you'd never ask. The tiger's name is *Arznel.'*

'Arznel,' Fox whispered to himself.

'A word of a foreign language,' Darig yawned. 'It could mean anything. Anyway,' he announced, completely changing the subject. 'I've said enough. The more you hear, the more you have to forget.

What would you like to do now; would you prefer to go hunting or should I let you rest?'

Fox gave a swift answer.

'Well,' he said. 'I am a bit tired. And I'm not very hungry.'

'Very well,' said Old Darig. 'You may return to your den. I'll see you, perhaps, this time tomorrow.'

The two foxes parted.

Fox had lied. He was hungry. Famished in fact. But now he was too overwrought to eat. What a story! He couldn't stop thinking about it, even after he'd reached his den. He nestled down in the grass bedding, and eventually, when his head stopped buzzing, managed to nod off. But how was he to know, that for him, sleep would never be the same again!

Dreamer

The place was very mysterious. The ground was covered in slabs of concrete forming a footpath leading to nowhere. Wire fences and cages circled every tree. Strong wooden walls surrounded the entire area, towering high into the sky, which was a blinding white. A large iron gate stood between the pillars, firmly shut, preventing all possible escape. The air was close and heavy, filled with the smells of rubbish, car fumes, cigarette smoke, stale pond water and cooked meat.

Fox crept slowly along the pavement.

He still couldn't remember how he came to be here. All around, he could hear humans talking and laughing, but could not see them. Their high-pitched, often taunting voices permeated the air, as if teasing him from the bushes.

He found the place stark and frightening, while struggling to walk; there was a strange force impeding his steps that he could not explain; an oppressive, magnetic feeling that seemed to be dragging him downwards, every nerve in his body tingling.

Silhouettes flashed by, of strange long necked birds, and large rabbit- like creatures with pouches in their bellies, but whenever Fox turned to see them, they vanished. He passed many smelly dustbins and tall, shady trees, until he came to an enormous glass cage. There he stopped.

Inside, a fearsome creature sat, with its back to the window. Its long tail was swishing impatiently. Its thick fur was striped orangey red and black. It turned around. The face was not very clear. It looked rather like the reflection of a tiger, in a shallow puddle- but clear enough. Long whiskers, triangle ears and a pair of large, pale eyes - *Arznel* -the tiger.

Fox trembled and stared in awe at this magnificent, legendary beast, now standing tall.

He did not expect the tiger to speak.

'Rrrrrrrrelease...,' he boomed. Arznel spoke in two voices, which both rattled the cage. The deep, organ tone voice overlapped with the, shrill, strangled voice, and it made a most blood curdling sound. '…mmmmmeeeeee!'

Fox staggered backwards as the shadow of the great tiger loomed over him. He pressed his gigantic paws against the window, condensing the glass with his breath. 'Rrrrrrrrrrelease… mmmmmeeeeee!'

Fox shrank to the ground, eyes bulging from his skull, fixed irresistibly upon this creature.

Then, the tiger's chest swelled, and it let out a roar so chilling, black thunderous clouds came to envelop the sky. Fox was hit by a blast of wind and lifted from his feet. The deafening roar continued to gust through Fox's eardrums even as he woke up:

'Rrrrrrrrrelease… mmmmmmmeeeee!'

'Ah!'

Fox nearly hit his head off the ceiling. He was still in the den, safe and warm, tucked up in the dry snug grass of his sleeping chamber. It took time for him to recover from that unusual experience. He lay back down in the grass, panting. What a strange dream, he thought. Old Darig would have to hear about it....

Old Darig simply nodded his head as the cub spoke, his eyes on the ground, looking thoughtful.

'The wind took my breath away!' Fox concluded. 'And that's when I woke up.'

Old Darig smiled, but it looked like a smile to mask his hurt.

'We've all had that dream, little one,' he said softly. 'It's normal when the story is new to us.'

'But it seemed so real,' Fox protested.

'Of course it did,' Old Darig cooed. 'All dreams appear real until you wake up.'

'But what should we do now?' Fox asked. 'The tiger asked to be released.'

Old Darig sighed and turned around at the mouth of his den, so that his face and tail pointed in the same direction.

'Little one, I'm sorry I told you that story. I didn't mean to upset you. I was just so angry at seeing those houses being built that I spewed an old tale about the demise of humans. Don't let it interfere with your sleep.'

Fox hung back in confusion. Why did Old Darig sound so dismissive now, of his own story?

'But Old Darig,' he pleaded.

'Little one, I once went through a phase,' he confessed. 'After what The Farmer did to my family, I wanted nothing more than to search for the great tiger. I wanted to journey alongside him to the land of the great cloud-forests and bring the world of Man to its knees. But in time, I grew up. I realized survival comes first. Here is home.'

'But what about the world?' Fox squeaked. 'Who's going to save it?'

Old Darig paused and climbed out of his den again, crouching to Fox's level.

'My dear little cub,' he said, plaintively. 'Don't make the same mistake I did. I wanted so much to be a hero, that I almost forgot my place as a true fox. When I realized that saving the world is impossible, I felt so empty. Take my advice, little one: mark your territory, and stick to it. Don't let your dreams precede your duties.'

Fox said no more.

The rest of the day he spent alone. He had told Old Darig he was off hunting rabbits, but in truth, he was doing everything but. He foraged the woods for anything he would allow himself to eat – roots, bulbs, worms, berries beetles, grass and a strange 'yellow brain fungus', growing on the bark of a gorse bush.

The cub felt he was using more energy searching for food than he was receiving from it. So when he returned to his den later that day, he was asleep in a trice.

Ever since Old Darig had put him out of his misery about his dreams of the great tiger, Fox had done quite well in not thinking about them. But it wasn't to be…

He now found himself wandering through a dark and richly growing forest. But this forest was unlike Lough Ine's. This place was vast and shut-in under a heavy mist. The air was moist and humid, thick with the perfume of so many flowers. Strange, two-legged animals jumped from branch to branch above Fox's head, hooting and hallooing as he made his way through the immense, waxy ferns. How astounding it all was.

But all too soon, the grand canopy that had kept the place so dark was stripped back, viciously, from all directions, and a burning sun cast its light onto the naked shrubbery.

Fox ran. He ran with his heart in his mouth, and did not look back, but could hear the droning of engines and the slicing and dicing of blades on wood behind him, until he reached a new area: an area starkly empty.

For miles around, there was nothing to be seen only dusty stumps and crusty branches, sticking out of the ground like drowning hands. Instinct dictated that Fox should keep running, despite the heat, and he did so until he reached a hill. Up the hill he ran, drawn by a curious sound on the other side. He was almost at the top when he noticed the sky was blackening. The dense, smoky clouds became burnished by red every time there was a loud BOOM from the other side of the hill.

Fox had not been frightened by the strange forest. He hadn't even been traumatized by the machines tearing it apart. But when he crested the hill and saw what was making all the noise, he couldn't help being overcome.

It was hard to tell who was who, what was what, for all he could make out was a sea of bodies, writhing grotesquely in the mud. Some were men, some were animals, some stood, some lay, all were fighting beneath a smoke-laden sky. The humans he identified as the two legged creatures wearing non-fur garments and wielding what he surmised as 'guns' – flames lancing from the tips.

Even the animals he could barely recognize, so strange and exotic were they. Only their fur, wings and scales marked them out, as they charged through the muddy, bloody mass, savaging their enemies with more than just teeth and claws, but with almost human-like weapons – sticks, clubs, spears…

Great balls of fire erupted from the ground, throwing bits of rock and metal through the dense, swirling air.

Fox pressed his belly to the ground and stared in absolute horror.

Just then, a familiar figure made itself known on the battlefield. The tiger leapt onto the ruins of a machine, and announced over the din – clear as a crystal-

'Ruuuuuuurrrr! No rest! No rest till we've won!'

And the last thing Fox saw before departing the gruesome scene was a net being cast over Arznel's head. Heavy steel balls wrapped tightly around the tiger's bulky frame and knocked him from his spot. Despite all the other sounds filling the air, it was the thump of the tiger's body against the ground that ultimately woke Fox up.

He nervously opened his eyes. Sure enough, he was at home, safe in his den. For a moment, he lay rigid, frequently trembling. His eyes were fixed open, in a wide, opalescent stare. He had never heard himself breathe so loudly.

Still mentally shaken, the cub tried to sit up, but his body refused to move.

He flexed his toes for some time until the warmth returned to his limbs, and once his heart stopped drumming, he was able to shift himself from the straw and bracken bedding. Someone needed to know right away.

It was dawn when Fox poked his head out of the den. He gave a nervous sweep of the area with his eyes; half believing this was another dream. The forest was still quite dark. Off in the distance, behind the tall conifers and below the hills, a strong orange glow could be seen as the early morning sun was beginning to wake.

The cub scurried along the narrow dirt track, in the shade of the grand horse chestnut trees. The wood sorrel and wood anemone were still asleep, closed delicately into their petals. Above in the canopy, the dawn chorus of blackbirds and finches was in flow, the little musicians chirping and twittering softly, while out on the Lake, the harsh screeching and squawking of a rabble of seagulls could be heard offensively clear.

Old Darig's den was found dug into the side of a leaf- loam covered mound in the centre of the forest.

Fox clambered up to the entrance, stuck his head down the hole and began yelling:

'Darig, Darig, come quick, I had another dream!'

Moments later, the old fox emerged, drowsily.

'What's the matter, little one?' he yawned, his eyes still crusted over with sleep.

'I had another dream!' Fox cried.

Darig flinched.

'Please little one,' he groaned. 'Not so loud. I just woke up. My ears can't bear your hollering. Now, what's troubling you?'

The words came tumbling out of the cub's mouth faster than Old Darig could comprehend them:

'*And there was – big fires! – and all the animals were fighting and the humans were, like, blowing everything up, and the sky was black and the – noise was, like, pow! Pow! And, and... and...*'

Fox stopped when he saw Old Darig's exasperated face.

'Okay little one,' he sighed. 'Do you want to try again? A tad slower this time?'

114

'Sorry,' Fox panted.

The cub took a deep breath and carefully told his story, slowly and in detail. Old Darig listened with care and with patience until Fox reached the end.

'It was such a huge battle,' he concluded. 'And it was so real. It had everything. It must have been a sign, it had to be! What do you think, Old Darig?'

The old fox smiled kindly.

'What do *I* think?'

The cub nodded anxiously.

'I think I've finally thought of a *name* for you,' said Darig.

This prospect did not appeal to Fox instantly.

'No, listen, I know it meant - wait, what?' he gasped.

'Yes, I believe I have,' said Old Darig proudly. 'You have an impressive imagination, and a unique gift for dreaming. Whether or not your dreams mean anything, it does not matter here and now. I think I've thought of a name that will suit you perfectly for the rest of your life. It's a simple name, but sometimes simple is better.'

Fox was speechless. Just for this special moment, he cast his worries aside and allowed his face to light up with anticipation.

Old Darig climbed from his den and stood looking down at the cub with his chest puffed out.

'No longer will you go by the title of 'Fox', he announced. 'And no longer will I have to refer to you as 'little one'. From this day forward and for all of your days to come, you will be known as *Dreamer."*

Reunited (All at Ease)

On the same morning as the young cub received his name, the time had come for him to say goodbye to his teacher.

Sitting on an outcrop of rock, on the edge of the hill, just outside the rowan grove, was Dreamer, formerly known as Fox. The day was bright and breezy, a warm sun bathing everything in white. The cub stared wistfully out at the lush landscape, with its whorls of colour and dazzling sun sheen. But all of this was tainted by the new houses on the hill.

After several failed attempts at convincing Old Darig that his dreams were special, the cub knew he couldn't win. Darig was simply having none of it. He seemed terribly sensitive to the topic, and did not wish to be perturbed further.

So now Dreamer lazed on the rock ledge by himself, trying to figure it out. Until the old fox's shadow was cast over him from behind. Dreamer hopped to his feet and faced the old fox, wondering what was afoot.

'It's all yours,' said Old Darig warmly.

'Huh?' Dreamer gasped.

Darig nodded, his eyes indicating the vast expanse of fields, shrubbery and fenland below.

'I'm very proud of you, young Dreamer,' said the old fox. 'You've completed your training. You are now a true fox. You no longer need an old dog like me to carry you around anymore.'

Dreamer felt rather taken aback.

'You mean,' he gasped. 'We won't be hunting or swimming or exploring anymore?'

'Not together, I'm afraid,' said Darig. 'But you'll be doing all those things by yourself, and as often as you want to. It's what all normal foxes do.'

Dreamer sighed; 'I guess I won't be seeing you anymore, then.'

'Nonsense,' Darig laughed. 'We both live in the same forest, don't we? I'm sure we'll run into each other all the time.'

Dreamer smiled weakly.

'Anyway,' the old fox concluded, sounding quite casual, as if it were no big deal. 'I'd better let you go now, the world is waiting.'

Dreamer turned back to the endless stretch of fields and hedgerows, before taking one last look at Darig.

'Well, goodbye,' he said, before taking off down the hill and into the green wilderness.

Old Darig grunted; 'Good luck, my son.'

The hedgerow was like an obstacle course of grass and bushes growing tall and out of control.

Dreamer wandered on through all of the thistles and blackberry brambles, excited now at the thought of being independent.

The cub found his time with Old Darig enlightening and he grew to love and respect the old fox. After all, he had no other father figure in his life. Saying goodbye to him was no joy.

But as the cub ventured further out into the flourishing fields, a sudden wave of relief swept over him. He was free. He could do whatever he wanted to do and go wherever he wanted to go, without Old Darig dictating his every move.

Although the old fox was wise and most helpful in Dreamer's quest to survive, the cub had always felt uneasy in his presence. Old Darig had always assumed that Dreamer was an ordinary cub with no secrets. Had he known that the cub had travelled to Lough Ine aided by a badger and a tasty hare, he would surely have been furious.

Not only that, but Dreamer was also a sort of 'vegetarian.' Apart from a few small rodents such as mice, rats or voles, he would never dare touch meat. Birds, rabbits and other attractive looking creatures were animals that Dreamer preferred to admire and respect, unlike any other fox who would hunt and eat them whenever possible.

If Darig had discovered any of this, there would certainly have been uproar. But now that this fear had subsided, Dreamer hurried on down the hillside, bypassing the new houses, with one objective in his mind: to find his friends.

Before returning to the woods, the cub felt he wanted to make up for all of the sunshine he had missed, by frolicking out in the open for a while. He did a loop around a vast plain of Yorkshire Fog and sheep sorrel, and back into the woods along a belt of shrubbery. Hopping a choked river beneath the branches of a willow, Dreamer was back in the shade of Knockomagh. The sweet scents of the ferns kept distracting him from the scents he was after – those of Badger and Hare! There seemed to be no trace of them, hereabouts.

Up on the Hill, he had more luck.

Through a blanket of green, prickly heather, where the purple flowers would not appear till next season, he moved, passing through a screen of pine trees, until he arrived at the fringe of Hilltop Warren.

As usual, the field was dotted with rabbits, lazing about with their white bellies in the air.

Dreamer kept his distance, not wishing to startle them. However, he did notice that one of the rabbits was unusually big. It was not Captain Spruce. He would have been greyish brown with a large bushy mane. This rabbit was reddish brown. Surely it couldn't be... or could it?

Dreamer edged his way up to the big rabbit, who was napping in the shade of a blossoming gorse bush, his face and ears covered in yellow petals from the branches hanging above his head.

Then Dreamer noticed a scar on his eyebrow. Yes! It *was* Hare! Dreamer hovered above him, wondering whether he should rouse his sleeping companion, or allow him to wake in his own time. The cub was too excited, and nudged Hare with his paw. But Hare's eyes remained closed, as he hummed a song and muttered in his sleep;

Running and hopping
And leaping through the air
Life is but a dream
When you are a hare

With that, Hare yawned, turned on his side and proceeded to snore. Dreamer grew so impatient; he stepped on his friend's tail with his front paw, digging his claws in! Hare sprang awake so suddenly; he walloped his head off a branch and caused a shower of petals to sprinkle down like yellow confetti.

'Ouch!' he cried. 'Son of a...'

Dreamer struggled not to laugh.

'Hi Hare!' he sniggered.

When Hare finished rubbing his head and opened his eyes to see Dreamer standing in front of him; he jumped and walloped his head off the same branch again, causing a second shower of yellow petals.

'F-Fox,' he gasped, staggering backwards whilst rubbing his head. 'I haven't seen you in, err, how long has it been?'

Dreamer made his way behind Hare and helped him to stand upright, before sitting back down to face him.

'I'm not sure how long it's been,' he said amiably. 'Seems like a long time, really. But I'm back now.'

'I see,' said Hare nervously. 'Well um, how have you been? Err, *where* have you been?'

'Just been in the woods,' said Dreamer casually. 'I needed time to cool off.'

'Oh, okay,' said Hare, taking a furtive step backwards. It was clear that Hare still believed Dreamer had turned predator. 'Did you do anything interesting, like, err, 'hunting' for instance?'

'Yep,' said Dreamer smiling, finding his friend's grovelling amusing. He planned to keep it going for a while, just for sport. 'I did a lot of hunting. It was fun.'

'Oh really,' said Hare, putting all four paws on the ground, as if ready to bolt for his life. 'That's good for you, really, really, really good. What did you hunt, might I ask?'

'Hmmm,' said Dreamer playfully, now getting a great kick out of Hare's awkwardness. 'Mushrooms, berries, slugs, mice... and other creatures.'

'Oh,' said Hare, trembling. His voice tightened with worry as he spoke.

'Any... long eared... fluffy tailed ... harmless... innocent... cute and loveable...'

'No, no, no,' Dreamer laughed finally. 'I didn't eat any hares!'

'Oh thank heavens for that,' sighed Hare, allowing himself to collapse on the ground with relief. 'Because I forgot to mention earlier; we hares don't taste as good as we look.'

Dreamer shrugged; 'Whatever you say.'

The two friends walked together around the field, making the most of the glorious sunshine. None of the rabbits seemed bothered by the sight of Dreamer. They must have remembered him as 'the friendly fox.' They appeared to be comfortable and happy in his presence. Hare, too, had relented. Now he and Dreamer were just the same as they had been on the journey.

'So did you do anything interesting while I was gone?' Dreamer asked.

'Well,' Hare began. 'I've been spending a lot of time with the rabbits. They've kindly accepted me as one of their own. I live here in the Warren now, in a form over by the rowan trees. My guess is the rabbits needed a strong, reliable animal to protect them from danger. They made a wise choice.'

'Oh yes,' Dreamer laughed. 'A very wise choice: a hare who sleeps in the bushes while a fox sneaks into the Warren!'

Hare grunted. 'Shut up.'

When the pair had walked the entire circumference of the meadow twice, they slumped down in the grass.

'Hey,' said Dreamer suddenly. 'I forgot to ask; where's Badger?'

'Oh, he's spending time with his new mate,' Hare replied. 'Her name is 'Holly,' a sow badger.'

'Really?' gasped Dreamer. 'Badger's found a mate?'

'Mmm, yes unfortunately,' Hare mumbled. 'I'd avoid them if I were you. Those two are drooling over each other. Sickening, really.'

Dreamer paused.

'Badger once told me that when he reached Lough Ine, he wanted to find a 'female' to be his 'mate'. What does that mean? What's a female? And what's a mate?'

Hare sighed.

'I'm far too tired and depressed to talk about that right now,' he muttered. 'I can't believe Badger can keep a mate and I can't. Who do I have to box to get one?!'

'What happened with you?' Dreamer ventured to ask.

'Ah, y'know,' Hare mumbled. 'No pleasing some people. I've had three mates, myself, so far. Lost one in a boxing match, to some other horse- faced home-wrecker. The same thing happened with my second! What is it with females and their preference for these big, brawny, numb-skulled layabouts?'

Dreamer paused.

'What about the third?' he asked.

'Eh, she just left when she heard me singing. Shallow floozy.'

Hare put his head down and continued to brood.

Dreamer sat beside him, only half listening. A number of things were on his mind. His dreams still bothered him deeply. He had been thinking about them all day. Not only that, but what was this whole business of having a mate? Of all the topics Old Darig had taught him, 'females' was not one. To Dreamer, they remained a mystery, as many other things did.

Towards dusk, the sun hid behind the distant mountains, allowing beams of golden light to crack through the bushes and branches of Knockomagh Wood, where families of blackbirds, starlings, thrushes, tits and finches were hurrying home to their nests in the canopy, to feed their younglings. In the shadiest areas of the forest floor, amid dew covered pond sedge and ferns, all of the primroses, violets and wood sorrel were beginning to close in for the night.

Dreamer and Hare shuffled through the hanging vines and twigs of Bubblelump Swamp, until they reached the pond. It had not changed since the cub last saw it; still slime covered and foul smelling, with dead branches protruding from the surface, where flies buzzed and zipped around mindlessly.

'Evening, Tadpole,' said Hare, as he stuck his head into the long rushes. Dreamer followed up behind and saw the tiny, young frog paddling around in the pool of brown, murky water; his big, bulbous eyes staring curiously upwards as usual.

Beside him, up in the drier part of the swamp area, tucked into the rushes and wrapped in warm, crusty grass, was the mysterious 'bird egg' that Dreamer and his friends had seen on the very day they arrived in Lough Ine.

'Badger and I have been visiting this little fella every day,' said Hare, looking at a blinking Tadpole. 'He's growing up really fast. I can finally see his arms and legs now.'

'What about the bird egg?' Dreamer asked. 'Do you think it's gonna hatch soon?'

'I doubt it,' Hare sighed. 'Badger says that birds' eggs only hatch when their mothers sit on them. I tried sitting on this egg the other day, but when Badger saw what I was doing, he lost his mind and pushed me into the pond. Lousy know - it - all.

We've been doing our best though; bringing more dry grass every day to keep it warm, but it's no use. I reckon there's nothing inside that egg only a rotten yolk!'

Dreamer gave a nod.

'I wonder how Tadpole found it,' he said.

'He told us, remember?' said Hare. 'Apparently, it was floating around in the water. It must've fallen out of a tree. Either that, or the mother mistook her egg for a poop!'

Dreamer bent down towards Tadpole's tiny face.

'Do you remember me?' he asked, smiling.

Tadpole giggled and splashed the water about with his long tail.

'You Fox!' he squeaked.

Dreamer rolled his eyes and gave a nervous laugh. 'Err, good... memory... Tadpole!'

It was not long before the sky had well and truly darkened. The forest was cloaked in black. Stars began to appear far above, where no bird could reach.

They studded the navy sky, glinting and twinkling brightly. The warmth in the air had dropped, and was now moist and chilly.

Dreamer and Hare made their way to the northern wing of the forest, where a large mound of rocks was found. Beneath, lay Badger's freshly dug sett. A deep black hole could be seen in the shade of the largest boulder, with a curtain of dry grass and ivy hanging down in front of it. A dusty carpet of brown leaves and moss was scattered around the outskirts. Hare scurried to the entrance and poked his head down the hole.

'Badger, you lazy git!' he shouted playfully. 'Come out, we have a visitor!' Moments later, the face of Dreamer's seemingly long lost friend appeared out of the dark hole.

'Hare, you pesky little...' he scolded. 'I told you not to disturb me tonight! Why, I ought to - Fox?'

'Hello,' smiled Dreamer as he rushed to greet his companion emerging from the sett.

But before a word could be said between the two, another face appeared out of the sett; a pretty one. It was a sow badger, with twinkling amber eyes and flowing white hair. She was just slightly smaller than Badger in size.

'Oh, Fox,' Badger stammered. 'This is my mate; Holly. Holly, this is my friend; the one I've been telling you about. We just call him Fox.'

'Actually,' the cub interrupted. 'My name is 'Dreamer' now.'

Badger and Holly nodded, wonderingly.

Hare paused for a second.

'WHAT!' he shrieked. 'You never told *me* that! And we spent the whole frickin' day together!'

'Sorry,' said Dreamer, defensively. 'I was just waiting for us all to be together, so I could tell the story once.'

'Well go ahead,' said Badger. 'I'd like to know what you've been up to. You had us all very worried, you know; disappearing like that.'

'I didn't mean to upset you,' Dreamer explained. 'Really I didn't. But when you told me what real foxes are like, you scared me. I thought I was going to turn into a monster and gobble you all up! That's why I ran away; to protect you. But I've decided -I don't want to be a normal fox.'

'You don't?' said Badger.

'Nope,' said Dreamer, shaking his head. 'If I were a normal fox, I'd have to live alone and eat my friends!'

Hare laughed nervously and shuddered at the thought.

'That's good news,' said Badger curiously. 'But it still doesn't explain how you got your name.'

'Well...' Dreamer began.

The cub told his companions about his encounter with the wise Old Darig, and everything he did during his time with him. He then told them of the story he had been told, about Arznel and the fate of the world.

'Oh I know that one!' Holly interrupted. Her voice was soft and pleasant.

'You do?' said Dreamer, cocking an ear up.

'Yes,' said Holly. 'My parents used to take turns telling me that story all the time when I was small.'

'Did it ever give you nightmares?' Dreamer asked.

'Well, no,' said Holly. 'But it did frighten me a little when my father told it. When my mother told it, she would always try to leave out the violence. Why? Did it give *you* nightmares?'

Dreamer proceeded to tell his friends about the disturbing dreams he had been having, and how they were the reason he had earned his name.

'Oh right,' Badger stuttered. 'That is strange, no doubt.'

'Well,' said Holly. 'I suppose it's only normal to have scary dreams if you've been told a scary story, right?'

Dreamer dismissed this with a shake of his head.

'These were more than just dreams,' he said. 'These could have been signs, messages, 'warnings' even.'

'But how?' asked Badger, still perplexed. 'How are these dreams so special?'

'Because,' Dreamer explained. 'They showed me things I've never seen before. I saw animals from different parts of the world; animals with spots, animals with stripes, animals with tusks! Some animals were smaller than us; others were as big as trees! And, I saw *humans.*'

'Interesting,' said Badger, scratching behind his ear.

'But that's not the strangest thing,' Dreamer continued. The cub went through the most bizarre details of his dreams. He described how some of the animals he saw were using 'weapons', and described exactly what the weapons looked like.

Then, referring back to his first dream, he described how Arznel the tiger was encased in a glass box, calling for help.

'Maybe,' Dreamer concluded. 'If we go and search for a place that looks just like the place in my dream; we can set the tiger free and save the world!' 'Okay,' Badger hushed, raising a paw. 'Let's all come back down to solid ground for a moment. No need to get carried away.'

Dreamer protested; 'No seriously -'

'It's alright,' Badger interrupted calmly. 'I believe you. We all do.'

Badger then turned to face Holly and Hare.

'Don't we?' he said, winking.

Holly gave a reassuring smile and nodded.

Hare sat on the ground, looking as though he had not listened to a single word; eyes glazed over.

'Huh?' he said, shaking from his stupor. 'Oh yes, of course I loved your story, Dreamer. It was great. Very funny.'

Badger grunted and turned again to face Dreamer.

'Anyway,' he said. 'I know how tense you must feel after having dreams like that, but don't go worrying about everything you saw in them. We can't control what might happen. Maybe your dreams 'are' special, maybe the great tiger 'is' real, who knows. But until something amazing happens, I think we should all forget this whole business of nightmares, and humans and war, and move on, especially you, F- Dreamer.'

The cub stared at the ground for a while, then took a deep breath and sighed.

'I wish I could forget it,' he said, lifting his eyes from the ground. 'But I can't. Those dreams... it's like... it's like they were meant to be. I can't forget them.'

'You're not trying hard enough,' Badger snapped. 'Think ordinary happy thoughts; Lough Ine is a safe and peaceful place. There are no 'wars' here. Humans can't bother us. Spring is in full bloom and all is well. Try filling your head with thoughts like that.'

Dreamer paused for a bit, and allowed Badger's advice to filter through. Anything was better than worrying. He looked around at his companions, with their warm, sincere faces. He suddenly, and strangely, felt more cheerful, as if a ray of light had broken through and dispelled all his worries like a puddle.

'Maybe you're right,' he gasped, looking at Badger. 'Maybe I shouldn't worry. Not yet, anyway. Not until my dreams start happening for real. Anyway, dreams can't hurt me!'

Dreamer peered around at the lovely shady wood, and the moon cradled in the sky. Then he muttered: 'We *are* safe here.'

'That's more like it,' said Badger with a broad smile.

'So do you feel better now?' asked Holly.

Dreamer nodded. 'Much better,' he beamed.

'Good,' said Badger, stretching and yawning. 'Now, I'm famished. Who wants to help me find a few snails?'

Signs of Summer

It's true, that if you take an ordinary picture and crush it into a ball- there is nothing you can do to make it perfect again. No amount of flattening, pressing or fiddling is going to return that picture to its former clarity.

Dreamer's friends had done quite well in trying to ease his mind. He soon found the stranglehold of worry around his thoughts loosening, and that he was able to engage in all the banter and high-jinks of his peers: gallivanting about the woods and warren with them, day and or night, getting up to all sorts. Night time was always a barrel of laughs. Unable to see each other properly in the dark, they would play a game of 'bumpers,' chasing each other around and not knowing who they were running into! They played hide and seek, pile-up, catch and battle tag until they were worn out and muddied.

But, as with the crumpled picture, Dreamer's mind could not settle back to what it once was. Always lurking in the recesses of his memories, suppressed under the assurance that all was well – was Arznel.

There could be no denying, that outside the shaded comforts of Lough Ine, lay a world calling for help.

One morning, however, while out searching for breakfast with Badger, he noticed the weather was steadily changing. The sun beat down, warmer and brighter than ever before, flowers of many different kinds were bursting into full bloom and the treetops overhead were thickening so vibrantly, as to block sunlight to the forest floor.

'What's happening?' asked Dreamer, as he sat in the middle of the woodland glade, fascinated by this metamorphoses.

Badger sniffed the air with relish.

'Ah,' he sighed. 'Summer- It's on its way!'

Days passed and the summer unfolded. Suddenly, it appeared all the world had become magical. All greenlife that once lay hidden became five feet tall and lush. The canopy became heavy with fresh new leaves, fanning the forest floor with a sheet of green. The old oak and chestnut trees returned to vigour, their crowns vast and full. The rowan and hawthorn trees around the Warren began to sprout their red berries. A wave of colour swept over the Hilltop as the heather finally turned a light pinky purple. Within the woods, nature unveiled another of her little wonders – the bluebell glade. All over the clearings and along the pathways, the bright, bulbous flowers carpeted the forest floor in their thousands, filling the air with an emollient aroma. Around the edges of the wood and hedgerows grew another plant that was new to the cub, called 'foxglove.'

Everywhere, birds welcomed in the season with their songs. Treetops, fences, bushes and hedges were lined with thrushes, blackbirds, starlings, wrens, robins, wagtails, gold crests, yellow hammers, blue tits, chaffinches and myriad others, all chirping and twittering their symphonies, sometimes individually, other times joining in together for a euphonic chorus.

The friends made sure not to waste a moment of this heavenly weather, though Badger did have some difficulty in persuading Holly to join them. His own eyes had begun to desensitize to the light, but hers were unaccustomed to such a thing. However, with the forest canopy so dense with new leaves, daylight could scarcely break through, and soon Holly was able to join her restless companions in their escapades.

Each day, they visited Tadpole and the bird's egg in Bubblelump Swamp. They would chat, joke, tell stories and entertain him with their own circus acts, sometimes having to wrestle Hare to the ground before he could attempt singing. The infant frog was always delighted to see them, if frustrated at not being able to leave the pond, yet.

Back on Hilltop Warren, the rabbit-clan leader, Captain Spruce, had kept his promise. Whenever he and his fellow conies managed to have a chat with resident birds in the area, they would tell of how a friendly fox had come to Lough Ine. This, of course, made interesting news; news which spread and found its way around the many regions of Lough Ine – from the forest, to the surrounding flatlands, even as far as the Lake itself, where a whole community of creatures lived. All were thrilled to hear that a friendly fox existed. Some even looked forward to meeting him, for they had yet to hear a fox speak, and they had heard that this one had some particularly interesting stories to tell.

Funnily enough, a handful of lucky animals did get to meet Dreamer. They would be going about their usual business when a young fox might approach them from the shrubbery. Instead of acting on instinct and fleeing, they would trust the rumour they had heard and begin to make small talk with the fox. When it was confirmed that the fox was Dreamer, the conversation would carry on, and soon, over a short time, Dreamer had scored himself a host of new acquaintances.

It was a time so fleeting that felt so long, a time Dreamer would come to appreciate as the happiest time of his life.

But happiness in itself is often fleeting, and one day, Dreamer began to discover just how close he was, even in Lough Ine, to the enemy…

He was on one of his habitual strolls, taking time to savour his surroundings, until he reached the cottage ruin. Suddenly, everything went back into focus.

What *was* this thing?

He had been passing it every day but had had no time to find its origins. How out of place it was, this blundering, stone contraption in the middle of the woods, with its triangle structure and shattered walls. It was as if the forest was trying to hide it, under layers of moss and fallen branches. But nothing could hide the questions – who built this and when?

'How're things, Dramer lad?'

Hm? Somebody had caught his scent.

Dreamer turned to his left to see Craggy, the hedgehog, clambering out from underneath the Fallen Beech. Dreamer was still in a daze and had to shake his head before replying.

'Oh hey, Craggy. How have you been?'

'Yerrah, grand,' said the old boar, who was usually quite grumpy but managed to put on a cheery face for a specimen as rare as a friendly fox. 'The newborns are keeping me fine n' busy. Only born yesterday and already full o' spikes, harharhar!'

Dreamer smiled broadly at the hedgehog, whose own spiky quills were beginning to turn grey. But he couldn't help asking:

'Craggy, one thing- those ruins over there, all covered in moss- where did they come from?'

'Hmph?' said the hedgehog, as he pulled his plump, greying body out of the crevice beneath The Fallen Beech and into the sunlight. 'Oh dat ould thing,' he exclaimed. 'Dat used to belong to de Forest Ranger.'

'The Forest Ranger…?' Dreamer gasped. 'A human?'

'Yeah, yeah,' said Craggy, lifting his chin. This was clearly no news to him.

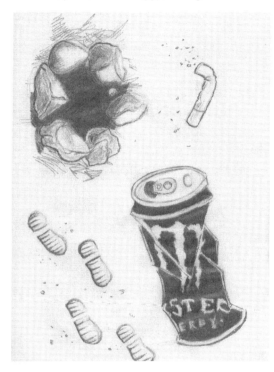

'He's been gone a fair while now.'

'But what was he doing here?' Dreamer asked.

'Twas his job to protect de place,' Craggy explained. 'Knockomagh's an old forest doncha know. Twas never planted. Twas always here. Not many o' dem forests left now.'

'No way,' Dreamer gasped. 'Why would a human want to protect us?'

'I dunnah,' said Craggy, sleepily. 'Spose we can't judge em all de same.'

Dreamer's brow twitched, and he decided to be on his way. Thanking Craggy for the information, he set off down the hill.

But as he walked, the concept of friendly humans began to weaken rapidly, when he came across another mind boggling enigma.

A small circle of stones was found in the middle of the clearing, only a small circle. But in the middle of them, the ground had been dug out and scorched black. Soot and ashes were scattered around the scene, along with bits of silver paper and very odd aluminium cylinders.

Dreamer now felt cold, despite the wave of heat streaming down through the branches. He sniffed gingerly around at the mess. The ashes were foul and bitter to the nostrils, and caused him to sneeze worse than any flower. The little crushed cylinders smelt strongly of rotten apples. Sticks had been used to poke the burning circle, and on the ends of them, was a sticky, pink residue. Those at least, smelt quite nice, and Dreamer gave one a daring lick. Whatever the goo was, tasted deceivingly delicious, and he backed away, for fear of what would happen if he ate the whole thing…

Before he could continue his investigation, a small, dark figure darted across his path ahead. He wavered by the stone circle, every nerve pulsing.

Who goes there?

Rationally, he decided whatever it was, could not have caused this disturbance, and trotted after it.

In a tangle of shrubs, Dreamer was relieved to find Wesley, the stoat, poking his head out. He had been gorging himself on a stolen egg. Yellow yolk smeared his kitten-like face and dribbled onto his creamy undercoat, the rest of him being a rich nut-brown. He tried to speak, but with a full mouth, ended up gagging and squirting some out his nose.

Dreamer managed to laugh. 'Stealing from birds' nests again, are we Wesley?'

The cub had developed a talent for acting like he wasn't worried.

'It was just lying there,' said Wesley with a cheeky grin.

'Sure it was,' said Dreamer, in mocking tones. 'I bet you climbed the highest tree in Knockomagh to pinch it! Right from under the mother's bum!'

'Na-ah,' Wesley insisted. 'It was just lying there, in a flimsy lil' ball o' twigs! That careless bird practically invited me!'

'What careless bird is this?' Dreamer asked, smiling.

Presently, there came a rustling from the nearby bracken, followed by a long, alarmed, clucking call.

Wesley gulped.

'Oops! Gotta go, Dreamer. I'll catch ya again, sometime!'

With that, the stoat hurried off into the undergrowth. No sooner had he gone, than Flapjack, the pheasant, erupted out of the scrub, in a fit of panic.

He was a large, cinnamon coloured bird, with an ink-blue head, red eye patches and long tail feathers. His ancestors had originally come from Asia, and although pheasants are well established in Ireland, Flapjack, for some reason, retained his Far Eastern accent.

'Oh, harrow, Dreamer,' he panted, trying to steady himself. 'Rearry nice to see you. Forgive me fo sounding so hasty, but I am rooking fo one of my eggs.

It mysteriousry vanished a short whire ago, and I suspect it was storen. Did you see anyrun pass by who may be the curprit?'

Dreamer smiled slightly. 'Sorry Flapjack. Can't help you.'

The pheasant shrugged his wings, looking disheartened.

'Very werr, then,' he sighed, eyes on ground.

Then Dreamer deliberately started to cough, muttering the name 'Wesley' under his breath.

'Ah, Wesrey!' Flapjack beamed. 'That stupid hairy weasow is goring to pay! Much apprecration, Dreamer!'

With another burst of clucking, Flapjack scuttled off into the woods on foot.

Leaving him at it, Dreamer went on his way.

At the edge of the Lough Ine Panorama, he stopped and gazed out upon the breathtaking landscape. Although his eyes rested on the flourishing hedgerows, and on the Lake, which sparkled a cobalt blue; seagulls squawking and squabbling on the strand – Dreamer's mind was on something less trivial.

Between stone cottages and stone circles, litter and foul stenches, something wasn't right. Something was at work here. Had the summer attracted *other* visitors? Was Lough Ine really such a small, undiscovered sanctuary?

Old Darig did say that the world wasn't getting any bigger. Animals once believed that the world went on forever, but when the humans began destroying what apparently did not need to be destroyed, to make space, it became clear- there isn't enough for everyone...

In a bid to calm his nerves, Dreamer set off for the Lake. Once he reached the bottom of the hill, plodding through rows of larch and spruce trees, the clues showed no signs of letting up.

He stopped in the middle of the beaten track. He peered around. And he realized.

'Spruce and larch trees,' he whispered to himself. 'Evergreen.' He looked back up the hill. 'All the other trees,' he thought. 'Deciduous.'

The (non-native) pines at the bottom of the hill grew in straight lines... rarely does anything in nature grow in a straight line.

'Craggy was wrong!' Dreamer gasped. 'Not *all* of Lough Ine is natural.

These trees were planted!'

Not far from where he sat, confirmation lay in full view. A stump. And another stump. And another. Perfectly, clean cut stumps.

Suddenly, all the more obvious clues came rushing back.

Stone cottage.

The snares on Hilltop Warren.

'We were idiots!' Dreamer cried. 'Of course the humans know we're here!'

Dreamer dashed through the pine rows and into a golden, wavy meadow. It was here he came upon the Duck Pond, where Bill and his mate, Branta, were frolicking in the crystal water. Their twelve little ducklings paddled in a seemingly infinite line behind them.

Bill was a healthy sized bird, with grey plumage, orange legs, a yellow beak, black tail feathers and an emerald green head. Branta and the ducklings had a less extravagant appearance, simply a light, dowdy brown on their fluffed up feathering.

Dreamer did not have to wait long to be noticed as he stopped on the bank, panting.

'Dreamer, how are you doing!' the father duck greeted warmly, ruffling his wings.

The cub stared, with a weight of dismay and betrayal on his heart. He didn't know how to react.

'How long have you known about this?' How can you act so carefree?' were just some of the things he felt like screaming, but he quickly relented.

No. Bill is a genuinely cheerful, happy-go-lucky bird, and a family bird. Of course he had to don a bright attitude, for his children. Perhaps Bill didn't see the felled trees or the campsite as a threat to his pond. *Hold your tongue, Dreamer, hold your tongue.*

'Unbeatable weather as usual!' the father duck beamed, paddling closer. 'I can never get enough of it.'

'I guess so,' the cub muttered.

'I tell ya,' Bill rambled. 'You're lucky to be living in such a fine forest. I took the kids in there earlier and my, my, the flowers! The bluebells and snowdrops, and, and, and bluedrops and snowbells!'

'Oh try not to twist your words,' scolded Branta as she floated up beside him. 'You're setting a bad example.'

'I'm just being creative,' Bill protested.

Dreamer allowed himself a giggle, when the twelve little ducklings made their way up behind Bill and began to climb up on his back, their tiny webbed feet clambering all over him, splashing and bobbing, causing their father to capsize.

'Give us a ride, give us a ride!' they demanded.

Bill found himself sinking.

'Careful children,' Branta warned. 'Your father isn't the soaring eagle he used to be.'

'Oh I'll show you,' he said, challengingly. 'Come on, kids, let's make some storm waves!'

The bumptious rabble of ducklings all cheered.

Bill turned to Dreamer, looking like he was under tremendous pressure. 'Sorry, Dreamer,' he said, trembling. 'I'm going to have to let you go. This lot can be quite a wing-full!'

Dreamer smiled understandingly and watched the father duck paddle furiously out into the Pond, with five eager ducklings piled on his back and the rest trailing behind, grabbing onto his tail and wings.

The cub turned shakily and ventured back into the woods, following a trail of primroses, no longer able to smell them. All thoughts of the Lake had been momentarily shelved, as he wondered what to do.

No, he was not going to tell his friends. He had already annoyed them with the issue of Arznel, with which he had received no support. That anxiety was his alone. It was too happy a time; who was he to try and upset them with talk of humans, when so far, they had not caused any major damage? What was the worst that could happen if he kept it to himself?

The next clue he came across was more offensive than frightening. His nose detected a repulsive smell coming from somewhere uphill, to the west side. He followed it up, trundling through the holly and ivy until he hit upon even more unexplored territory.

Old Darig had always said: 'mark you path and stick to it. That way you won't get lost, you won't get hurt, and you'll know where the food lies.'

This was just more of the old fox's moot advice. Dreamer didn't see the point in confining oneself. Small as the world may be, it was certainly bigger than that!

The woods came to an abrupt end, against a bramble covered wall. And beneath the wall, in a high, festering pile, were sacks upon sacks of rubbish.

Dreamer kept his distance and breathed through his mouth. There must have been fifteen to twenty of the black, bursting sacks, and among them was what Man would call a suitcase! There was also a large, soiled mattress. Bottles, cans, packaging and countless baby nappies spilled out onto the forest floor, choking the vegetation. Some of the nappies had swollen in the frequent rain; swollen to a staggering size! They were only one safety pin away from a really slimy explosion.

As he stared, Dreamer wondered if this was an act of evil, or stupidity.

The sacks had left distinct, flat, skid trails behind them, from where they had been thrown. Holding his breath, Dreamer leapt over the waste and onto the wall, clambering up the flattened brambles to see what was on the other side.

It should have come as a shock, but it didn't. He hadn't seen one of these since the day Hare was nearly run over by a metal monster. The road was quiet at the moment.

Against all instinct, he set himself down on the concrete surface and began a little journey, knowing very well where it lead. Rounding a few corners, heading down a steep slope, he found the road running past the Lake.

'Well, here I am,' he thought.

Above his head, in a giant flock, flew some new arrivals to Lough Ine – swallows.

'Hello Dreamer!'

'Hi Dreamer!'

'Evening, Dreamer!' they chirped, flooding through the pale aqua sky.

The air around the Lake was cool, fresh and salty. Its water was calm and sparkling under the evening sun. Only gentle wavelets disrupted its serenity. The surrounding rocks were sharp and coated in layers of heather, spaghm moss and scented mayweed. The sounds of angry, squabbling seagulls could be heard on the other side of the Lake. On one of the more distant rocks, a tall black cormorant could be seen preening its outstretched wings.

The Lake itself, however, was surrounded by a stone, plastered wall. Dreamer hopped it to see the strand. Foam seethed and bubbled on the shore, where shells, seaweed and pebbles were strewn about amid the gentle waves.

There, at the edge of one of the rockpools, Dreamer was met by Pierce, the grey heron.

'Ah, Dreamer,' he called, pulling his beak from the water. 'Good to see you this fine day.'

Pierce was a warm and charming bird, albeit constantly frustrated at trying to catch a fish. Below the rippling surface of the rockpool, an assortment of small aquatic creatures hid among the coral, causing the hapless heron a great deal of stress; crabs scuttling under rocks, anemones withdrawing into their body shelters, blennies camouflaging in the mud, shrimp dodging the hungry beak that went for them repeatedly.

'Are you having trouble?' Dreamer asked rhetorically.

'Why not at all, my four legged friend,' Pierce laughed, his voice quivering with suppressed fury. 'I'm just playing with the little buggers before I send them to meet their maker.'

SPLASH! SPLASH!

Pierce struck out again and again at a small shoal of shrimp, but they somehow kept eluding him.

'Blast it!' the heron panted.

Dreamer cocked an eyebrow.

'Maybe you should try somewhere else,' he suggested.

'Oh, not at all,' Pierce insisted politely. 'A little perseverance and I'll have one of these stubborn little water wigglers skewered on my beak, yes sir! Besides, I've already tried everywhere else… Ay up, is that an eel I see?'

The heron pitched forward again and plunged his whole head into the rockpool. Dreamer watched dumbfounded as Pierce splashed and floundered about in the water, before lifting his head and stopping abruptly.

'Uh oh,' he murmured.

'What is it?' Dreamer demanded.

'I believe I just swallowed a periwinkle,' said Pierce, worriedly.

'Oh,' said Dreamer, unhelpfully. 'Will you be okay?'

'I don't know just yet,' said Pierce. 'But perhaps it would be better if I took a short break.'

'Oh, okay,' said Dreamer, slipping away. 'Um, good luck.'

But as soon as the fox had left, Pierce was back on the edge of the rockpool. After a moment of watching and waiting, the persistent heron spied his prey and attacked. This time with success. Pulling his beak from the water he found a little butterfish squirming helplessly on the end of it.

'Hizzah!' he applauded himself.

Hopping from rock to rock, Pierce attempted to carry his prey down to the shore, when all of a sudden there came a most irritating screech from above, and a shadow fell over the unsuspecting heron. Looking up, he witnessed a berserk herring gull swoop down on him. Pierce opened his wings to take flight but was instantly mowed down by the impact of his aggressor's feet. When he managed to stand up, he found the gull had gone – along with his snack.

Dreamer was on the other side of the Lake when he heard the distressed cry of a heron:

'Curse you bloody gulls!'

But knowing he was too far away to enquire what the matter was, he carried on his jaunt around the shore.

Just then a magnificent mute swan floated by noiselessly on the Lake's gentle waves. But this pearl-white beauty was no stranger to the cub.

'Evening Emur,' he called, walking along the shoreline beside her.

The swan took her head out from underneath her great wing and swivelled her long neck to see him.

'Hi,' she muttered in a small voice, before swimming gracefully onwards, behind a large, barnacle coated rock.

Emur was a shy and secretive swan. Assuming she was happier alone, the other Lake creatures rarely made an effort to talk to her.

And the last acquaintance Dreamer had the pleasure of meeting that evening was an otter named Skip.

The great water dog rose from the Lake and clambered up the steep, sharp rocks, where he sat down to feast on a freshly caught purple urchin.

He then spotted the cub down on the shore, gazing up at him.

'Ahoy there, me aul flower,' he shouted in a throaty voice.

Dreamer smiled.

'Ahoy Skip,' he called back. 'Good fishing?'

'Ah,' said Skip. 'The oorchins an' fish an' crabs are boitin' loike mad these days.'

Dreamer smiled again and climbed onto another level of rocks to be closer to the admirable otter.

'Well you're having more luck than Pierce back there,' the cub jested.

Skip laughed, as he maintained his hold on the purple urchin. 'Poor aul feather bag. Oi'll haff to lend him a paw.'

Dreamer sniggered, and used his highpoint to admire the Lake properly, with its picturesque setting.

'Quoite a soight, yeah?' Skip mused.

'Mmm hmm,' said Dreamer, who was trying to calm his thoughts more than anything else.

'Did oi mention this Lake is actually unique?' Skip asked.

That was a good enough distraction.

'Dreamer turned to the otter with full attention.

'It is?'

'Ah, rarest of the rare, it is.'

'How, Skip?'

'Oh, now that's a tall tale that requoires toime to tell,' said Skip. 'But oi'll tell yiz this… no ma'her where ya go, anywhere in the whowel land, y'ill never foind another salt wa'er lake!'

'Really?' said Dreamer. 'This is the only salt water lake in the world?'

Skip nodded. 'As far as we know, yeh.'

'Wow,' said Dreamer. 'How's that?'

'Look aeuwt there,' said Skip, pointing his snout to the horizon. 'This used t'be an ordinary freshwa'er lake… till sea levels begun to roise… n' flooded in here! Ha! Now this lake is just loike the sea! I see all sorts comin' in here: seals, sharks, lobsters, jellyfish, the woorks.'

'Hm,' said Dreamer, wondering if in fact, he could eat fish…

'Anyways,' said Skip. 'Oi gots a hungry family needs feedin.' Oi'll haff to let yiz go.'

'Okay, Skip,' said Dreamer turning to leave.

'Laterz,' shouted the otter. He polished off his catch and scurried down into the comfort of his holt, the entrance of which lay underwater, to nurture his wife and otter cubs.

Skip was in his prime, a truly wise and strong otter. His proficiency in the water was unmatched, with his oily, sleek fur and powerful rudder. And his knowledge of life in the sea was irrefutable; his cubs always enthralled by the stories he told, especially those about the legendary 'blue whale.'

But in some ways, Skip was an unusual otter. For example, when he had gathered enough bones and shells from around the shore or after meals, he would stack them in a high, neat pile, and then, standing at a distance, would throw stones at them, knocking the pile back down again. It was a sort of game he enjoyed playing by himself, a game which had greatly improved his aim…

Back into the woods, Dreamer went, desiring only a good sleep and some fun with his friends the next day. After a day like this, he could have done with a laugh or two.

But on his way up the hill, as if he hadn't enough surprises, Dreamer caught another scent. Only this one, was fresh. Putting his nose to the ground, it became stronger as he gained height on the hill.

But drawing his head back, he realized he did not need his nose. The footprints were all too clear. They trailed through the withered leaves and crushed ivy, curling around the path ahead.

'Oh, no,' the cub gasped.

Into the clearing, half way up the Hill, he found the boots had stopped at the great oak where Nuala, the owl lived.

The tree stood alone in the glade, sky scrapingly tall, sturdy and bent ever so slightly to one side under the weight of its immense crown. Its trunk was draped in moss and textured with mushrooms and polypody ferns.

Why the tracks stopped here, Dreamer had no way of knowing, but he quickly became fearful. Who had come to the woods? What were they doing? Was his owl friend okay? Had she been kidnapped? Stuffed? Eaten? Caged?

'Nuala!' he cried. 'Nuala, are you up there?'

No response.

He dashed to the base of the tree, where the thick buttress roots fanned out over the forest floor like great webbed claws. Looking straight up, where the crown of the oak seemed to be tickling the sky with its galaxy of florid shaped leaves, Dreamer shouted again:

'Nuala!'

Even still, no reply.

'Oh no,' he trembled. 'What have they done?'

'NUALA!' he boomed.

At last, the figure of an aged, long eared owl could be discerned, staggering to the edge of her nesting hole.

'What, what, what?' she grumbled, shaking her bushy, tufted head and stretching her neck.

'Nuala, are you okay?' Dreamer demanded.

'Hmph,' said the owl. 'I was.'

Her fiery orange eyes bored into his even from such a distance. 'Must you be so intrusive?' she scolded. 'Have you no concept of the importance of sleep to us owls?'

'Sorry,' Dreamer sighed, relieved, but ready for the admonishing of a lifetime.

'As you should be,' Nuala went on, stiffening her dark brown feathers. 'Why, I'm so affronted right now, it shall take me all day to fall asleep again. My schedule has been utterly obscured.'

'Sorry, Nuala,' said Dreamer again, backing away. 'I was only checking to see you if had been, I dunno, harmed...'

Nuala straightened her posture. 'I have no time for this nonsense,' she huffed. 'I'm asleep even as I talk. This is terribly out of the ordinary for me. Think better of checking up on me in future, won't you. I'm quite capable of looking after myself, don't you know!'

With that, the owl turned, and bumped her head off the top of the entrance. Muttering a polite curse, she stooped lower, and disappeared.

'See you later, Nuala,' Dreamer muttered. '...Not!'

He was almost out of the clearing, pondering over the tracks he had followed, when he stopped and thought:

'No, I'm not done yet.'

He raced back to the oak and sniffed around the mighty buttress roots. He felt foolish at not having discovered earlier – there were *two* sets. They were dotted around the tree as if in a chase pattern. Up the moss- furred trunk of the tree, Dreamer sniffed, and then, he saw it.

Using a fatally sharp blade, somebody had carved into the trunk, a symbol.

Dreamer drew back and stared. All became quiet. Not even the sound of birdsong fretted the tight silence. Dreamer kept staring, the crude laceration holding his gaze, as if drawing him in. Sap leaked from the golden opening, like tears running down a gnarled face.

What is this?

His heart palpitating was the only movement he could feel, while he stared, thoughts of menace and destruction plundering through his mind. Had the tree been marked for demolition? Were more markings to come?

After what seemed like long and edgy standoff, Dreamer sighed and allowed his head to droop. He realized he had become sick from worry. No one ever listened; no one ever took him seriously. If something was to happen, he thought, let someone else fret about it. Let the loggers come, let the builders come, let it be a wake up call to those who rebuffed his warnings.

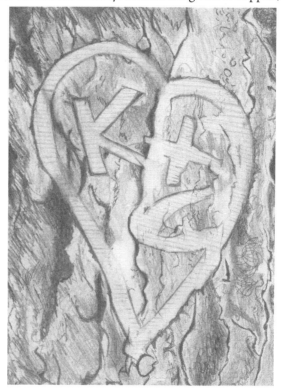

With a sweep of his tail, the cub set off up the track, where only moments before, two young humans had been walking, hand in hand. The symbol was theirs, a heart, with an arrow through the side and their initials set lovingly in the middle.

Today was not a day to worry. Not today, at least.

The Lake

CRASSSHHH!!!

Hare charged through the woods ahead of his friends. They were in the middle of another game of catch and, as you may have guessed, Hare was winning. He skidded to a halt at the fringe of the forest and hunkered down behind a hazel tree to catch his breath. Then peering excitedly around, he caught sight of Dreamer traipsing wearily through the shrubbery. The hefty forms of Badger and Holly were not long joining him. The three pursuers glared fiendishly at their fleeter footed companion.

'What's wrong, Dreamer,' Hare teased. 'Got a thorn in your paw! And you, lovebirds, maybe if you keep your eyes on me instead of each other, you'll stand some chance of catching up!'

Hare turned and bent over, mooning his friends with his fluffy tail wagging in the air.

Dreamer, Badger and Holly huddled into a circle and conferred.

'Gah, when I catch him I'll-' Badger seethed.

'Calm down,' Holly counselled him. 'I'm sure your plan will work.'

'What was the plan again?' Dreamer asked.

'Okay,' said Badger, combing his ears back and talking in a more subdued tone. 'It's really simple, anyone could've thought of it. By 'running' after Hare, we don't stand a chance of catching him, right? Obviously. But, if we 'walk' after him instead, we'll save strength and prolong the chase! And Hare will have to keep running whenever he sees us! That way, when he's worn out, we can surprise attack him!'

Dreamer and Badger both cackled.

But then, Hare's high pitched voice chimed in from a distance:

'Badger's like a snail
He's getting old and frail
And if he tries to catch me
You know he's gonna fail! Hah!'

Badger seized up with anger again.

'You scrawny little -', he barked, charging after an already out of sight Hare.

'Badger!' Holly called after him. 'I thought you said no running!'

Holly turned to a giggling Dreamer.

'What is it with you males? Everything has to be such a blooming challenge!'

Dreamer smiled and shrugged his shoulders, innocent in the matter once again.

By the time the friends reached the foot of the hill, all but one of them, were too tired to go on.

'Hey,' said Dreamer suddenly. 'I forgot. It's evening time now. That means Skip is free to show us around the Lake!'

Badger and Hare were less than enthusiastic, dragging their feet through the shrubbery.

'Aww, do we have to?' Hare panted.

'Well,' said Dreamer, rather miffed. 'We've never really seen the Lake before. Not up close anyway. It might be fun.'

'Nah, you go ahead,' said Hare, clutching his knees.

Dreamer turned to Badger, with a look of high expectation.

'Sorry,' Badger wheezed. 'It has been a long day. Plus I swim like a brick!'

'Holly?' Dreamer squeaked.

Holly, who was sitting under the shadiest beech tree, just shook her head.

'Wish I could, Dreamer,' she said, ruefully. 'But any more daylight and I swear I'll evaporate!'

'We'll wait here,' Badger promised.

'I don't know how long I'll be,' said the cub.

'Don't worry,' Hare yawned, laying down in a bed of ferns and curling up. 'We're not going anywhere.'

Dreamer hung his head and was off, muttering,

'Suit yourselves.'

The cub came to the stream that divided the forest from the meadow; a narrow babbling brook flowing peacefully under a stone arch. Dreamer stood on the edge of the bank, wondering whether he should jump across or swim.

It was then he noticed movement below the surface, creasing the still water. Due to the sun's brutal glare reflecting off the surface, Dreamer was unable to make out what was causing the stir. Until suddenly, the familiar bulky form of an otter erupted from the stream, showering the cub in a spray of droplets.

Dreamer shrieked and fell forward into the stream, causing an even bigger and louder splash.

Skip was helpless with laughter while watching the victimized cub haul himself from the water and onto the opposite bank.

'Oi wuzz waitin foor that mowment all daey,' he howled, doing a triumphant backstroke. 'Oi got ya good, didn' oi!'

Dreamer shook himself dry and smiled nervously. 'You got me,' he admitted.

Skip chuckled.

'Juss givin' yiz a li'hil practice beforr we go see d'Lake. Lots morr swimmin to dew befoor this day is aeuwt.'

'Oh,' Dreamer panted. 'Great.'

The otter led the fox around the rim of the Lake, sticking discreetly to the shade of the surrounding rocks. Skip chose a flat, limpet covered rock as a vantage point for himself and the cub. The rock was sheltered under an overhanging ash tree. Beyond, the Lake spread out and glistened like a white, jewel encrusted plate.

'So,' Dreamer began, shyly. 'What exactly makes this lake so special? Apart from being the only salt water Lake in the world.'

'Well, y'see,' Skip began. 'It's not juss wun thing. There's lots o' things that set this Lake asoide from all others.'

'Like what?' Dreamer demanded.

'Well it's hard to say,' said the otter. 'Unless yiv seen fer yourself. Loike, sometoimes, 'specially in the summer…' the otter began.

Dreamer leaned forward.

'Yes?'

'Sometoimes in the summer,' Skip went on. 'It seems, anyway, that the stars fall from the skoy, and land here in the Lake. Oi've seen em moyself, gli'ering in the shallows.'

'The stars fall from the sky?' said Dreamer incredulously. 'And land in the Lake?'*

Skip nodded. 'And that's not all.'

'How so?' asked the cub.

Without a word, the otter stooped and picked up an empty scallop, indicating for the cub to watch. Skip flung the shell out into the Lake with a splash. Before it could sink, Dreamer witnessed to his astonishment, the water opening up in a narrow, swirling circle! The scallop was caught up in the angry, spinning water and sucked to the bottom of the Lake!

'Whoa,' cried Dreamer.

'And sometoimes that happens,' the otter concluded.

Moving on, the fox and the otter soon reached the top of a high, smooth slope, running steeply down into the water. Hardly any moss or shells smeared its flat stony surface. It was here, Skip pointed out to Dreamer a little island out in the middle of the Lake. The island was narrow and boomerang shaped, layered with shrubbery. A large square section of rock jutted out of one corner.

'Y'see that oisland,' said the otter. 'That's where the aul *castle* used t'be.'

'Castle?' said Dreamer, perplexed.

'Great big heouses, that heumans used to build,' Skip explained. 'They down't build heouses loike that anymorr; juss lots an' lots o' lil ones.'

'Oh,' said Dreamer. 'So there was a castle right there in the middle of the Lake?'

'That's roight,' the wise otter smiled.

Dreamer laughed:

'How do you know all this?'

'Ah, y'know,' said Skip, modestly. 'We otters've lived on this lake fer longer than any heuman. These storries are passed deown frum generation t'generation. Moi young tots might be telling your young tots some daey!' Dreamer laughed weakly, still not having the faintest inkling as to where children came from.

'What happened to the castle anyway?' he continued.

'Toime,' said Skip. 'Toime ba'ered it deown to soize. But y'can still see some o' the feowndation today, if yiz look careful enuff.'

146

'Can you?' Dreamer gasped, straining his eyes at the distant island. 'I don't see anything.'

'It's that square piece o' rock,' said Skip. 'But if y'wants a clowser look, it's neow problem.'

'A... closer... look?' Dreamer stammered. 'How? The island's all the way out there.'

'Swim it!' said Skip, simply.

'Swim?' gasped the fox. 'You expect me to swim out there!'

'Ya have paws, downcha,' the otter teased. 'What's the bodder?'

Dreamer gulped. 'That's a lot of water.'

'The morr the merrier,' Skip laughed. 'What, have ya not swam beforr?'

'I have!' said Dreamer, defensively. 'You saw me swimming today!'

'That wa'er was barely up to your showlders!' the otter mocked. 'C'mon, this'll be a noice challenge foor ya! Oi does it all daey.'

Dreamer paused to emphasize his next point:

'You're an otter.'

Just then, the sonorous croak of a heron could be heard coming from the ash tree across from them. Pierce rose from his large stick nest above in his heronry, and glided over to Dreamer and Skip, with slow and languid wing beats, before setting himself down on top of the great slope.

'Impossible to sleep in this heat,' he yawned. 'How are we all?'

'Dreamer here is gonna swim fer uz,' the otter grinned, playfully.

'Oh are you really,' exclaimed the heron. 'Well have fun, I'm sure you'll -'

'I'm not swimming!' Dreamer snapped. 'Thanks for trying to encourage me, but I prefer being dry! Anyway, my friends are waiting for me back in the woods, so good - bye.'

Dreamer turned around, prepatory to leaving, but being in such a hurry, and a bad mood, he missed a step! The cub tumbled helplessly down the slope, images of sky, lake and rocks flashing back and forth before his eyes as he rolled, skidded and bumped in a chaotic descent. Skip and Pierce sprang to their feet and quivered, unsure of whether to scream or laugh, while watching the ball of orange fur bounce and slide uncontrollably downwards, followed by a trail of dust. There was a loud KA - THUNK as the misfortunate cub finally made contact with the brilliant blue water that had been waiting for him.

Skip scrambled down the slope, accompanied by Pierce who was hovering just above. Both friends edged their way up to the fizzing, rippling water, where the cub was still submerged. Skip and Pierce looked at each other. 'What've oi dunn!' the otter gasped.

Backing up and drawing in a great breath, Skip prepared to dive in and save the young fox. But just as the otter's front feet left the ground, the water below opened up again and Dreamer's shocked face rushed up to greet him!

'Whoa!' Skip cried, as he threw himself backwards and landed flat on his back, the cub soon landing on top of him. Dreamer then eased off and sat himself down. Spitting up water and shaking himself dry, he looked at Skip spitefully.

'That was for earlier,' he rasped.

Skip smiled respectfully.

'Touché.'

Pierce danced around the scene. 'Dreamer, are you alright?' he shrilled.

The cub nodded.

'I shouldn't be, but... I think I'm okay.'

'Oh, thank heavens for that,' Pierce sighed.

Skip threw a backward glance and examined the slope before chuckling:

'We should call that thing a rock sloide!'

The three animals fell about laughing, after which Pierce piped up:

'Well, Dreamer, I guess you deserve a break from us after that. Shall we walk you home or can you make it by yourself?'

Dreamer gave a mysterious grin.

'Mmm,' he said. 'I don't think I'm ready to go home yet. Skip, is it too late to go to the island?'

Skip looked taken aback by the cub's unexpected boldness.

'The oisland's always there if y'want it,' he offered.

'Okay!' Dreamer cheered, as he stood up and dived right back into the water, striking out towards the distant bed of rock.

Pierce glanced at Skip.

'I say, I think you've got him hooked!'

Pierce was the first of the three to reach the tiny island. He perched on top of the square rock piece and watched the water for a moment, wondering who would reach him first. It didn't take a genius' guess. Skip slithered out of the water, and snorted once to expel droplets from his nose. Dreamer followed suit, clambering onto the shore, his sopping wet fur plastered to his skin. It was as though he had become twice as heavy, and had to roll around in the sand to dry himself off.

The three animals took time to admire the ruin of the castle, whose glory was lost in the chasm of time. They couldn't imagine what it must have looked like back in its prosperous days, for all that remained was a bramble covered corner piece. It was as if the guards of the castle had returned in the form of thorns, to continue their duties. The island itself had shrunk catastrophically, from the rising water in the Lake, which had flooded in from the sea.

'Whatcha make o' that, ah,' Skip smiled, looking at the mesmerized cub.

'It's... wow,' said Dreamer, still marvelling at the eight foot tall structure.

'Hmph, oi know,' Skip agreed. 'Oi pass this place every daey and it still baffles me.'

'More impressive from up here,' Pierce chuckled, from on top of the rubble. The heron opened his wings and began to preen, while off in the distance behind him, a different bird flew, each wing beat sounding like a clap of thunder. None of the friends could have mistaken Emur the swan. She soared in the air as gracefully as she swam, before dropping downwards and skiing along the surface of the water. Looking to her side, she spotted the animals huddled together on the island, but then simply paddled onwards as if she had not, and disappeared behind another island.

Dreamer looked at Skip confused.

'What was that for?' he asked, offended. 'Why did she ignore us?'

'Ah, y'know,' the otter grunted. 'Swans; so full o' their own proide. Probelly thinks she's too good fer us. Oi wouldn't worry abeouwt it.'

'Just a bit stuck up,' Pierce added, failing to sound polite.

Dreamer shook his head and peered into the crystal water, where a kingdom of egg wrack seaweed gently swayed. Knobs of limpets and black bunches of mussels clung to the submerged rock, occasionally bubbling to show signs of life. But then, an entirely new creature floated by between the leathery stems of the seaweed- a fish.

Dreamer had never seen one before, especially one so big. This one had a bronze - green back, and three different fins. It drifted on by, and was almost instantly followed by another. Dreamer watched as a whole shoal moved across the shallows, their glossy hides catching the dying sunlight. Something about these strange fish made Dreamer's stomach rumble. In fact, the rumbling in the cub's belly was so loud, that Pierce heard it from his preening perch.

'In need of a feed?' the heron laughed.

Dreamer looked up at him curiously. 'Pierce, what kind of fish are these?'

The heron parachuted down to the cub and sat beside him, peering into the water.

'Oh my, pollack!' he blurted out. 'Num, num.'

'Can you eat these fish?' Dreamer asked, suddenly unable to control his drool.

'Oh I'm pretty sure you can,' said Pierce, before adding, 'if you can catch them.'

'Why, do *you* not catch them?' asked Dreamer.

Pierce snorted and laughed.

'Ee gad, would you look at those fish, young fox, they're bigger than me!'

'Oh,' said Dreamer. 'Um... does Skip catch them?'

'Yes, I'm sure he can catch the buggers with his eyes closed and - say, where is Skip?'

Dreamer and Pierce glanced around to see that otter had decided to slip away unnoticed.

'Must be going for a dip on the other side of the island,' Pierce suggested. 'It would have to be the other side if these fish haven't been scared off yet!' Dreamer stared wistfully into the water, at the still passing shoal of pollack. It had been so long since he had eaten anything substantial. With meat usually forming the bulk of a fox's diet, Dreamer was simply not getting enough nourishment.

'I see,' said Pierce, knowingly. 'You're half starved.'

The cub nodded. Pierce paused.

'You know what,' he announced finally. 'I think I shall give this Pollack fishing a go. Ludicrous as it is, I can't allow you to waste away.'

Dreamer smiled broadly, as the heron stepped up to the edge of the water and carefully nominated his target. Each fish seemed so enormous. Pierce knew catching and carrying one was not an option. His only hope was to kill and drag it ashore with all his might.

'Who am I kidding,' he muttered to himself. 'The fish stand a better chance of catching me! But no, I must not let the young fox down, he's depending on me. I must land one of these monsters before Skip returns and shows me up!'

'What're you doin'?' came a gruff, throaty voice from behind.

The startled heron jumped and turned to see that Skip had indeed returned.

Pierce stood his ground.

'Our little fox friend is hungry,' he explained. 'I was hoping to catch him one of these pollack.'

Skip raised an eyebrow in question.

'You? Catch a polluck?'

Pierce nodded defiantly.

'Are ya mad!' cried Skip. 'That'd be loike me troyin' to catch a cow!'

'It shouldn't be too difficult,' Pierce insisted. 'I'm an experienced water bird.'

Skip continued to rankle his friend.

'You've trouble catchin' shrimp ya silly -'

Pierce began to clear his throat loudly, trying to drown out the otter's criticism.

Stepping into the water, the heron sought out the fish he had selected earlier. Then he crouched. He waited. He drew his head back...

Skip and Dreamer both leaned forward with anticipation. Pierce catapulted his head forward and stabbed his slender beak into the shallow. A jet of blood spurted to the surface, diluting the water! Pierce wrestled for a moment, his beak impaling the still living fish, who went about trying to drag the heron under! Pierce pulled and pulled furiously, his long neck hunched up to breaking point! But the fish, oblivious to its own fatal injury, continued to resist the heron's efforts to haul him in. Swishing its tail and flapping its fins at lightning speed, the pollack caused Pierce to lose his grip and splash into the reddened water, before zig zagging on through the shallows, leaving behind it, an obvious blood trail. Pierce struggled and squirmed in the water, and while Skip dived in to help him, Dreamer made it his mission not to lose the wounded pollack. He waded out into the deeper end, following the line of pinky red water. The fish was able to move considerably fast, despite its wound, so right before it slipped out of reach, Dreamer threw himself on top of it and pinned it down with both paws.

Filling his lungs with just enough air, the determined cub plunged his face into the water and carried the pollack ashore, which by now was barely kicking.

Dreamer deposited his catch on the strand and the three tired, wet animals sat down to feast. Nothing needed to be said. But Skip didn't see it that way.

'Ye make it look difficult,' he laughed.

'Oh come now,' said Pierce, pointedly. 'For creatures who don't catch big fish on a regular basis, I think Dreamer and I did quite well for ourselves.'

Skip smiled. 'Ah, I'll grant ya that.'

The animals made short work of the pollack, dividing its juicy supple body up three ways, discarding the head and guts. Pierce pecked and nibbled at his snack delicately, while Skip wolfed his down in one go. Dreamer gobbled his up with the most intense relish.

Skip lay back and burped loudly, using a fishbone as a toothpick.

'Good?' he asked his companions.

'De - lish,' Pierce beamed.

'I feel a bit guilty,' Dreamer sighed.

'Why so?' asked Pierce.

'Well,' said Dreamer. 'We really gave that fish a nasty ending. What must his friends think of us?'

Skip and Pierce both stifled laughs.

'Dreamer, don't feel guilty,' Pierce reassured him. 'Fish are cold blooded. They can't feel pain, body or heart! Why, you could pick up a fish and whack him off a really sharp rock and he wouldn't even blink! In fact, he couldn't blink; no eyelids, you see!'

Dreamer giggled, now more at ease. He also felt better physically. The fish, he found, had given him a new energy that he had not felt in so long. Glancing from the remains of his meal to Skip, he asked the otter: 'Skip, I never have much to eat back in the woods. Is there any way you could catch a fish like this for me every day, whenever you're finished feeding your family? I just get so hungry all the time.'

It looked as though Skip's heart had sunk.

'Aw ya poor rascal,' he said, with the deepest sympathy. 'Sure oi'll fish fer ya! Thing is though, you'll have ta come lookin foor me. Oi ain't gonna go traipsin' through the woods lookin' fer you, with one o' these buggers kickin' and squirmin' in me meouth!'

The gratitude was as plain as day on Dreamer's face. 'Thank you,' he sighed.

The three animals lay in the shadow of the ruined castle for some time hoping to sleep off the meal.

But this peaceful respite was not to last. How could they rest, while lying so fully exposed to a titanic flock of scavengers?

Dreamer, Skip and Pierce were all woken from their stupor by the ominous sounds of screeching and cawing coming from far above. A menacing dark shadow fell over them, as danger closed in from every angle.

'Oh, barnacles!' cried Skip, as he and his companions witnessed the ravenous flock of gulls that were circling them thuggishly. The flock was a mixture of both herring gulls and great black backed gulls. The herring gulls were smaller but much more numerous, with their blue - grey backs, black wing tips, white heads and pink feet. The great black backed gulls were less in number, but larger in size, with their uniformly black backs and gigantic sharp, red tipped bills.

There was a cacophony of noise in the air; the flapping and clapping of countless wings, the clicking and clacking of so many bills, the shrieking and shrilling of all the birds joining in together for a malicious chorus of death.

The three animals backed up against the wall of the castle, completely beleaguered by these encroaching aggressors. Then Skip's voice could be heard above the racket:

'Get rid o' the fish! Get rid o' the fish!'

Dreamer volunteered, and sprang upon the remains of the pollack, frantically using his hind legs to sweep head, guts and bones back into the water. But the gulls, furious at seeing their plunder tossed into the Lake, upped the volume of their angry screaming and descended upon the three trapped friends. Dreamer received a gash across his nose and forehead from a pair of razor pointed mandibles. A large gang of gulls clouded around him while the rest continued to circle the island in preparation for their landing.

Skip instinctively pawed along the ground in search of the nearest rock. After finding a jagged square one, the otter skillfully lobbed it at the marauding scavengers. The rock struck home, taking out one of the gulls in a welter of white feathers. But this was not nearly enough to fend off the attack. On the contrary, this only fuelled the gulls' aggression! They screamed and chattered in a berserk rage, wings opened out fully like gargoyles, bills flashing wildly.

Dreamer broke free from the gang that encircled him, and rushed to join his friends, who were being harassed and shoved; gulls hissing and shrieking in their faces. More than fifty of the bullies now swarmed the island, occupying nearly every inch, and pushing the three stranded animals towards the edge.

'What now?' cried Pierce.

Even the wise otter, Skip, was stuck for an answer. Roaring, he bulled forward, smacking, clouting and battering his way through the throng of birds, clearing temporary areas of space. But each time it seemed the gulls were retreating, they turned in mid air and landed right back down on the island again; retaking the exact spots from which they had been driven.

It wasn't long before the defiant otter was overwhelmed; gulls clambering up his back, raking and slashing at his flesh.

'Into the wa'er!' he bellowed at his onlooking friends.

Dreamer and Pierce stood rooted to the spot, trembling indecisively.

'NOW!' Skip roared, as he himself, scrambled to the edge of the island and shot straight into the Lake, with a cloud of the ever feisty gulls still hovering over the screen of water. The rest of the birds closed in on Pierce and Dreamer, snapping and cawing.

'Pierce, just fly away!' Dreamer cried, glancing at his friend.

'I'm not leaving you here!' the heron whimpered. 'But at the same time, I don't think I can carry you - aah, aah aah!'

Pierce found himself being jabbed in the wing by a great black backed gull, with others crowding around to join in. The heron spread his wings to fly, but the immense rabble of gulls hindered his escape. Pierce then stabbed out with his own beak, in a futile attempt to fight back, before disappearing under a jumble of feathered savages.

Dreamer swallowed his fear and lunged at them from behind, but the birds turned and bounced him back out. The cub rolled on his back and stood up to see a shady pair of the larger gulls stalk towards him. Against his will, Dreamer deserted the battlefield and leaped into the water, with both gulls pursuing him. Knowing it was his only hope, the cub took a quick breath and vanished into the deep end.

It was then the whole world went silent, silent as the grave. All the sights and sounds of the land rolled back into nothingness. It was dark. The cub could see nothing in the hard black vault below him. With his breath knotted in his chest, Dreamer fought all temptation to surface. Ignoring the tightening pressure around his chest and ribs, he continued to wait in the dark, cold and silent.

And then a ray of sunlight glimmered down through the surface. Dreamer could feel the water warming on his back.

And then he looked down below and gasped, releasing the trapped bubbles from his lungs.

On the lakebed below, the sunlight had revealed a most blood curdling sight. The bottom of the lake had become a graveyard. Dead and decaying starfish still clung to rocks, streamers of flesh and slime hanging from their bodyparts. Shells and skeletons of much marine life lay strewn about among the coral, with some kind of pale green gas spewing from their carcasses.

Dreamer flailed his paws wildly, climbing upwards through the water to reach the surface. But just as he was taking his first breath, something else happened. The water around him began to swirl. Waves churned up from nowhere. The cub could feel his legs being sucked at from beneath as the whirlpool opened up to claim him! Kicking and flailing desperately, Dreamer managed to yank himself free of the spin-cycle.

He broke surface, and normality rushed back in an instant. Air, sunshine, land and of course, noise. The squawking and cawing of gulls still emanted from the island as Dreamer pulled himself ashore, hyperventilating.

The gulls who were still thrashing Pierce around, spotted the cub and hopped over to him en masse, closing in for the kill once again.

Dreamer, far too tired, far too hurt, far too saturated and far too shaken to put up a fight, simply collapsed on the ground and lay back to accept his fate.

The gulls couldn't believe their luck, and fell upon him.

But before they could as much as pluck one strand of hair from his head, a great white cannonball ploughed into them, scattering gulls left and right.

Emur made a barbaric sight! She crashed through the crowd, lashing out and biting with her hard, knobbly beak and using her mighty arched wings as clubs, pummelling and pounding without mercy. A swathe was cut through the horde of birds, and they couldn't get away fast enough. The swan barked like a dog, clearing the little island of every gull, in only a few moves. When the last gull had flown, the place was carpeted with feathers, some of which belonged to poor Pierce the heron. He and Dreamer lay among the carnage, still alive, and well enough to look up with astonishment at their saviour.

Emur had her back turned, and was still watching the gulls' retreat with her wings raised. She panted heavily, still trembling from the battle.

Dreamer and Pierce helped each other up, before tottering over to the great swan. She looked at them, with their stupefied expressions.

'Emur,' Pierce gasped. 'That was something else!'

Despite her shortage of breath, the swan blushed.

'Well, you know, it looked like you needed help.'

'We should get ourselves attacked by gulls more often!' Pierce joked. 'If it encourages you to socialize with us!'

The animals shared a laugh, and then up from the water, just off the island's tiny coast, the otter cautiously poked his head.

'Over already, is it?' he shouted. 'Oi was just abeout to make moi meove!'

More laughs followed as Skip clambered ashore and shook himself dry. 'Oh, ahoy there Emur,' he greeted. 'Moi goodness, y'missed a foine show there, oi'm tellin ya.'

'Ah, it was nothing,' Pierce gloated, trying to take the credit. 'All in a day's work. As long as Pierce, the *great* heron is on duty, you needn't-'

Emur lifted her wing and gave Pierce a slap on the back of his head.

He flinched and shook it.

'Sorry, ma'am...'

When the friends had vacated the island and gathered together back on the shore, dusk had well set in. The rosy sky tinged the hills, and tinted the Lake gold and scarlet. A cooling draught whirled in from the sea, relieving the day's heat.

Emur was thanked and praised profusely for her help. Warm goodbyes followed her as she winged her way home to the opposite shore.

Dreamer, Skip and Pierce sat on the strand for another while, still speaking highly of the swan, with whom they had finally broken the ice.

'I tell you I had no idea Emur was capable of such mettle,' Pierce babbled. 'And I certainly didn't think she'd ever use it to help us!'

'Aw, yeah,' said Skip, who had finally been told the true story. 'Watch out fer them swans. They may look all calm an' graceful but when threatened er angry, they can become as vicious as dogs!'

But to change the subject, Dreamer, who up until this point had seemed quite introverted, brought up the issue of what he had seen on the lakebed.

'Skip,' he asked. 'When I was hiding under the water, I saw some things, some ugly things. Creatures were dead, and rotting. It was just... just awful. What happened to them?'

'Oh that', said the otter. 'Oi fergot to tell ya abeout that. Well, foorst of all, ya needn't woory. Y'see, in the summer when the Lake heats up, a lot of the sea loife that's trapped in the Lake doies off. Coz there's nowhere forrem' to hoide. And yeah, it's a manky soight, but after a whoile, there's a foine influx of new loife comin in frum the sea. And they'll breed, and the whole Lake'll be back t'normal. That's just nature, son.'

Dreamer was pleased enough with this answer.

'That's good to know,' he sighed.

Pierce grunted. 'I knew all of that.'

The forest was dark and damp. Only the silhouettes of the fir trees could be discerned, as Badger, Hare and Holly waited at the verge, watching the final trace of light drag itself down behind the horizon.

'I bet he's drowned,' said Badger, worriedly. 'Aw, why didn't we go with him.'

'How long has it been now?' Holly asked.

'The sun was splitting the trees when he left us,' said Badger. 'Hare and I fell asleep while waiting for him.'

'Oh, that's not good,' said Holly. 'Maybe we should start searching for him.'

'I'm afraid of what I'll find,' said Badger. 'Or worse, of what I won't find.'

'Well all of this sitting around and chin wagging isn't going to bring him back,' Hare retorted from a nearby scots pine. 'Oh, wait,' he added. 'Is that him?'

Sure enough, the moping, bedraggled form of their missing friend could be identified, making its way limply through the trees. Badger, Hare and Holly rushed out to greet him.

'Dreamer, we're really sorry we didn't go with you,' said Badger. 'It was irresponsible of us to let you out there by yourself.'

Dreamer by now was fighting the droopiness of his eyes. Sleep was all he could think about, and although he appreciated all this care and attention, he found his friends were really hampering his journey home.

'Oh my, you're hurt!' cried Holly.

'What was it like anyway?' Hare asked.

'It was...,' Dreamer yawned. 'Ugh... never mind.'

* the 'stars' that allegedly fall from the sky, is actually 'phosphorous' that glows on the lakeshore every summer, and it does indeed resemble twinkling stars!

Encounters

A soft evening sun bloomed out over the hills, touching Hilltop Warren with a warm red glow. The rabbits were indulging in another of their summer feasts, rollicking around the plain to crop the sweet grasses.

Dreamer, Badger and Hare were there too, sharing in the laughter and merriment. They lay in a bare patch of earth under the hawthorn tree where Captain Spruce lived, watching the rabbits play and squabble. Usually, the field was dry and patchy, but with a warm sun and scattered showers, there grew food aplenty. Jokes, stories and poems were swapped, games were played and bellies filled, until running became a matter of indigestion and cramps. The trio was greatly entertained by a couple of brown bucks, who sat quarrelling over a leaf of clover, when there was plenty more to be found.

The music of the song thrush above their heads complemented the jubilation.

'Our best evening yet,' said Captain Spruce with a smile as he eased himself down beside Badger, who then shifted himself aside to provide room for the big rabbit. 'Ah,' he sighed. 'It's times like this I always feel alive. You're never too old for a bit of fun in the sun.'

Badger nodded and looked around. 'Hey,' he said suddenly. 'Where's Hare?'

Spruce grunted; 'Err, I believe he's over there.'

Hare was seen out in the middle of the field, surrounded by a small crowd of spellbound looking rabbits.

'So there I was,' he gloated, ears combed back. 'Surrounded by a gang of [twenty] hooded crows, right? All of them twice my size, with sharp claws and teeth that could skin a donkey!'

A rabbit raised his paw.

'Yes?' said Hare.

'Crows don't have teeth, do they?'

Hare paused.

'Well these ones did. Anyway, there I was, surrounded by [thirty] of the wasters, completely alone. While my two unconscious friends lay cheering me on, I prepared to finish the fight myself. The hoodies attacked, but I was ready. They came at me with dagger bills, but I held my ground and gave them such a clobbering! There were teeth and skin and feathers flying everywhere! And when the dust settled, all [forty] crows had met their doom!'

Hare's story was followed by silence. Some rabbits clapped, others tried to smile. The crowd began to clear.

'You're leaving?' Hare gasped. 'But don't you want to hear about how I wrestled a giant rat and saved my friends?'

While Spruce and Badger were immersed in conversation, Dreamer's eyes had wandered wistfully out over the field, detached from all festivity. He noted how the sun was splitting through a row of scots pines on the Hill's fringe, creating lines of black silhouettes.

'Hmm,' Dreamer thought. 'Just like the stripes of a tiger.'

These lazy summer evenings were beginning to feel like a stalemate. Each day came down to the same thing- play, snack, sleep, play, snack, sleep.

And always hovering over him, like a nagging reminder, were those darn *dreams* he'd had, all those weeks ago. His friends had told him not to worry. Dreams are dreams and nothing more. They don't foretell anything, they don't provide answers.

If that was true, then why did they bother him so? Why could he not quell these infernal thoughts of a tiger named Arznel, and a daring journey to rescue him? Oh, how Dreamer hungered for adventure.

As much as he adored the simple pleasantries of life in Lough Ine, nothing could compare to the journey to find it. How he longed to relive that rush, that dangerous, daring feeling of uncertainty, of having a goal.

The dreams he remembered vividly- green wooden fences, an iron gate, a pond, a concrete path winding its way through what looked like vast parkland... not to mention the huge glass cage that contained Arznel himself.

How hard could it be, to set out and scour the countryside for a place such as this?

He half enjoyed dreaming about the tiger, and about the great battle, because they were different to the dreams he regularly suffered – those of hounds, of shotguns, of houses spreading out over the land, devouring trees and hedgerows, of smelly waste avalanching into the streams and lakes.

Sometimes Dreamer felt angry at Badger and Hare, because in his heart he knew – that they had the very same dreams. Yet Arznel was his dream alone. His solution.

To set free this once mighty leader, to unite all creatures, to rise up and deliver a still beautiful world from the thrall of the humans – this was a life for Dreamer. This, he planned.

A berry dropped from above and hit Dreamer plunk on the nose, waking him from his thoughts. He looked up.

'Sorry,' squeaked a thrush.

Dreamer smiled.

'No worries.'

'Come here, Badger,' said Spruce. 'Your mate, Holly, I haven't seen her in ages. What's the problem there?'

'Aw, nothing, nothing,' Badger reassured, in a disheartened tone. 'She still isn't used to the whole daytime scene. I don't blame her. By right no badgers should show their faces at this time.'

'Hmph, fancy that,' said Spruce with a dry laugh. 'You and your motley friends are beheld as heroes around here. The rabbits still talk about your amazing journey. I'd imagine every bird and rodent in the whole of Lough Ine would be chuffed seen in public with you.'

Badger laughed shyly.

'Well, we don't see ourselves as heroes.'

At the other side of the meadow, where the Warren met the woods, a young rabbit named Catkin pottered about by himself, sampling the odd leaf of chickweed or jenny here and there. Within the Warren, Catkin was reknowned for being cheeky and troublesome. Disobeying direct orders not to wander too far from home was just a minor offence to the plucky little buck. It was he who had been caught in the snare that time, but the experience had taught him nothing.

After chasing an orange tip butterfly, he was led to a patch of untouched grass, and set about nibbling. As he ate, he became concious of prying eyes watching him. He sprang up. He listened. His radar ears twitched. Nothing. He turned his head gingerly. The meadow, the woods, the bramble bushes. No sign of danger.

'Hmph,' he muttered. 'Captain Spruce worries too much.'

As he set out for home, a movement caught his ear and he turned back to the brambles again. And sure enough, the glowering eyes of danger peeped out from the shade of the blackberries. Catkin couldn't move. The eyes then moved forward and Wesley the stoat materialized out of the shadow. Catkin's eyes locked on his.

But while most predators would simply spy their prey and pounce on it, Wesley proved he was not like other predators. He was a stoat: the uncrowned king of hunting.

He allowed his facial expression to become one of sincerity and friendliness. His warm, welcoming eyes bored into Catkin's. Then, the stoat began a strange, ritualistic dance. Keeping his head still, he moved his body from side to side, as if keeping time to a beat.

It wasn't until the young rabbit had become so entranced by what he was seeing that Wesley decided to cast aside his friendly charade and transform back into the ravenous killer he truly was. He bared his cat - like fangs and fell upon the helpless Catkin, knocking him off his feet. Catkin squealed and thrashed out with his hind legs. Wesley hissed and growled, clawing Catkin all over, contriving him to bare his neck.

But suddenly, to answer the cries of the distressed rabbit, Captain Spruce hurled himself recklessly at the stoat, tearing him away from his capture.

Wesley hit the ground but spun to his feet instantaneously.

'Run, Catkin, run!' cried Spruce, a split second before Wesley ploughed into him with numbing force. The two animals rolled about on the ground, pummelling each other wildly with their paws. Teeth and claws flashed. Catkin danced around the scene, wondering how to help. The young rabbit was overcome with fear and guilt.

'Dammit Catkin, run, now!' Spruce choked out as Wesley's claws sunk into his chest.

Catkin trembled and then took off sobbing.

Spruce broke away and drew a kick to Wesley's face and then tried to stand, but the stoat shook off the pain and lunged again, tackling the rabbit leader to the grass. The melee was about to continue until Dreamer grabbed Wesley by the tail and pulled him off the Captain. The stoat bucked and thrashed with his arms, spitting and squealing as if in a tantrum. To let him go would have been most unwise. Dreamer held fast on the stoat's tail, while Badger and Hare arrived to assist Captain Spruce to his feet. The three of them limped away together, back to the Warren. When Dreamer felt it was safe, he relaxed his grip on Wesley's tail.

'Way to cost me dinner!' the stoat chided, looking venomously at Dreamer while nursing his tail.

'Wesley,' Dreamer gasped. 'Why?'

'Why what?' Wesley spat. 'Why did I get hungry? You got a lotta' nerve; attacking me like that.'

'Captain Spruce is our friend!' Dreamer protested.

'No!' Wesley corrected him. 'He's *your* friend! Nearly all the animals around here are *your* friends, even your enemies! We can't all be like you! For everyone else, life goes on!'

With that, Wesley stormed off back to the woods.

Dreamer arrived back at the Warren to find Captain Spruce surrounded by a crowd of well - wishers.

'There's nothing to worry about, everyone,' said Spruce loudly.

'Oh yes there is!' said Violet pointedly. 'Your kittens are going to be born soon and I'm not raising them without a father!'

'I wouldn't miss it for the world, dear,' said Spruce in a more subdued tone, before announcing,

'Alright, everybody, I'm sorry for the way our feast turned out. It was going so well, but summer isn't over yet and thankfully neither are our lives, so let's all get some rest before anything else goes wrong.'

Dreamer, Badger and Hare thanked the Captain profusely for allowing them to take part in the rabbits' fun and games and wished him a quick recovery.

Catkin on the other hand had been scolded by nearly every rabbit in the Warren and was now at home at the bottom of his burrow, hiding from their abuse.

The field was now void of rabbits.

Only the three companions were left, sitting on the bare patch of earth under the same hawthorn tree. They were still trembling from the evening's recent drama. It took Dreamer a while to understand why Wesley had acted the way he did. Badger explained how stoats and rabbits are natural enemies like so many other animals, and how the fight between Wesley and Spruce only appeared strange because he had befriended both.

'Wesley has nothing against Spruce, I'm sure,' Badger concluded. 'He just needs to survive, and rabbits make good food for the stoat.'

'I wish we could make them get along,' said Dreamer.

'Only if you can make rain fall up,' Badger returned. 'Think about it: if I made friends with all the snails and worms I eat, I'd be as skinny as a twig by autumn. Wesley needs to be a predator. You'd be driven to do the same if you didn't have Skip to go fishing for you every day.'

Dreamer put his head down and muttered inwardly:

'If Arznel were here, he'd make us *all* get along.'

'Gosh, this is dreary,' Hare commented. 'Tell ya what: let's forget this whole ugly incident ever took place and go for a jaunt around the woods.'

'Way ahead of you,' said Badger, climbing to his feet.

'Oh, you're way ahead of me, eh?' Hare laughed.

164

'No Hare, I'm not challenging you to a race,' Badger corrected him.

The three friends trekked through the outskirts of the woods together, chatting and enjoying the fragrance of the ferns and bluebells. Until Badger began to suffer an unprecedented bout of hay fever and Hare got stung by a bee. Dreamer found himself looking at one friend lying on his left, sneezing and spluttering, and his other friend on his right, wailing with pain and cursing.

Dreamer couldn't help noting how the honeybee looked. Orangey yellow fur with thick black stripes.

'Hmm,' he thought. 'Just like a tiger.'

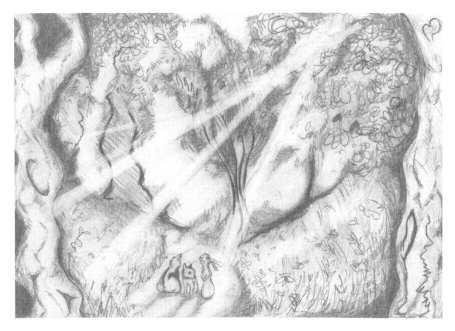

The three companions wandered on through the shade of the trees, with nowhere to go in particular.

'Okay, it's settled,' said Hare, still clutching his nose. 'I won't tell Holly about your flower trouble, if you say nothing to anybody about my encounter with Buzzy Buzzworth back there.'

'Deal,' said Badger, still sniffing and wiping his eyes.

Hare halted and glared at Badger.

'What are you laughing at?' he asked.

165

'Nothing,' sniggered Badger, staring at Hare's swollen nose.

'No, tell me!' Hare demanded.

'Nothing,' Badger insisted. 'I was just thinking about the rabbits earlier - scuffling about like that - what a crowd!'

Hare narrowed his eyes suspiciously, before turning and marching on ahead. Badger sniggered and whispered in Dreamer's ear; 'Doesn't his nose look like a berry?'

Dreamer stifled a laugh.

Coming to the Ranger's Cottage, Badger proposed:

'Hey, we haven't seen Tadpole in a while. Should we visit him before he starts to wrinkle?'

'Yeah,' said Dreamer.

Then Hare coyly made his suggestion:

'Race ya?'

'Oh, you and your races,' exclaimed Badger. 'You make everything so flippin' easy on yourself.'

'I'll slow down a bit for you,' Hare offered. 'Come on, it'll be fun. You did well the last time we raced - you came third!'

'If it'll keep you quiet,' Badger grunted. 'Fine, we'll race.'

Hare cackled with triumph and darted to the starting line, which happened to be the Fallen Beech. The sleeping hedgehog family inside were unaware of the three young animals lining up just outside.

'Right,' Badger announced. 'On your mark... get set...'

Quite unexpectedly, Badger took off through the trees by himself without saying 'Go!' He trundled ahead as fast as he could, out of sight.

'Cheater!' cried Hare, as he streaked off in pursuit of the lead.

Dreamer followed up behind instantly, trailing in Hare's shadow.

Badger was found hobbling clumsily along by himself, flattening grass and crushing bracken.

So this is how it feels to be winning, he thought.

Suddenly, Badger was pulled up short, when a great cloud of dust hit him in the eyes. He coughed, shaking the brown powder from his fur and looked down to see a cluster of the most peculiar looking mushrooms – flesh coloured, club shaped mushrooms with holes on their heads; holes for secreting their spores when touched.

'Puffballs,' he gasped, and an idea formed in his mind. If there was one way to slow Hare down, it was by stamping on –

Whoooooooooosh!

'That's what you get for cheating, you big cheater!' Hare called back, after flashing him by.

'Drats,' Badger cursed. 'Maybe next time,' and he continued to run as fast as his four stumpy little legs would allow. 'If I can just come second,' he panted. 'Then I'm still doing better than last time!'

And that's when a large shadow was cast over him. He looked up and saw Dreamer soaring overhead and landing in front of him, vanishing into the oaks.

Badger decelerated.

'At least I can't come fourth,' he panted, still heading for the Swamp.

The three young animals stampeded through the forest, with Hare in the lead of course. He stopped abruptly and looked back, almost out of breath. There was no sign of Badger. He had obviously fallen behind. It would take him all day to catch up. A ray of sunlight slanted down onto an empty path.

But where was Dreamer?

He must have taken a wrong turn and gone off in some other direction leading away from the Swamp. Either way, another victory for Hare seemed most likely.

He quickly turned and resumed the race, zipping in and around the trees, until he came to a large patch of brambles. They towered tall and thick; long winding stalks with bushes of sticky green leaves, bristling with sharp thorns.

Believing there was no time to go around, Hare opted to go through. He bulled forward recklessly, headfirst into the thorny, spiky, sticky bushes. Only then did he realize just how vast and aggressive they were. He desperately struggled his way through; twisting, biting, breaking, pulling, bending, snapping. Leaves and stems wrapped themselves around Hare's ears, arms and legs, tightening as he moved painfully forward. Thorns, sharp and nasty, dug into his fur. Moving was becoming less and less of an option.

'I ... have ... to get ... out of here!' he muttered. 'The last thing I want ... is Badger passing me out!'

Eventually, Hare emerged from the other side of the bushes, but it was too late. He could venture no further. His legs had been completely constricted by the long thorny brambles. Trapped, Hare collapsed and lay helplessly on the ground, trying to chew his way out without hurting his tongue.

And just when he thought his situation couldn't possibly worsen, Badger came shuffling along. He was happily taking his time.

'See you at the finish line, Hare,' he chuckled, as he made his way towards Bubblelump Swamp.

'No, no, no!' Hare sobbed, lying in a mournful heap. 'I don't believe it!'

Meanwhile, Dreamer had strayed too far from the racing area, in search of a short cut, and found himself wandering through the far north side of Knockomagh Wood; the place he had explored the least. It was a nice, breezy area, all the trees so spaced apart.

He slinked around each tree, watching a lizard dart from one sun patch to another and listening to the grasshoppers chirrup, and at the same time, wondering where his friends had gone. By now, he thought, Hare must have won the race.

Turning to leave this newfound area, Dreamer felt the air being punched clean out of his lungs as he found himself staring into the most beautiful eyes he had ever seen. Gasping, he took a wide jump backwards.

The eyes belonged to a young vixen. Her fur was a darker shade of red than his; almost, blood red. The tips of her ears curled back slightly, like the petals of a lily, and those eyes - Dreamer felt like he could fall into them and drown.

'Do you mind?' she said playfully, equally as surprised. Her voice was sweet and melodic. 'You nearly blew me away.'

Dreamer felt stupidly numb. The vixen regained her balance, and noticed the cub was staring with a quivering jaw.

'You seem lost,' she said. 'Are you new here?'

After what seemed like an embarrassingly long silence, Dreamer replied in a faulty voice; 'Err, kinda?'

'Oh right,' said the vixen, easing herself down and swishing her long, bushy tail elegantly. 'So you moved in a short while ago? Hmm, I've never seen you before, do you have a name, crazylegs?'

The cub was now happy to answer that once dreadful question. He steadied himself and cleared his throat. 'Dreamer,' he replied, sounding the slightest bit more confident.

'Dreamer,' the young vixen exclaimed. 'That's an unusual name. All the foxes I know are named after flowers.'

'What's your name, then?' asked the cub.

The vixen blushed and hid her face behind her tail.

'Why?'

'Because I told you mine,' said Dreamer smartly. He was enjoying this now. The vixen opened her mouth to speak but was cut off by a loud, rather irritating voice in the distance;

'Fuchsia, where didya go? C'mon, are we going hunting or not?'

Another fox emerged from the distant pine trees (a not so attractive looking fox). He was sandy brown and a piece of his ear was missing. One of his front teeth curled out over his lower lip, making his face look like that of a rat. Although he was older looking than Dreamer, he seemed slightly smaller in size.

He spotted the cub and growled ferociously, his flanks rising.

The vixen kept her back turned to this grouchy little fox, and continued to face Dreamer. She closed her eyes with exasperation and sighed;

'That would be my mate, Comfrey. He's not the most patient of foxes. Well, it was nice meeting you, Dreamer.'

With that, the pretty, young vixen turned and hurried to join her mate over by the scots pines, trying to lure him away from the fight.

'Is that what you get up to every time I let you go ahead o' me,' he whined, walking his mate back into the thicket of the forest. 'Who was that mongrel you were talking to?'

The vixen rolled her eyes.

'Relax, Comfrey, I'm just getting to know a neighbour.'

Long after the vixen had gone, Dreamer stared into the patch of trees where he had last seen her. It took time for him to awake from that drowsy, blissful state. But before he could evaluate his performance, Badger came hurrying up behind him, panting.

'Dreamer, Dreamer, come quick!' he cried excitedly. 'The egg is hatching!'

A Little Miracle

Dreamer hurriedly followed Badger up the Hill. They tore their way through the blossoming undergrowth and ran helter skelter up a dirt track. Ash and oak trees hunched over them on both sides forming a natural tunnel of greenery. Up and up and up they ran, dodging tree and bush until they reached the brow of the Hill. They skidded to a halt near the pond.

Hare was already there, crouched over the water (and for some reason, he was covered from head to toe in thorns, like a hedgehog.)

Tadpole bobbed about in the murky brown water, with his tiny head above the surface. His bulging eyes were wider than ever, fixed upon the bird's egg in the rushes.

It wobbled from side to side every few seconds. A tiny crack could be seen on its upperparts, gradually travelling down and around the egg. Dreamer and Badger knelt beside Hare, lowering their heads to the leaf cluttered water and raising their tails like a couple of flag poles. All the companions waited and watched, mouths open, tails wagging, hearts drumming with anticipation.

Soon, a little hole appeared on top of the egg, and out of it, slid a long, slim beak. Bits and pieces of shell crumbled and fell from the egg, allowing a pair of small, greasy wings to unfold.

Spellbound, Dreamer and his friends watched as the egg finally shattered all over and fell to pieces. There, lying in the soft rushes, amid the ruins of its former prison, was the tiniest bird any of the companions had ever seen. It had a long spear- like beak, small squinting eyes and was completely naked. The bird wriggled and squirmed in the rushes, cheeping and gurgling.

The friends went silent, while watching this little miracle struggling to sit upright.

'Ain't that a sight,' Hare gasped, turning to face Badger. 'Wait, are you crying?'

'No,' Badger sobbed, covering his face with his paws.

'Oh that's just pathetic,' Hare snapped. 'You're lucky Holly isn't here to see you get all emotional, ya' big softy ya'.'

'I'm not crying,' sniffed Badger, wiping his eyes.

'Bah,' Hare muttered in disgust. 'Don't try to defend yourself. Just look down there at that poor innocent child. What are its first memories of you going to be? A big, grey, hairy monster, weeping like a cub with a sore tooth! Pull yourself together!'

'Am,' Dreamer interrupted. 'Question: What kind of bird is it?'

A hush of silence fell over the friends. They all lifted their paws to scratch their heads at the same time.

'Beats me,' said Hare, looking down at the tiny creature sitting contentedly in the rushes, chirping and pecking at the egg shells.

'Is it a duck?' Tadpole suggested, gazing up from the water.

Badger shook his head.

'I'm afraid not, Tadpole. Good guess, though.'

Tadpole blinked.

'Is it a wobin?' he squeaked.

Badger smiled weakly at the young frog.

'No, Tadpole, it's not a robin.'

Tadpole persisted.

'Is it a ladybird?' he asked.

'No, Tadpole,' Badger dismissed. 'A ladybird isn't even a bird; it's an insect... good guess though.'

The animals sat together and pondered.

'Well, I'm stumped,' Hare announced. 'Does anyone have any ideas what kind of bird this is?'

Every face was blank.

'Well somebody in Lough Ine must know,' said Badger.

Dreamer thought for a while: what animal in Lough Ine is old and wise? Instantly, Old Darig popped into the cub's head.

'No,' he thought, shaking his head and squeezing his eyes shut. 'I can't let Old Darig see my friends. He'll kill them. And he'll be angry at me for *not* killing them.'

After rummaging through his mind, Dreamer finally thought of an animal whose knowledge of birds must be infallible.

'Nuala, the owl!' he cried. 'She'll know for sure!'

'This had better be worth my time, young fox,' the owl yawned, gazing down at Dreamer from her hole in the giant oak. 'We've had this discussion before. You are not to disturb me while the sun shines. What is your request?'

'I have a question,' Dreamer pleaded, looking up at the owl. 'About a bird.'

'A bird?' Nuala yawned, fanning her face with her wing. 'Do go on.'

Owls have a reputation for being the wisest of birds. It's not true. Their hunched shoulders and thoughtful eyes bestow them with an eminent appearance, when in fact, they may have the all brain capacity of a chicken. Nuala however, lapped it up, resolving to appear prim and prissy at all times.

'My friends and I,' Dreamer continued. 'We found an egg. It hatched earlier this evening. We want to know what kind of bird it is.'

'Very well,' said Nuala. 'Describe this bird to me.'

'Well, it's small,' said Dreamer. 'Err, very small. No feathers?'

Nuala looked annoyed.

'That could be any newborn bird,' she protested. 'Does it have any other distinctive features?'

'Well,' said Dreamer. 'It has a long beak.'

'A long beak, you say,' said Nuala. 'Sounds like a woodcock or a jack snipe or perhaps even a curlew. But before I make a mistake, which is quite unlike me, tell me where you found this egg.'

'Actually,' said Dreamer. 'It was my friend, Tadpole, who found it. It was floating around in the pond where he lives.'

Nuala paused and her great orange eyes went out of focus. Dreamer could hear her mumbling to herself.

'Sandpiper, no, oystercatcher, no, redshank, no, no, no! None of these birds live in the woods. Hmmmm.'

Nuala then asked:

'Is this pond anywhere near a stream?'

'Well yeah,' said Dreamer. 'A tiny little stream runs into it.'

'I see,' said Nuala, leaning forward on her perch. 'My guess is, that egg must have tumbled out of its mother's nesting burrow in the bank of that stream, and floated down into the pond where your friend found it.'

Dreamer's face lit up and his tail began to wag.

'So you know what kind of bird it is!' he asked excitedly.

Nuala blinked smugly and nodded.

'There's only one bird I know of,' she began. 'That has a long beak and lives near streams.'

After receiving his answer, Dreamer hurried back to the Swamp, and in his excitement, tripped over a pine root and tumbled down to the edge of the pond, where his friends were waiting.

'Well?' asked Hare, as if not noticing the cub's fall. 'Did the owl know?' Dreamer rose and shook himself clean, before glancing down at the baby bird in the rushes, still chirping and flapping.

'Hello, *Kingfisher*,' he said.

Fuchsia

It did not take long for the friends to discover that baby kingfishers are difficult birds to look after. They're delicate, and require warm nests at the back of tunnels, in special chambers, feeding on small fish such as eels or shrimp.

Dreamer had received this knowledge from Nuala. It was something the owl loved to do; once asked a question, she would not only answer it correctly, but give a long list of extra information. In other words, she just wanted to show off.

It was safe to assume that the rest of Kingfisher's family had already grown and fledged. This little kingfisher's survival, at least for now, depended on those who found her.

Dreamer and his companions were forced to sit by the pond for the rest of the evening, discussing how to take care of the infant, with their zero years of combined experience. Being left to lie helplessly in the rushes left her open to a multitude of dangers; starving to death, freezing to death or being snatched by a rat, a stoat or a mink.

Kingfisher was blessed enough to have hatched from her egg alive, with scarcely any incubation. It now seemed growing up, was going to be as difficult as hatching out.

The friends had to act quickly, as the sun was setting. Without warmth, the feeble, naked, young Kingfisher would surely perish in the cold.

Fortunately, a number of birds did agree to lend a helping wing. After hurrying down to the Lake, Dreamer summoned Pierce, the heron, who was more than willing to catch a few small rock pool fish for the young bird every day.

'It would be my pleasure,' he beamed, alighting on a shore rock. 'I'm always searching for something new and interesting to do. Feeding this youngster ought to keep me good and busy. Wait till I tell Emur.'

'Thank you,' said Dreamer, graciously, before scampering off to the edge of the wood, where he came upon the Duck Pond.

Bill and his family were elated at being offered the task of watching over Kingfisher day and night, to make sure the newborn bird was safe and well. 'Say no more, Dreamer,' said Bill, scuttling out of the water and flapping his grey wings. 'We'll take great care o' that little hatchling, won't we, Branta?' 'Absolutely,' said the mother duck, climbing from the pond and shuffling up beside her mate. 'We'll treat it like it's one of our own.'

All of the paddling ducklings frowned with jealousy.

'You're the best,' said Dreamer, leaving in a hurry.

Meanwhile, back in Bubblelump Swamp, Badger had finished digging a small round tunnel, the length of his arm, into the bank of the pond. Just before the sun fully set, Pierce, Emur, Bill, Branta and the twelve small ducklings all arrived at the pond, carrying materials with which to build a nest. After much swift, yet careful co - operation among the birds, a perfect nest was built at the back of the tunnel. It was constructed mainly from fish bones and twigs, with lockets of fur from Dreamer, Badger and Hare. The three companions watched with Tadpole as the birds completed their work. Even Emur the swan was happy to pitch in and line the nest with some of her downy feathers. Her primary feathers were amazingly big.

Pierce joked; 'Ee gad, Emur, the child could use one of those feathers as a hammock!'

Emur laughed; 'You should see my nest. When I'm in moult!'

Kingfisher was carefully lifted in Badger's paw, and placed gently into the nest. The young bird seemed comfortable and content there, gurgling peacefully.

The entrance of the tunnel was just about big enough for the other birds to stick their heads in and feed the youngling.

All of the animals cheered when Badger withdrew his empty paw. The job was done, for today. With every generous input, it seemed most likely now that Kingfisher would grow up healthy and safe after all.

Dreamer and his friends stopped by the pond everyday to visit this once helpless, naked, blind, creature; now safe in the right paws (and wings).

But that was not the end of Dreamer's troubles. Something new had taken hold of him. Some outer force. Something he could not begin to explain. Suddenly, the world began to move in slow motion. He walked as if walking through water. He became lightheaded; a bittersweet sensation. A strange, 'fresh' feeling suffused his senses. His heart swelled, sometimes hurt. He lost his appetite. More than before, his thoughts had been invaded. All ambition to set out on adventure had been numbed; numbed by a different desire. A vixen named Fuchsia.

Dreamer found she was the driving force behind his latest predicament. One thought of her; that silky crimson coat, that long, flowing tail, those eyes that reflected all the good things under the sun- and his whole being burst into euphoria.

Affable, an original song

Pick up the phone my dear
And bathe me in your light
Coz I'm shadowed by the fear
That you're gone and out of sight

Without a spark of certainty
You stand out as the one
In my eyes you defy gravity
While your face brings out the sun
Falling in deeper
And suddenly I'm weaker

So you took the stage that night
Without furthermore ado
And you never shined so bright
When the crowd belonged to you

As I sit and watch my world
Spinning dizzily away
Realization has unfurled
That my life is yours to save

Shot by magic on the street
When your silhouette took shape
I never thought we'd meet
So I couldn't help but gape

When I crash and burn with nothing
To whisper of my name
I'll fix my gaze upon you
And pray you feel the same
Falling in deeper
And suddenly I'm weaker

So you took the stage that night
Without furthermore ado
And you never shined so bright
When the crowd belonged to you

As I sit and watch my world
Spinning dreamily away
Realization has unfurled
That my life is yours to save...

He had to find her. He was not sure why, but every fiber in his body told him to. He spent the remainder of his summer evenings searching for her.

He wandered the woods; pacing around every tree, log, bush and rock, he circled the Lake; watching and waiting by the water in the hope that she might appear; he wandered out into the surrounding fields, hedgerows and meadows; stopping every now and then to listen out for the distinctive sound of a vixen screeching somewhere in the distance. But no such sound was heard.

During his lone search, Dreamer would often lift his nose and sniff the wind, hoping that it would be carrying the lulling scent of the vixen, which still graced his nostrils. But his sharp nose detected nothing, save for the usual aromas of the forest.

When it became clear that he was having no luck during the evenings, Dreamer began searching during the night. Again, he was met with disappointment. Yet he continued to try; searching all of the usual places; at dawn, in the mornings, the daytime and soon, the evenings again; always returning to the spot where he'd met her, hoping, and willing her to appear.

But the young vixen was nowhere to be found.

Dreamer was lost.

Even the company of his best friends could not cheer him up. He always trailed behind them during their strolls, reluctant to talk or play, stuck with a heavy sickening loneliness. He never laughed when Hare made a fool of himself tripping over, running into a tree, getting tangled in bushes, falling into mud holes or attempting to sing.

He was withdrawn. Cut off. Lethargic.

Badger and Hare grew increasingly worried about him.

It was dusk when the two friends found themselves hiding behind a mound of crusty copper leaves, watching Dreamer from a distance as he sat under an ivy covered beech tree, staring blankly up at the pink sky, with his head in the clouds. Darkness was seeping into the forest. The black trees were framed against the fading sky; the air cool, and heavy with the fragrance of damp, dew covered ferns. A magpie could be heard in the distance, chattering loudly. In the treetops nearby, a woodpigeon cooed.

'What's wrong with him?' Hare whispered, as he and Badger stayed crouched down, spying on their troubled companion. 'He looks like he was just hit on the head by a falling pumpkin. Is he ill, or wounded or... or is he thinking about those 'dreams' again?'

Badger continued observing Dreamer for a bit and shook his head dismissively.

'No,' he said finally. 'None of those things.'

'How do you know?' asked Hare, cocking up his ears.

Badger took his eyes off Dreamer and glanced at Hare.

'Do you remember when *I* was like that for a while?' he said.

'Yeah I do,' said Hare. 'You were so boring.'

Badger smiled; 'Maybe so, but do you remember *why* I was like that?'

Hare blinked; 'No, not really.'

Badger smiled.

'I had just met Holly,' he said. 'It was my first encounter with a female of my own kind. I felt like I was under a spell. I couldn't stop fretting about what she thought of me. It was very confusing. But before it could get to me, I decided to conquer my fear and ask Holly to be my mate. That wasn't so frightening. The worst she could have done was say no. Thankfully she didn't. So then, my strange feelings became great feelings!'

Hare scratched his head, looking quite glum.

'Okay,' he mumbled. 'What did any of that babbling have to do with Dreamer being a big, depressed furball?'

In annoyance, Badger clapped a paw over his forehead.

'Dreamer's not depressed!' he snapped. 'In fact, he's the opposite! He's over the moon; happy! He just doesn't realize it yet. Don't you see; he's found a female!'

Hare nodded and allowed his ears to droop. He stared at the ground and went silent.

'Oh,' he sighed. 'I see. Hmph.'

Badger looked at Hare with a raised eyebrow.

'What's wrong?' he enquired. 'Are you crying?'

'What, no!' snapped Hare, shrinking back and frowning. 'I'm just ticked off! Both of you have found female companionship and I'm still messing up every mate-ship I get into! I can't find anything long-term! Who'd have thunk it: me: the loner.'

Badger laughed and slugged Hare on the shoulder playfully. 'Your time will come,' he said reassuringly. 'There are plenty of fine female hares around here, I'm sure. In fact, I think I saw one earlier in the Warren... She was alone.'

In the blink of an eye, Hare was gone.

Not knowing what to do or where to go, Dreamer sat in a mournful heap, in the shade of the tall beech, watching the blue evening clouds take the shape of two foxes running together. He rolled over and snuggled up to the moss, pretending it was her.

'Who was she?' he pondered to himself. 'And where did she go?'

It wasn't long before the cub began having unhappy, defeatist thoughts:

'What if she was just another dream?' he went on. 'What if she never existed and was just imaginary? Hmph. At least it was a nice dream this time.'

In retrospect, the cub began to realize the absurdity in his previous dreams.

'What was I thinking,' he gasped.

A magic tiger? An epic journey? Saving the world?

'They were right,' he thought. 'They were all right.'

It was a story. They were just dreams. There was no great tiger out there, waiting to be rescued. And if there was, what could *he* do? He was one creature. One. Alone. Against a world of unimaginable dangers, on a futile journey.

And the humans? What could animals possibly do to withstand the mounting power and ferocity of the humans?

'It would have been like mice against bulls,' he sighed.

They were right. 'Hunt and sleep'. That's what life is all about.

The cub yawned and climbed sluggishly to his feet, before shaking the leaves and moss from his fur.

'Maybe I'll just go to sleep,' he sighed, out of pure self pity. 'Hopefully then I'll dream about her again.'

The cub turned and picked his way through the woods, in the direction of his den. The blanket of bluebells on the forest floor had already closed in for the night. The sky was now almost navy, save for a bright ribbon of pink trailing between the dark clouds. Up above, the fleeting silhouette of Nuala could be seen quartering the area, scanning the ground below for rodents. Her wings were soundless. All seemed perfectly quiet now; still and calm. All Dreamer could hear was the sound of his own paws crunching the leaves and twigs on which he thread, while still making his way home.

He loved the dark. Now he could imagine she was walking beside him.

Suddenly, even in the settling gloom, he caught a glimpse of a tail; a bushy, red, white- tipped tail darting behind the trees. He gasped and followed it. Hurrying around the corner, fast but silent, Dreamer found two foxes.

Sure enough, one was Fuchsia.

Dreamer's heart nearly convulsed, knowing now that this spellbinding beauty was no figment of his imagination.

She was all too real; wandering delicately beneath the trees, unaware of his transfixed eyes.

But the other fox happened to be Comfrey, Fuchsia's mate.

Dreamer had forgotten about him.

He trotted up along the narrow dirt track, ahead of his mate. The two foxes were making their way home, after a brief but successful hunt. Dreamer trembled with excitement. There she was; the vixen with whom he had been infatuated for so long. Now was his chance to find out where she had been; where she lived.

After waiting until both foxes were a good few meters ahead of him, Dreamer crept from behind the tree and followed them, making sure to keep their bushy tails in sight. Luckily, the wind was on his side. The two foxes ahead moved quite slowly; plodding through the undergrowth and taking their time. Dreamer had to be careful not to catch up too fast and risk being heard. He patiently, and silently, slinked his way around every mossy tree trunk that crossed his path, holding his breath and tensing his body. His paws touched the ground so lightly, no print was left. Forward he crept, with care and with caution. Old Darig's techniques were already proving their worth.

Fuchsia and Comfrey appeared to be talking to each other as they walked. Dreamer could not understand what they were saying; it sounded like faint muttering and mumbling.

It wasn't long before the two homebound foxes began to pick up the pace. They slipped away from Dreamer's sight, into the darkness. Dreamer rushed to the spot where he had last seen them, and proceeded by following their scents and tracks. Along the forest floor, he snooped and sniffed, combing the ground with his sharp nose, until finally, he reached the den of Fuchsia and Comfrey.

It was a small, round hole in the ground, concealed under layers and layers of colourful, withering leaves.

Dreamer dropped to the ground, only a short distance from the den, and hoped that his red fur would camouflage among the orange loam. He watched in tense silence, as the two foxes padded towards the den entrance together and squatted down. Comfrey had been carrying a big, wet bundle in his mouth the entire trek. He turned to his mate, opened his jaws and let drop to the ground, a dead rabbit.

'C'mon, Fuchsia,' he whined. 'Why won't ya' have some o' this?'

Fuchsia looked pitifully down at the slain creature lying by her paws. Her eyes were filled with guilt and sympathy.

'I'm not hungry,' she sighed.

Comfrey grunted; 'You always say that. You always say you're not hungry. O' course you are! You're a fox; we're always hungry. Now come on, dig in!'

Fuchsia hesitated and shook her head. 'No thanks,' she insisted.

Comfrey growled.

'I went to a lotta trouble fer you today,' he said in hurt tones. 'I caught ya' a thrush in the field, and ya' didn' want it. I went to the Warren by myself n' chased that scar faced hare fer as long as I could and ya' didn' even cheer me on. An' then I caught this rabbit an' ya' don't want that either? What do you want?'

Fuchsia yawned; 'Right now, I just want some rest.'

She seemed very fed up.

Comfrey sighed; 'I give up.'

The two foxes hunched over the hole in the ground and prepared to climb in. Satisfied, Dreamer decided to take his leave. Lifting himself from the ground, he turned to make his getaway, only to step on a dry branch.

There was a loud 'crunch' as it snapped in half. He gasped and flinched. He stood completely frozen, with his back to the two foxes nearby.

You could hear a pin drop.

Over by the den, Comfrey sprang alert. He pricked his ears and listened intently.

'Didya hear that?' he hissed, glancing about him with piercing eyes. 'Something's out there.'

'Well, yes,' said Fuchsia, bluntly. 'Lots of animals hunt at night. It could've been a hedgehog or a badger.'

Comfrey lifted his nose and sniffed the cold night air, and then growled. 'It's that fox again!' he snarled. 'The same one I caught ya' hobnobbing with the last time!'

'No, Comfrey,' Fuchsia pleaded. 'Leave him alone, he's done nothing wrong!'

Comfrey growled again;

'Why does every dog want what I got? When I find that li'l sneak, I'll turn him inside out!'

With that, Comfrey reared up and bounded into the darkness.

Dreamer gulped fearfully and scurried behind an old, rotting log for cover. He hunkered down in its shade and tried to disappear from view. Comfrey's ponderous paw steps drew dangerously closer. The raging little fox circled the area just on the other side of the log.

'When I find ya', I'll ring your neck!' he muttered. 'You stay away from my mate, y'hear! She's mine!'

Comfrey searched around tree trunks and under ferns, puffing and snorting.

Dreamer was curled up under the log, his belly pressed to the ground. Every nerve tingled.

This was the last thing he wanted. He was not in the least bit afraid of Comfrey. Not at all. A beating he could endure. It was a beating in front of Fuchsia he dreaded.

'Oh no,' the cub winced. 'If she finds out I like her, what do I do?'

He remained as motionless as a rock, while blending into the darkness.

Suddenly, Comfrey let out a cry of triumph.

'Aha!' he announced. 'I've found your tracks! And your scent! Your tail is mine, you li'l grasshopper!'

Dreamer gasped, hearing Comfrey approach. His paw steps were now louder and more menacing than before. The cub panicked and glanced around, frantically wondering what to do. There was no time to run, nowhere else to hide, and he had not the desire to fight. His heart hammered. His blood froze.

Comfrey spotted the log. Fox tracks led to it. The small prints trailed along the ground and stopped just there, where the scent of fox was strong. Comfrey galloped towards it, his fangs fully bared, his claws fully splayed. He leapt upon the log and glared down the other side.

Nothing.

The ground beneath lay empty, though the smell of fox lingered.

Comfrey called out in annoyance; 'If I catch ya', I'll skin ya' like a sheep! I'll squeeze the maggots from your eyeballs! I'll rip your spine out through your tail and use it to clean my teeth after I eat ya! I'll-'

To intervene, Fuchsia rushed to his side and waved her soft bushy tail in his face. This had a calming affect on him. The angry, jealous fox was lulled.

'Comfrey,' the vixen pleaded sweetly. 'Just forget it. It's been a good night, don't ruin it.'

Comfrey puffed sulkily.

'Let's just catch up on our sleep, shall we?' Fuchsia suggested.

'Bah,' Comfrey grunted, as he stormed back to the den entrance. Fuchsia sighed and hurried after him.

The two foxes slipped underground together.

Believing all was calm again, and believing he was safe, Dreamer crawled out from *inside* the hollow, festering log. He sneezed and shook the moss and earwigs from his fur. He then paused and allowed his body to relax. Peering over at the hole in the ground, Dreamer smiled. He now knew where Fuchsia lived. He would never lose her again.

Dreamer did not wish to invade the vixen's privacy, but to carry on wondering if in fact she was *real*, he feared, would have driven him demented. No. Surely this was the right thing to do.

'Well,' he thought. 'At least I know she lives in Lough Ine.'

But that wasn't enough. He wanted more. 'If only she would notice me again.'

Little did he know, she already had.

Fuchsia had been born the previous spring, the only sister of three cubs. Her original home had been down by the Ilen River, roughly three miles west of Lough Ine. Unlike Dreamer's family life, Fuchsia's did not come to a cruel and sudden end. It was instead steeped in peace and happiness the whole way through, each day filled with sleeping, playing and later hunting lessons.

But this simple, cliché of a lifestyle did not always appeal to the bright eyed cub. She had a spark. Always she had felt as though something was missing. So when the time came for her to leave home, adventure was her main priority.

Trespassing on farms, stealing from dustbins, sneaking into porches to drink from dogs' water bowls - all this seemed to suffice. Most of the time, Fuchsia had the stealth and the fortune to get away in time. But one night, she had neither.

Prowling around someone's lawn, on one of her habitual raids, Fuchsia did not expect to be disrupted. Yet, as she rooted through an overflowing dustbin, she mustn't have been alone for long, because down from the window sill sprang a ginger cat! The chase did not last long, the startled fox fleeing the scene in time. But her escape came at a price, for in her surprised state, the young vixen had run straight through a washing line, and ended up galloping through the nearby fields with a pair of boxer shorts over her head. Although the danger of the ginger cat had passed, Fuchsia soon found herself in an entirely different predicament.

As she hurried home, the garment she wore around her neck became snagged on a blackthorn branch. Fuchsia was whipped off her feet and hit the ground. For the rest of the night, she lay there, hopelessly tangled up in both blackthorn twigs and boxer shorts alike.

By morning she was exhausted from struggling. The item of clothing she had accidentally picked up the previous night acted like a noose around her neck. She lay amid the grass, breathing heavily, feeling completely helpless. Until something quite peculiar happened. Fuchsia was aware that she was lying in the middle of a warren, but to see one of its denizens hopping up to her?

The rabbit approached slowly, gingerly, pausing to stare and twitch every now and then. Fuchsia had not the strength to keep her eyes open, let alone break into chase. And at this point, she certainly did not have an appetite. So she lay there, and closed her eyes, expecting the rabbit to simply pass on by.

186

But no, the rabbit approached sure enough, and was soon crouching over the entangled vixen. To this day, Fuchsia still doesn't know why the rabbit did what he did, but perhaps he had witnessed one of his comrades trapped in a snare, and knew all too well the anguish. One thing was for certain, he knew Fuchsia was in no position to harm him, and so he began chewing through the legs of the boxer shorts. Fuchsia didn't protest. In fact she didn't make an effort to move at all. For a while, she believed it was all part of a fevered dream. Only it wasn't, for the rabbit eventually finished his task and carried on down the field.

Even though she was free, Fuchsia could not move for a long time. Maybe she was frozen stiff from lying in the cold field all night, or more likely again it was because a creature whom she had been taught to prey on had kept her alive in a different way. It was that incident that had deterred her from ever again harming a rabbit. And it was her near death experience that had taught her to appreciate all life. Never again did she harm bird or beast. She would strive to survive some other way.

Fortune must have played a significant role in the vixen's life, for one day, while out foraging far from home, she discovered Lough Ine; a forest rich in plant and fungal matter. Here, she knew she could survive. And it was here she met Comfrey, a fox slightly older than she was. Fuchsia's mother had always told of the importance of mating and this seemed like the ideal opportunity. Despite his gruff ways and proneness to being offended easily, he was a good provider and genuinely cared about Fuchsia's welfare, though was ignorant of her vegetarian lifestyle. Overlooking his flaws, Fuchsia continued to see him as 'sweet'.

What could not be understood was why Fuchsia *refused* to mate with him! Animals usually get together for one reason - mating. Giving birth and keeping the species alive. That's all. No emotional attachment, just survival. But Fuchsia did not feel like sacrificing her freedom and body, for a life of worrying about other lives, not yet.

Comfrey didn't understand this, and was constantly frustrated, following her around and waiting for her to give in.

Just when she was considering it, she met Dreamer, and all thoughts of raising a family with Comfrey were put on hold again. Who was that mysterious handsome fox?

Exposed!

The first rain came hard and fast. Dark nimbus clouds gathered and burst over the hills and Lake, sending sheets of torrential rain down over the dry, deprived land. It pelted down heavily, turning earth to muck, swelling streams and flooding fields. In the forest, curtains of cold, clear water cascaded down from the treetops, like a tropical monsoon. The canopy became heavy and full, some branches exploding into jets of ice cold water, until it passed, and the sun returned to find it had a lot of work to do.

Dreamer was licking his lips as he made his way back from the Lake. He and Skip had been fishing again, and now the cub had mastered the art of fishing for himself– using his tail! It was this little achievement that put a spring in his step, after he'd crossed the brook and begun climbing the Hill...

Fuchsia and Comfrey were asleep in their den. It would be dusk before he would see them again- from a distance of course. Dreamer had grown tired of trying to entice the young vixen. He had left his scent on virtually every tree, but she never noticed, or pretended not to. Whenever he barked or cried from nearby, to assert his existence, Comfrey would lure her away from the path, where she had stopped to listen. The whole summer had gone by, but Fuchsia and Comfrey just seemed inseparable. What drove Dreamer to keep trying, he did not know.

Once he reached the Hilltop, he clambered up the tall, heather covered rock ledge, and gazed across at the beauty of the landscape. He closed his eyes and put his nose to the wind, drinking its icy freshness.

It was then he decided to visit Tadpole and Kingfisher. He headed down the other side of the hill, moving through the swaying Scots pines and Douglas firs, and into the dank, smelly swamp. There, he was met by all of his friends at once.

Badger, Holly and Hare sat on the bank of the pond, lazing sleepily in the rushes, while watching Tadpole dabbling about in the brown water, his long tail flicking and wagging.

He was now ten weeks old; a froglet. His arms and legs had developed dramatically. He was also much bigger in size. His friends no longer had to strain their eyes to see him.

Kingfisher was perched at the edge of her nesting hole, glancing around and chirping with pleasure. She still appeared vulnerable; being so small and featherless. Nevertheless, she was safe. Her companions were on constant guard for danger, and with their daily inputs of dry grass, locks of fur and wood peelings, her home was always fine and warm.

Pierce, the heron, stood on one leg, ankle deep in the shallow outskirts of the pond. He had captured a mouthful of shrimp in one of the Lake's rock pools earlier, and had fed them to the young bird, straight from his beak. He was now merely staying by the pond for company.

The duck family were there also, huddled together in one of the pond's corners. The twelve ducklings swam in crazy circles, around and around their parents. Bill sat almost motionless, frequently paddling with his webbed feet. Branta bobbed about beside him, watching her children while humming a song.

'Morning Dreamer,' yawned Badger as the cub plodded over and sat beside him.

'Morning,' said Dreamer softly, curling up.

It sounded like the insects of the swamp were having a party. Or perhaps they always sounded that way, only no one had been quiet enough to listen. Unseen grasshoppers and crickets chattered and clicked somewhere in the long grass. Butterflies, both tortoiseshell and red admiral, fluttered and danced freely and carelessly around the stinging nettles. Honeybees hummed with pleasure while burying their faces in every flower they could find, guzzling the sweet nectar inside, allowing beads of pollen to cling to their jackets. Dragonflies hovered above the pond, their wings flapping so rapidly they could hardly be seen. Common flies, bluebottles, skimmers and chasers all zipped and buzzed around the marshy ground and mud puddles.

Some of the blackberries had fermented, and the wasps feeding on them became drunk. They droned about gracelessly, bumping into trees and each other, stinging at random.

But there was no vivacity in the animals this morning. They were quite happy to lounge about and do nothing. Hare stood outside the circle, flicking his long ears and waving his arms around wildly, trying to swat the pesky flies that nipped at him.

'Buzz off, you brainless little buggers!' he scolded. 'Get away from me! A million against one is not a fair fight!'

Pierce had more luck with his insect problem. He swiftly snatched a damselfly out of the air with his long beak and gobbled it up.

Bill muttered: 'A damsel in distress.'

Dreamer, Badger and Holly did not have much to say to each other. The night before had been a busy one.

Badger and Holly were out on one of their nightly hunts, and insisted on bringing Dreamer with them. Badger understood that his friend was feeling rather confused about the Fuchsia situation, and wanted to help take his mind off it, at least for a while. Dreamer was happy to join them.

And so, the three animals had a long and successful night together. They gorged themselves on the very best of everything- the rain having drawn out the earthworms from the soil's deeps. They shared scrumptious blackberries. They even met some other friendly faces who were out sharing the balmy night – Nuala hunting fieldmice, Craggy and Bertha gathering seeds and acorns for their piglets, and Flapjack the pheasant, who for some reason, seemed more agitated than usual.

'Stoopid cuckoo!' he had cried, running through the woods. 'Stoopid tresspassah! You bring shame to my famiry! Dare you stick your liar's bum in my nest! *Gobblegobblegobble!*'

'What's wrong with him?' Dreamer had asked.

Badger shook his head.

'Nothing we can help him with.'

So the three friends stayed out all night, sampling this, sniffing at that, and watching a flock of the peculiar pipistrelle bats, before the arrival of a lazy morning.

If only they knew…

Dreamer, Badger and Holly were now too tired to do much else, other than sit by the pond and watch over Tadpole and Kingfisher. The companions noticed how much the two infants had in common:

They were both newborn pond dwellers, both without parents, and were both restless and eager to grow.

At first, the companions were worried about what they'd learned - kingfishers eat frogs!

But with all these little similarities, and because they were being raised together from such a young age, it seemed likely that the pair might indeed become the best of friends.

'So Dreamer,' said Holly, sitting up. 'Have you heard the news?'

'No,' said the cub. 'What's happened?'

'Nothing bad, if that's what you're thinking,' Holly chuckled.

'It's Kingfisher. Her eyes have opened. She can finally see.'

Dreamer had noticed that the little bird's eyes had changed. Her once tiny, squinting eyes were now wide open and twinkling.

'That's great,' said Dreamer, genuinely pleased, but too tired to show it.

For some time, the dull monotony dragged on. That was, until Hare became restless.

'I'm bored,' he groaned, scratching behind his ear. Badger grinned and seized his opportunity.

'Well, go for a swim!' he laughed, lifting his heavy paw and patting Hare on the back so hard, it knocked him into pond with a mighty splash. Tadpole clung to a floating twig for dear life as the waves swept over him. It was almost like a miniature storm. The animals were in gales of laughter. They clapped and shrieked and squealed at the sight of Hare twisting and flopping about the pond, splashing and spraying water around, like a whale trapped in a rock pool. Kingfisher chirped and bounced up and down with amusement.

Hare emerged from the water, saturated and covered in mud. He wore a face like a thundercloud.

'Oh, that tears it,' he growled, springing forward from the pond and landing on Badger's chest. Badger gasped and rolled with Hare back into the water. The animals found it impossible to contain their laughter, while watching the two friends playfully wrestle. Water and mud flew in every imaginable direction. Pierce and the duck family had to evacuate the pond and take cover behind some rushes. Badger and Hare continued to fight in comical fashion; rolling and tackling, rising and falling, splashing mud into each other's eyes before charging again. Hare reared up and leapt upon his opponent's back. Badger piggy- backed Hare around the rim of the pond, waiting for him to drop off.

But because the animals were so distracted, and making such a rumpus, they did not hear 'the outsider' creeping up behind them.

The bramble bushes rustled violently and twigs snapped under the paws of the big creature as it drew closer to the pond, wondering what all the commotion was about, and who was making it.

Before Dreamer and his friends had time to run away or hide, they were caught...

Out of the bushes, with a dead pheasant dangling from his jaws, stepped Old Darig.

He gasped and dropped his catch to the ground with a sharp thump, and stared in disbelief at the amount of different species congregating together in front of him; ducks, badgers, a heron, a hare, a froglet, a kingfisher hatchling and a fox cub.

The fox cub he knew well - or so he thought.

'SCATTER!' cried Hare.

The animals fled. Hare shot into the woods like an arrow, Badger and Holly trailing behind him, Pierce opened his wings, flapped and ascended into the sky, Bill, Branta and the ducklings scampered clumsily into the bushes together, tripping and stumbling, while back in the pond, Kingfisher rolled backwards into her chamber and Tadpole disappeared underwater.

But Old Darig made no effort to pursue them. He just stood glaring fixedly at Dreamer with a look of shock- horror on his face. The cub sat frozen and speechless, Darig's eyes bored into his. The old fox's words cut the silence like a knife:

'Dreamer,' he gasped. 'What's going on? Who were those animals?'

The cub gulped, and then stood up with a sudden burst of defiance.

'Those were my - my friends,' he managed to burble out.

Old Darig cocked an eyebrow. 'You're... friends?' he said frostily.

Dreamer nodded, still trembling. He knew what he was in for. And he wasn't looking forward to it.

Darig paused and allowed his head to droop. He then took a deep breath, raised his head and opened his eyes, trying to recover himself.

'Young fox,' he coolly began. 'Did I teach you nothing about the world? Did I not teach you how to be a real fox, or did I waste my time?'

Dreamer said nothing, and braced himself.

Old Darig paused again and resumed, this time, more aggressively.

'A 'real fox' does not have 'friends'!' he shouted. 'Especially not with animals he should be hunting and eating! What on earth possessed you to socialize with birds, and and and badgers?'

'They're my friends!' Dreamer snapped.

Old Darig recoiled at the cub's rebellious remark.

'Don't say that again,' he warned. 'Coming from a fox, it simply sounds wrong. The animals I saw you with - you should have been picking them out of your teeth, not playing with them! It's a disgrace to the animal kingdom!

An outrage! What would your mother think if she ever caught you betraying your own kin like that?'

'I barely knew my mother,' Dreamer retaliated. 'She didn't live long enough to teach me what you did. I didn't know what it was like to be a real fox until I met you. Before that, it was my 'friends' who'd helped me survive!'

Old Darig growled:

'Your 'friends' are your natural enemies. I taught you that. They may have helped you in the past, but now you know better. Or at least you should. A true fox would never -'

'Well maybe I'm not a true fox!' Dreamer shouted. 'Maybe I prefer being different. Maybe I prefer having friends, instead of being a lonely killer!' Darig frowned and grunted.

'You know what's worse than all this,' the old fox concluded. 'You were dishonest with me. We spent quite a long time together. I thought *I* was your friend. I thought I was helping you. The thought of helping you made me feel useful and needed. After all, my son and daughters were all killed by The Farmer's hounds, lest you forget. Much of my life was spent alone and sad. I didn't think I'd ever get another chance to raise a cub. And then I met you. All that pain and misery was washed over. You were my new son. Our time together made an old fox feel young again, even happy. And I thought you liked spending time with me. Little did I know- you were just covering for your *friends*.'

Dreamer was struck by sudden sympathy.

'No,' he pleaded, in a softer tone. 'I really did want you as my teacher. I had a great time, honestly. I just didn't want you to hurt my friends. That's why I didn't tell you about them.'

Old Darig, with a look of defeat on his face, twitched his whiskers and sighed.

'I once considered myself a wise fox,' he grunted. 'Hmph. Wise foxes are not so easily fooled by children. Maybe I too have a lot to learn.'

There was a dark silence.

'I'm sorry,' said Dreamer in a quivering voice, as he backed slowly away through the bushes, into the shade of the trees. 'But I can't be a normal fox. I'm really thankful for all your help and advice but it won't change me...

I remember you saying once, that we survived because we were chosen for something great. Well sometimes I believe I am, but whatever that is, I can't do it as a normal fox. Sorry, but I need to be different.'

Leaving Old Darig standing by the pond, Dreamer turned and vanished deep into the woods, where the first leaves of autumn were beginning to fall.

Dreamer and Darig would not speak again for a long time. But the division between the two foxes was not the saddest thing to happen in Lough Ine. for the animals were unaware that a storm was coming.

But this wasn't the sort of storm that brought rain, thunder and lightning.

No. This was a different kind of storm, one more dreadful.

One day soon, the wind that blew through Lough Ine would be carrying the smell of cordite…

BOOK ONE
-PART THREE-

Fighting for Lough Ine

Many Changes

Winter had come again, like an uninvited, unwelcome, and yet unavoidable relative; taking what it wanted and leaving nothing but a barren, white landscape. Upon its arrival in Lough Ine, the bitter season snatched the warmth from the air, pinched the light from the sun and shoved the leaves from the trees, scattering nuts and berries all over the forest floor.

Flowers could bear no more of this rude and reckless visitor, and waited underground until it left. Gone were the primroses. Gone was the bluebell glade, the anemone, the wood sorrel, the fox glove. All hid beneath the rotting red loam of the fallen leaves.

Making itself at home, the winter dragged in blankets of snow and frost, wrapping every tree, bush and rock in its rimes of icicles, and leaving everything to languish under its intense cold.

The creatures who could endure the company of such an unruly guest were forced to scavenge for whatever morsels it hadn't devoured. Nuala, the owl, stored in her secret larder, as many mice and rats as she dared to catch. Squirrels, voles and fieldmice gathered precious grains and fruit, and stashed it away in any chamber that remained untouched by winter's greedy, grasping claw. Some, who had had enough of such tension, excused themselves. Craggy, Bertha and all the juvenile hedgehogs, ate their fill and retreated deep under the Fallen Beech for a long, blessed snooze.

Those who had the fortune at being warned of winter's approach, quickly made themselves scarce. The swallows assembled in their gargantuan flocks and embarked on a perilous six week journey south – believing anything, no matter how dangerous, was better than staying behind with that abominable beast called winter.

On top of the white capped Hill, sitting dozily in the shade of an evergreen holly bush and overlooking the shiny frozen landscape, was Dreamer the fox, now almost fully grown. Time had treated him well. He had certainly become a fine animal, blessed with a lustre red coat and impressive bushy tail. At nearly two years old (fourteen in fox years), this was his second winter. He had been living in Lough Ine for roughly a year and had known his friends for about the same length of time.

But there were some things time could not heal; things Dreamer could not simply 'grow out of'. As usual, his mind was restless, his heart longing. As a cub, he had had an obsession with danger. Whether he feared it, or yearned for it, danger was always a part of Dreamer's being. Lately however, as the fox sifted the scents of the wind and watched the clouds closely, he could not help but feel that this danger he had been so unduly preoccupied with, was now closer than ever before…

Dreamer slinked out from beneath the holly bush and stretched his lithre body.

'Nothing I can do about it now,' he thought, trying to grant himself some solace. 'What happens, happens. If there's one thing I should worry about now, it's finding food.'

Indeed, food shortages were the prime concern of most wildfolk in the sanctuary since winter arrived. No one was going to listen to the far-fetched nonsense of an overwrought fox now.

'Oh well,' he thought, making his way across the rock-face. 'I'm sure nothing will happen in the next few blinks.'

Just then, as if fate had nothing better to do than use his heart-strings for puppetry, Fuchsia and Comfrey were seen snooping around the pine section in the distance, after a fruitless hunt.

'Hmph,' Dreamer grunted, watching them slip behind the trees. 'I'd almost prefer danger.'

For months, he had been admiring the vixen from afar, with painful longing in his heart. But she never noticed him. As her beauty grew, so too did his jealousy. Comfrey had won, and Dreamer had given up all hope of ever being with the fair vixen.

Dreamer strolled down into the bare, leafless wood, keeping to what was left of the shade. Since the once prodigious canopy had receded, he longed for shade, although dark winter nights came without a star.

It didn't take long for him to meet Badger and Holly, who had also aged healthily.

Badger was now almost a meter long and exceedingly heavy. His dark grey coat grew wild and shaggy. He looked for all the world like a bear. His mate took on a more elegant look; her fur growing smooth and straight.

The badger couple were crouched around an oak root, the ground riddled with little holes.

'Any luck?' Dreamer asked.

Badger shook his head gravely.

'Not a nibble,' he replied. 'I don't know what's happened to all of the earthworms, but we can't seem to find any no matter how far down we dig. And when we do find some, they're rarely big enough to feed a sparrow... and you?'

Dreamer nodded.

'I caught a couple of mice today. And Skip caught me a trout yesterday. Still though, this weather keeps me looking for more. I could eat a thistle.'

'Mmm,' Badger muttered. 'We all know the feeling.'

Dreamer came close to smiling when he saw Holly.

'Nice to see you out at daytime again,' he said wryly.

Holly replied rather moodily:

'The sound of my belly's growling kept me awake.'

Dreamer had already resumed his stroll.

'I hope you succeed,' he called back, as the badgers continued to comb the ground afresh.

Further on down the hill, Hare was found scratching the snowy ground, an area formerly occupied by the bluebells.

Hare's coat had turned completely white. It was a winter metamorphoses he had to go through to camouflage from predators in the snow.

'Find any grass yet?' Dreamer enquired.

Hare sighed loudly.

'It's like searching for a furry, four legged worm.'

Dreamer sniggered; 'Badger and Holly would've liked that.'

Hare stood up on his hunkers and dried his wet paws on his fur.

'Grrr,' he said loudly. 'I tell ya, if winter had a face, I'd cock my leg on it!'

'I'm sure you'll find some eventually,' said Dreamer reassuringly. 'I mean, grass can't fly south! It's under all that snow, no doubt. Just keep digging.'

Hare saluted with his paw; 'Will do.'

Presently, Kingfisher fluttered down. She had become one of the most dazzling birds in Lough Ine, with her aqua blue feathers and bright orange under parts. On the tip of a low beech branch, she perched.

'Hello Kingfisher,' said Dreamer. 'You're alone? Where's Tadpole?'

Kingfisher giggled.

'You keep forgetting, silly. We call him *Frog* now.'

'Oh right,' Dreamer blushed. 'Well, where's Frog then? Surely he hasn't gone off hibernating without saying goodbye.'

'No, he's coming,' Kingfisher chirped. 'Just wait.'

Moments later, the restless little amphibian came hopping around the trees, over mounds of snow, before finally reaching his friends by the oak.

At almost a year old, he was fully grown. He was light green with blotches of brown, had long legs and his usual big bulbous eyes.

'H-h-hi everybody,' he shivered. 'My gosh it's cold isn't it, are you cold, I know I am, gosh I hope I don't freeze to death. Have any of you eaten? I haven't, oh, I hope I don't starve to death!'

Frog was a terrible hypochondriac. He was constantly concerned about his health and safety, a change in character none of his friends had expected. As a tadpole, he had longed to leave the pond and be free to roam dry land. And now that the time had come, he rarely wanted to leave.

'You're alright, Frog,' Dreamer assured. 'I'm sure you'll survive. Besides, today it's *my* turn to worry.'

The friends all looked fixedly at the fox.

'What do you mean?' asked Hare. 'What's worrying you?'

Dreamer realized he was being inappropriate. It was wrong to lay these troubles upon his friends so suddenly, especially Kingfisher and Frog, it being their first season.

To Hare he whispered, 'Can I speak with you for a minute?'

The two animals slipped off together behind the great oak tree, where the love- heart carving was beginning to heal over.

'What's up?' asked Hare.

Dreamer cast his eyes about nervously and then leaned in close to his friend.

'Do you remember when I was having those dreams?' he whispered.

'Oh, come on,' said Hare irritably. 'We're not still dusting that fossil, are we?'

'Listen,' said Dreamer forcefully. 'Back then, I thought we would have to *leave* Lough Ine to find danger… but now…'

'But what?' said Hare, almost yawning. 'You think danger is coming here?'

Dreamer nodded. 'I can sense it.'

Hare rested his head against the trunk of the tree and began banging it gently.

'What kind of danger, exactly?'

Dreamer lowered his eyes to the ground.

'I don't know,' he admitted. 'But the wind; sometimes it's like it's screaming at me, proper 'death' screams. And the clouds; they take shapes, shapes of… I'm not sure what, but very unpleasant.'

Hare paused before saying, 'You, my friend, need sleep.'

Dreamer sighed extremely loudly.

'I mean it,' said Hare. 'Weary body, weary mind.'

The two friends stopped talking when they realized they had company. Kingfisher fluttered down from the midpoint branches of the oak. Frog hopped from around the corner.

'You're taking an awful long time,' said Kingfisher. 'What's all this about?'

'Yeah,' said Frog. 'It sounds pretty bleak, whatever it is.'

Hare smiled. 'It's nothing, fellas.'

Then to Dreamer,

'Seriously, a good, long sleep.'

Dreamer hung his head in defeat.

'Yeah, Dreamer,' said Kingfisher, pretending to understand the matter. 'Learn to chill out!'

Hare grunted. 'You might want to rephrase that, Kingfisher. Wrong season.'

Dreamer broke into smile at this.

'R-r-really, D-Dreamer,' said Frog. 'Y-you worry too much!'

The fox couldn't help laughing now.

'Okay, Frog,' he conceded. 'I will try to stop worrying. For now. But you might have to put up with me again later.'

Hare spread his arms. 'No problem. If we can tolerate Frog, we can tolerate you!'

A snowball splatted into Hare's face.

'No fair!' squeaked Frog's voice.

Hare stooped and rolled up a snowball of his own. 'Come here, you little squirt! Prepare to be buried!'

Dreamer set off into the woods with a now lighter heart. Of all the animals in Lough Ine he had come to know, he had chosen only four as his truly 'best' friends, the same four: Badger, Hare, Frog and Kingfisher. They had always managed to put his mind at ease.

Unfortunately, due to Holly's refusal to surface during the day, Dreamer rarely had the chance to see her anymore, and felt rather distanced from her.

Suddenly, he struck luck as a tasty brown rat darted across the snow covered path in front of him. Dreamer was on him instantly and snapped the rat up in his jaws. After throttling it, the rat proved a snack, but Dreamer's appetite was undimmed. Tired, the fox thought he should rest first before resuming the hunt. And so, he padded off towards his den.

He didn't make it far.

A Dark Premonition

On the way to his den, Dreamer came across something quite unexpected... and very much unwanted.

Making his way through the forest, the fox brushed passed several snow festooned branches, until he reached a clearing, where his nose was suddenly hit by a foul stench. From somewhere up ahead, behind a wall of pine trees, some unfamiliar fumes wafted into his nostrils. Curiously, the fox scurried over to where he believed the smell was coming from, unconsciously following a trail of litter; aluminum cylinders, emerald green glass shards, silver wrapping, paper cups, apple cores and wrinkly, yellow fruit skins.

Dreamer halted and stared wonderingly at this mess strewn all over the forest floor. He took a few steps forward, now fully alert. As he edged ever closer to the gap in the trees, the smell became visible, as the air began to blue...

And without warning, he felt his blood freeze as the ghostly face of a tiger materialized out of the trees and hovered over him. Once again, it was difficult to see the tiger's face, with the net obscuring his features. It hung from his ears and was wrapped tightly around his body, like a thick, white spider's web; steel balls flattening his fur against his skin. Instead of his once mighty roar, Arznel let out a chilling moan, which shook the snow from the trees; a moan of pain, a moan of want. And just like that, he turned, and melted back into the pines.

'Wait!' Dreamer called after him. 'Arznel, wait!'

The fox bounded into the trees in pursuit of the tiger, but quickly grinded to a halt as a most horrific sound blasted his ears; worse than the moan of the tiger, worse even than the boom of a gun. It was a deep, bellowing horn of a sound that ripped through the sky with its volume. Dreamer squeezed his eyes shut with pain, and realized it was not one sound, but hundreds of different noises coalescing into an almost explosive din.

Dreamer pried his eyes open, feeling the rush of wind on his face, and nearly gagged at the frightful sight that met him. Where once, fields and groves lay snoozing peacefully under a calm sky- a monster now rampaged. A vast, concrete structure of wide, twisting roads, lanes, bridges, railings, signs, lights; crisscrossing and running over and under each other. Wheel-machines streamed up and down this superhighway like an infestation of fireflies, honking and screeching. Green and purple smog enfolded the sky, from where came a rain; a rain so potent, it melted the weeds from the walls.

As Dreamer turned to run, he felt something crunch beneath his front paw.

Looking down, he saw a set of white sticks and a round rock lying amid the ashes – and a scattering of some orange fur! Dreamer wobbled and fell to the ground, becoming tangled in the fox bones! He found his head had become wedged inside the ribcage, and he rose to shake it off. But the skeleton seemed to tighten its grip, and Dreamer quickly ran out of air, collapsing to the ground. The roar of the traffic beside him began to dwindle, as did he.

When he woke, all was eerily quiet. He shot up.

Snow. Trees. Ivy.

He was not in his den. He was outside in the open.

'Oh no,' he gasped.

Dreamer was accustomed to dreams - but hallucinations?

He set about dashing through the trees in search of his friends. Fear gave him an unnatural boost of energy, and before he knew it, he had topped the Hill. By the edge of the pond in Bubblelump Swamp, he found Badger and Holly.

They were sitting side by side, trying to keep each other warm, when the fox hurried to them, shaking.

'Are you okay?' asked Badger, leaning forward.

Dreamer was still chasing his breath when he said:

'We need to find Arznel!'

'Excuse me?' said Badger. 'What on earth brought all this up again?'

'He came to me again,' the fox replied. 'In a dream. Or some kind of dream. He showed me what will happen to Lough Ine if we don't do something about the humans.'

Badger and Holly both recoiled and stared fixedly at the fox.

'What!' shrilled a tiny voice. Frog leapt from the pond and landed by Dreamer's feet. 'What's going to happen to Lough Ine?' he cried, staring up at

Dreamer with an anxious little face.

Dreamer couldn't find it in himself to answer.

'Is it true?' enquired Kingfisher, fluttering down from the scraggy old pine and landing on the snow –caked ground. 'You saw Arznel again? Wait, who's Arznel?'

'We have to find him,' Dreamer persisted, as if ignoring Kingfisher. 'We have no choice. The humans are destroying the world, and if we let them, they'll turn to Lough Ine and do the same.'

Dreamer could see the stupefied expressions on the faces of his friends, but this did not stop his spiel.

'If we find Arznel and release him, he'll help us fight back! Lough Ine will be saved. The whole world will be saved!'

'Stop. Right. There,' Badger growled, raising one paw and covering his face with the other. 'This is pure dribble. Dreamer, what did I tell you before? I told you to forget this whole business of war, and tigers, and humans and whatnot. I told you to move on and think happy thoughts. What in the blazes made you start dreaming again? Have you been worrying about this the whole time?'

Dreamer shook his head.

'Not the whole time,' he admitted. '…not since… I met Fuchsia…but today, Arznel *came* to *me*! It must be a sign. If we continue to do nothing, nothing will change!'

'Oh for the love of,' Badger rolled his eyes. Holly licked his ear in a bid to calm him. 'Nothing needs to change, Dreamer!' he shouted. 'Since we got here, nearly four seasons ago, I haven't seen a single human!'

'But they've seen us,' Dreamer shot back. 'They're here all the time, they know all about us; how could you be so naïve in thinking they don't? The litter, the carvings, the snares on Hilltop Warren!'

'Well if that's the worst they can do, it's a small price to pay,' said Badger dully.

'It is not the worst they can do,' Dreamer yelled. 'Don't you agree the humans are terrorizing us? They killed our parents. And I've seen them destroy our homes to make way for their own.'

'That. Does not. Happen. HERE!!' Badger shouted, pointing a claw at the ground. Holly came between Dreamer and Badger, trying to keep them apart.

'Boys, that's enough,' she asserted. 'Winter's a hard enough time without being narky at each other.'

Dreamer's eyes drilled through Holly and hardened on Badger.

'Lough Ine is a sanctuary,' he said coolly. 'Because the humans – *made* – it a sanctuary! Who's to say they won't change their minds! All this wood, all this building space! It's a bigger haven for them than it is for us!'

Badger's eyes widened and his chest puffed outwards.

'Honey, no!' cried Holly, restraining him.

From the brambles on the rim of the Pond, Hare eaves-dropped. He crouched, flattening his ears against his back, listening only to Dreamer.

'Hmmm,' he muttered. 'Looks like all that practice I've been doing wasn't a waste of time after all.'

Discreetly, Hare slipped off, back to Hilltop Warren.

'No, no, no,' Badger yelled. 'I'm not having this discussion again! There isn't going to be a war, Dreamer, and if there is, we're not taking part. This is where we belong, at home in the safety of our fields and our forest. If the humans had any intentions of destroying it, we'd know. You are not going to drag me off on some foolish, pointless journey, to find a tiger who may not even exist!'

'Then why does he come to me?!' Dreamer cried, his voice faltering out of tune. 'Why can't I put him out of my mind? How come he shows me things I've never seen for real? How can that not be a sign?'

Badger recoiled. It sounded like Dreamer was genuinely pleading for an answer.

The fox's eyes were damp and doleful.

'I don't think I'll ever find peace of mind until I find-that-tiger!'

Badger bit his lip.

'Think, dream and fantasize all you want,' he said in a subdued tone. 'But don't bother me with it. I have everything I ever wanted right here, a good home, a good mate; nothing but peace and normality. I won't have you disturb it for the sake of a blind idea. And like I said, if there is a war, I will not fight. Good day. Come on, Holly.'

The two badgers shuffled off into the gloom of the forest. Holly looked back at Dreamer with a sympathetic smile before disappearing.

Angrily, Dreamer shouted after them,

'You won't have a peaceful life when the humans get here!'

Dreamer looked down at Frog and Kingfisher, who were standing still in the snow, stiff from both cold and dismay.

'I'm sorry you had to see that,' he said.

There was silence for a bit, while Frog searched for his voice.

'Oh it's fine, it's fine,' he said at last. 'It takes more than a little tiff to scare me,' and under his breath he added, 'or a little less.' Anyway, I better go and leave you be.'

Frog did a back-flip into the Pond.

Splash.

Kingfisher was left to confront Dreamer alone.

'Don't worry about Badger,' she said, lamely. 'He's just grumpy coz it's so cold and he hasn't had his dinner yet. Give him time.'

Dreamer nodded.

'Thanks, Kingfisher,' he said, dully, watching the little bird disappear into the treetops in a flash of blue and orange.

Alone, and lost in a fog of anxiety and confusion, Dreamer wandered miserably home.

Meanwhile, up on the ledge of the Hill, another fox stood, watching his former pupil fade from sight.

Old Darig's once fine chestnut coat was now flecked with silver and grey. The wise fox was now truly old and frail.

'Such a shame,' he muttered to himself. 'That young fox is capable of so much more. He could have been a great hunter, a great father. But no. He would rather spend his time gallivanting with his natural enemies. How very disappointing.'

Making his way upwards through the snow and evergreen shrubbery, Old Darig reached the Lough Ine Panorama.

He closed his eyes and waited for the frozen wind to hit him like a wall. Sifting the scents, deep into his chest, Old Darig opened his eyes.

'Without a doubt,' he muttered. 'Danger is coming. But what kind, and how soon, remains to be known.'

More than a Feeling

There was no let up to the skinning cold. One day blended into another without any change in temperature. This interminable stark weather was beginning to take its toll. For those not hibernating, Lough Ine had become a scene of business; creatures scurrying around frantically, searching for and stocking up on, anything they deemed vital for survival.

In Hilltop Warren, the rabbits had been debating survival methods. It was suggested that a party of rabbits be sent out of Lough Ine to find and raid gardens for carrots and lettuce. Captain Spruce dismissed this idea immediately. He said that not only would this mission be insanely dangerous, but also, it was more than likely the wrong season for growing vegetables, thus the journey would be wasted. The rabbits would simply have to continue scrounging for grass amid the icy desert.

The birds of Lough Ine were experiencing further troubles. Flapjack the pheasant had to be extra vigilant while roaming the ground for worms and other insects, as he was in constant danger of being ambushed by some starving predator. And as the forest floor was so hard from ice, his beak was often not powerful enough to penetrate the surface, which seemed to give the worms below a fine protective shield. But to add to the despair of the poor cinnamon coloured bird, it was *shooting season*. He was reluctant to venture too far out into the fields and marshes, for the threat of hunters was now constant.

Since November, Flapjack had been spotting them out in the pastureland, while foraging some two miles from Lough Ine. Of all the birds these men enjoyed shooting; Flapjack knew that pheasants were most popular, so he decided to keep his head down. Literally.

At the edge of the forest, where Knockomagh Wood met Hilltop Warren, Dreamer was on his way up the hill. A fat little robin perched on the path ahead of him, poking through the snow and rolling bits over, before flitting off once it saw him coming. Under a snow wreathed bramble bush, a family of wrens huddled together, trying to summon some warmth. Dreamer stopped and watched as a little blue tit clung to the side of a beech tree, peeling off strips of bark to reveal some tasty grubs. Once he reached the outskirts of the Warren, the fox noticed Hare was skulking around over on the eastern side of the hill. He seemed to be immersed in some kind of important business; running to and from the trees, sometimes stopping and pausing.

Agog, Dreamer edged his way over to Hare in the distance. On reaching him, Dreamer was surprised to find that his friend was holding a long, curved yew branch in his paw, with a long strand of braided flax binding both ends. Slung on his back were a couple of old primrose leaves, rolled up into a cone shape so as to hold dozens of perfectly straight, thinly peeled sticks; duck feathers fixed on the backs of them. This odd little apparatus was strapped to Hare's back with several rushes. Once Hare spotted Dreamer approaching, he turned and faced him, saluting like a soldier. The secret was out.

'Hare,' Dreamer gasped. 'What in the name of snowflakes have you done to yourself? What- what is all this? What is that thing you're holding? And that thing on your back?'

Hare raised his yew branch and twirled it in his paw skillfully.

'This thing,' he began. 'Is my 'bow'. And on my back, are my 'arrows'. And over there, is my 'bull's-eye'.'

Dreamer glanced over to the trees where an old sawed stump lay facing out, with its countless rings showing. These indeed acted, as Hare himself put it, as a perfect bulls-eye.

'What's going on?' he asked, now fully engrossed in Hare's project.

Hare paused and looked up at the white, rolling sky.

'Captain Spruce once told me an interesting story,' he explained. 'Interesting but sad. He said how, a long time ago, before the time of the gun, humans used to hunt animals with this type of weapon. Even though it's not as deadly as the gun, it still did a lot of damage. Did you know that 'bears' used to live in Lough Ine? And wolves? And wild boar!'

'Go on,' said Dreamer impatiently.

'Well,' said Hare. 'That story reminded me of the one *you* told. You know, about your dreams! You described how the animals were using the same kind of weapon, only *against* the humans.'

'I remember that,' said Dreamer.

'Well,' said Hare. 'Believe it or not, your dreams inspired me to take up 'archery'. I got some of the rabbits to help me make the bow stave. Frickin' nightmare, that was. We nearly stripped Knockomagh Wood bare looking for the right wood. Pine is too stringy, birch is too hard. Oak branch snapped and hit me in the family conkers. Voice sounded like a wren-chick for days…As it turns out, yew is the best choice.

Hah! The rabbits think I'm a bit mad, but I don't mind.'

'You can't blame them,' said Dreamer, still adjusting.

'I used to practice a lot whenever I wasn't around you or Badger', Hare went on. 'I didn't want Badger knowing, in case he'd copy me and get better at it. And I didn't let you know either, in case you'd tell him! But it was worth the time I spent alone. I think I'm finally getting good.'

Hare whipped an arrow from his quiver and fixed it to his bowstring. (A hare's eyes are on the sides of its head, so Hare had to turn his face almost away from the target to aim.) He drew it back to breaking point, narrowed his eye, and let fly!

The sleek missile cut through the air as fast as light and struck the tree stump hard, sticking in cozily among a bunch of other arrows.

Dreamer was aghast.

'What d'ya think?' Hare laughed. 'I started out with close range and only started on long range the other day. How many other animals do you reckon are doing this right now?!'

Dreamer gasped, utterly dumbfounded.

'I've never seen anything like this before in my life. Except in my dreams, of course.'

Hare smiled. 'And check this out,' he said, taking an arrow from his quiver and showing it to Dreamer up close. It was tipped with something pearl white and frightfully sharp.

'What is that?' gasped the fox.

'Shark tooth,' said Hare. 'One on the end of each arrow… Skip wasn't lying when he told you about all those sea creatures coming into the Lake. One shark skull was all it took to supply me. I found it floating around on the shore one morning and the idea just hit me. Painful work, though. Imagine having three thousand teeth in your mouth!'

Dreamer shook his head. It wasn't yet March, but it seemed Hare had already gone mad.

After a brief silence.

'To be honest with you,' said Hare in a more subdued tone. 'I'm not doing this for fun.'

Dreamer's eyes widened with anticipation. He did not need to ask the inevitable question, for Hare understood well enough what the look in his friend's eyes meant.

'I'm training for war,' said Hare at last. 'You know, just in case your dreams are trying to tell us to.'

Dreamer beamed with joy.

'You believe me?'

Hare nodded.

'Like I said, just in case.'

'But – but,' Dreamer stammered, half smiling as he spoke. 'Weren't you the one who tried calming me down the other day? Weren't you the one who tried convincing me that I was being irrational?'

'Living in denial,' Hare confessed. 'That's all I was doing.' With that, he quickly loaded his bow and loosed another arrow at the tree stump. It found its mark with a loud SMACK, shattering some of the other shafts.

'Impressive,' Dreamer commented, nodding his head slowly. He was delighted he had someone on his side. But then it became apparent war was not the only thing on Hare's mind.

He sighed; 'Not impressive enough, unfortunately.'

'What do you mean by that?' Dreamer asked.

Hare unhooked his bowstring and tossed it aside.

'Look over there,' he sighed, pointing over at the Warren while hanging his head.

'I don't see anything,' said Dreamer.

Indeed the Warren was blanketed by a dense white haze.

'Okay,' Hare groaned. 'Follow me and I'll show you.'

Hare led Dreamer through a gap in the hedge, into the Warren, where they had a clear view of the snowy field.

'Here we are,' Hare panted, halting at a hawthorn tree and gazing out into the field.

'Can you see her?'

211

'See who?' asked Dreamer.

'Just look,' said Hare.

Out in the middle of the field, Dreamer saw a beautiful young doe. Brown was her colour, save for her white belly, under parts and socks. She sat in the snow, pawing at the ground with a look of frustration on her sweet face.

'Her name is *Lyla,*' said Hare. 'Daughter of Captain Spruce.'

Dreamer was puzzled. 'She's your mate?'

'Was,' said Hare. 'But she decided to end us, because we were being ridiculed for our differences.'

'Before you go any further,' Dreamer interjected. 'She's a rabbit. You're a hare...'

Hare's ears stiffened. 'So?'

'Well,' said Dreamer pointedly. 'It's not exactly normal.'

Hare snorted. 'Isn't it obvious to you that nothing we've ever done is normal? We were never brought up normal! We never had the chance.

Personally, I've come to like it that way; I like standing out!'

Hare threw another glance over at the young rabbit in the field, who was by herself outside the circle of other rabbits.

'I've tried everything to win her back. I even saved her life, you know. Some nasty half-eared fox was stalking her, so I darted past and got him to chase me instead of her. But she's adamant we can't be.'

'Well, okay,' said Dreamer. 'I know the feeling. But you can't blame her for avoiding you. I mean, a Hare with a bow and arrow is rather intimidating. You might be scaring her off.'

'Really?' said Hare. 'I thought it would impress her.'

'You may be trying too hard,' said Dreamer. 'Anyway, if you want advice on females, stay away from me!'

'Oh,' said Hare. 'You're still having trouble?'

Dreamer nodded.

'It's been so long,' said Hare. 'What's taking you to pluck up and try courting that vixen?'

'I can't,' Dreamer sighed.

'Why not?' Hare asked.

'Because,' Dreamer explained. 'That nasty half eared fox that chased you - is her mate.'

'Ouch,' said Hare.

'I know,' said Dreamer.

The two friends watched as the little doe wandered further into the distance, all the time scratching the ground.

'You know,' said Dreamer cryptically. 'There is one thing you could do.'
'What's that?' asked Hare anxiously.

'Well,' Dreamer suggested. 'There is an awful food shortage up here. And playing with your bulls- eye doesn't seem to be helping the situation.'

'And?' said Hare impatiently.

'I think you should go over there and give Lyla a helping paw.'
Hare paused. His eyes warmed. 'Do you think she'd like that?'

'How could she not?' said Dreamer. 'Digging through that snow is hard work. Go on. Help her find some grass. That ought to break the ice!' he added drily.

Hare smiled nervously and began a long awkward journey over to where the pretty doe sat.

Indifferent, Dreamer turned and ventured back into the woods, unsure of where to go.

Again his mind was preyed on by a number of troubles. He knew he had to find the fabled tiger, Arznel, but when, where and how? And who would join him on this journey? He and Badger had been avoiding each other for days. The pair had been inseparable since the morning they met, but the prophecy of war had deeply divided them, for both were very different in their outlook.

Badger's only ambition was to settle down with Holly and start a family. But Dreamer, on the other hand, was eager to set out on an adventure, leaving Lough Ine and everything behind.

The fox had now lost two animals whom he had once regarded highly, the first of course being Old Darig.

As Dreamer came into to a clearing in the forest and looked skyward, he could have sworn he saw two dark clouds merging together to form a sinister skull. Shuddering, he tried to ignore it.

Precious Moments

Badger and Holly lay together under a heatless sunset. The final flicker of light seemed to wink at them from behind the white mountains, leaving strips of pink and yellow across the evening sky.

The two badgers were sheltering from the cold under a clump of brambles, using each others' bodies to generate warmth. Their thick grey coats protected them from the otherwise painful thorns.

It was coming up to hunting time and the couple had decided to rest out in the open during dusk before setting out at nightfall.

'It looks so warm over there,' Holly yawned, watching the sun- burnished mountains.

'I know,' said Badger. 'This cold spell could go on for another few moons. But we'll be okay. Food is rare, but it's not gone. We always manage to pull through. And we have our sett. You can always trust that to be warm. Surviving this winter won't be as difficult as everyone's saying.'

Holly smiled.

'And our cubs are due in spring,' she said joyfully. 'I simply can't wait for that season to come around.'

'I know, neither can I,' said Badger, sitting up.

The thought of being a father always excited him.

'How many younglings do you think we'll have?' he asked.

'Oh, it's hard to say,' giggled Holly. 'Could be anywhere from one to five.'

'Well,' Badger mused. 'It doesn't matter about the number. We'll make brilliant parents. We'll take care of the little terrors for a good two or three months; feed them, entertain them, love them and then teach them how to survive on their own... yes, and we'll watch them grow... and they'll raise their own families... and by then we'll be old and... and grey.'

Holly laughed.

'Don't get carried away. I don't even want to think about letting my babies go before I've even had them!'

'Sorry,' Badger blushed.

'Anyway,' said Holly. 'We have to think of names for them.'

'We could name them after their father!' Badger beamed, instantly regretting this suggestion. 'Oh, right...' he added.

Holly smiled sympathetically.

'I know,' she said softly. It must be awkward not having a proper name. But why is that, Badger? Why did you never give yourself a name? Or your friends, they could have given you one. Have you ever thought about that?'

Badger nodded.

'I used to think about it,' he sighed. 'I guess I'm just used to being called 'Badger."

'But would you like a name?' asked Holly. 'Because I could think of one for you.'

Badger glanced at the sunset.

'There was a time when I didn't think I'd need a name,' he confessed. 'The first few seasons of my life were spent alone, so I had no one to address me. Then I met my friends. Ever since then, I've haven't had a lot of time to think of names. I've been too sidetracked. But yes, maybe it's about time I did go by a proper title.'

'Okay then,' said Holly happily. 'I'd be delighted to think of a name for you.'

'Thank you,' said Badger, looking his mate in the eyes.

'And your friends,' Holly added. 'Hare, and Frog, and Kingfisher; they need names too. I find it silly that after all this time we're still calling them by *what* they are, instead of *who* they should be.'

'You're absolutely right,' said Badger nodding. 'This is one matter we've neglected for too long.'

'Then it's settled,' said Holly. 'You all get names. Just like Dreamer did. When was the last time you had to call him Fox?'

Badger suddenly went sullen.

'Yes,' he muttered. 'Dreamer...'

'Oh, I'm sorry,' Holly exclaimed. 'I didn't mean to bring that up again. I know you two haven't been seeing eye to eye lately.'

'No, it's fine, Holly,' said Badger. 'I've been meaning to talk to him for a while now. I just don't know what to say that'll make him snap out of this phase he's going through. Again.'

Holly smiled sincerely.

'I'm sure he'll come around eventually,' she said. 'I mean, he can't keep worrying about nothing forever.'

'He'd better wake up soon,' Badger grunted. 'Because it annoys me. It really annoys me that Dreamer and I went to so much trouble finding Lough Ine and settling down, and already, he wants to leave! On some silly journey to find a fictional tiger so we can rebel against the humans. How ridiculous is that! He's completely deluded!'

'Now, now, he's still your best friend,' Holly hushed. 'Even if he is slightly deluded.'

'But it's not just that,' Badger went on. 'But why would *we* want to fight? Forget the other animals of the world; let's just focus on Lough Ine. What business do we have with the humans? This is a nature sanctuary, protected *by* humans *from* humans. Men can't cut down our trees, or pollute our water, or hunt us. We're safe. This is our little paradise. We should be happy. I don't want to be dragged away from all this without a reason.'

'You won't be,' said Holly reassuringly. 'Because there is no reason. We are safe.'

There the conversation ended.

All traces of sunlight were gone and hunting time had arrived. Together, the badgers emerged from the brambles and shuffled off into the woods.

At early dawn, down in the Swamp, Kingfisher and Frog had to say a temporary goodbye. For frogs, winter is an important time because it's mating season. Huge numbers of frogs gather en masse in ponds and bogs to mate, before laying their spawn the following spring. But this did not happen in Bubblelump Swamp. For some reason, there weren't that many frogs around. Most were already hibernating. Many ponds were frozen over, making the mating process difficult. And because Frog did not have a mate, he decided to do the next best thing - hibernate. He believed a long winter's sleep was well overdue.

'Enjoy the rest of your winter,' he said as he burrowed into the rushes and stuck his head out for a final look at his friend. 'I hope you find it easier than the rest of us.'

Kingfisher was perched on one of the low, overhanging pine branches.

'Are you sure you want to go to sleep now?' she asked. 'I mean, you haven't even said goodbye to the others.'

Frog sighed.

'I searched for Dreamer and Hare for as long as I could,' he said. 'But I didn't want to stray too far from the pond incase I'd get lost and freeze into a statue.'

Kingfisher giggled.

'How bad? At least then you wouldn't leave... What about Badger and Holly?'

'They know,' said Frog. 'I met them last night and I told them I was planning on hibernating soon. If I go missing, they'll know where I am.'

Kingfisher nodded.

Before striking off, Frog added:

'You will say goodbye to the others for me, won't you?'

'Of course I will,' Kingfisher promised. 'After I come back.'

'After you come back?' Frog was all concern. 'Why, where are you going?'

'Oh, just fishing,' said Kingfisher. 'Somewhere outside Lough Ine.'

'Why outside Lough Ine?' asked Frog. 'What's wrong with here?'

'Well it's a little hard,' Kingfisher explained. 'Nearly all of the ponds are frozen and the Lake is being hogged by the otters and herons. I thought I'd have more luck out in the country, you know, in the streams.'

'Hmmm, the streams,' said Frog. 'That's a good idea. At least you know running water can't freeze. I'm sure you'll find plenty ticklebacks.'

Kingfisher chuckled. 'There called 'sticklebacks'.'

'Oh, whatever,' Frog blushed. 'Anyway, I'm afraid I have nothing else to say, apart from 'good luck,' of course.'

'You too,' said Kingfisher earnestly, flapping her wings. 'I'll see you in spring.'

With that the little blue and orange bird fluttered off up into the white gloom, leaving Frog below at the pond by himself. Looking around at the Swamp for the last time, he made his way out onto the slippery sheet of ice, faltering and skating every now and then until he found a small hole. With a hop, a skip and a jump, Frog plopped into the water and swam for the bottom. There he set about burying himself in mud, where he believed he would be staying for a whole month or two.

Little did he know, he was only to remain there for a few hours, before duty would call him to the surface.

Into the Blizzard

And then it happened.

Dreamer was strolling through the woods on the same morning, on a full belly. He had been chasing a mouse earlier and had followed it all the way back to its home in the stream bank where he devoured the whole family. But don't be quick to judge. It wasn't like Dreamer to take lives, nor was it like him to take a life and not feel guilty about it. In the midst of the winter turmoil, animals were sure to starve - therefore Dreamer justified his actions by believing it was either him or the mice.

On the way back to his den, he was met by Hare, who was sitting sulkily on a beech stump with his ears down over his face.

'You're the image of happiness,' said Dreamer wryly as he approached. 'What happened after I left you with Lyla yesterday?'

Hare groaned;

'Once she saw me coming, she ran off.'

'No,' said Dreamer sympathetically.

'Mmm hmm,' Hare sighed. 'Maybe you're right. Maybe it's wrong for a rabbit and a hare to be together. Oh, and I acted like such a nutcase to get her back!'

Dreamer cocked an eyebrow; 'Acted?'

But before another word could be said, there came a clattering noise from above. Dreamer and Hare craned their necks to see Kingfisher tumbling down through the icy branches of the canopy, crashing into branches and breaking twigs during her chaotic landing. She appeared to be in a tremendous panic.

'Run!' she screamed, as she blindly hit the ground with a thump and buried herself in snow. Only a bird shaped hole was left.

'Kingfisher!' Dreamer gasped as he pawed through the snow in search of his feathered friend.

'What in the name of frozen whiskers is wrong with you?' cried Hare with a frown, as Dreamer rolled Kingfisher's shaking little body from the snow. She lay there on her back, coughing and wheezing, too overcome with fatigue and trepidation to speak.

'What's all this about?' asked Badger as he came forth from the trees. Holly's unborn cubs had a bottomless appetite. The to-be father was busy scrounging food for his mate again.

For a brief moment, Dreamer and Badger glared at each other coldly, before all eyes fell upon Kingfisher.

She had almost broken free from her state of terror, and was now sitting upright, still trembling, either from the cold, or from what she had seen. Her friends hovered above her, all staring down, anxiously awaiting the urgent report.

'Well, what is it?' Hare was impatient.

Kingfisher held her breath and gazed up at all of the bewildered faces around her.

'We're under attack!' she announced.

Everybody gasped at once.

'Attack?' Badger exclaimed. 'How? By what?'

'A hunting party,' said Kingfisher. 'A *human* hunting party. I saw them while I was out fishing. They're coming our way!'

Badger looked abashed. He turned and slumped to the ground, numb, stiff and silent.   , .

'Where are they?' asked Dreamer. 'How far away?'

'Um, um, quite far still,' said Kingfisher. 'But they'll be here soon, I know it!'

Badger stood up and faced the little bird.

'That's preposterous,' he said angrily. 'If they're so far away, then how do you know they're coming here? They'll probably turn around before they're even anywhere near Lough Ine.'

'Nah ah,' said Kingfisher dismissively. 'They're coming here, I know it, I heard one of the dogs say it.'

Dreamer raised an eyebrow. 'They have dogs with them?'

'Yes,' said Kingfisher, nodding furiously. 'Three big, brown dogs, with red collars.'

Dreamer paused as his mind spun back to that awful night when his whole family were butchered by three such dogs. Could these three that Kingfisher spoke of possibly be the same?

'What did the dog say?' asked Dreamer, interrogating her.

'Well,' said Kingfisher in a quivering voice. 'When the hunters were finished hunting, I saw them all walking across the field together, towards the road. I was watching from the stream. The dogs were running ahead of them. They sounded really excited. One of them was very loud. He said something like "Yay, we're going to the woods!"

That's when I flew back here, so I could tell you.'

'The woods,' Dreamer gasped. '... There aren't that many other wooded areas outside Lough Ine... they *must* be coming here!'

All hearts were set racing.

'Oh, it was awful,' Kingfisher continued. 'Some of the men were carrying dead birds.'

Badger slapped the ground with his paw, sending a spray of snow through the air.

'No,' he growled. 'I refuse to believe this. Lough Ine is a nature reserve. Humans aren't allowed to hunt here.'

'Well humans have a habit of bending their own rules!' Hare snapped.

All eyes turned to him.

'That's right,' Hare continued. 'Humans will often do what they want, whether it's right or wrong! From what I hear, it's forbidden to shoot hares! Well that Farmer spared my mother no mercy! And let's not forget "badger baiting," eh! We all know that's not allowed. And even if it were, I don't see how any human could be sick enough to try it. But look at *your* family, Badger. Did those men care about their so called 'laws' when they tethered your mother to a post and let her be mauled to death by those hounds? I think not. Believe me, these men will hunt whenever and wherever they want!'

Badger frowned and went sullen again.

'How much time do we have?' asked Dreamer.

Kingfisher seemed lost for words.

'I -I don't know,' she sobbed. 'They seemed quite far away when I saw them. And they could be stopping to hunt in the fields along the way. Maybe an hour. Or less. Before we hide, we should warn everybody.'

'Oh hoho no,' Dreamer growled as he sped to the edge of the wood and gazed out at the distant white hills. 'No hiding. Not this time. We've been doing that for far too long.'

'What are you planning on doing?' asked Hare as he, Badger and Kingfisher followed him to the verge.

'I'm going to stop them,' said Dreamer concisely. 'I'll make sure those men don't set foot in our home.'

'Don't be a fool, Dreamer,' said Badger. 'You don't stand a chance against those men. Humans are too strong and advanced for us. I'm sorry, but we're powerless to stop them. We always have been.'

'We always have been, yes,' Dreamer echoed, turning back. 'But we don't always have to be. We can change that today. Or at least I can. I'm not asking you to follow me. In fact, I'd prefer if you didn't.' Then turning away again, he said: 'I'd be better off alone on this mission.'

'How exactly are you going to 'stop' these men?' asked Badger with a touch of sarcasm.

'I'll do whatever I can,' said Dreamer sternly. 'I don't care if I lose every drop of blood in my body, I'll find some way of stalling them! They're not going to see Lough Ine today.'

'Oh for the love of...' Badger groaned. 'Listen Dreamer, you are seriously starting to stroke my fur the wrong way! What you want to do can't be done!'

Badger then began to drone on in the most defeatist tone. 'Face it; we're always going to live in the shadow of the humans. We're always going to be second best to them. Wherever they came from, they own the world now, and we're just tenants! Look, they haven't wiped us out yet, so let's just do our best to survive before they do.'

'NO!' Dreamer roared, in a blind temper. 'I'm sick of it! I'm sick of living in fear! The only reason we haven't fought back is because we're so convinced we can't. We don't know any different! Well not me. I'll try stopping them nonetheless.'

'Please,' said Badger calmly. 'Enough time has been wasted. We'd be much safer underground. Let's just go to our homes now and wait for this ordeal to blow over.'

Dreamer stubbornly made his way down the slope.

'You're right,' he said smartly. 'Enough time has been wasted. If I am to do anything, I have to do it now.'

With that, Dreamer broke into a gallop across the field.

Badger snarled.

'Didn't you hear what I said?' he shouted. 'We'd be safer underground! The hunters won't find us there!'

Dreamer paused and turned back for a final few words before his departure. 'The dogs would find us!' he cried.

On saying this, the fox disappeared into the white gauze of mist, leaving his friends behind to feel both guilty and insecure.

'He's right,' Hare sighed. 'There's no escape from these hunters if they come.'

'Hmph,' Badger grunted as he trudged off back into the woods. Kingfisher flapped her wings and took to the air.

'Where are you going?' asked Hare.

Kingfisher replied from above: 'I'm going to wake Frog!'

Dreamer felt like a fish out of water. Through the shimmering white fields and fenland he ran, leaving behind light paw prints. He ran fast and reckless, puffing and panting, trying to ignore how weary he had already become. It was not until he reached a certain hedgerow that he stopped and looked back. He was no longer in the vicinity of Lough Ine. This was the furthest away from home he had strayed since he was a young cub on a journey. But now Dreamer was on a new journey; not to find his home this time, but to save it.

Loneliness and fear did not strike him until Lough Ine was out of sight. He was alone in the white wilderness, with no cosy forest to protect him from the sub zero wind that blew strongly through him. There was nothing but fields upon fields, all bordered by hedgerows as far as he could see, completely blanketed by snow.

Dreamer was greatly daunted as he stopped up to gaze out upon this vast expanse of white. Drawing on every ounce of strength and courage, he marched purposefully on through the intensifying blizzard. Snow was now whirling down. Icicles and snowflakes clung to his fur and whiskers, setting him back over and over as he slogged painfully down one mound and up another. On and on, through the lonely countryside, the fox went, stumbling and staggering under the pressure of the bitter cold. The sharp wind buffeted him again and again, dogging his steps and blurring his vision. But despite all this, he never failed to make progress.

The air and the blizzard had of course made him feel numb and stiff, but a great sense of adventure and exultation had swelled up inside him, and this helped him feel warm. He now had a real purpose - to save his home and his friends. It is never easy for a fox to be respected by other animals, as he is always seen as a ruthless predator. Yet the animals of Lough Ine had accepted Dreamer as their trustworthy friend and ally, and he was ready to repay them. He was not willing to let them suffer under the boots of their greatest enemy. Somehow, he had to hinder these barbaric hunters from reaching their goal.

Time passed, but Dreamer was not sure how much. A half hour perhaps, or more. It seemed like quite a while since he set out, and now he was afraid he didn't have long. He couldn't help feeling as though he were too late, that perhaps the hunters had already reached his home.

The fox could feel his spirit beginning to stagger under the combined assault of cold, exhaustion and thirst. The wind whipped through his coat, ruffling his fur and penetrating his skin. Every inch of him ached. Before venturing much further, he knew he was in dire need of water. With a small stroke of luck, Dreamer came upon a little rivulet, trickling by under a row of snow wreathed fuchsia bushes. After tottering over to the bank, Dreamer collapsed in the snow and tried to regain his breath before taking a drink.

It was when he lost all feeling in his body that his mind started to wander. Great waves of nostalgia swept over him as he reminisced on the bright, funfilled days of the summer. Playing catch and battle tag in the woods with his friends, rolling around and lazing in the dry summer grass of Hilltop Warren, finding shapes in the clouds of the cerulean blue sky, chasing and identifying insects, sniffing the newly blossomed bluebells and primroses - these were just some of the things he vividly remembered.

How long ago it all seemed now.

He then remembered his long busy day out on the Lake with Pierce and Skip. How he wished he could relive that day. In retrospect, being attacked by seagulls was a lot more fun than the situation he was currently facing.

'I'm sorry,' he whispered, with beads of tears rolling down his face. 'I can't go any further than this. I've failed you all.'

More time passed. Climbing shakily to his feet, Dreamer peered into the stream, intending to lap up a few cold mouthfuls. But to his astonishment, he noticed *two* reflections in the water. Looking across the stream, he saw

Kingfisher perched on one of the fuchsia branches.

'No way,' he breathed.

Kingfisher giggled.

'You're a mess. It's a good thing we found you in time.'

Dreamer gasped; 'We?'

Turning around, he was pleasantly surprised to see Hare bouncing excitedly towards the stream bank, bow in paw, and quiver full of arrows slung on his back.

'Worn out already?' he jeered. "I could have travelled twice this distance, running backwards!'

Dreamer was gobsmacked.

'Oh, you'd make great fun for those dogs,' Hare went on playfully. 'Leaving all those tracks behind for them to follow. Good thing we found them first. Hah! And then we find you sheltering under a tree with what - one leaf left on it?'

Dreamer was finally able to laugh.

Frog poked his head out of Hare's quiver.

'Speaking of shelter,' he asked. 'Do you think you could maybe find some? I didn't haul myself out of hibernation so I could wander out here and catch my death.'

Dreamer was still caught between the spasms of relief and despair. 'I told you not to follow me,' he said.

'Oh yes,' said Hare as he leaned over the stream bank and began slurping up water loudly like a parched horse. 'And let you wander out here by yourself to screw everything up!' Finishing his drink, Hare turned to Dreamer and concluded: 'A word of advice, Dreamer – if your friends ever try to help you – let them.'

At that very moment, to give Dreamer a further morale boost, Badger came hobbling up the field, over cushions of snow. Dreamer couldn't help smiling at his arrival.

'Not a word,' said Badger with a smirk as he slumped down beside the bewildered fox.

Dreamer gave a knowing nod. The presence of his friends had invigorated him with a new hope and a new energy. Despite the nagging fear of the journey ahead, he couldn't stop himself from feeling giddy with happiness.

'The hunters are close,' said Kingfisher sternly. It was obvious she had been practicing her 'grown up' voice along the way. 'I saw them again; they're in one of these fields. But not for long. They'll be headed for the road soon.'

'Road?' said Dreamer.

'Yeah,' said Kingfisher. 'Just one, narrow straight little road with no bends. The hunters have parked two of their wheelie- beetles there.'

Dreamer paused and thought for a moment.

'I have an idea,' he announced.

The Diversion

Along the snowy ground, went three sets of paws, and the shadow of a little bird circling them all the while. Frog sat astride Badger's head, wrapping himself up in his white stripe for warmth. Together, the five companions braved the open countryside.

The cold no longer bothered them, for they were too happy in the company of one another.

Field by field, stream by stream, fence by fence, mound by mound, they progressed further out into the unknown. Dreamer had been out here only once before with his two original companions, Badger and Hare, but he could scarcely recognize it now. And for the two little ones, Frog and Kingfisher, being so far away from home for so long was an entirely new experience, which daunted and frightened them both. But with so much at stake, and with such an important task to carry out, they were made route out all the courage and charisma in their beings.

Very soon, the time came for them to test just how reliable Dreamer's plan was.

'There they are!' shrieked Kingfisher as she swooped down from the air, looping around her friends' heads. 'They're just ahead of us, in the next field!'

The five companions hurried to the edge of the field and hunkered down behind a gorse covered ditch. Kingfisher flitted into the branches above, while below, Dreamer, Badger, Hare and Frog huddled together in the shade, trying to conceal themselves. Only their frozen breath could be seen outside the bushes, rising in white puffs. Then began a long, eerie silence.

The animals waited nervously for their enemies to pass by.

'Do you see them?' whispered Hare to Kingfisher above.

Kingfisher peered tentatively through the twigs and spines. Outside, all she could see was an eerie white haze.

'Not yet,' she whispered. 'But they're coming. I know I saw them.'

'How many?' Dreamer hissed.

'I don't know,' replied Kingfisher. 'But it looked like a whole bunch. And yeah, three dogs.'

The uncomfortable silence drifted on. The nervous tension among the friends grew.

'Oh, where are they?' Hare whined. 'I don't know whose tail I'm sitting on.'
'Ssshh,' Kingfisher hushed. 'Do you hear that?'

The friends listened intently from the bushes.

In the distance, they could hear a babble of voices; loud, rough, *human* voices approaching slowly, with heavy crunching footsteps. Slowly and stealthily, Dreamer lifted his head to chance a peek over the ditch.

He could make out nothing at first, but the voices and footfall were all too clear.

Then, out of the white haze, the hunters came. Three, four, 'five' of them, some tall, some small, all with hats, jackets and wellingtons. Each toted a gun of some description. A belt of ammunition was tied around the waist of each man, and two of them were holding green satchels, in which to keep whatever game they had shot.

As they marched casually through the field, passed the ditch where Dreamer and his friends were hiding, the three monstrous hounds sniffed excitedly around the ground behind them.

Dreamer watched them come closer; his body rigid with fear. Gulping, he sank back down into the bushes with his companions, where Kingfisher joined them. Every mouth was dry. Every heart was racing. The hounds were right on the other side of the ditch. The companions could hear them sniffing, scratching and slobbering.

Suddenly, the gorse bush above shook violently as the head of one hound came crashing in! He hovered there for a moment, panting and drooling, looking clumsily about him. He seemed unaware that a small group of animals were huddled just beneath his chin; only a thin layer of branches and twigs keeping them hidden from his view. The hound was breathless from running all day, so he focused on panting with his mouth, rather than sniffing with his nose. Had he taken but one whiff, he would have instantly caught the scent of his prey. Fortunately, he did not get a chance. From nearby, there came a loud whistle, followed by a 'Here boy!'

In a flash, the hound was gone. His loud paw steps could be heard dwindling into the background.

Dreamer and his friends remained still, recovering from their close encounter. Usually, instinct would have been to run, but fear often causes animals to freeze.

When it was thought they were safe, the companions crawled from the bushes and stood up. Hare's fur was wet, from droplets of the hound's drool splashing on his head.

'Honestly,' he said. 'I can't believe we survived that.'

Everybody nodded.

Dreamer climbed on top of the ditch and gave himself an almost clear view of his surroundings. Through the haze, he could discern the five hunters making their way down the hill, towards the gate, with the three hounds cavorting behind them, tails wagging.

For a brief moment, Dreamer focused on the hounds.

'Those *are* the hounds,' he said to himself. 'I knew it was them all along. Next time I see those hounds, I won't be hiding.'

Dreamer hopped off the ditch and rejoined his friends. 'Okay,' he said. 'Let's go over the plan one more time: we want to create a diversion - by separating the men from their machines, and the dogs from their men. And this is how we do it: first, we beat the hunters to the road...'

O' Connor angrily opened the door of his prized Wranglers convertible jeep, and sat in. He sparked up a cigarette and inhaled deeply.

'Two ducks and a woodcock,' he muttered. 'We've been out here fer two bluddy hours an' all we manage t'get are two ducks an' a woodcock.'

The Farmer waited impatiently for the rest of his hunting party to sit in before starting the engine. The dogs were kept in the back seat; being held carefully by two of O' Connor's hunting pals - Collins and Leonard.

Collins was a young man of the local town, with short bleached hair and freckly skin. At twenty one, this was his first hunting trip.

Leonard, who lived and worked as a farmer on the nearby peninsula, was a middle aged man with wavy black hair and short stubbly beard.

'So what'll we do bies?' asked O'Connor, seeking approval from his two buddies. 'Will we chance de woods or what?'

'I'd say we should,' said Leonard. 'We're having no luck around here, like.'

'Fair enough,' said O' Connor, gleefully. 'Roll down your window there and tell Sully where we're going.'

The two great Wranglers jeeps were parked side by side by the gate. The other jeep carried the remaining two members of O' Connor's hunting party - O' Sullivan and Mac Sweeney.

O' Sullivan was a heavy, red faced man with brown curly hair. He lived not far from where the jeeps were presently parked. He was also a farmer who owned and hunted on all the land on the west side of that very road.

Mac Sweeney was a well built, muscular young man from the local fishing village. He had a mop of light sandy hair and unmissable brown eyes. He played rugby for his village's team and had only recently, during a simple pub conversation, been talked into hunting.

'A great bitta' craic,' he was told it was.

'We're going to try de woods, Sully,' shouted Leonard across at the other jeep.

'Grand job,' said O'Sullivan.

O' Connor stuck the keys into the ignition and started the engine, only to quickly turn it off again. He turned back to his two pals in the back seat, his elbow sitting on the head rest. Leonard and Collins wondered why he looked so serious all of a sudden.

'Remember now,' said O' Connor solemnly, glancing from Leonard to Collins and back. 'Not a word of this t'anyone.'

Collins shrugged his shoulders.

'I wasn't gonna say nathing, Connor,' he said defensively.

'No, come here now, Collins, I'm serious,' said O' Connor. 'Do you've any idea what'd happem to us if we were caught hunting down by de Lake?'

'I do, but like -'

'I'm being dead serious, Collins,' said O' Connor, his dark eyes wide open and boring into Collins'. 'Tis snowing like mad today, so no one's around. We'll have wan look around de wood and see if there's any pheasants er shnipe n' come shtraight back here, understood?'

Collins nodded.

Both jeeps pulled out onto the road, gravel crunching under their heavy tyres. Although it was only the afternoon, the headlights flashed on on both vehicles, so as to see through the mist. The day was so dark you'd think it was six o' clock in the evening.

Down the narrow little road, the jeeps went, one gamely following the other. Further on down the road, the haze was beginning to thin out. O' Connor could finally see the narrow stretch of road ahead of him. After travelling another fifty yards or so, he caught sight of something lying in the middle of the road. He instinctively jammed on the brakes, threw off his seat belt and stepped out. The jeep behind had no choice but to grind to a halt also.

'What's de hold up?' shouted O' Sullivan out his driver's window.

'Two seconds,' said O' Connor as he edged his way up to the greyish black figure he had spotted in his headlights.

There, lying in the middle of the road, on top of the grassy strip, was a dead badger.

All of the hunters vacated their jeeps and surrounded it.

'Christ, he's a big fella in't he?' gasped Mac Sweeney.

'Must've been fairly stupid too,' laughed Collins. 'He forgot to look both ways!'

While the men all stood around admiring the size of the badger, and prodding it with the barrels of their guns, and while the suspicious hounds sniffed at its carcass, Hare emerged from the roadside stream, covered in mud. He glanced over at the group of men, who were still wondering what to do with their find.

'I wonder how long Badger can hold his breath,' Hare muttered. Pulling an arrow from his quiver and fixing it to his bowstring, Hare took aim at one of the jeep's front tyres. The shark- tooth gleamed. It seemed likely to do its job. TWANG!

The jagged missile buried itself in the jeep's front tyre, causing air to come hissing out. The front of the jeep slowly sank to the ground, its tyre now almost fully flattened.

Hare frantically loaded his bow again and positioned himself near the second jeep, which was parked behind the first. Stringing the arrow back and lining up his target, Hare let loose and effortlessly burst one of the jeep's rear tyres. Air squirted out of the fractured rubber, dragging the back of the jeep down with it.

'Yes!' Hare secretly applauded himself. 'I bet even Skip couldn't hit a target like that!'

With both tyres successfully punctured, Hare turned and bolted into the nearest fuchsia bushes.

'Well,' said O' Connor, scratching his bald head and looking down at the motionless badger. 'Looks like we'll have ta move him.'

'Whah?' gasped Collins. 'Move him?'

'Sure we have ta,' said O' Connor. 'Lookit the size of him. If we squash him, there'll be blood all over da windshcreen.'

'We'll never be able te move him,' Mac Sweeney protested. 'He's a monster of a size.'

'Course we can,' said O' Connor confidently. 'We'll all catch hold ob 'im tegethor and dump him over de ditch there.'

'Fair enough then,' said O' Sullivan.

Just as the men were crouching down to take hold of Badger's arms and legs, a blue and orange thunderbolt whizzed past their faces and circled above in the air.

'Whoa,' all the hunters gasped, jumping backwards and looking up.

Kingfisher was skirting and diving through the air, spinning and dancing with Frog on her back, to add to the distraction. She boldly swooped down on the hounds and teased them by fluttering her wings like a hummingbird.

The hunters watched on in awe. The hounds snarled and barked furiously.

Kingfisher then wheeled around and shot into the field, with the hounds galloping after her, yapping and jumping.

'Come back here ye stupid clowns!' O' Connor bellowed.

'Um, lads,' Collins interrupted. 'Where did the badger go?'

The three hounds ran along the full length of a snow festooned hedgerow and halted promptly.

They had lost the bird. And they had also lost their human masters. With a rough snowstorm brewing, it would be difficult for Ripper, Gnasher and Thrasher to find their way back to the jeeps.

'Dammit,' shouted Ripper, the hardiest of the three. 'We shouldn't have chased that bird. We're miles away from the jeeps!'

'No, we have to find that bird,' pleaded Gnasher, the softer, more 'willing to please' one.

'What, why?' asked Ripper angrily.

'Coz it was strange,' said Gnasher. 'It was blue n' shiny. The Farmer would be really pleased with us if we caught it.'

'Let it go,' said Thrasher, the dopiest of the dogs. 'I'm freezing my tail off out here.'

'There was something else too,' Gnasher went on, ignoring his brother. 'I could've sworn that bird had a 'frog' on its back!'

'A frog on its back?' said Ripper questionably. 'The cold must be really getting to you.'

'Yeah,' Thrasher slobbered. 'Or else, or else The Farmer put a drop of whiskey in your water bowl!'

'Enough!' snapped Ripper. 'Let's just get outta' here.'

But before the dogs could venture one step in the direction of the jeeps,  Kingfisher flew out of nowhere and skimmed past their noses before twirling back up into the air.

She made sure the dogs could see her. Frog clung desperately to her back, his tiny arms wrapped around her neck as she flitted up and down through the air.

'Can they see us?' asked Kingfisher.

'I don't know,' Frog squeaked, his eyes firmly shut.

Kingfisher dropped out of the air again and looped around the dogs' heads, tormenting them.

'That's the bird!' Gnasher cried.

The three hounds bounded through the snow in pursuit of Kingfisher and Frog, who were now gliding close to the ground, corkscrewing now and again to provoke the dogs even further.

A kingfisher's body is not designed for such acrobatics, so Kingfisher had to push herself beyond her every limit.

'Try not to be so scared,' she shouted back to Frog.

Frog replied in a panicky tone:

'That's asking a lot right now!'

'We have a job to do,' shouted Kingfisher. 'We have to get these dogs lost. We need to keep them chasing us for as long as we can! Try making them angry!'

'Job done!' cried Frog as he daringly looked back and saw three furious faces approaching fast; fiery, hateful eyes, sharp teeth bared and ready for a kill, ponderous paws beating the ground trying to pick up speed.

'Well, make them angrier!' Kingfisher suggested, while clinging to the wind.

Frog gulped and chanced another peek back. He puffed up his chest and began flicking his long tongue like a typical frog.

'Shoo hounds,' he jeered. 'You don't really want a frog in your throat, do you!'

The hounds found this extremely irritating and barked incessantly, while running at full stretch.

'Are they annoyed?' asked Kingfisher.

Frog shut his eyes and clung on to his friend's neck even tighter.

'Please fly faster!'

Deeper and deeper into the frozen wilderness, the hounds were drawn, until soon; they were clueless as to their own whereabouts. All around, the snow blew in heavy gusts.

'Where's the bird now?' asked Thrasher.

'Forget the bird,' cried Ripper. 'Where are we?'

Meanwhile, O' Connor and O' Sullivan were busying themselves fixing a couple of spare wheels onto their jeeps, while the other men stood around idly.

'How in the name of God did we both manage to borst our tyres?' O' Connor said for the fourth time, while jacking the jeep up off the ground.

'Must be a bad road,' Collins remarked, as he stood out on the road with the other men.

O' Sullivan was working on the second jeep, attaching the spare wheel and tightening the bolts.

'I dunnah,' he muttered. 'Tis strange.'

'What's strange now?' asked O' Connor.

'I was checking the tyre,' said O' Sullivan. 'And I found this.'

'What's dat ould yolk?' O' Connor gasped, as he took the peculiar little object in O' Sullivan's hand - a thin, sharp stick, about ten inches long, with a duck feather on the back and what looked like an ivory spike on the front. 'Ow.' O 'Connor nicked his finger when he touched it. A glob of blood leaked onto the snow.

'No idea what it is, or where it came frum,' said O' Sullivan. 'But I found one in yore tyre too.'

O' Connor shook his head and proceeded to lifting on the spare wheel, frequently sucking his finger.

'Looks like something de Indians would use on de cowboys,' he muttered.

Collins paced back and forth on the road, peering into the stream and bushes.

'Lads, I'm seriously wondering where dat badger went,' he said.

'Never mind de badger,' said O' Connor huffily. 'I'd be more worried about de dogs. We can't go anywhere till dey come back.'

'They'll come back when they hear de engine going,' said Leonard.

Once the bolts of the fresh wheel had been tightened efficiently, O' Connor stood up, flexed his fingers and wiped his brow. But before he could open the jeep door, he spotted something in the field opposite; a bright red figure, skulking around on the horizon. It stopped moving once O' Connor made direct eye contact with it. It stood perfectly still, staring back.

As he got a closer look, O' Connor realized what it was.

'Look lads,' he whispered loudly. 'A fox!'

All the hunters gathered together where O' Connor was standing and peered into the field.

'Where?' asked Collins.

'Away over there,' O' Connor whispered, pointing. 'Can you see him?'

'No,' said Collins, scanning the field.

'How c'n ya miss him,' Mac Sweeney quipped. 'He's de only red thing out there.'

'I see nathing any'ay,' said Collins, giving up.

'Ah come on Collins, look over there,' said O' Connor forcefully.

'Where?' said Collins again.

'Ahead,' said O' Connor.

'A head?' said Collins dimly.

'No, I mean ahead, there, ahead!'

'Where?'

'You're looking left. Look dead ahead. No, that's right... now you're looking up. Jaypers, look ahead! That's left again... don't look at me, is there a fox on my face?'

O' Connor fixed Collins' head in place with his hands. 'Right over there, ya ding dong.'

'Oh right,' said Collins at last.

In the distance, at the edge of the field, the hunters could all make out a beautiful red fox, staring back at them.

'A nice wan, in't he?' Mac Sweeney commented.

'He is,' said O' Connor with a devious grin. 'I reckon he'd be worth a few bob. If we sold his coat.'

'That's illegal now in't it?' said Mac Sweeney.

'Tis I'd say,' said O' Connor, lifting his chin. 'But nobody has to know we shot de fox, like. We could just say my wife found de coat in de attic and wants to sell it.'

'Fair enough,' said Mac Sweeney. 'But... you don't have a wife.'

O' Connor smirked.

'Nobody has to know dat either. Come on, let's go after him.'

One after the other, the five hunters climbed over the gate, into the field.

'Ah,' gasped Collins. 'Wedgie!'

'Quiet!' O' Connor hushed. 'Don't scare him off.'

The shot guns were cracked open and loaded each with two Eley cartridges, while the rifle was filled with seven Remington shells.

'Safety off, bies,' whispered O' Connor.

All the guns clicked.

'Okay,' said O' Connor, as they slowly advanced. 'Spread out, spread out, spread out!'

The five hunters put space between each other and formed a long line. Together, they crept silently towards the distant fox.

Dreamer turned his back and pretended not to notice them approaching.

Offering himself as live bait, he held his ground.

When he could hear their footsteps, he knew they were close, and that's when he darted up the hill.

The hunters took aim, fingers on triggers.

Yet, there was silence.

'I can't get a clear shot,' Leonard groaned. 'There's too much snow falling.'

'Ah shazbock,' O' Sullivan mumbled. 'It's a snowstorm. We'll never catch him now.'

'Yeah we will,' said O' Connor. 'Look, look, he's still there!'

Dreamer stood on the white slope up above the hunters, frequently hidden by the waves of snow that swept past him in the maddened wind. He was still within their scope.

'Come on, come on,' O' Connor ordered.

Abandoning stealth, the hunters charged up the hill.

Dreamer was off again, courting death. His heart pounded behind his ribs. Up and up and up the hill, he led the hunters, until they were lost in the intensifying blizzard. The icy wind howled and whistled around them, so loud, they couldn't hear each other shout. Snow whirled around their bodies, like little twisters trying to suck them up. The hunters stumbled about, unsure of whether they were searching for the fox, or searching for their way back to the road.

But one thing was certain: neither the road nor the fox could be seen anymore.

'Flip it!' cried O' Connor. 'We're lost!'

On the other side of the hill, under a naked hawthorn tree the animals had chosen as their rendezvous, sat Hare.

He twitched his whiskers and stroked his bow nervously, frequently pacing back and forth or peering around outside for any signs of his friends.

'Where are they?' he mumbled. 'We agreed to meet here. Am I under the wrong tree?'

On saying this, there came the sound of rapidly flapping wings from above and Kingfisher alighted on a branch. Frog shakily climbed off her back and jumped to the ground.

'Never again,' he panted. 'Never again.'

'Where's the rest?' asked Hare.

'They're coming,' said Kingfisher. 'The plan seems to be working.'

Moments later, Badger came trundling along into the shade of the hawthorn. 'All's going well so far,' he panted. 'We definitely led those hunters on a wild- goose chase.'

'Well done,' said Hare earnestly. 'I'll bet those dogs couldn't play dead as well as you did.'

Badger laughed.

Frog was trembling terribly.

'Don't worry,' said Kingfisher. 'It won't be this cold at home. We'll have trees to shelter us from the wind. And you can go back to sleep.'

'It's not just the cold,' said Frog. 'I'm just afraid those hounds might have tracked us down.'

Just then, the brambles behind the hawthorn began to rustle.

Frog shrieked and dived behind Badger.

Dreamer burst out of the bushes, much to Frog's relief.

'The plan was a success,' he announced, in between attempts to catch his breath. 'We stalled the hunters and damaged their machines. The hounds are now lost out in the eastern fields, and the men, lost in the west. We've created a fine mess for them.'

The companions cheered and jumped about, play fighting.

'But it's not enough,' he said in more serious tones. 'Eventually the men and the hounds will meet up again. And the machines have been repaired. I wasn't expecting that.'

'So what are you proposing?' asked Badger, letting go of Hare's ears. Dreamer paused. His voice then carried a tinge of fear.

'The hunters are going to reach Lough Ine,' he declared at last. 'And we have to race them.'

'Okay,' said Hare questionably. 'But when we get home, what then?'

Dreamer shook his head.

'I don't know,' he confessed. 'Coming out here may have been a mistake. And forget the part where I said 'may have.' There was no way we could have fully stopped the hunters. All we managed to do was bide ourselves more time by wasting theirs. All we can do now is... I suppose... anything we can.'

There was a hushed silence. Frog piped up.

'Does this mean I have to ride on Kingfisher's back again?'

Dreamer looked up from the ground and nodded.

There was no hesitation.

The five companions hastily made their way out from underneath the hawthorn tree and right back into the blizzard, on a desperate race against time, hoping against hope, that it wasn't already too late.

The Siege

Swimming around at the bottom of one of the Lake's many rock pools was a little tompot blenny. The tiny shore fish had been swept into the rock pool earlier, due to strong winds out on the Lake. But, having a memory of not more than three seconds, this bothered him little.

Around in circles, the little blenny swam, exploring and re - exploring his surroundings. A couple of red, jelly like anemones clung to the walls of the rock pool, displaying their impressive stinging tentacles in the hope of catching a passing shrimp. A few rays of white light slanted down through the sheet of bladder wrack seaweed on the surface, betraying the presence of a crab. He stood in one spot for a time, bubbles frequently hissing out from his armoured mouth, before scuttling off under a rock. Around and around the little tompot blenny swam, finishing another two laps of the rock pool, when all of a sudden, to break his new routine, a long, yellow, pointed bill sliced down through the surface of the water and tried to grab him. The blenny got the fright of his life, and instinctively dashed under a rock for shelter. But unbeknown to him, this was the same rock the crab was sheltering under! The crab couldn't believe his luck, and while the blenny had his back turned, he opened his pincers and sidled over to make his move...

'Oh bother,' Pierce scolded himself. 'Missed him.'

The grey heron was hunched over the rock pool, trying to single out some breakfast.

Knowing he wasn't going to have much luck in this spot, he opened his wings, took to flight, and set himself down by the shore. Wavelets rolled in and washed around the heron's spindly ankles before ebbing back out into the Lake. Empty mussels, limpets, cockles and scallops were washed in and out with the angry shore.

Pierce glanced up at the brooding storm clouds. While a blizzard raged out in the countryside, conditions in Lough Ine were relatively calm. Only a mild wind disrupted the stillness of the trees and Lake, swaying the branches and stirring the water. Occasionally there would come a strong gust, dashing waves against the rocks. But the storm seemed a comfortable distance away. Presently, Emur the swan came paddling by from behind one of the little rock islands. She helped herself to a patch of bladder wrack seaweed that had been pinned to the pier by the waves.

'Another day in paradise,' said Pierce brightly.

Emur nibbled politely and swallowed.

'For us at least,' she replied. 'I pity the woodlanders.'

'Oh, I wouldn't go fretting my feathers off over them,' he said cheerfully.

'The woods have seen many winters, and always its creatures have pulled through. Let's be grateful nothing has changed for us, eh? There are still plenty of fish biting and the cold doesn't seem to be causing us any anxiety.

No need for us to scrounge for food or hibernate, no sir.'

'I guess so,' Emur yawned.

'Dare I say it,' Pierce went on, closing his eyes and lifting his head. 'But I believe this could be the best winter yet. We've held up easily so far and we've avoided a lot of storms. Just look at that storm over there; it's passing away. And soon, it'll be spring, and we won't have all these worries. Yes Emur, I believe all is going well... Emur?'

The swan had grown tired of the heron's rambling, and paddled away.

Above on Hilltop Warren, at the edge of the snowy field, Captain Spruce poked his head tentatively out of his burrow under the hawthorn.

For a moment, he peered around, sniffing the air, his long ears pricked up and searching for movement like a couple of radars. With safety confirmed, he crept from his burrow and thumped the ground with his foot.

'They're gone,' he announced. 'You can all come out now.'

All around the field, rabbits began popping out of their burrows, filling up the surface of the Warren until the place was again bustling with grey and brown bodies digging and nibbling.

For a while, the Captain sat by himself near his burrow, watching his comrades. He then spotted his daughter sitting across from him. She was pawing at the ground, rather listlessly.

Squatting down beside her, he looked around once.

'Still shaking?' he asked.

Lyla just nodded, barely acknowledging him.

'That was a close one,' he said. 'Those two foxes were spying on us the whole time. If we hadn't spotted them sooner, our party would be one less now.'

'Well luckily that didn't happen,' said Lyla in a sort of abrupt tone.

'Forgive me for sounding like an over - protective old fuddy duddy,' said Spruce. 'But I'm certain those foxes had their eyes on you.'

'So?' said Lyla. 'I escaped didn't I?'

'I'm afraid luck is not enough,' said Spruce sagely. 'You must be wiser.'

'What do you mean by that?' asked Lyla.

'There's no need to be so adventurous,' said Spruce. 'You wandered too far out into the middle of the field, where any predator could have snatched you up with ease. By rights, every rabbit should always stick close to its burrow.'

'But I hate being cooped up so close to home,' Lyla griped. 'What's the point in being free if you can't enjoy it?'

Spruce smiled, looking slightly hurt.

'You're three months old and already it sounds like you want to leave home.'

'I don't want to leave home,' said Lyla. 'I just want the freedom to run around and see where I'm living; see what home looks like from a distance; see what's behind this and under that. I don't want to be tied to one place. It makes me feel like I'm caught in a snare.'

Spruce smiled again.

'You're a free spirit,' he said warmly. 'I can tell a normal life isn't enough for you. You're fuelled by excitement, and not routine. Well, I suppose I can't always hold you back. Some day, when I'm far too old to chase you, you'll be off getting up to all sorts of mischief and you won't have me to haul you out of it.'

Lyla blushed.

'But don't be too anxious to leave home just yet,' Spruce warned. 'Take it from someone who knows. Believe it or not, I wasn't always a fussy old wind bag. When I was your age, I used to venture out into the country all the time. Not alone of course. Oh, the things my friends and I got up to. A couple of times, we snook into someone's garden to steal some carrots and lettuce and spinach. We could have been killed! In fact... one of us nearly was...

Lyla, let me just tell you this. Cockiness kills. The outside world is a treacherous place. You may survive one thing to be claimed by another, so there's never a need to feel invincible. Danger hides in many places and takes on many forms. You can never be careful enough. I hope you're prepared for that.'

Lyla nodded. 'I am now.'

Fuchsia and Comfrey made their way eastwards through the woods, back to their den. A song thrush skipped along the ground, with its head tilted to one side. One may have thought she was listening, but in fact, she was searching the ground for fallen berries or seeds. Her head was tilted because like hares, her eyes were on the side of her head. She took to the trees once she sensed the two foxes coming.

Fuchsia was trailing behind her mate, who was in a sulk. He moped along with his head down, nattering away to himself. Fuchsia felt something needed to be said.

'Don't feel bad, Comfrey,' she soothed. 'Those rabbits were genuinely too fast. I'm sure we'll have more luck next time.'

'What d'you mean *we?*' he snapped, turning back sharply. 'I'm the one who does all the hunting. And even at that, you don't eat anything I catch you.' 'Yes, I do,' said Fuchsia. 'In my own time.'

'Well, we'll see,' said Comfrey. 'All I have to do is think of an easier way of catching those rabbits. Maybe I can dig them out of their burrows.'

Fuchsia forced a laugh.

'You know,' she said. 'Maybe we should give up on the rabbits.'

Comfrey halted and glared at his mate. 'Are you serious?' he gasped.

'Well,' said Fuchsia. 'It seems all we ever do now is hunt and sleep. When was the last time we had fun? Winter is a dreary enough time without being bored stiff on top of it all. We used to swim in the stream, play in the mud and chase each other through the woods.'

'We were cubs!' Comfrey snapped.

'But it was great,' Fuchsia beamed. 'We were so happy.'

'We have more important things to worry about now,' said Comfrey. 'Like survival.' Then he added bitterly;

'It should be easy, since we have no cubs to look after!'

Fuchsia's lip drew back in a half growl.

'Is mating all you think about!?' she hissed inwardly.

'Anyway,' Comfrey grunted. 'We'd better get some shuteye. Maybe we can ambush those rabbits later in the evening.'

'What is it with you and the rabbits?' said Fuchsia, wishing she had sounded angrier. 'We have food buried. And besides, there are plenty roots and bulbs around! You're just wasting precious energy with all that chasing!'

'Someone has to provide,' said Comfrey.

Fuchsia sighed. 'This is going around in circles.'

Comfrey sniffed the den entrance and slipped underground. Then he popped his head back up and said: 'You coming?'

Fuchsia nodded, looking defeated, and followed him.

She had always tried to make the relationship work, but Comfrey's pig-headedness knew no bounds.

Her feelings for him had deteriorated. Gruff and bossy as he was before, he was now quite simply insufferable. Any bit of 'sensitivity' or 'charm' in him was long gone. She could deny it no more - her mate was a nuisance. A nuisance with less sense of humour than a pine cone. Fuchsia knew something needed to change... She thought about this while lying beside the snoring fox.

Down at the bottom of the hill, just outside the woods, lay the little meadow. It was almost completely blanketed by snow save for the numerous bunches of cottongrass that peeped out the top.

Wesley the stoat scurried from one clump of grass to another, carrying in his mouth, a freshly captured bank vole. Satisfied with his catch, the stoat was on his way back to his hollow under the footpath, when suddenly he sensed a little vibration in the ground. It wasn't much. At first. But it grew. He stopped up and listened out, his little rounded ears standing on end. Somewhere, not too far ahead, a sort of rumbling sound could be heard growing in volume. Whatever the sound was emanting from approached fast; its weight trembling through the earth. Wesley could feel it under his paws. Whatever it was, must have been big.

The stoat slinked his way through the grass and snow and reached the edge of the meadow. Peering gingerly through a temple of cottongrass, Wesley had a clear view of all that lay ahead.

To his front left, the silver Lake churned in the wind, to his front right, the towering forest covered hill stood, its trees shaking their heads, and in between the two, lay the road.

And it was there, Wesley found what was making the noise. After seconds more waiting, the stoat spied a plume of brown dust rising from around the corner of a patch of chestnut trees. The rumbling noise filtered into the sound of crunching tyres. Wesley recoiled with fright and dropped his vole when he witnessed two metal monsters appear from around the corner. They were green in colour with black roofs and between them had many heavy wheels.

Wesley did not run. Maintaining his curiosity, he held his position and watched as the two Wranglers jeeps slowed down, turned and parked themselves under a snow bearded oak. The noise stopped. Silence followed.

Wesley tensed his body when he saw the men step out of the vehicles. Still the stoat stayed put.

Humans were not new to him. He had often seen humans roaming about in Lough Ine before, during day lit hours; hill walkers, bird watchers, families going for picnics, people swimming in the Lake. But what were these men up to? On a freezing cold day when hiking would have been dangerous and swimming, insane, what business did these men have in Lough Ine? To Wesley's horror, he discovered they were armed. Each man wielded some sort of gun, and to add to the stoat's dismay, three big brown hounds were released from the rear of one of the jeeps. Wesley needed no bidding. Off he went, back into the meadow, leaving behind his catch.

'All set, bies?' asked O' Connor, dropping a cigarette and stamping on it.

'We are,' said O' Sullivan.

'Lads is this legal?' asked Collins.

O' Connor guffawed loudly.

'It doesn't matter *like*. Dere's no one around.'

'Sure, we could get arrested if we're caught, like,' Collins queried.

'Do you see any squad cars?' said O' Connor pointedly.

'S'pose not,' Collins sighed.

Cautious as he was earlier, O' Connor had relaxed somewhat when he'd reached the sanctuary, having met not a single car on the way over.

'We'll be grand,' said O' Sullivan brightly. ''Tis only a bitta' shooting, like. Tisn't harming anyone.'

'Fair enough, then,' said Collins finally.

The three ever diligent hounds cavorted and danced about, eagerly awaiting their orders.

'Go on, bies, go on!' O' Connor urged, resting his gun underneath his arm and clapping his hands. 'Find us a pheasant! Find us a pheasant!'

The hounds almost tripped over each other, scarpering into the shade of the forest. Together, the five men followed, passing a big blue sign that read:

Knockomagh Wood Nature Reserve
Tearmann Dulra Choill Chnoc Oghma

National Parks and Wildlife Service
Pairceanna Naisiunta agus Fiodhulra

In the heart of the forest, Flapjack sat pecking the snowy ground. His mate, Andiae was back at the nest on the hillside. The cock pheasant was still overshadowed by the thoughts of his children. Every day, the guilt of not having saved them haunted him. Part of him knew from the beginning that a cuckoo had snook an egg into his nest. Had he but acted sooner and removed this false egg, he could have prevented the tragic deaths of his ten unborn chicks. Andiae was equally distraught.

While these melancholy thoughts whirred about his head, Flapjack was unaware of the ivy bushes rustling behind him. It wasn't until sticks started breaking that he became conscious of danger.

Hopping to his feet, the pheasant hurriedly ran along the forest floor and into a nook in some holly and ivy. There he nestled down under the serrated leaves, fully hidden from sight (but not from smell). Believing he was safe, he sighed with relief and allowed his ink blue head to sink comfortably into his own fat.

'That ras a crose one,' he muttered.

Without warning, the holly and ivy stalks behind him shook and shivered. Flapjack spun around and found himself staring into the eyes of a hideous hound.

The pheasant let out a loud, strangled squawk and flapped his wings in a frenzy! The hound pounced but narrowly missed him; as-Flapjack fluttered off up into the canopy, only to be spotted by a band of hunters below.

Leonard swiftly aimed his shotgun upwards and squeezed the trigger. Following an ear splitting bang, there came a wisp of smoke and flame. Flapjack dropped from the air and landed in a heap in the snow, some of his brown and cinnamon feathers drifting down on his lifeless body. Thrasher scurried over to where the dead pheasant lay, and grabbing him by the neck, carried him back to his master in his mouth. 'Good boy,' saidO' Connor.

Thrasher allowed the pheasant to fall. O' Connor picked it up by its legs and handed it Leonard.

'I believe this is yours,' he smirked.

Leonard put the carcass into the green sachet.

'Nice shot, bie,' said Mac Sweeney.

'Cheers,' said Leonard, as he opened his shotgun and discarded the empty cartridge on the ground. He sniffed the chamber.

'Aahh,' he sighed. 'I love de smell o' sulphor.'

He passed the gun around for Collins and Mac Sweeney to sniff too.

'Nice alright,' said Mac Sweeney.

The hunters pressed on, following a dirt track east into the forest.

249

The echo of the first gunshot was heard all over Lough Ine. It had sent a gigantic wave of birds into the sky. Robins, thrushes, blackbirds and myriad others all burst forth from the treetops and bushes in a blind panic.

Even the birds of the Lake were aware of the brewing tumult.

'What in the name of catfish?' cried Pierce, as he glanced over at the woods.

Emur glided up to the heron on the shore, her usual calm, demure face now flushed with worry.

'What's happening?' she breathed.

Skip emerged from his holt up on the shore rocks and looked up at the panicking birds overhead.

'Dearie me,' the otter gasped. 'Looks loike the heumans have broken an eould promise.'

Fear ran through Lough Ine as fast as the wind. After hearing the first fatal shot, and the distressed cry of a pheasant, animals all over the woods, fields, hedgerows, meadows and Lake began to fear for their own lives, even small fry that the hunters were not interested in; mice, rats, shrews and voles practically clambered over each other, desperately seeking somewhere to hide.

Rabbits on the Hill froze and stood like statues, their senses inflamed. Barely twitching their whiskers, they listened out for another strange, loud popping sound.

The sound was even heard underground:

'What's going on?' cried Fuchsia, as she stuck her head out of the den. 'Stay down!' Comfrey snarled from below. 'D'ya wanna get us both killed!'

The two foxes retreated into their sleeping chamber.

While most frightened birds took to the air, many of the game birds preferred to hide. They quickly took shelter under whatever bushes, logs, stumps or rocks they could find, hoping for the danger to pass. But they were easily flushed out by the sharp nosed hounds. Ripper dived behind an old hazel log and barked madly, causing a startled woodcock to come zipping out, flapping its mottled brown wings rapidly. The fat little bird rose into the air, much to the delight of the hunters below. The sound of gunfire rang out again. O' Connor, O'Sullivan and Leonard fired a trio of bursts, blasting several branches out of the oak tree above. They all missed.

The woodcock climbed further into the air, wheeling, spinning, corkscrewing, unsure of where to go. It seemed almost out of range. After quickly pumping a bullet into the chamber of his .22 rifle, Mac Sweeney excitedly pointed it upwards, and, not even taking the time to aim, pulled the trigger.

With a loud CLAP, the woodcock was cut out of the air.

It landed in a cushion of snow and was immediately retrieved by Ripper. There was absolute awe among the hunters.

'Jaysus Christ!' O' Connor bellowed. 'How didya do dat?'

'No one's ever hit a woodcock with a rifle!' cried O' Sullivan.

'You're a natural!' beamed Leonard.

'Piece o' piss,' said Mac Sweeney smugly.

Ripper left the dead woodcock by O' Connor's feet. O' Connor handed it to Mac Sweeney.

'No one's gonna believe y'shot him with a rifle,' he said. 'You'll be laughed out of the shebeen!'

'You shoulda' brought your camera phone, Liam' said Mac Sweeney to Collins.

When the novelty had temporarily died down, O' Connor announced: 'Come on, anyway. We'll see if there're any ducks around here.'

Old Darig climbed shakily from the mouth of his den. But he did not dare leave it. The sounds he had heard were too obvious to ignore. The old fox emerged only half way out of the ground, and stared sadly at the amount of terrified rodents scrambling past him on the forest floor.

It was every fox's dream to have this much food displayed in front of him, but Old Darig did not have the heart to even attempt catching any of these mice or shrews, for he understood their trauma. The old fox was weak with sadness.

'I knew this day was coming,' he sighed. 'But I didn't think I'd live to see it.'

Old Darig closed his eyes and withdrew underground.

O' Connor led his hunting party eastwards through the ring of scots pines. The men talked on a range of different topics, none of which had anything to do with hunting; mainly sport, women, cars, current affairs, neighbours. And then they came upon what they were looking for. 'Lads, come look at this!'

O' Connor beckoned quietly, peering through a gap in the trees. The four other men edged up to The Farmer and gasped. Just outside the screen of scots pines, at the edge of a little meadow, was a little duck pond - full of ducks!

'Jaypers,' gasped O' Sullivan. 'We should come here more often. The place is teeming with targets!'

Collins stifled a laugh. 'They're like sitting ducks!'

'Shush,' said O' Connor. 'They don't know we're here... on the count of three...'

All the guns clicked.

Bill and all of his family and friends sat huddled together in the pond, bobbing gently about. Sure enough, they had heard all of the distant shots earlier, and were severely tempted to fly away. But Bill insisted they stay put. A decision he would later regret.

'If we fly, we'll be doing exactly what they want us to do,' he'd said previously. 'I know what these men are like. If we keep our heads down, there's a chance they won't find us. So remain calm everybody. This'll be over.'

The nervous ducks did as they were bidden, and sat in icy silence. A silence all too soon shaken by an explosion of noise. A series of gigantic splashes erupted from the pond, spraying down on the surprised ducks. It was an ambush.

Smoke and sparks spewed forth from the barrels of five booming guns. Panic instantly ensued among the ducks. They flapped, fluttered and flew, screeching and quacking.

The salvo continued, guns hopping and jolting, banging and booming.

Most of the ducks were lucky enough to survive the slaughter, taking frantically to the air, while being pursued by pellets and shells streaking past their wings. Bill and Branta escaped into the woods on foot, their twelve matured offspring waddling clumsily behind them. Soon, not a single living duck was left in the pond. A smell of sulpher hung in the air. A shower of white, grey and emerald feathers drifted down and settled on the red, bubbling water. In there, floating lazily around, were five slain ducks.

A look of ugly satisfaction crossed O' Connor's face. He looked at his fellow hunters.

'Wan each,' he grinned.

Meanwhile, the three hounds, Ripper, Gnasher and Thrasher were off by themselves on the other side of the wood, busily sniffing around the ground in circles, periodically stopping at tree trunks and rock piles. They were on the trail of a scent.

'I think it leads up this way,' said Thrasher. 'What are we looking for again?' asked Gnasher.

Before Thrasher could answer, Ripper sighed loudly, while sniffing a bare patch of ground with no snow.

'Mmmm,' he said. 'Rabbit. Most of its tracks are snowed over, but its scent is nice n' strong. And you know what they say - where there's one rabbit, there's a warren!'

The three hounds made their way up the steep, tree covered slope, towards Hilltop Warren, where the tables were set to turn.

The Eleventh Hour

Captain Spruce stood in front of his daughter in a protective pose. His chest was puffed up, ears and tail erect, paws raised.

The rabbits of Hilltop Warren were motionless, alert. Staying close to their burrows, they were prepared to make a break at the next sound or movement that could spell danger. Many had already fled underground.

'Well?' said Lyla, who was still hidden behind her father. 'What now? Are we going underground or are we just going to dawdle out here like a couple of fence poles?'

'Hold on,' Spruce hushed. 'I want to make sure we're safe. Those shots seemed quite far away; the bottom of the hill, maybe. If we don't hear anymore, we'll stay outside. If we do, we'll retreat. But for now, stay behind me.'

'I'm not a newborn,' said Lyla sulkily. 'I can protect myself. Anyway, why are we so uptight? I thought hunting wasn't allowed here.'

'I know,' muttered Spruce. 'I thought that too.'

The head rabbit then jumped unexpectedly.

'What's wrong?' asked Lyla.

'I have a scent,' he said, his voice carrying a tinge of fear. 'Oh my, it's getting stronger!'

The rabbits witnessed to their sheer terror, three large, vicious hounds bounding out of the scots pines ahead, like something straight out of a nightmare.

Captain Spruce hollered at the top of his lungs:

'SCATTER!'

The rabbits instantly dashed down into their burrows, just as the hounds were scorching across the field, barking like demons.

'Come on, underground now!' yelled the Captain, ushering everybody into their holes before turning to run alongside his daughter to his own burrow.

The two rabbits were the last ones left out in the field. The hounds torpedoed towards them, tongues lolling from their mouths.

Lyla scampered down through the main tunnel, ahead of her father, who was still only at the entrance.

The hounds reached him quickly and dived through the air. Captain Spruce instinctively froze and faced them, believing his doom was at hand.

255

But Dame Fortune was on his side.

For out of nowhere, an arrow whistled and struck Thrasher in the left shoulder. He yowled with pain and staggered about in circles, the sharp missile protruding from his body. The hounds halted and growled, looking around for the responsible perpetrators.

With them distracted, Captain Spruce turned and hurried down the shaft of his burrow to safety.

The hounds made no effort to pursue him. In fact, they had forgotten all about the old rabbit. They were more interested in finding out who the sniper was.

Then, to satisfy their curiosity, and to kindle the fires of rage, Dreamer leapt forth from the hedge. He had been running all day and was now going purely on 'second wind'. But Dreamer stood, and stood boldly, glancing at each of the hounds' faces, his eyes burning into theirs.

Badger then slid down the ditch beside him, carrying in his paws, a thick club fashioned from a hazel branch. Hare followed suit, bow in paw as ever.

Kingfisher, mounted by Frog, perched on the topmost branch of the overhanging hawthorn tree. She had been riding on Badger's head most of the trip, and Frog on hers.

'Just in time,' Dreamer panted.

'We would have been earlier if Hare hadn't got his tongue stuck to that icicle,' Badger grunted.

Hare recoiled.

'Says the one who had us all waiting while he carved himself a club out of a frickin' branch!'

'Not now, fellas,' said Dreamer, his eyes still on the hounds.

Ripper, Gnasher and Thrasher couldn't contain their excitement.

'It's him!' Ripper gritted out. 'The one who got away from us last winter. I know it's him. His scent never left my nostrils. Watcha say we finish what we started!'

The hounds snarled venomously and set upon Dreamer and his friends, but surprisingly enough, Dreamer was just as nimble and fierce. For it was at that moment, he became a different animal. All shrewdness, all stealth and tactical planning left him. The usual careful, cunning fox was now a vengeful beast, sacrificing all for a bloodbath. The distance between he and Ripper closed, and as they crashed into each other, the fox was immediately tumbled over by the hound's greater size and weight. Ripper pinned him down with his paws, and searched for the nape of his neck. Dreamer thrashed out wildly with his limbs, screeching and spitting.

Gnasher and Thrasher danced around the scene excitedly, looking for an opening, before turning their sights on Badger and Hare. The two friends stood side by side, every nerve pulsing.

'It's been a while,' said Hare, arrow notched to string. 'Since our last scrap.' Thrasher pulled the arrow from his shoulder and lurched forward, but Badger swung his club in a mighty arc and batted him across the snout. The hound yelped and fell flat on his back. Badger followed his blow and jumped upon his foe.

Gnasher made a drive for Hare, but Hare sent an arrow for his skull. Gnasher dodged aside and rammed Hare to the ground. Hare roared with pain as sharp claws scored his flesh and pressed him down. The hound opened his jaws wide, lips tucked above his gums. Hare saw his fate written in those terrible fangs.

But as luck would have it, a pebble whipped Gnasher on the head. He looked up at the blue thunderbolt whizzing by.

'Nice shot,' laughed Kingfisher.

'Thank you,' said Frog.

The two friends fluttered off over the ditch, with the livid Gnasher behind them.

Hare jumped to his feet, to see his two companions locked in a deadly embrace.

Dreamer was suffocating. He and Ripper had been grappling like creatures possessed, and now the hound had the fox by the scruff of the neck, throttling him. Badger and Thrasher lay wrestling on the ground, tails in each other's mouths, claws in each other's sides.

Hare didn't know who to help. It was a coin- toss.

'I could easily regret this,' he mumbled as he flung himself upon Thrasher, biting deeply into his rump!

Alarm bells sounded in the hound's head as the long bucktooth pierced his flesh. He dropped Badger and glared at Hare, who just smiled nervously and did what he did best - ran. How he ran, with Thrasher gallumphing after him.

Badger rolled to his feet and set off to assist Dreamer, who was turning purple under his fur. Ripper was squeezing the life out of him, jaws secured around his neck.

Until Badger came in from the left and blind- sided him. The hound flew head over tail and landed heavily in the snow.

Dreamer climbed falteringly to his feet, wheezing some god- given breaths. He nodded his gratitude to Badger, who was nursing his shoulder. But both friends had to focus again.

Ripper was getting up.

There was no escape. The companions were stranded in the wide open field, totally hemmed in by three merciless hounds. Their only options, it appeared, were fight or die.

Below in the forest, O' Connor and his hunting party ambled along a dirt track that wound its way up around the hill. The day had rewarded them with five ducks, one woodcock and a pheasant.

'So far so good,' said Leonard. 'D'ya want to keep going or should we pack it in for de day.'

'Might as well keep going,' said O' Connor. 'We can't go anywhere till dose flippin' dogs come back.'

'Ah well, how bad,' said O' Sullivan. 'Gives us more time here I spose. Should we check if there're any pigeons or shnipe around deese parts?'

'Ashir, why not,' said O' Connor. 'We're here now; we might as well make it count.'

The five hunters continued to stalk through the woods, gaining height on the hill as they climbed the spiralling steps. The steps had been put in place many years ago by the Forest Ranger. But he never intended for them to be used by men such as these.

The hunters tore through the branches, where the zebra spider was planning on weaving her web in spring, crushing a robin's nest hidden among ivy, and with a simple skid of the boot, filled in a rat's hole! The men marked their progress with a trail of empty cartridges, cigarette butts and green beer bottles, one of which now trapped a shrew...

Nuala the owl crept to the edge of her nesting hole in the great oak and chanced a peek down over the side.

The five interlopers passed by slowly, chatting animatedly amongst themselves, their footsteps crunching the snow. The long eared owl heaved a sigh.

'It appears we will never be truly safe,' she muttered to herself. 'The humans have broken nature. Nature is not the unstoppable force it once was, capable of regrowing, reproducing every time it suffered. The humans have grown in strength, in number. They now believe the world belongs to them, rather than they belong to the world. With eyes so blinded by greed, power and technology, how can they be aware that other life exists?

A time will come when their towns will spread, and overshadow the beauty that once was the countryside. Yes, I've heard stories from the outside. I'm certain of what is to come. Forests will become timber, bogs will become turf, fields - construction sites.

And this - this veritable haven I once called Lough Ine, is the latest victim. It's hunting today, it's logging tomorrow. What does it take to get these strange creatures to see sense?'

Nuala sighed again and shuffled off back into her hole.

The battle on Hilltop Warren was standing still.

Dreamer and Badger circled the savage Ripper, growling and glaring. The hound may have been outnumbered but he easily had the strength of both his adversaries. He boiled venom, scowling into the eyes of Dreamer, then Badger, who were both keeping their distance.

Ripper reared up and flew at Dreamer, just as the hawthorn tree at the meadow verge burst open and Gnasher tumbled out after Kingfisher. The little blue bird skimmed past Ripper's nose, causing one hound to career into the other! Ripper and Gnasher lay tangled up in the snow.

Dreamer and Badger saw their chance and hurled themselves
at the bewildered dogs.

Hare ran like the wind, around and round the meadow, arrows dropping out of his quiver at every turn, as Thrasher pursued him all the way. He gasped and puffed, knowing his life depended on keeping up the pace.

Kingfisher was rapidly tiring out. She had to frequently land on the ground or in the bushes to stretch her wings and neck, not to mention deposit Frog. But now, she was needed again. Hare was in a royal mess.

'Hold on tight,' she said to Frog.

'Why, what are you - aaaaaaaaágh!'_

The bird dropped from the air and clung to Thrasher's head, pecking and jabbing at his hairy cranium. Frog bounced around on her back, like a man at a rodeo.

Thrasher grinded to a halt and began shaking his head; yapping and snapping, but Kingfisher held on like a limpet.

Hare, believing he was still being chased, galloped on, until he spotted Thrasher on the other side of the meadow.

'Oh.'

He searched along the ground for his bow, and once he found it, he notched his last arrow to its string.

'My turn to save you,' he muttered as he lined up his target.

The arrow whistled through the cold winter air, and struck true!

Thrasher was rubbing his head into the ground, with his tail in the air, when it came from nowhere and impaled him! Searing pain shot up through his spine, as the long shaft went in one side of his tail and came out the other! His howl echoed for miles around.

Kingfisher and Frog were able to rest in the snow, after Thrasher took off running across the meadow, as if trying to escape what was in his tail.

A fox and a hound fought like it was their destiny to kill each other. Dreamer and Ripper rolled through the snow, in a jumble of red and brown fur; jumping, falling, rising; snorting, snarling; slashing, biting, tearing. Dreamer fastened his teeth in Ripper's leg, as the hound tried to keep him down. When the pain became too much, Ripper let go, and was bowled over by a swift scratch across the face. Now Dreamer was on top.

Badger had Gnasher in a tight headlock. The hound was wriggling free, when suddenly he was unable to move. Hare had arrived, and lay on Gnasher's lower body. Both friends contrived to keep the hound still.

Once again, Kingfisher and Frog came to the rescue. The bird flew low, and Frog pelted Ripper with a snowball! The hound snarled, taking it in the eye. Kingfisher and Frog perched on top of the hawthorn tree. Ripper abandoned Dreamer and stood barking incessantly at the base of the tree, jumping up and down.

Dreamer shakily lifted himself from the ground, his body riddled with lacerations. He appraised the situation.

'We're getting nowhere!' he shouted at Badger and Hare, who were still using their bodies to pin Gnasher down. 'We have to lose these dogs!'

'Easier said than done!' Hare groaned, keeping his arms tightly wrapped around Gnasher's legs.

'Any idea how we're going to lose them?' asked Badger.

Dreamer nodded and darted half way across the field, despite a terrible limp.

'I think I know a way,' he shouted. 'Follow me quickly!'

'What kind of idea is this?' asked Hare, to which Dreamer replied:

'Unreliable, foolish and likely to backfire!'

With that, he was off.

Badger and Hare looked at each other and nodded, before springing up and taking off.

Gnasher scrambled up and pursued them.

'The only things ye're gonna lose are your heads!' he bellowed. 'Come on, Thrasher, forget the arrow, you can pull it out later.'

The two hounds raced across the field, soon accompanied by their brother, Ripper.

Dreamer, Badger and Hare sped towards the edge of the Warren, Kingfisher and Frog gliding above.

The five companions burst through the bushes and scarpered into the woods, followed instantly by the hounds. Dreamer ran fast and graceful, adrenalin acting like a natural narcotic on his sprained leg. Hare ran at his usual dizzying speed, while Kingfisher flapped painfully through the air with Frog as a burden on her back, hanging on for dear life.

But Badger! Oh poor, slow Badger! When the others had just outdistanced the hounds, he had fallen hopelessly behind! Ripper, Gnasher and Thrasher gathered around him as he jogged clumsily around the trees. The hounds set upon him, but Badger instinctively dove under Ripper's legs, and scrambled on, making an apparent bee-line for an earth patch on the ground. On this earth patch, grew a cluster of the unmistakable – puffball mushrooms! Badger skidded to a halt and watched the hounds' advance, insanity dribbling from their gums. Once close enough to smell their foul breath, Badger clapped his paws flatly down on the puffball mushrooms, releasing a brown cloud of their deadly spores! The hounds stopped in their tracks, coughing, sneezing and spluttering as Badger slipped off to join his friends. But little time had been bought.

For the hounds were off again, at full cry. With bloodshot eyes and runny noses, they homed in on their prey. The animals stampeded through Bubblelump Swamp and down the dirt track, kicking up snow in their wake.

'This way!' cried Dreamer, as he turned and bolted up a narrow secluded pathway between encroaching bushes of holly, ivy and bramble. All of the animals trailed after him. And it was here, the chase climaxed.

Dreamer had led his friends, and his enemies, to the Lough Ine Panorama. The five companions stood bunched onto the ledge of the hill, where the drop was terrifying. A gushing river wound its way around the foot of the hill, over two thousand feet below.

The animals halted at the edge before turning to face the hounds.

They approached slowly, baring their blood stained teeth, foam bubbling from their mouths as they growled, panted and growled some more.

'You should have just stayed down!' Ripper snarled. 'You should have just given up!'

Hare peered down over the edge of the hill and felt his stomach tighten. 'Dreamer,' he said questionably. 'You need to be more careful with your plans. This one certainly lacked something.'

Cornered, the friends inched backwards, until they were wobbling on the very tip of the ledge.

All at once, the three hounds leapt upon Dreamer and his friends.

In the blink of an eye, Dreamer, Badger and Hare dropped to the ground and huddled, allowing Ripper, Gnasher and Thrasher to sail over their heads and down over the edge. The companions watched on as the hounds shrank from view, hitting every bump and bush on the hill's cliff-like escarpment. Once two thousand feet had passed them by, the hounds plummeted into the river, one after the other. Three large ripples followed three large splashes after Ripper, Gnasher and Thrasher walloped the surface of the water.

Dreamer and his friends could make out the shapes of three miserable dogs climbing onto the riverbank, dejected and defeated. They wandered the bank for a moment, tails literally between their legs, before shaking dry, and collapsing.

Silence.

'I stand corrected,' said Hare. 'That was an excellent plan.'

Dreamer laughed nervously:

'My original plan was for *us* to jump off.'

Hare said no more.

'What now?' panted Badger.

Kingfisher fluttered down and perched on the ledge.

Frog slid off her back and directly into a puddle, where he drank and swam and relaxed for a few blissful moments.

'Dreamer,' Kingfisher gasped. 'The hunters - they're coming up the hill!'

Dreamer paused.

'Good,' he said. 'Let them.'

'But w-we can't fight them,' Frog protested.

'I know we can't,' said Dreamer. 'Not like this. We'll need help. And lots of it.'

Badger gasped, 'you mean ...'

'Yes,' said Dreamer. 'Driving these hunters back will require an all out rebellion.'

For a moment, nothing else was said. The friends needed time to process what they were hearing.

Then Dreamer took a deep breath.

'Come on,' he said. 'Let's get ready. There's not much time.'

The animals made their way off the ledge and back up towards the Swamp.

Dreamer trailed behind them. Pain and exhaustion stung every inch of his body.

'Arznel,' he muttered, his eyes closed. 'My body is spent. Give me strength. Give us all strength. There is so much left to do.'

Every second counted. In the short time that followed, the five companions found themselves frantically scurrying in and around the woods, trying to rouse as many animals as they could. They called up trees, under logs and rocks, down holes and crevices, in through hollows and clefts. They went around to every nest, burrow, sett and form, stirring up a tremendous bedlam. Hare collected his arrows, and Badger, his club.

After reaching Hilltop Warren, Dreamer paused and allowed a macrocosm of words to fill his mind. Where the words came from, he had no idea. They seemed to just flow in from nowhere. He barely understood what half of them meant; nevertheless, he was pleased with how they sounded.

He peered around once to make sure he had an audience. He couldn't see anyone, really, save for a few rabbits tentatively poking their noses out of their burrows. There was no time to wait for them. Dreamer just began, and hoped everyone could hear him:

'Friends of Lough Ine!' he declaimed. 'Children of the earth. Do not slumber, do not cower, for a whole world balances on the edge of abyss! For too long, we have been living under a black cloud. For too long, we have stood idly by and accepted the suffering of our kind, without question, without objection.'

The bushes began filling up with birds. Some rabbits crept fully out of their burrows and listened as Dreamer continued.

'This world was ours first and still is by right. No one knows when the humans first arrived or when they turned hostile, but what we do know is, they have pushed us! Every day, for infinite days, everywhere, they have pushed us. We have been disregarded, disrespected. They see us as lesser creatures, put here to survive and nothing more. They think they can do whatever they want to us, to this world.

But now, having crossed into our sanctuary, they have pushed us too far! Today, they will pay! For every tree felled, for every mother snatched away from her younglings, they will pay!'

Some rabbits cheered. Birds warbled and shuffled on their perches. More rabbits came out, more birds arrived. Dreamer's voice rose in volume and in passion.

'We will not allow good and beauty to be sacrificed on the altar of greed and exploitation! We will not allow the freedom of our way of life succumb to the blindness of theirs! We will prove to them, that they are not alone in this world! That we are here, we are real and we are angry! And they cannot make us go away! Today, for the first time, animals will run *towards* danger!'

Dreamer's voice rang out like steel. It echoed around the Hilltop, resonated down to the surrounding fields and hedgerows, coursed through the ground, was carried by the wind from tree to tree, until the young fox's words had fallen on the ears of many.

Badger put a paw on Dreamer's shoulder.

'Not bad,' he said.

The fox turned to his friend.

'I'm not done yet.'

The five companions made their way to the edge of the woods, still shouting orders as they went.

'Come on out of your hidey holes, animals,' cried Hare.

'Assemble on the field, everyone,' shouted Badger. 'And feel free to bring some sticks and stones with you.'

'And don't keep us waiting all day,' added Frog.

What Goes Around...

O'Connor wandered a few paces ahead of his pals who were walking in single file up the narrow pathway. The Farmer always liked to feel as though he were in charge, and being at the front of the group gave him that sense of authority.

The men were nearing the top. Light poured onto the path ahead of them, where the bare treeless Hilltop stood.

'Not a bad day, lads,' said O' Connor brightly. 'We all got something at leasht.'

'Yerrah, yeah,' said O' Sullivan. 'I reckon we should make diss our regular spot.'

'I dunnah, lads,' Collins queried. 'I'd say we should head off fairly soon before someone reports us fer trespassing.'

'Go away outta dat, willa,' O' Connor rebuffed. 'Who's going t'report us if no one knows we're here, like.'

'Just t'be safe, y'know,' said Collins.

'Ah, Collins, relax.'

O' Connor dropped another cigarette and looked around. 'Those bluddy dogs,' he grunted. 'Where did they go?'

As the hunters pressed on, they did not notice the bramble bushes on the side of the dirt track rustling. Hare furtively emerged, up to his waist in leaves. He watched the men pass by in front of him.

Slipping an arrow from his quiver, Hare fixed it to his bowstring and took aim.

Mac Sweeney suddenly let out a cry.

All the men turned to see him limping around with a little dart protruding from his leg.

He was cursing and swearing with pain.

'Agh,' he hissed, pulling it out and placing a hand over his injured thigh. 'Where did dat come frum?'

Presently, a white, furry figure jumped from the bushes and landed in the middle of the path.

'Holy -' gasped O' Connor.

The men stared in awe at the big white hare that had just stopped to look at them. He twitched and blinked curiously.

'Lookit dat,' whispered Collins.

'What's he holding?' said Leonard.

'What's he wearing?' asked O' Sullivan.

'Never mind dat,' O' Connor laughed. 'A shtuffed hare'd look good on my mantelpiece!'

Pointing his shotgun, O' Connor fired.

But Hare had taken to his feet before O' Connor could even touch the trigger. Snow squirted up from the ground.

'After him, lads!' The Farmer bellowed.

The hunters gave chase, with Mac Sweeney dragging his sore leg behind him.

Hare made sure the hunters could see him at all times, deliberately moderating his speed as he scampered down the hill; his fluffy white tail always in view as the men stumbled and trundled after him.

'I can still see him,' O' Connor panted. 'Come on, come on, come on!'

Hare led the men through a small clearing and up an alternative route to the Hilltop. He then halted and bolted up a slope to the side of the path, through trees and branches, out of sight.

'It's grand, it's grand,' said O' Connor. 'He can't have gotten too far.'

The men were about to continue the chase. But instead they froze. You would have to have been standing among them, to believe what they saw. From atop the steep, tree covered hillock, an avalanche of animals came spilling down. Rabbits, hedgehogs, stoats, squirrels, minks and martens all thundered down the slope, screeching, mewing and snarling with truculence. They were headed by a fox; the very same fox the hunters had lost track of earlier. Galloping alongside him were two badgers and a hare; the same hare who had led them into this clever trap. Then came the birds; a great wave of them, flapping and fluttering down through the canopy, cheeping, tweeting, shrieking and shrilling. Among them was a dazzling kingfisher, mounted by a little frog. The wildfolk made a formidable sight. They charged in all their strength, fuelled by a red wrath.

The men panicked and fumbled with their guns, but before they could do anything to repel the deluge, they were bombarded by a hail of sticks and stones. Pebbles and twigs whipped and clattered at the bewildered hunters as they turned to run, but they were unable to escape the onslaught. The animals rushed into them, milling around the men's ankles like a giant, moving carpet.

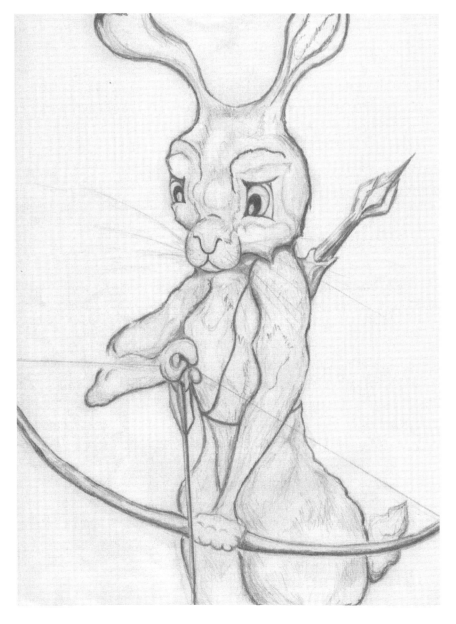

Minks and stoats leapt up, biting and scratching, rabbits clung to legs, birds descended on the men's heads, pecking and raking. The slow hedgehogs were unable to do much, simply being there for morale support.

'What the Jaysus is going on here?' cried O' Connor, as he kicked and shook all the rodents out of his pants and wrestled with the duck on his head.

It was a mad ambush.

The men were surrounded; some animals clambering up their legs and backs, the rest encircling them, hissing and spitting. The air was thick with birds of so many kinds, including several crows and hawks that had been summoned from the outer fields.

The hunters looked as though they were wearing coats made of fur and feathers.

They kicked and staggered their way through the throng of wildlife, and ran hell for leather through the woods, waving their arms and kicking their legs wildly, until every mammal and bird had dropped off. The men had received a number of cuts and gashes; their clothes tattered.

'What in the name of the Almighty!' cried O' Sullivan.

'Calm down, calm down!' O' Connor hushed. 'It's probelly mating season or something. De animals are angry coz they think we're interfering with their territory. Tis normal.'

The hunters watched as the horde of animals approached again.

'BANG!'

'BANG!'

'BANG!'

The hunters steadied themselves, pointed their firearms and opened up. A rabbit and a couple of crows fell to the snow, but this did not halt the animals' advance. On they came, in all their grandeur, hell bent on vengeance.

O' Connor trembled.

'Back to de jeeps!' he shouted. 'Back to de jeeps!'

The hunters abandoned the battlefield and doubled back down through the woods, back along the winding dirt track, panting and wheezing. During their retreat, they were buffeted by the birds all the way, who were swooping down now and again for a peck or a jab, some dropping rocks and pebbles on their heads, others simply - dropping their droppings!

At last, the bottom of the hill was reached.

269

The men hurried out from under the cover of the trees, flung open the doors of their Wranglers jeeps and dived in. Pebbles and rocks clattered and pounded against the rooftops and windscreens, as the persistent birds continued their assault. Beaks and talons raked and scraped at metal. The swallows had no idea what they were missing.

O' Connor heaved a sigh of relief and sank down into his driver's seat, trying to catch his breath.

Collins and Leonard sat in the back, while O' Sullivan and Mac Sweeney sheltered in the opposite jeep.

'Dat was freaky,' Collins panted.

'Come on, Connor,' said Leonard. 'Let's take her out of here.'

But O' Connor, vindictive as he was, had no intention of leaving. There was a glint of insane anger in his eye as he spoke.

'Embarrassing is what dat was,' he rasped. 'Embarrassing!'

The Farmer stroked his shotgun like a prized pet.

'What are you saying?' asked Leonard.

'What am I saying?' O' Connor spat. 'Is dat really how you want to end de day? Us gettin' chased out outta de wood by a few furry feckers!'

'Let it go,' said Collins.

'I will not let it go!' O' Connor boomed.

'What's your plan, so?' asked Leonard.

'We go back in there and sort that shower of maggots out!' The Farmer declared.

'Ya can't be serious,' Collins gasped.

'Am I not?' O' Connor barked. 'If anyone had seen dat! We'd never hear de end of it!'

'No one saw,' said Collins.

'We saw,' said The Farmer. 'Dat's bad enough. Look, we're going back in and dat's dat. Alright! We'll be in an' out in two minutes. So load up.'

The Farmer made some hand signals to O' Sullivan in the other jeep.

O' Sullivan squinted his eyes. It was difficult to see through all of the stones that were raining down, splitting the windscreens and denting the roofs.

O' Sullivan shook his head and threw up his hands.

'I don't know what you're saying!'

O' Connor mouthed the words:

'We're going back in!'

O' Sullivan stared blankly.

O' Connor sighed and rolled down his window just a narrow slit and put his mouth up to it.

'We' re going back in!' he bellowed.

O' Sullivan was dumbfounded.

'What did he say?' asked Mac Sweeney in the back seat.

'He said we're going back in,' gasped O' Sullivan.

'Whah?' gasped Mac Sweeney. 'Is he mad?'

'J'know what,' said O'Sullivan. 'I don't blame him. We've been having a good day and we shouldn't let something like dat ruin it. Come on, so, we'll make it quick. Belt up.'

The engines roared to life. Revving up, the two great Wranglers tore off into the forest.

Many of the marauding birds were struck down. Feathers of various sizes and colours popped into the air as numerous thrushes, starlings, blackbirds, wagtails and crows were knocked from the air.

The jeeps stormed on, on a reckless rampage; crushing plants and logs, churning snow into puddles, obliterating branches, bushes and vines. The ground was ripped up; the great tyre tracks sizzling in the snow. The jeeps rocked and juddered along the stark, lumpy ground.

And then, the animals came into view. A jumbled mass of furry bodies charged down the hill in droves, seemingly unafraid of the metal giants powering towards them. The animals swept over the jeeps like a tsunami over a beach. Rabbits and hedgehogs bunched together, allowing the jeeps to pass harmlessly over their heads. Stoats, minks and martens leapt onto the bonnets, windscreens and roofs, hanging on with their claws. A handful of animals were mowed down.

O' Connor jammed on the brakes and sent a number of rodents and vermin catapulting through the air. O' Sullivan copied this tactic and cleared his jeep of the sticky assailants. Both jeeps sat still, engines rumbling.

The animals rallied together, jostling and clambering over each other, clawing and butting at the doors. The birds clouded over the jeep in their multicoloured flock. Wesley splayed his claws and slashed the jeep door from end to end. Captain Spruce hurled his shark-tooth spear and split the rear widow down the middle. Craggy, the hedgehog was in the process of jamming a big round rock up into the jeep's tail pipe, but never got far in his sabotage.

It appeared the hunters were under siege, with no escape. The animals were enraged, berserked, frenzied. It didn't look like anything could stop them. Then, the windows rolled down and the long black barrels of the hunters' guns slithered out.

The animals shrieked and scattered, dashing behind trees and down holes, but many did not get away in time, for the hunters did not hold back. They unleashed a volley of fire, and riddled the forest floor with smoking craters. The guns hopped and jolted, pellets and shells changing direction and crisscrossing through the air.

Panicking animals ran in circles, some dodging the fusillade, others being hit and splattered. Several rabbits and birds met their ends. The animals broke up and scattered throughout the area.

The engines rattled again and the wheels kicked up snow and earth, and the jeeps were off again.

O' Connor gave a nervous laugh.

'Well, we sure showed dem,' he announced, with a tremor in his voice. 'S'pose we better get going now, anyway. Maybe we can catch a few more of de divils on ee way out.'

In the blink of an eye, the windscreen shattered under the impact of a great white bird.

The swan launched herself at the jeep and landed on it, feet first. She barked and flapped, clinging to the dashboard.

O' Connor gasped and spun the wheel in an abortive attempt to shake the bird off, but there was no time. Instinctively, the men unbuckled their seatbelts, threw open their doors and bailed out. The swan took to flight right before the jeep crashed directly into a tall beech tree. There was an awful crunching sound as the jeep wrapped itself around the great gnarled trunk.

O' Connor, Collins and Leonard scrambled to their feet and gazed at the wreckage. The front of the Wrangler was in ribbons, crushed up to nearly half its length. The windscreen was reduced to a carpet of sparkling shards of glass and its two front tyres were ruptured. The bonnet was buckled into a perfect triangle shape, revealing a gutted engine. Gas spewed from the carburetor.

O' Connor's face paled.

The men turned to see that the swan had been accompanied to the forest by an otter and a heron. The three newcomers made their way through the trees, away from the second jeep which was still at large.

It slowed down in front of the three men and O' Sullivan jumped out.

'Are ee alright?' he cried. 'Will I ring da hospital?'

'I'm grand,' said O' Connor, still assessing the damage and brushing glass from his coat.

'We should call a tow- truck,' Collins suggested, still quivering.

'No!' O'Connor shouted. 'Then de whole parish will know we were here. Let's just fetch a rope and drag her home ourselves!'

'I think there's one in the back of my jeep,' said O' Sullivan.

But before a move could be made, all the men had to drop to the ground as a deafening, fiery explosion erupted only a few feet behind them, shredding the canopy. A gout of fire rose and ballooned from the skeleton of the Wrangler, tendrils of flame shooting out here and there. The beech tree moaned its song of death, before toppling over and hitting the ground, creaking and sparking. A pall of thick black smoke roiled into the sky, followed by ash and a sprinkle of flame. Burning pieces of charcoal showered down from above, settling where the five men lay.

They shakily stood up, numbed to the core. They stared at the cooking jeep and tree, allowing their eyes to adjust.

'Well,' Collins breathed. 'What now?'

Fire!

*D*reamer stood on top of the steps, his eyes transfixed with fear on the orange glow behind the trees, a cloud of blue black smoke suspended menacingly over the treetops.

The animals had all stopped in their tracks once they heard the great noise. It was certainly louder and more frightening than any gunshot.

Having grouped together on the slope, they watched in mounting terror as the dreadful forest fire spread. The wind carried its flames from tree to tree, setting every branch and twig alight.

Dreamer slowly turned around to face his companions.

Badger, Holly, Hare, Frog, Kingfisher, Captain Spruce, Violet, Lyla, Catkin, Wesley, Craggy, Bertha, Nuala, Bill, Branta, Andiae, Emur, Pierce, Skip and a host of others stared back at him, with a look of dismay on each of their faces.

'What is it?' Lyla sobbed.

'It's called fire,' Spruce breathed. 'I've always known what it is, but I never thought I'd see it in Lough Ine.'

'Are we going to die?' Lyla sniffed.

'No, no, no,' Spruce whispered softly, hugging his daughter close.

'Hmph,' said Wesley. 'Don't make any promises y'can't keep, bucktooth.' Spruce glared at the stoat. 'Quiet, vermin!'

'Err, perhaps we should all go home and wait for the fire to pass,' Pierce suggested.

'Easy for you to say,' Bill complained. 'Your home is by the Lake. We here in the forest - we're dead ducks!'

'Please,' Dreamer interrupted. 'There's no time for all this bickering... no, we can't go to our homes. The fire would find us no matter where we hide. We just have to accept what we can't prevent.'

'When you're quite finished stating the obvious,' said Nuala from an ash branch. 'We'd like to hear a plan.'

Dreamer paused momentarily, but the roar of the fire prompted him to

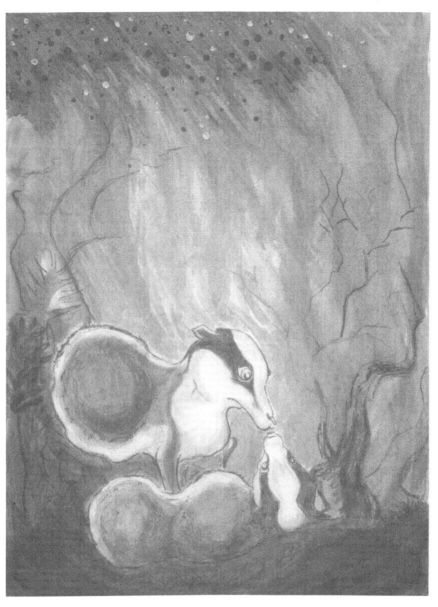

speak.

'There isn't really a plan,' he conceded. 'Anyone who wishes to leave may leave. But I'm staying. The hunters are just as afraid of this fire as we are. I plan to use that against them.'

'Are you off your rocker?' cried Wesley. 'You'll be fried to a frizzle!'

'Maybe, maybe not,' said Dreamer. 'But I can't leave, not yet. This is where my dreams have led me. This is what they were all about. I can't let this opportunity pass me by. Does anyone at all want to join me?'

This may as well have been a rhetorical question, for Badger brandished his club and Hare fixed an arrow to his bowstring. The others simply nodded. 'I'm just taking my daughter out of here,' said Spruce. 'But I will return.' Dreamer smiled broadly. 'Thank you. All of you.'

The hunters were trapped.

The burning beech tree lay across their path, blocking the exit of the second jeep. They stood around, fuddled and flustered, realizing the enormity of their actions. O' Connor had his hands on his head.

'Oh my God, oh my God,' he gasped. 'What're we going to do, lads? Should we just run off home now or should we try putting de fire out?'

Collins was on the verge of crying.

'I feel sick,' he gasped. 'I didn't want this.'

'Cut de crap, Collins,' said O' Connor. 'Think o' something quick lads.'

'There should be another way out,' said O' Sullivan. 'Alright fellas, pile into my jeep there an' I'll take us out. If anyone asks later, we weren't here!'

'But how do we explain dat?' cried Leonard, pointing at the flaming wreckage of the other jeep.

But before another word could be said, an arrow pinged off the Wranglers' bonnet. The familiar screeches and howls of a horde of charging animals could be heard emanting from above on the slope.

'Oh, please not now,' O' Connor sighed.

Within seconds, the sound of gunfire rang out again.

Further east, Fuchsia and Comfrey were running speedily through the forest, heading upwards.

'Faster,' cried Comfrey as he overtook his mate. 'We have to reach the Hilltop.'

Fuchsia dashed in and around the trees, trying to catch up to her mate.

'Wait,' the vixen panted. 'Won't the fire reach the Hilltop?'

'Just keep running,' Comfrey ordered.

'I think the Lake is a better idea!' Fuchsia shouted, but Comfrey was out of sight.

The area of forest that the two foxes were running through had thus far been untouched by the fire, but the heavy pungent smell of smoke was everywhere in Lough Ine.

Old Darig squeezed out of his den and stood bolt upright.

The looming black cloud hung over the woods, growing in size with every passing moment.

'That's not a rain cloud,' he muttered.

Sniffing the air, Old Darig realized immediately what was happening and took off through the woods, his frail body causing him to falter and limp. The fire raged unchecked, inexorable, out of control. Flames jumped from one tree to another, growing larger and brighter. Cascades of sparks and burning pitch shot skyward, as black ash smuts filled the air. Black acrid smoke billowed into the sky, blocking out daylight. It was as though nightfall had come early.

But it appeared an even greater fire raged in the hearts of Dreamer and his followers, burning all traces of apprehension, for they stood in the middle of the turmoil, driving against the hunters with all their might.

O' Connor and his company were sheltering behind the doors of their jeep, pointing their shotguns and rifle over and under, firing haphazardly.

But the animals kept coming. They charged from the undergrowth, hurling sticks and stones before returning to their hiding places, others recklessly charging towards the men, only to be struck down. Any animal that got too close was kicked away, or butted with the back of a gun.

Badger and Hare knelt behind a birch log, loosing arrows and chucking stones. Skip hid across from them, behind an ash tree. Never did his aim prove more useful. Picking up a large rock in his webbed paw, he hurled it through the air. The stone passed through the jeep's windscreen with stunning accuracy. Shards of glass cascaded down all over the busily shooting hunters. They could bear no more of the arrows, sticks and stones clanking, pinging and glancing off their jeep, nor could they afford to waste any more time.

'Alright, screw diss,' shouted O' Connor, ejecting an empty cartridge. 'Sully, you reverse the jeep there like a good man. I'll deal with diss lot.'

O' Sullivan clambered into the jeep and threw his coat over the broken glass. He then revved up the engine, turned the jeep around, shifted into first gear and waited for his friends to gather up.

But O' Connor was determined not to leave the battlefield in defeat. For a time more, he sat shooting out at anything that moved, while flames licked at the tree trunks and treetops; the fire fuelling itself with every piece of wood it touched.

'Connor!' cried O' Sullivan. 'What in God's name are ya doing? Get in!'

'Two seconds,' said O' Connor, emptying his barrel into another rabbit.

'De whole shaggin' forest is coming down!' cried O' Sullivan.

'Nearly done,' said O' Connor.

Old Darig staggered out of the blanket of smoke, sneezing and spluttering. Opening his puffy eyes, he was astonished to see dozens of various animals, bravely and arrogantly defending themselves and each other.

'Unbelievable,' the old fox gasped. He then spotted a young fox crouching amid the scorched grass.

'Dreamer!' he cried.

But before the old fox could venture a step, a bullet streaked past his nose. He yelped and took a jump backwards, then paused to gather his wits.

'I'm an old fox,' he thought. 'But I'm also an experienced fox. I've been in more fights than all of these rabbits and otters put together. Perhaps it's time for one more.'

Leonard and Mac Sweeney both wrestled with O' Connor, trying to bundle him into the jeep.

'Dat's enough, Connor!' shouted Leonard. 'We have t'go!'

'Alright, I'm going, I'm going.'

Suddenly, Leonard could feel himself being knocked forward as a big, reddish grey fox leapt upon his back. Old Darig dug his claws in deep.

O' Connor and Mac Sweeney pranced around, fumbling with their guns. 'Hold still, Lenny,' cried Mac Sweeney. 'I'll blast him off ya!'

But before the shot could go off, another fox leapt from nowhere and butted the gun to one side, causing the shot to go astray.

O' Connor took aim at Dreamer, but in the nick of time, a pebble whipped his hand and The Farmer looked up to see Kingfisher swoop down on him, circling his head.

Dreamer fled with Old Darig away from the carnage, Badger, Hare, Kingfisher and Frog following not so far behind.

'Just when I think you can't surprise me any more,' said Darig wryly, as he and Dreamer slumped down behind a birch log.

'What are you doing here?' asked Dreamer, glaring at the old fox.

'Well let me see,' said Darig. 'Gathering a tiny army of small, weak and young animals to fight back against a gang of humans with guns - in the middle of a forest fire - a rather risky business, wouldn't you agree? Such a daring stunt requires the help of one more experienced.'

'Why would you want to help me?' Dreamer growled. 'I thought you were ashamed of me. You know, for going behind your back and mixing with animals you trained me to kill.'

'Not ashamed,' said Darig. 'Just slightly taken aback. Anyway, enough chin wagging. As you can see, we're in a bit of a tight spot.'

Flames washed over the forest; tall, roaring, orange, consuming the entire pine section around the base of the hill. They then climbed further up the hill, smothering the canopies of some deciduous trees, whipping at the forest floor, crackling, bursting, sparking.

The sky was pitch black, lost entirely behind the veil of thick, billowing smoke.

The animals could endure no more of the raging inferno. Most had already fled. The birds had left immediately after the first explosion. The courage they had been infused with earlier had been severely tested by the fight with the hunters, but the fire was more than enough to rekindle their fear, and so they flew.

Only Dreamer and his companions, along with Old Darig were left in the gutted woods. Together, they searched for somewhere unburned, where they could pause to breathe. Their senses were assailed by the horrible stench cloying the air.

It was a mad and confusing retreat. They dashed around burning trees, hurdling walls of fire, and taking frantic detours around falling branches and exploding stumps.

'Holly!' Badger cried, as a hail of sparks gusted around him. 'Holly!'

The pair had been separated while running. Badger was alone now,

279

stranded in the midst of the turbulence.

All of the animals had been fleeing quite far apart from each other; Dreamer alongside Darig up ahead, Kingfisher with Frog up above, while Hare rocketed on ahead, being the first to reach the Hilltop.

Badger and Holly had been trailing behind, and were now lost.

'Holly, where are you?' shouted Badger hoarsely.

The pulsating heat and smoke were unbearable. Badger coughed and spluttered furiously before breaking back into a run, until at last, he reached an unburned area of the forest. But it would not stay safe for long. Embers glimmered threateningly above in the canopy.

Badger collapsed on the ground, breathing rapidly. He looked around but couldn't see his friends through the fog of smoke. And he found that the flames hurt his eyes a lot more than daylight ever did. He then discovered, to his sheer dismay, that this was the same place the hunters had fled to.

The silhouettes of O' Connor, Leonard and Mac Sweeney disappeared into the grey haze, as they made for the Hilltop. They had been separated from the jeep by a falling tree, and had fled on foot, hoping that the jeep would find some way of following. With their exit below closed off by the fire and fallen tree, *up* was their only option.

But where *was* the jeep?

The ominous rumbling of an engine answered Badger's question. It zoomed out of the whirling smoke, bumping and rattling on the rocky ground of the hillside. For some reason, it no longer had a roof. The two men inside were fully exposed.

Then Badger gasped in horror as he caught sight of Holly staggering out of the burning trees, directly into the path of the oncoming jeep.

Badger roared with all his heart:

'HOLLY WATCH OUT!'

But she was too dazed to hear the warning.

She vanished under the shadow of the giant metal beast. There was a slight thump and the jeep jolted before passing on by. Badger sank to his knees and quivered.

'No,' he pleaded.

Hare, who had returned to the hillside to search for his friends, witnessed the incident. He sighed and shook his head, before grunting angrily and

taking to his feet.

No thoughts had he, just an instinct to do something incredibly stupid.

Down the hill he sprinted, towards the passing jeep. There by the side of the path, he crouched down and waited for his chance. The jeep juddered past, and with all the strength Hare still possessed, he leapt onto the mudguard above the back wheel, and gripped firmly to the seat with his claws. Just below his dangling hind legs, the wheel threatened to drag him under. The jeep sped on, so loud; the men did not hear Hare climb in. He slid down into the back seat behind O' Sullivan and Collins and quickly aimed an arrow at the driver.

But, spotting the intruder in the wing mirror, Collins spun around and grabbed Hare around the neck.

'Sully, there's a rabbit in the back seat!' he cried.

Hare dropped his bow and squirmed, kicking his legs and struggling to breathe as Collins lifted him up.

The jeep came to a dead end as a burning ash tree crashed down in front of it. Turning around, it did a U- turn back in the direction from which it had come.

Badger looked up from the ground and saw the jeep rattling by, Hare in the back being strangled.

All thoughts aside, Badger focused on saving his friend. Picking up a stick that resembled his club, and aiming carefully, he muttered a silent prayer and let it rip from his paw.

Whop, whop, whop!

The club twirled through the smoke filled air like a boomerang and hit Collins squarely between the eyes, knocking him senseless back into the jeep, as Hare jumped safely from the mudguard and landed in the settling dust. The jeep was gone.

Badger hobbled weakly along the smoldering ground, and crouched beside Holly. She lay on her side, among the ashes and tyre tracks. Badger nudged her broken body with his nose. She opened her eyes and forced a smile. 'Badger,' she managed to say, in a low, fading voice.

Badger couldn't speak. He sat by his fallen mate's side and laid a paw on her side. Her breathing was rapid. Holly blinked.

'I saw the way you fought today,' she said, clutching the last of her life.

'You were truly amazing.'

Badger was seized by feelings of helplessness.

'I was fighting to protect you,' he managed to choke out. 'And I failed.'

'No,' Holly coughed. 'No you didn't. No animal could have done more for his mate. I'm grateful.'

Tears heated up in Badger's eyes. He squinted, trying to fight them.

'I was looking forward to spring,' he whispered. 'But now I'll never see our cubs.'

'Of course you will,' Holly smiled. 'They're coming with me. We'll be waiting for you, in a different sanctuary.'

Badger nodded, his vision blurred, his heart heavy and clogged with grief. 'Live your life, Badger,' she said on her last breath. 'Stay with your friends. You can always trust them... to keep you happy... until you find me again.'

With that, Holly closed her eyes and silently slipped away. Badger stayed by her side, overcome with pain. For a while, he tried to will life back into her. But then he laid his head on her head and gave vent to his agony, sobbing uncontrollably.

Moments later, Hare came plodding along. He edged his way up behind Badger, trying to blink away the tears that hung unshed in his own eyes, and placed a paw on his friend's shoulder.

'We have to go,' he said.

Badger hesitated, and then limped with Hare up the Hill. And so, the fire spread again. What was once the 'safe' part of the forest was now consumed by the raging conflagration, until the whole of Knockomagh Wood was engulfed.

Near the top of the Hill, where both the companions, and the hunters had gathered, the battle was nearing its end.

...comes around

Dreamer and Darig, disorientated and exhausted, desperately climbed up the steep slope, with the fire chasing them all the way. Flames crept along the boughs of every tree, crackling and combusting.

'There's nowhere to go,' Dreamer coughed, flames nipping at his heels.

'Yes there is, just keep running,' Old Darig panted.

At last, the two foxes reached the Hilltop. There were few trees in this area to burn, yet the fire formed a terrible blazing ring around them, closing in slowly but surely.

While stopping for breath, Dreamer caught sight of another two foxes running up the hill just across from them. The small sandy brown one was speeding just ahead of the slim red one.

'This way!' shouted Comfrey.

'No, Comfrey, I'm not doing that!' said Fuchsia for the third time.

'Why not, it's the perfect opportunity!' said Comfrey looking back. 'All the rabbits are gone, so we can take their burrows! That way, we don't have to leave Lough Ine because of the fire! And if any o' the rabbits come back and find us in their burrow - it's easy meat!'

'That's horrible,' said Fuchsia.

'Oh, you and your damn soft spot,' said Comfrey. 'Can't you see this is ideal? All those burrows-just for us! Who knows, some of them might make a nice nursery!'

Fuchsia snapped.

'That's it, Comfrey,' she barked. 'I've had it. You have been a thorn in my paw since last summer. All I wanted was a mate to respect and care about me, not a mate who is rude and selfish and bossy and who wants nothing - but to *mate* with me! We're finished, Comfrey. Goodbye!'

Fuchsia turned on her heels and scurried back down the hill, intending to loop around the fire, but being in such a rage, she did not spot the falling tree.

Dreamer had spotted it first, but he hadn't counted on Fuchsia turning back.

It was a tall scots pine, creaking, splintering, bending and toppling. Fuchsia was nearing it, unaware that it was about to land right on top of her.

Of all the animals in Lough Ine, Dreamer had been worrying about her the most. All along, his friends were in his own company. He knew he could look out for them at all times, but Fuchsia - she was out of his care.

Crrrrrrrrraaack!

Down came the tree, with wisps of smoke and ember streaking behind it.

Leaving Old Darig to catch his breath on the rock-face, Dreamer galloped to Fuchsia's side.

But then – DISASTER!!

He was snatched abruptly from the air and choke-slammed to the ground. Comfrey held him down, savaging him with his teeth and claws.

'No, no!' Dreamer roared.

Fuchsia was still in shock, and did not move as the tree crashed down on top of her! Its trunk groaned, its branches bursting into a flurry of sparks and embers as it caged the vixen inside.

Comfrey seemed oblivious to this, as he mauled and thrashed Dreamer about.

'I've been waiting a long time for this, you little tapeworm!' he snarled. Dreamer squirmed.

'You would rather kill the one you hate than save the one you love!' he choked out, as Comfrey's paw crushed his throat.

Comfrey grinned through rat- like fangs.

'Love?' he laughed. 'She was just my latest! I've conquered many vixens- Fuchsia just needed more time.'

Dreamer roared and used his hind legs to throw Comfrey through the air. As soon as he landed, Dreamer bulled into him, almost breaking his ribs. Comfrey took one hit from Dreamer's head, and another from the pine trunk as his body smacked against it. He fell. He rose. He shook his head and steadied himself. Dreamer crouched, poised for further combat.

But, Comfrey took only one step, before stopping, and collapsing to the dust…

Fuchsia lay inside an air pocket under the tree, pinned to the ground by a twig through her tail. She coughed and wheezed, succumbing to the unbearable heat.

Then, against all instinct, Dreamer crashed in through the fire! Spotting Fuchsia, he gnawed on the stubborn twig until it snapped, while the fire singed his fur. Both foxes leaped through the flames again, and rolled on the ground together to quench their flaming backs!

They lay panting. All went quiet for a moment. The fire seemed to crackle and spark rather peacefully. Fuchsia then sprang up with a look of bewilderment on her pretty face, staring fixedly at Dreamer. Dreamer stared back, into the deep brown pools of her eyes. A burning leaf twirled down slowly, heading for Dreamer. Fuchsia quickly snapped it up in her mouth, and spat it out. Then they smiled at each other.

On the other side of the tree, Comfrey stood up and limped away, down the other side of the hill. Driven by fear and shame, he fled Lough Ine, and never returned.

Dreamer stared still, and then nodded. Fuchsia nodded back, and was off.

Dreamer peered around, through the ash in his eyes.

'Oh no!'

Where was Old Darig?

The great Wranglers jeep came shuddering out of the blaze, its engine spluttering from lack of oxygen. It made its way over the hill and slowed down by a mound of rocks.

'What happemed to de roof?' asked O' Connor, who couldn't be heard while they were speeding.

'Twas getting fierce smoky inside,' said O' Sullivan. 'So we let de roof down t'get some air.'

'There's even more smoke outside, ya pillock!'

Just as the jeep was about to pick up speed and head down the other side of the hill, a great big fox landed in the front seat, on top of O' Sullivan! The men all recoiled with fright, as Old Darig bit deeply into O' Sullivan's arm.

O' Sullivan screamed and let go of the steering wheel. It was then, the jeep's front wheels locked on left, causing the jeep to spin! Around and around, all the sights and scenery twirled in a tornado of blurred colour. The engine roared at an unhealthy pitch.

O' Connor struggled to sit upright, and struggled even more to load his shotgun, as the fox continued its relentless attack on O' Sullivan.

Collins reached from the back seat, his lips flapping in the wind, and straightened the steering wheel.

The jeep broke out of its free-spin, and took off like a torpedo. The hunters panicked and evacuated, leaping out over the sides and into the snow.

O' Sullivan jerked his arm free of the fox's grip and followed them, opening his door and bailing out, disappearing in a flash.

Old Darig, believing all of the men were gone, stood up and prepared to make his exit. But then he heard a sharp, metallic *clink* behind him. Turning around, he found O' Connor was still sitting in the jeep, his shotgun trained right on him.

Dreamer watched on helplessly as the jeep spun uncontrollably along, hitting rocks and bushes in a crazy pattern.

Then, after hearing a familiar *BOOM*, he saw Old Darig's limp body drop out and hit the ground.

Dreamer's heart sank.

O' Connor had already abandoned the jeep when it turned on its side, cutting a trench through the earth, colliding with a large rock and flipping upside down. Following a heavy crunch, the jeep lay in a cloud of dust, its wheels still spinning, its engine wearing out.

The hunters picked themselves from the ground, coughing and groaning. They limped and stumbled down the other side of the hill, out of the smoke, and out of sight. Only one stayed behind.

O' Connor searched around the ground for his shotgun. Without warning, he felt himself being bowled over. Dreamer lunged at The Farmer, tackling him to the snow and ashes, wrestling with him, pummelling wildly with his paws. O' Connor threw his clenched fist at the fox's face and swiped him off. As soon as he hit the ground, Dreamer sprang up again, glaring at The Farmer engagingly. Indifferent to the throbbing pain in his cheek, he growled and launched himself again, knocking The Farmer off his knees.

O' Connor flinched. He felt something hard jabbing him in the back - his shotgun!

O' Connor flipped himself over and grabbed his precious weapon. But there was no time to load.

Holding the gun by the barrel, O' Connor clubbed Dreamer with the butt, sending the dazed fox flying.

'I'll sort you out now in two seconds,' O' Connor growled, loading his shotgun and pointing it at the fox, as it crawled miserably along the ground. But this was all part of Dreamer's latest plan.

O' Connor put his finger on the trigger and aimed... but instinct told him to turn around. He relaxed his grip on the weapon.

There, right in front of him, was the jeep, lying upside down in a pool of its own diesel. And behind the jeep, another burning pine tree was toppling forward.

O' Connor quickly glanced down and noticed the fox had gone.

With no time to think, The Farmer ran as fast as he could, but barely escaped the gigantic explosion that flared up just behind him, in a fireworks bouquet of scraps and sparks. The entire area was swallowed up by an earth shattering blast.

Dreamer trundled wearily through the dense rolling smoke and collapsed. His strength waned, his body battered, he lay covered in dust, breathing quickly and hoarsely. The fox was sure his time had come. Nothing around suggested he was going to live. He only hoped that his story would be told. He hoped that his sacrifice, and the sacrifices made by all of his comrades, would inspire all animals to do as the animals of Lough Ine had done.

After thinking these thoughts, Dreamer closed his eyes and allowed the fire to surround him. The heat intensified again, the evil flames closing in, creeping further and further up to the fox's motionless body. He made no effort to escape. He just lay still and prepared his spirit to be carried away in smoke.

Then, he opened his eyes and saw a small winged creature appearing out of the haze.

'An angel,' he gasped deliriously.

Kingfisher fluttered down and perched herself on Dreamer's head, and pecked it.

'Get up!' she squeaked. 'Get up!'

Dreamer lifted his head and coughed.

'I know a way out!' Kingfisher squeaked. 'Follow me quickly!'

Flapping her little wings, Kingfisher was away, flitting and bouncing through the smoky air.

Dreamer rose painfully to his feet. Every joint in his body ached.

'Come on, hurry!' Kingfisher's voice was taut with urgency.

Dreamer moved downwards through the burning woods, in a slow, staggering gait. Flaming cinders and branches dropped down all around him, as if intending to miss him.

Kingfisher led Dreamer to the ledge of the hill; the same one the hounds had fallen from.

'Jump!' cried Kingfisher, circling Dreamer's head.

Dreamer gasped.

'What?'

'It's your only hope,' Kingfisher shouted. 'Go on, quickly. It was your idea in the first place!'

Dreamer gazed down at the blood freezing drop. He could feel his stomach in his chest. Although it looked like the stream had deepened from the melted run-off from the hillside.

'I don't know what'll happen to me if I jump!' he cried.

'The hounds survived,' said Kingfisher. 'Frog, Hare and Badger all survived. So will you. Now jump!'

Dreamer gulped and looked down over the edge again. His head reeled. The ground and the stream swayed dizzily, so very far below. Kingfisher was gone.

Dreamer looked back at the forest one last time, completely cloaked in fire. He wavered no more.

Squeezing his eyes shut and holding his breath, Dreamer leapt off the edge, and vanished into the unknown.

Promises

There was a sudden white flash.

All Dreamer could see was white. There was nothing else only white. It was as if the whole world had disappeared; rolled back into nothingness. Silence followed.

For a moment, Dreamer could hear nothing, only himself breathing.

Then, a familiar deep roar. But this was not a roar of pain or anger. Somehow, Dreamer distinguished Arznel's roar as one of hope and victory.

'*Ruuuuuuuuuuuuuuuuuurrrrrrr!!*'

As soon as the wondrous sound faded away, Dreamer sprang awake and found himself floating down the stream. The cold water sent a shiver up his spine. He gasped, flailed and twisted, and swam for the streambank. There, he scrambled onto a flat rock, trembling and coughing up water, drenched to the skin.

After wringing himself dry, he opened his eyes and sighed.

What was once a quiet, pristine place was now bustling with activity. Crowds of people had gathered just outside the Lake, cameras flashing. More wheelie beetles were parked around the base of the hill; giant, long, red ones, spewing water from their tentacles, big square white ones, and slightly smaller ones of various colours. Many of them had sirens blaring.

Dreamer turned to see that the fire had at last been put out. The forest was scorched grey and black. It looked gaunt and ghostly. Its trees were crusty and bent. The forest floor was packed with ashes. Some flames still burned, but were gradually dying down as the settling dust choked them. The cloud of smoke in the sky was breaking up and clearing away. Daylight had returned.

From the streambank, Dreamer could clearly see each of the hunters being shoved into the backs of long, white wheeled vehicles by other men in blue shirts.

The hounds were being led away too, in leashes and muzzles.

O' Connor was being taken away in a stretcher. He had been found earlier, dangling helplessly from the branches of a rowan tree. He was suffering from serious burns and smoke inhalation. He would live. Whether he would live and learn, was another matter. The hunters were whisked away up the road, never again to set foot in Lough Ine.

Dreamer grunted, almost satisfied with the closure.

'There you are!' squeaked a tiny voice from below. Dreamer looked down and saw that Frog had just emerged from the stream.

'Are you okay?' he shrilled, his eyes bulging.

Dreamer nodded.

'Just tired and sore,' he said. 'I'll be alright given time.'

The fox then noticed Badger sitting on the opposite bank, staring listlessly into the water.

'Is he alright?' Dreamer asked.

Frog shook his little head.

'Why, what happened?' Dreamer demanded.

'It's Holly,' Frog whispered.

Dreamer paused and allowed his head to droop.

'Oh... dear,' he muttered.

Just then, Hare limped over to join his friends. Kingfisher wasn't long following. She alighted on the streambank and waddled along. The animals stayed by the stream for a short time, keeping a fair distance between themselves and the swarm of humans by the Lake.

Nothing needed to be said. They were too grateful for being alive and together. It took time, but then they all hugged. Badger was the only one who didn't take part. Dreamer had almost fallen asleep on Hare's shoulder, when suddenly he shot up:

'Old Darig!' he gasped.

After wading quickly across the stream, Dreamer took only a few steps into the black forest, when he stumbled with exhaustion and collapsed. His friends crossed the stream quickly and rushed to his side. Badger, along with Hare, helped the fox to his feet.

Up through the burnt, dusty hill, the companions made their way. Ashes rose from their paw prints as they ran wearily upwards. Dreamer felt like the living dead. All strength was leeched as he dragged his body along, with no more than determination to find his old tutor, alive or not.

With fewer trees, the hill seemed so much smaller. It was not long before the animals neared the top.

Dreamer scoured through the ashes and charred pieces of wood. He circled every black tree and sniffed the smoky air.

When he was on the verge of giving up the search, he spotted something lying under a strangely 'unburned' rowan tree. Sure enough, there was Old Darig.

Dreamer hurried over and stooped in front of the old fox. For a while, he lay still and lifeless. But a smile soon broke across his face and he eased his eyes open.

'You made it,' he said, in a raspy voice.

'Old Darig,' Dreamer choked out. 'I'm so sorry.'

'...For what?'

'Everything,' Dreamer explained. 'For being so cold and abrupt with you. And for not helping you.'

Darig smiled again.

'Please,' he said. 'You owe me no apology. I'm the sorry one. You were right all along, Dreamer.' He coughed. 'I now wonder if you children are there to teach or to learn from. Because you had the friendship and trust of so many creatures, you were able to drive those men away. I was wrong to forbid you from seeing them.'

Dreamer said nothing.

He then noticed a nasty bullet wound on Darig's back. His blood stained the tree trunk.

'Listen to me,' the old fox continued, rapidly slipping away. 'That story I once told you... I'm beginning to think it's true.'

'I'll find him,' said Dreamer sternly. "I'll find Arznel. We're going to win this war!'

'Dreamer, no,' Darig breathed, gripping his last ounce of strength. 'What are the chances of -'

'No,' Dreamer sniffed, trying not to show emotion. 'I'm going to find Arznel. Animals are going to live in peace and safety, in a world clean and pure.'

Old Darig swallowed another mouthful of blood and nodded.

'So be it,' he concluded. 'It's about time someone did what you plan to do. And I couldn't have chosen anyone better to do it. You've always been a little reckless, Dreamer. But maybe that's what it takes. Go on your journey, son. Fight your war. I'll be watching you. But for now, I must go and find Eva. She's been very patient.'

'I'll see you again,' Dreamer sniffed.

But Old Darig barely got to hear these words, for he had already closed his eyes for the last time.

Dreamer fought all temptation to cry, and sat in mournful silence.

His friends watched from the nearby horse chestnuts. After some time, they edged their way up to him and slumped down.

Dreamer lifted his head and glanced at each of his companions.

'I'll be leaving soon,' he said. 'You already know why. I'm not asking you to follow me.'

'You already said that once,' Hare pointed out. 'And we were having none of it.'

Dreamer showed a hint of a smile.

'Well,' he said. 'If you're coming with me, you'll need proper names to go by. While we were travelling through that blizzard this morning, I came up with ones you should be proud of.'

There was a buzz of excitement among the friends.

Dreamer lowered his eyes on Frog, who was staring curiously back up at him.

'You are definitely something else,' he said. 'I can't think of any other frog who would haul himself out of his comfortable pond and throw himself into a dangerous and stupid adventure. Despite your size, you were with me everywhere I went today, offering your aid. I know you'll do the same again next time. That's why I've decided to call you *Aidey.*'

The frog smiled a broad smile, puffing up his chest.

Dreamer then looked down on Kingfisher.

'Where would I be without you,' he said warmly. 'Only one of us can fly. If it hadn't been for your keen eyes and unbelievable bravery today, who knows what would have happened. I'm sure those eyes of yours will help us again and again. That's why I want to call you *Keeneye.*'

The little blue bird chirped happily and ruffled her feathers.

Dreamer then raised his head and found himself looking into the eyes of Hare.

'I didn't think you'd have the patience to wait until last,' he said. 'So let me hurry up and name you.

Hare, there are few things you can't do. You can box, do archery, and ignore danger when your friends are in need of help. I would say you can sing, but let's not get ahead of ourselves.'

Hare laughed.

'But really,' Dreamer concluded. 'If there's one thing you can do that no other animal around here can compete with, it's run. So from here on in, you will be known as *Rush!*'

The hare shrugged.

'It beats being called Spot, or Pongo.'

Dreamer concluded by turning to face Badger, who still had that lost expression on his face.

'I know about Holly,' said Dreamer. 'It hasn't hit me yet that she's gone. I know she meant the moon and stars to you. But weren't you the one who told me about Spring Valley? You will see her again. But until then, much needs to be done. Holly wouldn't have wanted you to give up.'

Badger sniffed and nodded.

"A different sanctuary." He would grip those words forever.

'You dream of a cleansed world as much as I do,' Dreamer continued. 'You want the earth to be a place of never-ending joy and reverence. Well, it's not impossible. We can have this, but we'll have to fight for it. Like me, you will strive for victory, and you will have victory. So from now on, you will be known as *Victor*.'

The badger wiped his eyes and tried to put on a serious face.

Dreamer wandered ahead a few paces and turned back.

'Today was only a taste, my friends' he declared. 'Just a taste.'

Presently, there came from behind the burnt trees, a loud screech. The ground began to tremble. Branches snapped in their dozens. Dreamer and his friends gathered together cautiously and waited in suspense to find out the cause of such a commotion.

There was a flap of wings here, a furtive scurry there, first from one direction, then another, and before they could rub their eyes in disbelief, animals came plodding out of the shadows, one by one, two by two...

They had been summoned from the surrounding hedgerows, coppices and streams to assemble in Lough Ine; whole groups and families of stoats, pine martens, minks, otters, red squirrels, rabbits, hares, foxes, badgers and most amazingly - red deer. Among them were the animals of Lough Ine themselves, along with countless birds and water fowl.

They formed a semi circle around Dreamer and his companions, who were as bewildered as could be.

'How - wha - how did - ?' the fox stammered.

Nuala the owl perched herself on a surviving rowan branch and leered down at the friends below.

'News tends to travel quickly,' she said, actually smiling for the first time.

Captain Spruce stepped forward from the great rally, his shark-tooth spear standing a whole foot taller than himself.

'If and when this war ever breaks out,' he said to Dreamer, saluting with his paw. 'We'll be with you to fight it.'

Dreamer nodded at the rabbit leader, and then gazed at his magnificent army.

Hundreds of animals stood at his command, ready to follow him to Death's Jaws.

But then, Dreamer couldn't help singling out one of the foxes. It was Fuchsia. She stared at him seductively. It was she who had brought them. Dreamer stared back.

Later that day, when the humans had cleared away, the friends found themselves on top of the hill, over looking the damaged land. Soft light shone through the clouds. The afternoon was light and calm, the blizzard having worn itself out.

Victor and Rush sat side by side in the heather, while Aidey basked in a murky puddle. Keeneye preened herself on a dry, thorny gorse bush. Dreamer stood tall and straight, peering out over the stretch of smoldering remains. But strangely, he was not sad. In fact, he hardly felt any sorrow or despair at all, at least not now. Despite all that had happened, there was a strong undercurrent of excitement and joyful hope he couldn't deny. Spring was approaching.

He looked at the scars that Man had left on the his home, but he did not see them. Where there were black, burnt trees, he saw new bark hugging the old, and budding catkins opening their sticky eyes to the early sun. Instead of shrivelled, crusty branches, he saw a prominent canopy of fresh April leaves. Where there were ashes, he saw the quick return of grass to the forest floor, and could almost smell those sweet, sweet bluebells.

Who could grieve, when the sun would smile so heartily, and food would be so abundant!

Already, the heat from the fire had melted the snow in Hilltop Warren and the rabbits were enjoying a well earned feast.

It would be as though all those who died in the terrible battle were enjoying Spring Valley so much, they decided to share it with their still-living companions. For that too, they would be remembered.

Fuchsia sidled up behind Dreamer and nuzzled him gently on the neck. The two foxes sat together, keeping each other warm.

For the rest of the cool, breezy day, the companions remained on the top of the hill, observing the landscape, eager to begin the great journey.

Before falling into a trance, Fuchsia added:

I don't know what to say. This is all so sudden.'

Dreamer smiled affectionately at his new mate.

'What is?' he said smartly. 'The war or us?'

'Everything,' said Fuchsia. 'I'm half expecting to wake up at any moment.'

Dreamer rested his chin on Fuchsia's head and drew in her intoxicating scent.

'If this is a dream,' he said. 'It's the best I've ever had.'